Praise for the Liz Talbot M

LOWCOUNTRY BO.

"Imaginative, empathetic, genuine, and fun, *Lowcountry Boil* is a low-country delight."

– Carolyn Hart,
Author of *What the Cat Saw*

"I love this book. And you will too. This lighthearted and authentically Southern mystery is full of heart, insight, and a deep understanding of human nature."

– Hank Phillippi Ryan,
Anthony, Agatha & Macavity Winning Author of *The Other Woman*

"*Lowcountry Boil* pulls the reader in like the draw of a riptide with a keeps-you-guessing mystery full of romance, family intrigue, and the smell of salt marsh on the Charleston coast."

– Cathy Pickens,
Author of the Southern Fried Mysteries and *Charleston Mysteries*

"Plenty of secrets, long-simmering feuds, and greedy ventures make for a captivating read...Boyer's chick lit PI debut charmingly showcases South Carolina island culture."

– *Library Journal*

"What do you get when you cross a Southern mystery, a ghost of a warning, a love triangle and a savvy protagonist who will stop at nothing? Easy, you get a page turning read—*Lowcountry Boil*."

– Donnell Ann Bell,
Bestselling Author of *The Past Came Hunting*

"Boyer's deft hand at Southernese adds a rich texture to the narrative and breathes sass into the coastal setting, leaving no doubt that this author is a fresh new voice on the mystery scene."

– Maggie Toussaint,
Author of *Death, Island Style*

"It's a simmering gumbo of a story full of spice, salt, heat and shrimp. She had me guessing, detouring for a few laughs then doubling back for another clue right until the last chapter."

– The Huffington Post

"Twisted humor has long been a tradition in Southern literature (maybe it's the heat and humidity), and Boyer delivers it with both barrels. In lesser hands, all the hijinks could be distracting, but not in *Lowcountry Boil*. Boyer's voice is so perky that no matter what looney mayhem her characters commit, we happily dive in with them. An original and delightful read."

– Betty Webb,
Mystery Scene Magazine

"A fascinating story with the hint of ghost story mixed in with the mystery. With many plot twists and a very surprising ending, *Lowcountry Boil* kept me guessing all the way through."

– Fresh Fiction,
A Fresh Review and Fresh Pick

"Humor, a little romance, a charming location, and an intelligent detective with a few idiosyncrasies...*Lowcountry Boil* might be Susan M. Boyer's first mystery, but it's an outstanding debut. Here's hoping Liz Talbot mysteries become a staple in the mystery field."

– Lesa Holstine,
Lesa's Book Critiques

Lowcountry BOIL

**The Liz Talbot Mystery Series
by Susan M. Boyer**

LOWCOUNTRY BOIL (#1)
LOWCOUNTRY BOMBSHELL (#2)
LOWCOUNTRY BONEYARD (#3)
LOWCOUNTRY BORDELLO (#4)

Lowcountry BOIL

A Liz Talbot Mystery

Susan M. Boyer

HENERY PRESS

LOWCOUNTRY BOIL
A Liz Talbot Mystery
Part of the Henery Press Mystery Collection

First Edition
Trade paperback edition | September 2012

Henery Press
www.henerypress.com

This is a work of fiction. Any references to historical events, real people, or real locales are used fictitiously. Other names, characters, places, and incidents are the product of the author's imagination, and any resemblance to actual events or locales or persons, living or dead, is entirely coincidental.

ISBN-13: 978-1-938383-04-5

Printed in the United States of America

For Jim,
I could have looked the world over and not found a better man.

ACKNOWLEDGMENTS

I am so insanely, ridiculously blessed. My heartfelt thanks to everyone who helped me along the way to making this book a reality. There are many of you, and I have a clawing fear I'm going to have a blonde moment and accidentally leave someone out. Nevertheless, here goes.

Mega thanks to my family for their patience while I spent countless hours playing with my imaginary friends. Thank you, Jim, for making my life possible. Thank you to my mom, Claudette Jones, for sharing with me at an early age your love of reading, and my dad, Wayne Jones, for telling me at an early age that paper will lie still for anyone to write on it. Thank you, my brilliant sister, Sabrina Niggel, my first reader and fierce cheerleader, and my mega-talented brother, Darryl Jones, for inspiring and encouraging me to chase my dream. Thank you to the best, most supportive brother-in-law a girl ever had, Joe Niggel, and the best, most supportive sister-in-law, Danielle Jones. Thank you, Jennifer, Melanie, Jimmy, and Brandon, for forgiving me for not being like the other kids' moms.

Huge thanks to our extended family and friends for their long-term suffering and encouragement, especially Sandra and Wilson Childers. My dear friend Sandra was one of my first readers. Wilson thinks we can now buy a plane. His boundless optimism has helped me through the rough spots. Thanks, Casey Williams, the Queen of Pain—my Jazzercise instructor—also an early reader. I'd love to thank all of our family and friends by name for their years of encouragement, but you all know there are far too many of you. (Please refer to the first sentence regarding how ridiculously blessed I am.)

Mega huge thanks to my dear friends and critique partners who have read this novel so many times I bet they can recite it: Sarah Cureton, John and Marcia Migacz, and Bob Strother. Special thanks to Bob's wife Vicki for her support. Thanks to the members of the Greenville Chapter of the South Carolina Writers' Workshop not thanked above, my first critique group, bless your hearts. Here I know I'll leave someone out, and I'm so sorry: Phil Arnold, David Burnsworth, Kevin Coyle, Barbara Evers, Betsy Harris, Steve Heckman, Jim McFarlane, Dana Neilson, Valerie Norris, Carole St Laurent, Pat Stewart, and Steve Stewart. Thanks to those in the Saturday novelist group not already mentioned, Melissa Lovin and Melinda Walker.

Thank you, Kristen Weber, for giving me permission to tell my story my way, and then asking all the right questions to help me make it better. Thank you, Evan Gregory, for your efforts on my behalf and for helping me to do this my way.

Thank you, Donnell Ann Bell, for preventing me from setting my hair on fire many, many times. A special thank you to my new Hen House sisters and fast friends, Terri L. Austin and Larissa Reinhart for all the hand-holding and late-night Twitter therapy. Thank you to my friends at Sisters in Crime, the Guppies, Romance Writers of America®, Palmetto Romance Writers, and Kiss of Death Chapter of RWA®.

Thank you to everyone at the Warsaw, IN Hampton Inn for providing me with an ideal place to write without distractions, and for the endless supply of coffee, tea, and cookies.

Last, but certainly not least, thank you Kendel Flaum, for having a dream and taking me along for the ride—and for being a brilliant editor.

STELLA MARIS RESIDENTS OF NOTE

TALBOTS (Districts 3 and 4)

* Talbot, Emma Rae Simmons	Liz's Grandmother (Simmons: District 3)
* Talbot, Frank	Liz's Father; Retired (Talbots: District 4)
Talbot, Carolyn Moore	Liz's Mother; Active Volunteer
Talbot, Blake	Liz's Brother; Police Chief
Talbot, Liz	Private Investigator
Talbot, Merry	Liz's Sister; Director of Teen Council
Chumley	Liz's Parents' Bassett Hound

DEVLINS (District 1)

Devlin, Stuart	Michael's Father; Deceased
Devlin, Kate Sullivan	Michael's Mother; Retired
Devlin, Adam	Michael's Brother; Mgr Island Hardware
Devlin, Deanna Stevens	Adam's Wife; Works at Island Hardware
* Devlin, Michael	Liz's 1st Love; Owns Devlin Construction
Devlin, Marci Miller	Michael's Wife; Liz's Cousin; Bank Teller

GLENDAWNS (District 2)

* Glendawn, John	Owns The Pirates' Den
Glendawn, Alma Ferguson	Married to John; Owns The Pirates' Den
Glendawn, Moon Unit	Owns The Cracked Pot
Glendawn, Elvis	Unofficial Bike Patrol for SMPD

SULLIVANS (District 5)

* Sullivan, Grace	Liz's Godmother; Owns B&B; Psychic
Sullivan, Henry	Grace's Brother; Rector at St. Frances
Sullivan, Nancy Emerson	Henry's Wife
Sullivan, Mackenzie	Henry's Son; Town Solicitor
* Sullivan, Lincoln	Henry's Cousin; Mayor of Stella Maris
Sullivan, Mildred Kingsley	Lincoln's Wife

LIZ TALBOT'S CIRCLE

Stevens, Colleen	Liz's Best Friend; Deceased
Andrews, Nate	Liz's Partner; Private Investigator
Andrews, Scott	Liz's Ex-Husband; Nate's Brother
Rhett	Liz's Golden Retriever

STELLA MARIS POLICE DEPT

Talbot, Blake	Liz's Brother; Police Chief
Cooper, Clay	Police Officer
Manigault, Sam	Police Officer
Murphy, Rodney	Police Officer
Cooper, Nell Baker	Clay's Mother; Dispatcher
Glendawn, Elvis	Unofficial Bike Patrol

EXTRAS

Bradley, Kristen	Merry's Roommate
Causby, Troy	Merry's Boyfriend
DiTomei, Phoebe	Owns Phoebe's Day Spa
Harper, Warren	Town Doctor; Medical Examiner
Lyerly, Zeke	Owns Lyerly's Auto Repair
* Pearson, Robert	Talbot Family Lawyer; Councilman Dist 6

* Denotes Town Council Member

ONE

The dead are patient.

I know this firsthand. My best friend Colleen drowned in Breach Inlet the spring of our junior year in high school, and I didn't hear a peep out of her until last March—a month after my thirty-first birthday. It was a Friday night, a few minutes past nine, and I had just chased a rabbit into Falls Park, in the West End of Greenville, South Carolina. The rabbit was fast, for one so big. At the foot of the rock steps that led down from the street, he darted under the Liberty Bridge. We'd had a cold snap, and while the sidewalks of downtown Greenville bustled with restaurant traffic, the park was deserted except for me, the rabbit, and my partner, Nate Andrews.

Nate stopped one level up and sprinted towards the bridge. He passed the rabbit, cut through a planting bed, and jumped off the rock retaining wall into the rabbit's path. Nate raised his hands in a stop motion. "That's far enough."

The hare hesitated. He took a step towards me, and then glanced into the Reedy River. For a few seconds, we all listened to water rushing over rocks.

"Don't be stupid," I said.

Naturally, the rabbit pulled a gun.

He pointed it at me, then at Nate, waving it back and forth. "I'm not giving that bitch a dime."

Nate said, "Hey, buddy, we don't care." He reached towards his jacket.

The rabbit lunged toward Nate, pointing the gun like a sword.

Nate raised his hands.

While the rabbit was distracted, I grabbed my Sig Sauer 9 from the holster at the waistband of my jeans. "Put the gun down. Now," I said, as though bored with the routine task of whipping out a nine mil. I wasn't nearly as nonchalant as I sounded. It was rare for me to draw my weapon.

The rabbit swung back to me, waving what looked like a .38 caliber. "How 'bout you drop yours, blondie."

Nate slipped his gun from his shoulder holster and pointed it at the rabbit's foot. "You can't shoot us both."

The rabbit heaved his furry shoulders and burst into muffled sobs.

"Lower the gun, slowly," I said. "Put it on the ground and step back."

The bunny complied.

"Now take off the headpiece to that costume," I said. That evening, our subject had been playing Harvey in a local production of the Pulitzer-Prize-winning play about a six-foot-three rabbit visible only to gentle soul Elwood P. Dowd. Nate and I had staked out the theatre. We'd thought we'd be there another couple hours, but we caught a break when the rabbit stepped outside for a smoke. Harvey doesn't get much stage time.

He pulled off his furry mask.

"Peter Tyler?" The rabbit's name really was Peter. Once the mask was off, I knew it was him. His wife, our client, had given us a photo.

"Yes," he spat. He wiped his cheeks with his paw.

Nate handed Peter the subpoena. "You've been served."

I picked up his weapon, removed the bullets, and handed it back to him. "Have a nice evening."

Peter sat heavily on the low rock wall and dropped his head in his hands.

When I walked towards the steps, my long-dead best friend Colleen appeared on the swing that hung from a trellis beneath the bridge. I stopped short. I almost didn't recognize her. She looked fantastic, for a ghost. Her skin was clear and luminous, her long red hair a cascade of molten curls. She looked like a perfect version of herself, as if she'd spent a month at a high-dollar spa. But I'd known Colleen Stevens my entire life. It was her—-her funeral fourteen years earlier notwithstanding.

Tears pooled in her eyes. "Liz, come home."

Nate walked up behind me. "Let's grab a drink."

"I think I need one." I wasn't ready just then to own the truth that Colleen's presence signified.

"Come home," Colleen repeated. Then she vanished.

I shuddered and blinked.

Nate and I climbed the steps to Main Street. A guitar player set up by the fountain was covering Amos Lee's *Arms of a Woman*. Foot traffic was steady, and he'd drawn a small crowd. Nate and I waded through. We crossed the street and headed down to our favorite bar. The executive chef might object to my calling it a bar. The Mediterranean food was excellent, but for us it served as a neighborhood bar.

We settled into chairs at a table on the patio overlooking the Reedy River. Neither of us minded the chill, and my brain needed fresh air. I ordered pinot noir, Nate a Sam Adams.

I stared into space, wondering why in hell Colleen showed up in the park. I never questioned what I'd seen. I was born and raised on Stella Maris, a sea island near Charleston, South Carolina. If you grow up in the South Carolina Lowcountry, you're generally tolerant of ghosts, haints, spirits, and the like. Charleston County has more supernatural entities per capita than anyplace else in the country. Still, a ghost I'd played Barbie dolls with shook me in a way that specters rattling around antebellum homes didn't. I pondered what she might want from me. Ghosts haunt folks for a reason, right?

"Something about that guy bother you?" Nate asked.

"Peter? No, case closed. Why?"

The waitress laid down cocktail napkins and set our drinks on the table. When she stepped away, Nate said, "Something's bothering you."

Nate knew me well. For six years we'd sold information by way of discreet investigation out of our office, Talbot & Andrews, based in Greenville, South Carolina. Greenville is near the foothills of the Blue Ridge Mountains—on the opposite corner of the state from Stella Maris. We interned with the same Greenville private investigator before opening our own agency. Nate wasn't just my partner. He was my friend. I didn't want to lie to him, but I wasn't ready to tell him I was seeing ghosts. I shrugged.

Nate took a sip of his beer. "I thought since the guy was trying to screw his wife over, he'd dredged up unpleasant memories."

I threw Nate my most dramatic *oh puh-leeze* look.

He drew back, looked away. "Sorry."

I've never held it against Nate that his brother was my ex-husband, Scott the Scoundrel.

Scott owns a private equity firm that devours other companies for breakfast, has team-building meetings over lunch, screws one of their wives over cocktails, then fires half the team before dinner. He is the progeny of Satan, but disguises it behind a perfect smile and a good-ole-boy manner.

Nate is the same flavor of blond-haired-blue-eyed handsome, but Nate's a good guy. We handled criminal defense cases, insurance fraud, and an endless variety of romantic indiscretions. We'd also been hired to do such sophisticated tasks as locate a trailer missing from a trailer park, determine who left an old goat grazing in a judge's front yard, and track suspected UFOs.

We had bills to pay.

"It's nothing," I said.

Nate nodded and drank his beer. He knew I'd talk when I was ready. One of the things I loved best about Nate was that we could talk over a drink, or not.

I sipped my wine. *Come home,* Colleen had said. Home.

I'd built a life for myself in Greenville, four hours away from the island paradise that spawned me, where all the people who mattered most to me still lived. If you added up all the hours I spent trying to explain to my family how I could do that, I probably have years invested in justifying my presence in the Upstate.

After college, the reason was Scott's budding career. After I saw through his polished veneer, discovered what I'd married and divorced him, I stayed because my own career was established. Those were the lies I told myself, anyway.

The dirty little truth was I stayed away because my cousin, Marci the Schemer, had tricked Michael Devlin into a train wreck of a marriage, and they still lived on Stella Maris.

Michael was the man I should have married. And you can bet your mamma's pearls I *would* have married him had Marci not intervened. Stella Maris is a small town. The prospect of running into Michael and Marci at town picnics and Friday night football made me a little crazy. It was easier to live elsewhere and visit often. But Stella Maris would always be home.

Marimba music announced an incoming call on my iPhone. I pulled it out of my pocket and looked at the screen. My brother's picture smiled back at me.

I slid the arrow on the touch screen to the right and raised the phone to my ear. "Hey."

"Liz," Blake said. The tone of my name told me something was very wrong.

I waited.

"Come home."

I sucked in a lungful of air. "What's wrong?"

"It's Gram," he said.

Someone turned down the volume on the world. A giant bird beat in my chest, trying to get out. I stood, ready for flight. "What? *What?*"

"Liz, she's dead."

Like everyone else, at first, I assumed it was an accident.

TWO

Rain drizzled from dense, low-hung clouds the day we buried Gram. Sunshine would have been inappropriate attire for that somber Tuesday afternoon. I stood beneath the funeral home canopy feeling as if my whole body had been numbed for a root canal. It just wasn't possible that Gram lay without protest in that coffin. Emma Rae Simmons Talbot was the most vibrantly alive person I had ever known. It violated some law of physics that all her energy had vanished in a tumble down her deck steps.

Nate stood solidly beside me. He'd insisted on driving me home— had barely left my side since Blake called. This was only the second time Nate had ever been to Stella Maris. The first was the day I married his brother.

After we sang *Amazing Grace,* the army of mourners invaded Mamma and Daddy's five-thousand-square-foot lowcountry cottage. Each in turn, they murmured sympathies and made their way to the dining room, where Mamma's antique mahogany Duncan Phyfe table labored under a spread of food I couldn't bear to look at. Like a murder of crows, they roosted on the front porch railing, grazed off china all through the house, lighted in the screened porch, and gathered around the live oaks in the backyard.

I felt guilty for wishing they'd all leave. It was a comfort, really, that so many folks came to pay their respects. But it's hard to be hospitable when you're grieving, and I was exhausted from the effort of being gracious. And all that handshaking and hugging kept me popping into the powder room to wash my hands and apply sanitizer. That many people, you had to figure at least a dozen carried viruses.

Long hours later the crowd thinned to family and Nate. Aside from Mamma, Daddy, my brother, Blake, my sister, Merry, and me, this group included Marci the Schemer (Daddy's dead sister's only child) and Michael Devlin. As if that day wasn't bad enough.

In addition, there was a whole gaggle of Great Uncle Harrison Talbot's family. Great Uncle Harrison was my granddad's brother. Granddad had been waiting for Gram on the Other Side for twenty years.

We gathered in the living room and waited for Robert Pearson, the family attorney, to read the will. It hadn't struck me how barbaric this was, this custom of divvying up the remnants of a person's life as soon as they were buried, until the life being divided was Gram's.

I sat on the end of Mamma's buttery-yellow leather sofa beside my baby sister. Okay, Merry's twenty-nine, but she'll always be my baby sister. Her grip on my hand tightened. She looked crumpled, as if she was caving in from the weight of her grief. Fat tears slid down her cheeks. Although I'm two years older, four inches taller, and a few pounds heavier, we're reflections of each other. In many ways our thoughts, emotions, and reactions are identical. As if one set of wires got crossed, the ways we're different, we're polar opposites. Merry cried out her sorrow openly. Mine was a private heartbreak, to be nursed in a dark quiet place.

Blake, my older brother by one year, flanked Merry's opposite side and held her other hand. He tapped his foot and tugged at the collar of his crisp white shirt with his free fingers. Blake was the Stella Maris Chief of Police, but his daily uniform was more casual. His neck was unaccustomed to starch and a tie.

I was thinking not one of us gave a damn about the will—Gram wasn't even cold yet—when I took a gander around the room. Let me tell you, after studying the faces of the Talbot clan, I reconsidered my position. Vultures hovered among us.

Uncle Harrison's eager eyes avoided mine. Two of his grown children chatted quietly in the corner, more excited than grief-stricken. Marci the Schemer perched on the edge of her seat, something like triumph painted on her face. She glanced my way and caught me staring. Our eyes locked and the corners of her mouth sneaked up. I felt nauseous.

My eyes settled on Robert Pearson. He stood in front of the french doors that opened to the foyer, shifting from one foot to the other with this apologetic look on his face. Ridiculously young for the task at hand, he reminded me of Harrison Ford, circa the first *Indiana Jones* movie.

The part of the family attorney was supposed to be played by a gray-haired man with reading glasses perched on his nose—not the guy who married one of my high school girlfriends.

Robert cleared his throat. "If everybody's ready, I guess we'll get started." He waited for the murmurs and fidgeting to quiet and then forged ahead. "First I just want to say how sorry I am for your loss—*our* loss. I loved Emma Rae. Everyone on this island did. Her sudden passing shocked us all." Robert's eyes worked the room, finding each face in turn, sharing heartbreak with some, searching others.

He gripped the will with both hands. "I'll skip the formalities. Emma Rae had roughly eight hundred thousand dollars in various investments, which she left to her only surviving child, Franklin Talbot."

A wave of rustling swept the room as everyone squirmed in their seats. This was significant news, but not what they were waiting to hear. Everyone expected Daddy would get the money.

It was all about the land.

Protecting the land was a religion in our world.

Land was power in our world.

Robert continued. "With the exception of several personal items she wanted each of her grandchildren to have as mementos, her house, the contents, and the three hundred acres the house sits on, go to her granddaughter, Elizabeth Talbot."

I was stunned mute. My eyes and mouth opened wide (Mamma would later inform me) in a most unattractive expression that called to mind a freshly caught tuna.

A gasp—really it sounded more like a cat hiss—riveted everyone's attention to the wingback chair by the fireplace. My cousin, Marci the Schemer Devlin, stood. Her little bird-body trembled and her face flamed against her ebony pageboy. She stared Robert down for what felt like a Sunday afternoon. Then she pulled back her shoulders and stalked right out of that room. Michael followed her, offering an apologetic look to the room on his way out. No one spoke as the front door banged against the wall.

For a ten count no one moved. Then, as if someone flipped a fire alarm, our extended family cleared out in a whirl of hugs, tears, and glares. The exodus left Merry, Blake, Mamma, Daddy, Nate, and me alone with Robert, who sat down in a recently vacated chair. I glanced at

Blake and Merry. Two pairs of wide cobalt blue eyes, mirrors of my own, wore identical expressions of grief-laden shock. I turned to Robert for an explanation.

Robert prompted Daddy. "Frank, you may want to expound a little on the contents of Emma's will. I know y'all discussed the family holdings and how they would be distributed."

Daddy leaned forward on the sofa, his face sagging, eyes bloodshot. He was normally so young looking that strangers couldn't believe he was my daddy. His sandy blond hair was the exact same color as mine before I got my multi-toned highlights—not a speck of gray on his head. I couldn't believe how much the last few days had aged him. Mamma sat close beside him, one hand protectively on his leg.

Daddy coerced air into his lungs. "Your Grandmamma's property—the house and the land it's on—that's Simmons land. When my daddy died, I inherited the Talbot family land, acreage roughly double that of the Simmons tract. When the time comes, the Talbot land will be divided between Blake and Esmerelda, giving the three of you equal holdings." More often than not, Daddy calls Merry by her given name—Esmerelda.

Merry shifted beside me. Righteous indignation made it through her raw throat and swollen sinuses. "Marci gets nothing?"

I stiffened. Any sympathy for Marci the Schemer felt like a betrayal. Coming from my sister it was especially brutal. Merry was given to making allowances for Marci on account of her unfortunate childhood. I was not.

Robert glanced at Daddy. "This kind of thing is not unusual here, you know that. It's not about making anybody rich. It's about conservation." He cleared his throat again, his voice turning hoarse. "From what I gathered, Emma Rae felt that you, Liz, would be a good steward of the land."

"But I don't even live here, haven't in years," I protested. "Blake's the oldest...he lives on a *houseboat*..." Okay, it's a very nice houseboat. But at the time, I reasoned he could use a house.

Blake shot me a look that did not convey brotherly love. He is quite fond of his simple life on a houseboat moored at the local marina, and although he frequently meddles in my affairs, he is not a believer in reciprocity.

Daddy's devastated expression, so out of place on a face that seldom took life seriously, asked things of me I was unprepared to give. "Things have changed," he said. "You have responsibilities."

"I need air." I sprang up and bolted across the room. Through the dining room, into the kitchen, and out the back door, I made my way to the screened porch and collapsed on the swing.

It was too much to absorb. Gram's death had hit me like a battering ram to the stomach. How could I not have known this could happen? I hadn't spent nearly enough time with her in recent years. The guilt was thick on my tongue.

I was busy loathing myself when Colleen materialized beside me on the swing.

"Stay," she whispered. Since she died, Colleen didn't have much to say, but what she said swelled ripe with import.

"I can't," I told her. "My life's in Greenville now. I have clients. Friends. A renovated loft."

"*Important.*" Colleen had an urgent look in her saucer-shaped green eyes.

It hit me then that I had business with Colleen. "Have you seen Gram...on the Other Side?"

She shook her head slowly.

This alarmed me for reasons I couldn't parse at the time. "You've got to find her. Tell her... Can I see her? The way I see you?"

She shrugged and gave me an apologetic look. "Stay."

A tear slipped down my cheek. "I can't make any decisions today. Don't ask me to." I shut my eyes, shut her out, and just sat there, rocking slowly back and forth, holding myself.

I heard the back door open and close. When I opened my eyes, she was gone and Blake stood in front of the door, hands in his pockets.

"I need to talk to you." He sat beside me on the swing, right where Colleen had been seconds before, and loosened his tie.

"Blake, I can't stay here." I shook my head. "I love this place as much as you do..."

He turned to look at me.

"...but I can't make a living—"

The intensity in his eyes cut me off.

"Gram was murdered," he said.

* * *

Less than two weeks later, against Nate's vehement objections, my condo was on the market and my kiwi-green Escape hybrid stuffed with luggage and boxes of essentials. Rhett, my golden retriever, rode shotgun as I quitclaim to my life in Greenville. Marci the Schemer ceased being a force strong enough to keep me away from Stella Maris the minute Blake uttered those words.

I traded poor Nate for a ghost of a partner and moved home.

THREE

There are two ways to get to Stella Maris: by private boat or by taking the ferry from the Isle of Palms, our neighbor to the south. The ferry ride takes twenty minutes. Every time I make the trip, I get out of the car and watch as the town comes into focus. The old Beauthorpe homeplace sits at the corner of Main and Simmons, and in the backyard there's a silver maple with a tire swing I've swung on a million times. When I see it, I know I'm home.

My wheels touched the ferry dock just before noon that sunny Monday in early April. I called Mamma to let her know I was home.

"*E-liz-a-beth Su-zanne Tal-bot.*" Whenever Mamma's upset with one of us, she trots out all three names and enunciates each syllable. "Did your brother not tell you to stay in Greenville until he's caught your grandmamma's killer?"

"Yes, Mamma, he did." *Frank-lin Blake Tal-bot* apparently believed his dual status as my big brother and chief of police gave him two reasons to mind my business. I have never suffered his intervention a moment my entire life.

Mamma was silent, perhaps reflecting on how middle children were often difficult. Finally she said, "I'll change your sheets and air out your room."

"Mamma," I said, "I'm going to Gram's."

More silence.

"I need to be close to her."

She sighed. "I've got book club tonight, and a church meeting tomorrow. You'll come for dinner Wednesday?"

"Of course."

"I'll call Blake and Esmerelda."

I needed to call Esmerelda myself. I hadn't spoken to her in several days. And I'd have to call my brother. "Let me talk to Blake first."

"That's perfectly fine with me."

I ended the call after Mamma sufficiently admonished me to be careful. I knew she was rattled. Stella Maris was one of those small towns where you could leave the door unlocked for the plumber and not think twice about it. Our island home was unacquainted with violence.

As I drove with the moonroof open, windows down, through the streets of my hometown, the island reclaimed me. I slipped the clip out of my hair and let it tumble to my shoulders and whip in the wind. Rhett hung his head out the passenger window. The thick breeze was laden with the pungent scent of salt marsh, spiced with pine, and sweetened with magnolia blossoms.

Stella Maris is a sultry, windswept Eden. Blake, Merry, and I grew up here on clay-colored beaches with the salt air sticking to our suntans. Blake's toy soldiers defended our sand castles, and we learned to surf the foam-laced waves of the Atlantic that alternately caressed and pounded our playground. The island both nurtured and seduced us. My family's roots sank deep into the sand and anchored us here. Our souls are salt-water cured.

The island is roughly star-shaped, with the ferry dock at the south end of Main, between South Point and Marsh Point. The remaining three points of the star are Pearson's Point, Devlin's Point, and North Point. Two main roads crisscross the island—Main Street and Palmetto Boulevard.

I drove down Main past The Stella Maris Hotel and The Cracked Pot, the island's diner. Trees with border beds were wove into the sidewalk—even the main business district was green and lush. I bore right around the traffic circle bordering the park, made a three-quarter loop, and headed north on Palmetto Boulevard.

A few blocks down Palmetto Boulevard, businesses gave way to churches, then homes. Ancient, sprawling live oaks dripped Spanish moss and shaded neighborhoods. At the end of Palmetto, I turned right on Ocean Boulevard. A couple hundred feet later, I made a left into Gram's driveway. Palm trees lined the oyster-shell-and-gravel lane that approached the house and ended in a wide circle. I parked the Escape and stared at the life Gram had left me.

The house was architecturally schizophrenic. When Gram and

Granddad first built it in the sixties, it was likely considered a craftsman-style beach cottage. But they'd added on several times. The result was a sprawling yellow house with teak trim flanked by an assortment of porches. Elevated to protect it from storm surge, the house roosted on a four-car garage. A wide staircase lined with potted gardens beckoned me to the deep front porch where Adirondack chairs, a swing, and a hammock waited. As it had my whole life, the house utterly charmed me, spoke to me of rain on the tin roof and starry nights on the deck.

I let Rhett out of the car. He had bushes to water. I needed to see the ocean. Two acres of lawn surrounded the house that now belonged to me. At the edge of the lawn on both sides of the house was a maritime forest—nearly three hundred acres total. I owned the northeast point of the island. It was just sinking in, the responsibility of it. For the first time since Robert Pearson read the will, I wondered how I would pay the taxes and insurance, let alone maintain a fifty-year-old house. I had a little in savings. I could pad that when the condo sold, but I needed to scare up some clients—soon.

I rounded the front corner of the house and crossed the side yard. On the beachfront side of the house, sea oats and palm trees created the natural landscape that led out to the Atlantic. I couldn't see the ocean over the sand dunes, but the music of the surf and the warm salty breeze called to me.

As I reached the back corner of the house, something yellow fluttered in my peripheral vision. I glanced left and gasped. Crime scene tape outlined the back deck, stairs, and a large rectangle of sand.

How had I forgotten the house was a crime scene?

Someone murdered Gram here, in the place she loved most. I stumbled backwards, tears brimming in my eyes. Those horrid yellow streamers were a stark reminder: My home was forever changed. I swiped at my eyes with the back of my hand. All I could do for Gram now was find her killer.

I pulled out my phone and tapped Blake's name. "I'm at Gram's," I said when he answered. "Are you guys finished here? Can I take down the crime scene tape?"

He made a noise that was part growl, part roar. "I'll be right there."

I waited in the hammock on the front porch.

FOUR

Blake parked his Tahoe in the drive less than ten minutes later. Rhett came barreling across the yard to greet him. Blake, already in mid-rant when he climbed out of the SUV, stopped and stared at the dog. Rhett sat on his haunches, tongue hanging out of a sloppy grin.

"Hey buddy." Blake scratched him behind the ear. It's hard to hold onto anger when faced with a dog who's happy to see you. "Good thing Liz has you for a butler, isn't it?" Blake patted him on the side, and Rhett romped off to explore the yard.

Blake started towards the steps. "I should've known better than to've expected common sense from you."

"You should've known I'd never stay away."

One foot on the first step, he stared up at me. My brother's only two inches taller than me—he's about five-ten—but he works out. Edges of medium-brown hair peeked out from under his Boston Red Sox cap. His uniform consisted of a golf shirt, jeans, and leather boat shoes, no socks.

"Let's talk out back." He turned and headed around the house.

By the time I'd rolled out of the hammock and caught up to him, he'd ripped down the crime scene tape and wadded it into a ball. We climbed the deck steps and settled into Adirondack chairs. From here I could see over the dunes. Waves meandered in, toppled over themselves, and rippled towards the beach.

Not taking my eyes off the surf, I said, "At the funeral, all I could think was that she was gone."

Blake looked up the beach, away from me.

"She was still doing the Cooper River Run," I said.

Blake jerked with a half-chuckle. "And throwing themed cocktail parties. Last month it was Roaring Twenties. She was a flapper."

Tears raced down my cheeks. "She wasn't finished living yet."

Blake put his arm around me and squeezed me tight. "I know."

"When you told me her fall wasn't an accident—I don't think I really accepted it until I saw the crime scene tape."

"It's hard to credit."

I straightened in my chair. "I want to know how it happened." My grief fueled my resolve for justice.

"When I know something, I'll tell you."

"So, you don't have any leads?"

"I didn't say that."

"Blake, let me help."

"*Hell* no."

"I'm a trained investigator—"

"Who may be the next target," he said. "I can't make you leave, but I will not allow you to participate in this investigation. For Pete's sake, Liz, *I* probably shouldn't be working this case. We can't turn this into a family affair."

"It is a family affair."

"It's also an open police investigation." He took off his cap and ran his fingers through his hair. "This is hard enough as it is." Blake looked more stressed than I'd ever seen him. I felt awful that I'd added to his burden.

Then he switched gears. "You need to get a security system installed."

"I bet not a soul on this island has a security system."

"Some do. We're not as isolated as we used to be—lot more marina traffic."

"I'll look into it." I tried to appear cooperative. "I understand you don't have much to work with, but you know how she was killed. You'd tell any victim's family that much."

He shook his head in exasperation. "Look. Very few people outside the department know she was murdered. The dunes hid the crime scene tape from the beach. Everyone thinks she fell down the steps."

I squinched my face in one of those expressions Mamma is forever telling me causes wrinkles.

Blake continued. "Someone hit Gram over the head with a blunt instrument and placed her at the bottom of the steps to make us *think* she fell."

"How do you know that?"

"Because it's my job to be suspicious."

He picked up a seashell lying on the deck. "I thought it was odd there was blood on her head but not a trace on the steps. The head wound was the only mark on her. If she'd fallen down the steps, she'd have had other injuries. The autopsy confirmed it."

"So why haven't you alerted the media?"

Blake tossed the seashell over the deck rail. "Culprit thinks he got away with it, maybe he's less careful. Also, I've avoided the mass hysteria that will turn this island into Bedlam by the Sea."

"Who knows besides Mamma, Daddy, Merry, and me?"

"No one outside the department—except Mackie Sullivan. He's the town's attorney. I'm required to notify him."

Blake gestured with his head up the beach towards the bed and breakfast. "Oh—and Grace. I didn't tell her, she told me."

"Figures."

Grace Sullivan, my godmother, was our local psychic. She'd nearly drowned in the ocean when she was seventeen—white light and all that. Ever since, she'd possessed insights that fascinated some and scared others.

"Any idea what the murder weapon was?"

"There were small pieces of bark in her hair consistent with the firewood underneath the deck. The forensic team went over the house with a fine-tooth comb. No evidence anyone else was inside that night. Nothing obvious is missing. My guess, it happened out here."

"What makes you think she was moved?"

"The position of the body. She was face down in the sand at the bottom of the steps. She didn't fall. The blow came from behind. The killer would've had to've been on the deck when she came outside. She would've seen him—there's no place to hide. Motion detectors light this place like a football field on a Friday night."

Blake hesitated. "Also, I found a flashlight underneath the deck. It's possible she dropped it when she was hit from behind."

"Why would she have a flashlight if the outdoor lights were on?"

"No lights under the deck."

"Do you think she went down for firewood?"

"Nah," he said. "She had a fire going in the fireplace. But the log rack in the sunroom was full. TV was still on. Glass of wine on the table by her chair. Something else, the wind was up that night—near gale force. Hard to figure why she'd go outside."

"And Alma Glendawn found her around nine-thirty that night?" Alma and John Glendawn lived just down the beach, next to their restaurant, The Pirates' Den.

Blake nodded. "It was a fluke. Alma stopped by to bring her a slice of key lime pie when she left the restaurant. Gram loved the stuff. When she didn't answer the front door, Alma came around back."

"So what's your read?" he asked, like curiosity and stubborn had fought, and curiosity won in a points decision.

"It wasn't random," I said. "Probably has something to do with the land." The Stella Maris beaches weren't pristine by accident. Much of the land on our twenty-four-square-mile paradise had been in the same families for generations—folks who cherished our small town and were terrified of timeshares.

Others looked at our wide beaches and saw the potential for enormous wealth. Zoning regulations protected the island from exploitation. Still, the town stood one town council election and one real estate deal away from becoming its own worst nightmare.

"Did you notice how pissed Marci was about the will?" I asked.

"She didn't exactly try to hide it."

"But do you think she really expected she'd inherit?"

"She's the oldest grandchild. Always thought she was entitled to...well, whatever she wants."

I knew that better than most. "Do you think she's capable...?"

"Oh hell, yeah," Blake said. "But she's got an alibi. She was home with Michael. He wouldn't lie for her."

I mulled that. Thinking about Marci being home with Michael stirred up all manner of emotions, none of them happy. "How did you find out she had an alibi for a reported accident?"

"I'm highly skilled."

I nodded, but I was thinking about the turtles.

The summer I was six and Marci was eight, Gram bought Blake, Merry,

Marci, and me pet turtles. Gram taught us what to feed them, how to clean their tanks, and to make sure they spent time under sun lamps. Merry was only four, so Blake and I helped her take care of her turtle. She named him Ted. Mine was Susan Akin, after the reigning Miss America, and Blake's was Donatello, after one of the Teenage Mutant Ninja Turtles. Marci would never tell us her turtle's name. She probably never gave it one.

Against Gram's better judgment, Marci took The Turtle with No Name home to the rented duplex where she lived with her parents. Marci's mamma, my daddy's older sister, was one of those mothers who had too many of her own problems to pay much attention to her daughter, let alone a pet. Mamma generally avoided allowing us to cross the threshold of that sad, neglected home, but she occasionally relented, when she ran out of excuses to offer Aunt Sharon.

One day I was over at Marci's and The Turtle with No Name was splotchy, his eyes filmy. The tank smelled to high heaven, and what little water the turtle had was filthy. I told Marci the turtle was sick and needed to go to the vet. She told me to fuck off. By the time I alerted Gram, his symptoms had disappeared.

That evening, Merry's turtle, Ted, had splotches and milky eyes. He died before we could get him to the vet. Marci denied switching the turtles and Aunt Sharon pitched a hissy fit when Gram called her on it. Two weeks later, my turtle disappeared. I know in my bones Marci took Susan Akin, either for the pure-T meanness of it or to replace Ted after she'd killed *him*. Donatello lived to a ripe old age under tight security. The last occupant of Marci's tank died within a month.

I was only six, but I think I knew even then that something was bad wrong with Marci.

A flock of seagulls flew by.

"How do you know when the flashlight was dropped? It could've been there for months."

"Maybe," Blake allowed. "But I don't think so. Looked new."

"Where exactly was it?"

"I'll show you." Blake led the way down the steps. The space was adjacent to the garage and had a sand floor. "Over there." He pointed to the area in front of the stacked firewood.

It felt preternaturally chilly under the deck. A burst of wind swirled through, whipping my hair into my face and blowing sand. I rubbed my arms.

"I've got to get back to the office," Blake said. "Promise me you'll let me handle this."

"Don't ask me to make a promise you know I can't keep."

"Dammit, Liz—"

"I'll promise you this. I'll bring you anything I find. I'd never do anything to make you look bad. And I'll be careful."

His shoulders rose and fell heavily. "It's still a mess inside. I would've had someone clean up the print dust if I'd known you were coming." He turned and left.

I stepped back into the sunlight and surveyed the area one section at a time. What had Gram been doing out here that night in gale force winds?

A familiar ripping pain tore through my abdomen.

I staggered to the nearest support beam and leaned against it, holding my stomach with one arm, gripping the post with the other. Ovarian cysts, the gynecologist in Greenville had said. I squeezed my eyes shut. Bursts of light popped behind my lids. Somehow I was going to have to see a local GYN damn quick. Thank heavens the bad pains were rare.

Rhett's high-alert bark sounded from the front yard. I made my way around the house. Rhett ran a circle around me, then sprinted down the driveway and barked emphatically up Ocean Boulevard.

Catching up with him, I peered up and down the street. The only sign of life was an older gentleman in a baseball cap several blocks away walking in the other direction. Rhett kept barking at him, alternating *woofs* at me.

"What is it, boy?" I knelt and stroked his head. The man disappeared around a curve. Someone whizzed by on a bike. Uneasy, I scanned the area once more. If anyone else had been there, he—or she—was gone. I turned towards the house and called Rhett to follow. But I couldn't shake the feeling I'd missed something important.

FIVE

I grabbed my suitcase, garment bag, and makeup case from the back of the Escape. Another wind gust, too cool for the day, beat at my back as I climbed the steps. When I unlocked the mahogany and stained-glass door, it blew open. Oddly, the wind offered no resistance when I closed the door behind me.

I set my luggage down on the heart-of-pine floor in the foyer. Rhett followed as I wandered down the wide entry hall and through the dining room, where Gram had presided over holiday feasts. In the kitchen Gram's grocery list was still on the refrigerator, an open copy of *Southern Living* on the black granite-topped island.

I slipped into the sunroom that fringed the back of the house, hungrily exploring for more of Gram. The wall of full-length windows offered a panoramic view of the Atlantic. A half-completed crossword sat atop a stack of magazines in the sweetgrass basket by her favorite chair. I sank into the overstuffed tropical print and put my feet up on the ottoman. A soft throw spilled across the chair arm. I gathered it to me, nuzzled my face in it, and inhaled. Lavender. Gram's favorite.

Gram's life passed before my eyes. When I was little, she rocked me to sleep crooning Broadway tunes. She taught me to play Scrabble, Monopoly, and poker. We had slumber parties and watched old movies wearing pajamas, wide-brimmed hats, and pearls. She taught me which glasses were for champagne, how to shag, and why life isn't fair. She held my hair while I puked up the tequila I swiped from her liquor cabinet and she never told Mamma. It's not that she loved me more than Blake, Merry, or Marci. It was more that Gram and I were kindred spirits.

The doorbell chimed. Rhett raced towards the foyer and I followed. I glanced through the tall window to the right of the door. Kate

Devlin stood on the porch holding a casserole dish. I couldn't help but think of Kate as an old-fashioned Southern Belle—gentility personified. Her delicate ivory skin would never confess her age, though she was only a few years younger than Gram. Kate's dark-chocolate hair was no doubt the same shade it had been the day she married Stuart Devlin.

In a world where things went according to script, Kate would have been my mother-in-law. In my fantasies, she reflected a great deal on how I would have made a more suitable wife for Michael than Marci the Schemer. I fluffed my hair and opened the door.

"Hey, Kate." I stepped back to welcome her inside.

"Liz, darlin', I was hoping I'd catch you. I know you won't have time for cooking while you're settling in. I made you this chicken potpie." She handed me the dish.

Boy, word got around this island fast. "Well, thank you so much. Aren't you sweet? Please come in."

Rhett sniffed at the dish and whined.

"Stop that now," I admonished him.

When I looked up Kate had one foot on the top step. "Thank you, darlin', but I can't stay." She started down the steps. "I'm running late for a meeting at the church. Come by and see me real soon, you hear?"

"All right then." I waved. "Thanks again."

She was inside her dark blue Lincoln MKS and headed down the drive lickety-split.

The bottom of the dish was frosty. Women like Kate kept potpies, casseroles, and stews in the freezer ready to go for new neighbors and friends with any manner of emergency. She sure had gotten here fast—left in a hurry, too.

I put the potpie in the freezer. It hadn't thawed much, and I was banking calories. Mamma would not be serving a diet-friendly dinner Wednesday evening. I'd no sooner turned away from the refrigerator when Rhett started barking like a hound of hell.

I started back down the hall and heard a key turn in the lock. The door swung open. There stood Marci the Schemer in a red linen suit and heels. With her ivory skin expertly made up and every ebony hair in place, she looked like Snow White. One look into her eyes and you knew she had more in common with the Wicked Queen. Rhett barked as if he might like to devour her.

"What are you doing here?" I asked loud enough to be heard over Rhett.

She didn't appear intimidated by either of us, but she had a pissy look on her face. "Why don't you call off that mutt of yours."

"This is how he typically responds to trespassers." I matched her expression, or tried. I hadn't had near the practice at looking irritated. "Rhett, come here, boy."

He stopped barking and trotted to my side.

Marci closed the door behind her. "I'm hardly a trespasser here. I've had the run of this house my whole life, just like you."

"Well, you don't anymore. I'll take that key."

She raised one corner of her mouth. "My, my. Is that how family treats family? What would Gram say?"

"She'd likely say she didn't recall giving you that key, or she would've had the locks changed."

Marci's hard eyes never left mine as she laid the key on the secretary. "I've come for what's mine. Gram left me a piece of jewelry as a 'memento.' My choice. Said so right in that will of hers."

I stared at her for a moment. "Too bad you waited until I arrived to come by for it. Now that's all you'll get."

"Oh, you didn't think this was my first trip, did you?" Her eyes glittered with spite.

"If I find anything else is missing, I'll report it stolen."

"You haven't spent enough time here in thirteen years to know if anything's missing."

"Aren't you supposed to be at work?" Marci was a teller at the bank in town.

"Lunch hour." She started towards the stairs.

I held up both hands. "Wait right here. I'll bring Gram's jewelry box down."

"No need," she said. "I know what I want."

I raised an eyebrow.

"I'll take her engagement ring."

I felt as if I'd been slapped. She and I both knew that ring held no sentimental value for her. She'd likely sell it. She only wanted it because she knew I did. I gritted my teeth. "You. Wait. Right. Here. Rhett, stay. Guard." Guard wasn't a command Rhett knew, but Marci didn't know that.

I went upstairs to Gram's jewelry box and took out the ring. It was a lovely piece with two-carat, emerald-shaped diamond in a platinum setting. I found a small velvet box in her dresser drawer, slipped the ring inside, and hurried back downstairs.

Marci wasn't in the foyer. Wherever she'd gone, Rhett had tailed her. "Hey," I called out in protest.

Rhett barked twice.

I cursed under my breath and followed his bark through the french doors into the living room. Gram's style was tasteful, but eclectic. Her favorite piece had been a big green velvet sofa with wood trim and a row of fringe around the bottom. Marci sat in the middle of it, legs crossed, as if waiting for a servant to fetch her tea.

I laid the ring box on the coffee table. "I have things to do."

"Well, I can't stay." She didn't move. "It's not fair, you know."

"What?"

"You getting everything. You always were her favorite."

I closed my eyes and willed Marci to leave.

"Why don't you keep the house and let me have the land," she said, as if she were offering me a concession.

"Now why, exactly, would I ever consider giving you—of *all* people—any part of what Gram left to me?"

"Because if you do..." She leaned forward and lowered her chin. "I'll give you what you really want." A knowing, evil smile slid up her face.

"Get out of my house." I strode into the foyer and yanked open the front door. Rhett went to barking again.

Marci took her time getting up. She smoothed her skirt and picked up the ring box. "Think about it." She slithered towards the door. "I've taught Michael how to please a woman. He's much better than he was at twenty-two."

"Ooooh! Out. *Now.*" I shooed her out like a chicken had gotten in and slammed the door behind her.

I was shaking with anger. Could she really be so cold-blooded she'd try to barter her husband? Every time I saw the evidence of who—what—Marci was, it shocked me.

I went to the kitchen, pulled the potpie from the freezer, and put it in the refrigerator to thaw. I'd need comfort food tonight. And I needed a glass of pinot noir. I pulled a bottle from the wine rack, fished a corkscrew out of a drawer, and poured myself a glass. Rhett and I went out onto the deck, where I practiced synchronizing my breathing with the surf.

An hour later, my blood pressure had lowered considerably. What was I doing before Kate came by? I went back inside, sat on the edge of Gram's chair, and studied the room. She'd spent the last evening of her life here. What had she been doing? It was a Friday night. She was probably watching *Murder She Wrote* reruns.

I felt a draft.

Colleen appeared on the loveseat. "Stay."

"I'm staying, all right?" I leaned forward. "Would you please find Gram? Find out what happened."

Colleen turned transparent. "Can't." Her voice echoed.

"Why are you here if you can't help?" I shouted.

"*Merry.*" The whisper was so loud it filled the room.

"What about Merry?"

A whirlwind burst through the sunroom. Paper and plant leaves rustled. Picture frames toppled and hit the sofa table. Colleen vanished.

I glanced down and noticed the stack of magazines in the sweetgrass basket had slid across the floor. A yellow legal pad stuck out from a folded newspaper. I straightened the basket's contents and picked up the pad. There were two columns of names, in Gram's handwriting. The guest list for Gram's next cocktail party?

Lincoln Sullivan	Mildred?
Frank	Merry???
Grace	Mackie Sullivan
Michael Devlin	Marci
Robert Pearson	Olivia?
John Glendawn	HC/SD??

Lincoln Sullivan was the mayor, Mildred his wife. Frank must have meant Daddy, but why was Merry's name next to his instead of Mamma's? And why was Mackie Sullivan, Grace's nephew, by her name? He surely wouldn't be escorting her to a party. Olivia—one of my friends from high school—was Robert Pearson's wife. But what did HC/SD mean? Why all the question marks?

What was this?

I quickly realized the left-hand column listed the mayor and the five remaining members of the town council. Gram had been the sixth. But what did the names on the right mean? I flipped through the remaining pages of the tablet, but they were all blank. I pondered the list for a moment and tucked it away in the corner of my brain to percolate.

After feasting on Kate's chicken potpie—that rich gravy and buttery crust was all kinds of sinful—I took Rhett for a long walk on the beach. We walked south, towards town. The breeze was gentle on my skin. The mingled greens of pine, oak, and palm in the forest were deeper, the wild flowers lusher. Stella Maris was ripe in the falling light. I let my mind drift, soaking it all in. Rhett romped in the surf and chased shore birds.

We turned around halfway to the lighthouse at Devlin's Point. On the way back, my thoughts turned to Nate. We would operate in different cities now, but we hadn't dissolved our partnership. Already I missed our daily debriefing over drinks or dinner. I'd been gone less than twenty-four hours and I was concocting ways to convince him he'd always wanted to live on a sea island.

When Rhett and I got back to the house, I hauled the boxes with my office essentials inside. The living room was huge and had a wall of bookcases. There was plenty of room for my new office. I set up my wireless printer on a bookcase shelf. Then, I sat on the sofa, took out my laptop, and started a case file. Gram was my client.

I'd worked murder cases before, usually pre-trial investigation for the defense. I entered everything Blake told me into my standard interview form. "The following investigation was conducted by Elizabeth S. Talbot, of Talbot & Andrews Investigations, on Monday, April 4, 2011, at Stella Maris, South Carolina. On this date..." The format Nate and I use is a clone of the FBI's FD 302. Judges and attorneys like this. They become familiar with FD 302s in law school, and find the unambiguous bureaucratese soothing. I printed out the interview notes, dated and signed the page, and placed it in the file along with the legal pad I'd found in the sunroom.

I set my laptop aside, padded over to the Chippendale secretary that housed Gram's tower computer. I powered up the Dell and performed the equivalent of an autopsy on it. As expected, there was nothing there but recipes, emails of the forwarded-inspirational variety, and Internet bookmarks related to gardening and travel.

We'd left Greenville that morning before sunup, so by nine-thirty Rhett and I were yawning. We made our way up to the room that had been mine my entire life. Moving into Gram's room was something I couldn't bring myself to do.

SIX

I slept fitfully that night, and had one weird dream after the other. In the most vivid, I sat on the toilet in Merry's bathroom while Colleen lounged in the garden tub. The dream felt different from any I'd ever had before. It felt real.

Colleen snapped her fingers, spraying sparks from the tips. "Pay attention." She pointed at Merry.

Merry fluffed her hair in front of the bathroom mirror. She leaned in for a closer look and applied a coat of lip gloss. A smile crept up her face.

A dark-haired man came into the room. He stepped up behind Merry, buried his head in her neck, and wrapped his arms around her. She closed her eyes and sank into his embrace. He raised his head and stared at me in the mirror as he caressed my sister's breasts. His face came into focus as he grinned malevolently.

An electric current seared me and I jumped up from the toilet.

It was Michael.

"Seriously," Colleen said. "What do you think you're doing?"

I spun on her, primed to pounce.

"Sit. Watch." She gestured to the toilet.

Outraged, I sat back down on the toilet and propped my elbows on my knees and my chin in my hand.

Merry's eyelids parted with a soft moan. Then, her eyes shot wide open and she began to struggle.

Michael laughed and held tight. "You knew exactly what you were getting into."

Suddenly, I was flying backward through space. Merry and the bathroom got smaller and smaller, inside a circle that was rapidly shrinking. Then, POP! Merry, the bathroom, and the circle were gone.

I sat straight up in bed, disoriented.

It was morning and my phone was ringing. Sister-instinct told me it was Merry before I saw her picture on the screen.

"Guess what?" she said.

"What?" I might have been the teensiest bit cranky.

"I'm leaving Teen Council in Charleston."

Merry was the executive director of Teen Council, a Charleston nonprofit that sponsored programs for at-risk teenagers. She was devoted to "her kids," often spending her days off with them.

"What?" I asked through a yawn. "Why? You love your job."

"I'm going to work for a foundation with this awesome new concept. They help inner-city gang members who've been convicted of violent crimes—murder, rape, assault—reenter society after they've been paroled. Its focus is building bridges between rival gangs."

"Sounds like a suicide mission." I was alarmed, but knew from long experience the way to talk Merry out of something was not via direct approach. Merry was often a mulish crusader. "Besides, you won't like living in a big city."

"That's the best part." She squealed. "I get to work right here on Stella Maris."

"I don't understand." My deductive reasoning skills are sharper later in the day, after I've had coffee.

"We're building a high-rise, state-of-the-art facility right here at Devlin's Point."

A volcano erupted in my neck and spewed lava into my brain. "Are you insane? That goes against everything—you'll never get that past the town council."

"I'm speaking to the council tonight. I've talked to several members informally. Not Daddy, of course—you can't talk to him about building anything on this island without listening to a lecture about wildlife habitats and beach erosion. I'm pretty sure I have enough votes to get it passed."

With a vise grip on the phone, I took slow, deep breaths. The one thing Gram would never have stood for was building a high-rise, state-of-the-art *anything* on Stella Maris. There were a hundred reasons why oceanfront development was a bad idea. Merry had always been as passionate about protecting the island as the rest of us. I'd never in my life heard her speak derisively about protecting wildlife habitats. Apparently, the only thing she was more passionate about was habitats for hoodlums.

"Over my burnt and scattered ashes you will." I pressed 'end' to disconnect the call. Hopping mad, I flew into the yellow-tiled shower in the adjoining bath. I emerged moments later and stormed the walk-in closet, grabbing a pair of khaki capris and a lime green polo shirt.

I picked Mamma's number out of my favorites list, then put my iPhone on speaker and set it on the skirted dressing table. I sat on the chair and reached for my moisturizer. Had Merry been talking to Michael "informally," by chance?

All my life I've had dreams that, when examined later, seemed to have been a foreshadowing. Many times things are connected, but twisted. Just before Marci the Schemer tricked Michael into a sham marriage, I dreamed the flying monkeys from *The Wizard of Oz* carried him off to the Wicked Witch's castle.

But Colleen had never made an appearance in my dreams before. Somehow her presence gave this one more weight. Colleen had been trying to tell me something about Merry, which made me wonder what last night's dream could mean. Merry was capable of a great many things in the name of one of her causes. Fornication with My True Love, Michael, was not one of them.

Mamma answered on the fifth ring.

"Just exactly who does she think she is?" I asked.

"Good morning, to you, too, sweetheart," Mamma gushed in a tone sugary enough to induce a diabetic coma. "Why, some mothers complain they never hear from their children at all, and mine...well, they have been on my telephone line all morning. I am truly blessed. Just think, had you and your sister not intervened, I would be sitting here with nothing to do except finish the last hundred dozen cookies for 'The Most Fabulous Spring Bazaar Ever,' for which I am, as you may recall, the chairperson for the fifth year in a row. It will commence Thursday morning at eight a.m. sharp, family melodramas notwithstanding."

I knew right off I should have cooled down before calling my mamma. "I know you're awfully busy, what with 'The Most Fabulous Spring Bazaar Ever' and all, it's just that..." I searched for some reasonable-sounding way to put it and found none. "Merry has lost her mind. I would think that the long-term health and safety of every man, woman, and child on this island would merit a moment of your time."

"Liz, darlin', you really should reconsider your choice of vocation. Your flair for the dramatic far surpasses your skill at photographing fornicators."

"Do you *know* what she's up to?"

"She mentioned something about a fellowship hall for teenagers."

"Ohhh! I cannot believe her. Of course she's going to sell that sack of manure wrapped up in a lace doily with lavender sachets." Classic Merry. She'd spin this project as something Mamma would support.

Something tickled the back of my brain, and I wondered for a split second why Merry told me the truth. She had to know how strongly I'd oppose her plans, and she wasn't above giving the truth a coat of varnish for me just like she had for Mamma. I knew in that moment Merry was manipulating both Mamma and me, but I didn't know yet to what purpose.

I tried to speak calmly. "She told me she's building a youth center all right. But not a fellowship hall for Stella Maris kids. No indeedy. She *said* she was going to build a halfway house for gang members on parole. *Felons*, Mamma. *Murderers...rapists... From different gangs.*"

"*Surely* you misunderstood."

"She thinks if she isolates them on an island—our island—she can convince them to all play nice. There are going to be gang wars on the beach, for heaven's sake. Right smack-dab in the middle of Devlin's Point."

"Liz, you're talking crazy. Your sister doesn't *own* Devlin's Point, and the town council—"

"—is being hornswoggled just like you are."

"What do you—?"

"What I mean is, Merry has apparently conned enough members of the council into allowing some social engineers to use Devlin's Point as a Petri dish."

"Oh, dear heavens," Mamma murmured.

"I'm going to find Blake. You'd better tell Daddy."

"Oh, dear heavens," Mamma repeated. "I've got to run—my cookies are burning."

SEVEN

I found Blake that Tuesday morning right where he is every morning at eight: walking through the front door of The Cracked Pot, the island's diner. I slipped behind him and followed him inside.

Moon Unit Glendawn owns the place. She greeted him as the door closed behind us. "Well, good morning, Blake. How are you this bright sunny day?"

If she had been any more bright and sunny herself, she would have spontaneously combusted on the spot, leaving us to pour our own coffee.

"Doing great, Moony. Could use some coffee." Blake hung his cap on the coat tree.

Moon Unit caught sight of me behind him. "Well, Liz Talbot, as I live and breathe. Welcome home." She rushed out from behind the counter to hug my neck. Moon and I graduated from Stella Maris High the same year.

Blake stared at me as if he'd been hoping my presence in town was just a bad dream and was now dismayed by the contrary.

Moon swooped back to the other side of the counter and went about the business of getting us fed. "Coffee. Coming right up. Hash browns or grits?"

"Grits," Blake said. "With red-eye gravy."

My mouth watered. "Me, too, please. And could I have my eggs scrambled with cheese?"

"Sure thing." Moon tore off the ticket and spun it back to the kitchen.

This was the first time I'd been inside since Moon Unit bought the former Stella Maris Diner and transformed it into something that was part small-town diner and part tropical café. She'd kept the white and pink ceramic-tiled floor but added skylights and live plants. The most striking feature was the far wall. It was paneled in white beaded-board and covered in photographs.

Blake slid onto a stool and I took the one to his right.

I leaned in to him and spoke in an almost whisper. "When's the last time you spoke to Merry?" I reached into my purse for my hand sanitizer and squeezed a generous dollop onto my hand. I offered it to Blake, but he waved it off.

"I don't know," he said. "Day before yesterday? Why?"

Before I could launch into how our sister lost her mind, Moon walked over and poured our coffee. "I hear you got trouble brewing." She replaced the pot on the warmer and slid onto the stool behind the counter. Her inquisitive hazel eyes jumped from me to Blake and back as she slid the cream and sugar within reach.

"What?" Blake measured precise amounts of cream and sugar into his coffee.

She leaned closer and lowered her voice, "A little bird told me Merry's gonna build an orphanage over on Devlin's Point."

Blake stirred his coffee. I gulped mine.

"If you ask me," she said, "there are way better places for an orphanage. First hurricane blows through here, all the orphans will have to go stay at a shelter."

Moon leaned closer, in imminent danger of sliding off her stool. "That is, if you could get permission to put one up there in the first place, which everybody knows is never gonna fly."

"Camp." Blake took a long sip of coffee.

"What?" Moon Unit and I both drew back and squinted at him.

He set down his cup. "It's not an orphanage. It's a camp for inner-city kids. Not a bad idea, you ask me."

Moon looked horrified, and for possibly the first time in her life, was absolutely speechless.

I wasn't. "Is there an outbreak of crazy here?"

"Relax," he said. "It's not what you think."

Moon crossed her arms. "I'm just tellin' you, that's not what Tammy Sue Lyerly was tellin' over at Phoebe's Day Spa."

"Yeah, well, more than hair gets twisted over there," Blake said.

Coffee sloshed out of my cup as I sat it down. "I got the story straight from Merry, and—"

Blake put his hand on my leg and squeezed and I shut up.

No one squeezed Moon Unit's leg. "Everyone is still in shock over poor Emma's untimely departure for the hereafter, and she must be spinning in her grave already."

Blake pinched the bridge of his nose. "Look, some kids'll camp on the beach for a couple of weeks each summer."

Clearly Blake had missed the part about the kids being felons from rival gangs. And the high-rise, state-of-the-art facility. Merry gave Blake, Mamma, and me each a different story. What the hell was she up to?

Moon Unit grabbed our breakfast from the ledge and handed us hot plates. I let the first smoky bite of biscuit soaked in red-eye gravy melt on my tongue.

"Eh law." Moon shook her head slowly, switching subjects. "I don't think my mamma will ever get over finding Emma Rae."

"I need a little more red-eye," Blake said.

We had less than a minute of peace while Moon went around to the kitchen and came back with a bowl of gravy. She chattered on, and we both ate way faster than usual. Half a dozen bites later, I realized I'd missed a chapter in Moon Unit's monologue.

At least she was carrying on about her family and giving ours a rest. "Speaking of Little Elvis, I'm surprised he's not following you around already this morning, Blake. Isn't he late?"

Blake drained his coffee cup. "Since Elvis doesn't work for me, he can hardly be late."

"Well, he sure *thinks* he does," Moon said. "Whizzing around with a walkie-talkie in one hand, steering his bike with the other. *Patrolling,* he calls it. All day long. Some of these smart-assed teenagers around here have been making fun of him again."

Little Elvis Presley Glendawn was two years younger than me, but was developmentally challenged.

Blake looked at her and nodded once. "I'll handle it."

"He's smarter than those punks in every way that matters. He just won't grow up much more inside, is all." She softened and gave Blake a grateful smile. "Probably gets on your nerves a lot, following you around, reporting in and all that. It's real good of you to put up with it like you do."

"Sometimes he tells me things I need to know." He grinned. "Kinda like you do."

He ducked as she swatted at him with the morning paper.

"Heck, Moony," he said, "with you and Elvis around, I could cut a position from the patrol force."

"I don't know why I put up with you, I declare I don't," Moon said.

Blake looked at me. I drained my coffee cup as I stood. He laid a ten on the counter. "Breakfast was great, as always."

"It was fabulous," I added as we moved towards the door.

Outside, underneath the pink and white striped awning, I inhaled a therapeutic lungful of salt air. I looked at my brother. "What exactly do you mean, 'It's not what you think?'"

Blake took his time settling his cap on his head. He massaged his neck with one hand and gestured at me with the other. "I'm not getting in the middle of this."

"You already are."

"Just talk to Merry, okay?"

"I already have."

"Try again. Tell her I said she'd better tell you the truth or I will. And remember, she means well. That's all I'm saying. Except this: stock up on Guinness—Extra Stout."

"What?"

"For years, this family has done everything short of dragging you home by your hair. Now, when you should have stayed in Greenville, here you are." His eyes locked on mine. "You'll be seeing a lot of me. And I drink Guinness now."

EIGHT

By the time I got back to Gram's, the movers were waiting for me. All my furniture went into the empty bay in the garage. The movers hauled Granddad's mammoth mahogany desk up to the living room. It was a sentimental piece, and my desk was too contemporary to blend with Gram's décor anyway. While they worked I cleaned up fingerprint dust. At eleven o'clock they were backing out of the driveway.

I tried to humor my brother and talk to my sister, but Merry was mysteriously unavailable at work, at home, or on her cell. Fine. I'd take in the town council meeting that night myself.

I unpacked my clothes while periodically hollering for a ghost. Colleen had some explaining to do, but was unfortunately elsewhere. I needed to know if she was trying to tell me something about Merry's halfway house/orphanage/camp, or if Colleen's irritatingly cryptic clue had something to do with Gram's death. Either Colleen knew something I didn't, or she and I had different agendas. Our relationship needed more give and take. I made a mental note to speak to her about how maybe she could work on being a more cooperative ghost.

By two o'clock, I'd eaten a light lunch of hummus and pita and organized my desk. I slipped my Sig Sauer 9 into the bottom drawer. Daddy and Blake held the opinion that a Sig 9 was too big for a woman, but when I was in a situation where something might need shooting, I wanted heft. And I had an imaginary friend named Sig as a child, so there was a certain symmetry.

I pulled out the legal pad I'd found in the basket by Gram's chair and looked at it with fresh eyes. More than anything, it looked like some of my case notes—things I doodled when I was puzzling something out. I tapped my pen on the desk. The politics of solving Gram's murder would be complicated.

Blake had taken a job as a patrol officer right out of college because it was one of only two openings in town, and he wasn't qualified to teach Jazzercise. Five years later, Charlie Jacobs retired and the town council offered Blake the chief's job. He was flabbergasted.

He may have been an accidental police chief, but he was a good one. You take care of what you love. However, being a small-town police chief—even a good one—required little in the way of detective work. Most offenses fell into one of three categories: traffic, teenagers, or drunk and disorderly good-ole-boys. The culprits were of the caught-in-the-act variety. Clearly, he needed my help.

The Internet has made a PI's job infinitely easier. In addition to the paid database services I use, there's enough information available on public sites to make conspiracy enthusiasts head for the compound. When I don't know what I'm looking for, I start with birth records and sift through a person's life until I find a gold nugget.

I set up profiles on the computer for everyone on Gram's list, with electronic copies of original birth certificates for everyone except Mildred Sullivan. She and Marci the Schemer were the only two persons of interest not born on Stella Maris. Marci's birth certificate was easy to find—I knew she was born in Kissimmee, Florida, and I also knew the address on her birth certificate where my daddy's sister and her husband parked their RV the year Marci was born. Cypress Cove was one in a long succession of nudist resorts they'd visited until Marci was old enough to go to school.

I searched for Lincoln and Mildred's marriage license to find her maiden name, and hopefully, where she was born. Most often marriages happen in the bride's hometown. Lincoln was a decade older than Mamma and Daddy, and I'd never heard anyone say where Mildred was originally from. I couldn't find a record of them marrying in South Carolina or North Carolina.

I set Mildred aside and pulled criminal background checks for the others. I knew about Marci's teenage infractions—a DUI and a marijuana possession charge. I did not know that John Glendawn had been arrested for marijuana possession in 1961. He would have been eighteen at the time, and had obviously not pursued a life of drug abuse, so I hardly thought it relevant.

Everyone else came up clean, so I started on financial profiles, the love of money being the root of so much evil and all. I pulled up the Charleston County real property database. Everyone on Gram's list owned the property where they lived. John Glendawn also owned The Pirates' Den. Aside from mortgages, no one had any outstanding liens or judgments.

I drew a big circle around Marci the Schemer's name. She might have an alibi for the time of the murder, but she was damn sure guilty of something.

I glanced at my watch—five thirty already. I needed to get changed. My stomach began to knot up at the thought of a public debate with my sister. Merry was a fierce advocate for huddled masses every-where, and an end-justifies-the-means type. She would firebomb any obstacle that stood between her and saving the world. I expected no quarter. I stepped into the shower and let the pulsating hot water work the tension out of my muscles.

Forty-five minutes later, I scrutinized the results of my primp ses-sion in the full-length mirror. I'm a healthy five-foot-eight, size ten. The world of runway models would no doubt classify me as obese. I can live with that. My gray Ann Taylor pantsuit and pink blouse fit perfectly. The matching silk scarf, sandals, and handbag completed the ensemble. I pulled my hair back into a sleek ponytail, and my makeup was transpar-ent. I was ready for battle.

I gathered my essential equipment—camera, binoculars, laptop, bottled water, hand sanitizer, gloves, and notepad—and slid them into my orange Kate Spade tote. Then with a ruffle to Rhett's head, I headed through the mudroom and down the steps into the garage. God bless Gram, she'd never sold Granddad's van. He'd owned the only landscap-ing company in town, and his old white work van still sat in the garage next to Gram's darling little silver Cadillac convertible. I'd never get away with using Gram's car for surveillance in this town, but Granddad's would be perfect as soon as I had it serviced and the back windows tint-ed.

I climbed into the Escape, backed out of the garage and headed towards town. Time to find out what my sister was up to.

NINE

When I turned left on Palmetto Boulevard, Colleen materialized in the passenger seat.

I jumped, stepped on the accelerator, and made an exasperated noise at her. "Now you show up."

"It's a good thing you've got connections to local law enforcement," Colleen said. "The speed limit's thirty-five."

"Why are you speaking in complete sentences all of a sudden? So far, all I've gotten is cryptic monosyllables."

"I didn't have much to say before now. Besides, it was very dramatic, don't you think?" Colleen laughs like a donkey crossbred with a pig: *bray* snort-snort *bray*. She bray-snorted exuberantly. "Better watch where you're going."

I glanced out the windshield and jerked the wheel to the left, narrowly avoiding the sidewalk. "I can't be late to this meeting." I wasn't in danger of being late. But I wanted to be early and watch everyone else come in.

"Why on earth not?" Colleen rolled down the window and stuck her bare feet out into the warm evening breeze. "Trust me. I've been to a few. Town council meetings in Stella Maris are mundane madness. Tidbits of small-town life morph into high drama and comedy. What color should we paint the water tower? How do we round up the wild hog population? Should the council wear shirts and ties or matching golf shirts in the Fourth of July Parade? About as often as Haley's Comet swings by, there's actual business discussed."

"Tonight's going to be one of those nights." I slowed down for a stoplight and looked both ways before flooring it. It didn't cross my mind until much later to wonder how ghosts roll down car windows.

"You're worried about what Merry's up to," she said.

"What do you know about that?"

"If I tell you, this evening won't be nearly as much fun."

"You think gang wars on the beach sound like fun?"

"I think you should make sure that never happens."

"Dammit, Colleen."

"See you inside." She faded away.

At six forty-five p.m., I walked into the executive conference room. The mayor, Lincoln Sullivan, and his wife, Mildred, huddled in quiet conversation at the large mahogany table that filled most of the room. They stopped talking long enough to look at me with raised eyebrows and say hello.

"How are y'all?" I flashed them my brightest smile.

Colleen sat in a chair along the back wall. She motioned me over. "Council etiquette," she said. "The unwashed—you, me, Blake, and anybody else who wanders in by mistake—sit in chairs along the wall, not at the conference table."

I sat down beside her, leaned down, and fiddled with my purse. "Blake comes to these things?" I asked in a whisper.

"They like him to be here in case any police business comes up," Colleen said. "Usually, that means somebody's dog has to be penned up because he's fertilizing the neighbor's yard, or somebody's teenager went Goth and is scaring folks."

Colleen chattered on. "Most times, the only other unofficial attendees are the mayor's wife, Mildred, and Mackie Sullivan. This meeting's drawing a crowd." Colleen's eyes sparkled mischievously as spectators settled into chairs against the wall. "Merry has the whole town worked up. Wild speculation and mass hysteria—I love it. I haven't had this much fun in ages."

"Hey," I murmured. "What's Mildred Sullivan's maiden name?"

"How would I know?" she asked. "Oh. And who's going to fill your Gram's seat on the council? That's the other hot ticket."

Blake slid into the chair on my right. "Hey, Sis." His tone advertised neutrality.

"Hey," I said with a little smile. Then I asked him, "Do you know what Mildred Sullivan's maiden name is?"

"Not a clue. She's from Charleston, I think. Why?"

"Just curious.

The air pressure in the room shifted. Before I turned to see him, I felt Michael Devlin walk into the room. He took a place at the table across from Robert Pearson. At thirty-three, Michael looked better than he ever had: six-foot-three, toned and tanned, with black hair and a chiseled face that called to mind the Cherokee in his family. He must have felt me staring at him, because he looked up and our eyes locked. Something in his soft brown eyes connected with something in the pit of my stomach and twisted it. I looked away first.

"Oh boy." Colleen rolled her eyes.

I concentrated on breathing. Of course, I'd known he'd be here, but I'd thought I'd moved beyond the place where the sight of him physically hurt.

Fortunately, my sister staged a distraction. Merry made her way around the table in our direction, followed by the most accessorized man I had ever seen up close. Gelled hair, three shirts, necklace, bracelet, two rings, and one of those man-purse things. Something about him was vaguely familiar. Blake, Colleen and I stood.

"Liz, Blake," Merry said, "this is David Morehead. He's with the New Life Foundation. David, my sister, Liz Talbot, and my brother, Blake." People that didn't know us well would never have known from Merry's gracious tone that she and I were on the verge of unladylike behavior.

We all shook hands and exchanged pleasantries. Merry took the seat on Blake's other side. He squirmed.

More people filed into the room. I glanced at Colleen. Someone would soon be sitting on her lap. She must have had the same thought, because she took a seat at the table and swiveled around in her chair to face me. "They never use all of these chairs."

I gaped at her. I knew no one else could see her, but surely others could see the chair swivel. Nobody seemed to notice. From the other side of Blake, I could hear Merry talking to David Morehead.

"Stella Maris is divided into six districts. Originally the districts reflected the parcels of land owned by the town's founders. More recently the lines have been creatively redrawn as those families intermarried and then divided land in an estate," she said. "But the council has always consisted of one member from each of those families. According to the town by-laws, any family member residing in District Three can fill Gram's seat. If no family member volunteers, we'll have a special election. Then anyone living in District Three can be elected, family or not."

Colleen spun around in her chair. "Problem is, most of the family is already on the council."

"Would you stop that?" I hissed at her.

"Stop what?" Blake asked.

I stared at him for a beat. "Jiggling your leg. That's working my nerves."

"I wasn't—"

"I just need a few minutes of peace, okay?" I turned back to Colleen and narrowed my eyes. She smiled and swiveled back to the table. She had a point. Daddy held the District Four seat, which was made up of the Talbot family land. Michael, a family member by marriage, represented District One, the Devlin district. Gram had held the Simmons' seat. Before her death, our extended family made up half the town council. There was likely as much speculation about who would fill her seat as Merry's nonsense.

As police chief, Blake was ineligible. Up until the day before, I had lived in Greenville, several hours away. While Merry was a resident of District Three, she had expressed no interest in filling the vacancy, which was no doubt a relief to each and every member of the council. By Stella Maris standards, Merry was a subversive.

It didn't take much to be labeled a subversive in Stella Maris. Rumor had it—and I could have confirmed it—Merry had attended several anti-war protests and seen every Michael Moore movie. She turned up the volume on her favorite Dixie Chicks song and rolled down the windows of her car especially for Mildred Sullivan's benefit whenever the mayor's wife happened to stroll by within hearing distance. Mildred had organized a public smashing of Dixie Chicks' CDs after that unfortunate comment one of them made regarding the former president.

Colleen leaned back so far in her chair that she was nearly horizontal. Her head was in my lap. "They talked about it at lunch today. They have it all planned. There's going to be a special election. First order of business." She sat up before I could respond.

Mackie Sullivan entered the room and negotiated his way in our direction, eyes laser-locked on David Morehead. Blake, Merry, and I stood up, having been raised to a certain standard of manners, even when dealing with the insufferably pompous. David Morehead followed suit as Mackie sauntered to a stop, way too close.

Mackie extended his hand to David with a smile that reminded me of an eel. "Good evening, sir. I am Mac E. Sullivan, *not Mackie*. Mac. Short for Mackenzie. The initial 'E' stands for Emerson, a family name on my mother's side. I am counsel of record of this venerated assembly, and it would be my great privilege if you would allow me to welcome you to our fair municipality."

Mackie—we called him that just to irritate him—was never one to use five words when he could get in a hundred. Blake studied the floor. With remarkable self-control, none of us laughed out loud.

David shook the offered hand and smiled tentatively. "It's a pl—"

"Would everyone please be seated? It's almost time to begin." Lincoln Sullivan interrupted, magnolia syrup dripping from every word. He glared at his nephew, Mackie.

Mackie would have ignored him, no doubt, but we sat down immediately, grateful for intervention. The mayor smiled and nodded at us. He glared again at Mackie, who reluctantly took a seat.

Just as the grandfather clock in the corner struck seven o'clock, the last two members of the council, John Glendawn (Moon Unit and Elvis's daddy—District Two), and Grace Sullivan (Mamma's best friend and my godmother—District Five) took their seats. Plenty of folks in Stella Maris would give you an earful about having a psychic hold public office if you asked them, psychics being "of the devil" and whatnot. Fortunately, none of the other council members shared this view.

I hadn't seen Daddy come in, but he was seated on the far side of the table. He grinned at me. Blake might not be happy I was home, but my daddy surely was.

Lincoln Sullivan cleared his throat. "Looks like everybody's here. I guess we can get started." He peered over glasses perched on the end of his patrician nose. His gaze danced around the room and settled with undisguised curiosity on Merry. "We have a lot to talk about this evening. Young lady, we'll get to you in a moment."

The mayor paused eloquently, then continued. "You all are aware of our predicament due to the tragic passing of our dear friend, Emma Rae. Does anyone have a motion regarding the filling of her seat for the remainder of her unexpired term of office?" Lincoln looked directly at Robert Pearson (District Six).

"I move we hold a special election, six weeks from today," Robert said, apparently on cue.

"I sec—" Daddy raised his hand.

"I have something to say." Merry stood.

Daddy stared at her, irritation written on his face.

Lincoln eyed her over the top of his glasses. "Young lady, you are out of order. I believe I mentioned we would address your business momentarily."

"But what I have to say bears directly on this issue," Merry protested.

Mackie blustered, his most remarkable skill. "Pursuant to—"

"*Mac.*" Lincoln cut him off and turned to Merry with a look of patient kindness. "Well, ah, I'm sure we'll all be glad to hear it. If you'll let your daddy second the motion, as he was about to do, then I'll call for discussion, according to the Roberts Rules of Order." He smiled at her and then at the head of the Talbot family.

"I'm terribly sorry." Merry smiled back at him. "It's just that, I want to volunteer to fill the seat, so there's no need to *hold* a special election. I was merely trying to save the council some time."

You could have heard a mosquito in that room.

No longer smiling, Lincoln gaped at her.

The room erupted in a clamor of murmurs, whispered conversation, and nervous shifting.

Lincoln regained his wits and rapped his gavel. "Order, order everyone."

The room quieted.

Lincoln addressed the group. "This assembly will take a fifteen-minute recess while council meets in executive session to discuss this most interesting development."

"But—" Merry started to object.

"Elizabeth." When Daddy uses my actual, full name, he's serious. "Would you and your sister and her friend please give us a moment? You can wait in the lobby. I'll come get you when we're ready." He nodded cordially at David Morehead.

Merry collected her briefcase and her associate and stormed out of the room. Blake and I followed, along with the other spectators—all except Colleen, who stayed behind.

Merry strode to a far corner of the lobby and whirled to face me.

Fast on her heels, I glared at her, regaining my equilibrium and my voice. "Well, well, baby sister. You forgot to mention you were staging a coup."

"I have just as much right to that seat as anybody in this family," she said. "No one else wants it, and by the way, you aren't fooling anybody. You'll stay in Gram's house a week, max. Then you'll be headed back to Greenville and the beach house will be on the market. So don't pretend you give a tinker's damn what happens here."

"The *only* reason you're interested in that seat is so you have a better chance of shoving your big idea down everybody's throat." My nails bit into my palms as I clenched my fists at my side.

"How would you know what I'm interested in? You barely give me or anybody else here a passing thought anymore."

"I would hardly have to be a mind reader to know what's going on. Since when have you given the first damn about town government? This is so transparent, *please*. You're afraid I *will* stay—not that I won't."

Blake stepped between us, placing what the casual observer might have mistaken for a consoling arm around each of our shoulders. "Let's all just simmer down now."

"Stay out of this," we said in unison, both glaring at him.

"Afraid not, ladies." He kept his voice calm, the way you do when you're soothing a colicky baby—or a rabid dog. "As chief of police, I'm going to ask you once more, nicely, to simmer down. As your brother, I beg you on behalf of our entire family to please not embarrass us all by making a scene. You can brawl later."

I turned away from both of them and studied the painting on the wall to my left. It was a Civil War battle scene.

Blake continued in his diplomatic tone. "Now, I am interested myself, Merry, in where this sudden interest in civic affairs comes from."

"I'm not particularly interested in town government. But a family member has held that seat ever since this town was born, and there isn't anyone else to fill it." Merry gave Blake that look sisters always give their brothers when they want something. "You are ineligible, and Liz," she tossed her head and a glare in my direction, "won't be sticking around long. Who else is available?"

Blake looked out the floor-to-ceiling windows at the park across the street.

"Do either of you really want to leave it up to a special election?" Merry demanded. "We could end up with somebody who isn't *from here.*"

The faint tinkle of a warning bell sounded in my brain. Simultaneously, something outside caught Blake's attention. My eyes followed his and I gulped for air.

Humphrey Pearson, Robert's uncle, skated by on rollerblades wearing a body-sized placard strapped across his shoulders. The message was the same front and back: "New Laws, Not New Jails." Humphrey was stuck in 1969, and his favorite political issue was legalizing recreational drug use. He'd somehow gotten the idea that drug offenders were to be incarcerated at Devlin's Point.

Had he been wearing any clothes under the sign, his protest wouldn't have gotten nearly the attention. A crowd was forming.

Blake's tone never changed. "Maybe we need to bus in a few more folks who aren't from here. Freshen the gene pool."

Mildred Sullivan overheard Blake's remark. She glared up at him. "And to think, I convinced Lincoln to promote you when Charlie Jacobs retired."

Blake turned and looked down to meet her stare. "All due respect, Mildred, I hope that's working out better for you right now than it is for me." He reached for his cell phone. "Excuse me, ladies."

With a haughty look, Mildred glided off to the other side of the lobby and missed Humphrey's protest. Mildred considered it her duty, as the mayor's wife, to hold the community to high moral standards. She didn't hold with nudity.

Blake turned back to the parade outside and spoke into his phone. "Coop, I need you to come over to the town offices and escort Humphrey home." Clay Cooper was Blake's second in command.

I resumed trying to reason with my sister. "Hell's bells, Merry. Half the people in this town are from somewhere else. Folks from the mainland brought us cappuccino, Pad Thai, and designer hair color."

"People without history here see things differently," Merry said.

Public nudity crisis handled, Blake rejoined the conversation. "It's only a matter of time before someone whose great-grandfather was born elsewhere is elected to the council. Maybe we should let some new folks fool with it for a while."

"She's just trying to hedge her bets with this gangbanger scheme of hers."

"Think what you want," Merry said. "Just remember this: I care enough about what happens here to do something about it. You'll be back in Greenville by this time next week. Maybe you should run for city council up there."

"This is just as much my home as it is yours. And if you think for one minute—"

"Don't you live in a loft in downtown Greenville?" Merry interrupted.

Blake must have felt us regaining our momentum. "Liz, Merry isn't going to do anything that would hurt this island. She lives here, too."

I was getting cranky at the repeated reference to where everybody lived. Hadn't I just moved home? "I love this island just as much as the two of you. And you're both crazy if you think that hauling a hundred members of *rival gangs* who have been convicted of *violent crimes* over here won't hurt anything."

"I didn't say that. Merry?" Blake tilted his head and looked expectantly at her.

She examined her nails.

He exhaled loudly and looked heavenward for answers. When none were forthcoming, he lowered his gaze to meet mine. "Just because she has a proposal doesn't mean she shouldn't be on town council. She'd still just have one vote."

"The idea of developing Devlin's Point just turns my stomach, and I can't imagine opening up our home to that kind of risk."

"*Whose* home?" Merry goaded me once more for good measure.

"*My* home," I ground out through squared jaw. "*I'll* take the seat," I said. "I own property here. And I moved in yesterday."

Without a backward glance to either of them, I stalked down the hall, knocked twice on the conference room door, and let myself in without waiting for an invitation.

"...we have to seat a volunteer from the Simmons—" Lincoln

stopped talking and they all stared at me.

"Well, now you have two volunteers," I said.

Lincoln, Michael, Robert, John, and Grace all turned to Daddy.

Daddy sat there for a minute, staring at nothing in particular, doing this thing with his hand that he always does when he's considering something real carefully. He held his palm at a right angle and made a chopping motion on the table. Right, left, right left. Back and forth. Finally he looked at Lincoln. "Liz is older, and she inherited the Simmons estate. I move that we fill Mamma's council seat by appointing Elizabeth to her unexpired term."

Robert nodded. "I second the motion."

"Any discussion?" Lincoln asked.

No one said a word.

"Well, then," Lincoln said, "all in favor?"

By unanimous vote, I became a council member. I took a seat at the table. "I'd like to make a motion myself."

Lincoln gestured for me to proceed.

"I move we table the rest of tonight's business and adjourn so that I can educate myself on other matters before the council."

Daddy seconded my motion, and it also passed unanimously. No one, it seemed, was eager to discuss fellowship halls, orphanages, or jails. I braced myself to face my sister as we filed out of the conference room.

But the lobby was deserted.

TEN

After throwing the first Tuesday of every month on the bonfire of my sister's insanity, I was starving. I zipped over to The Pirates' Den—the restaurant John and Alma Glendawn owned on the north shore of the island. Since I was dining alone, I climbed into one of the high-backed stools at the mammoth mahogany bar that took up the entire street-side wall. I settled into the tropical print cushions and looked around in appreciation. I had missed this place.

It looked like the inside of an old ship—all varnished wood and portholes. The glass wall to my back featured several sets of french doors that led out onto an oceanfront deck. Saltwater aquariums containing a variety of tropical fish lined the left wall. And everywhere you looked, parrots—stuffed, wood-carved, ceramic, you name it. Steel-drum music wafted through the restaurant. The rich aromas of Jamaican spices and grilled meats and vegetables infused the air. My stomach growled.

John had arrived from the council meeting just in front of me. His returning to the restaurant rather than going home was an added bonus to a great dinner. I pulled out my hand sanitizer while I mulled how to approach the subject of who HC and SD were, and what their relationship to John Glendawn might be. That connection should tell me what Gram's list meant.

He puttered behind the bar and kept me company while I sipped a margarita and waited for my cheeseburger. He had the look of an ancient sailor, with sun-leathered skin and bright blue eyes. Gray hair curled out from under the well-worn captain's hat that was pulled down low and cocked slightly to one side.

Maybe I was biased, or maybe it was the salt air, but my taste buds insisted the cheeseburgers at The Pirates' Den were the best to be found. I devoured the three-napkin masterpiece John put in front of me.

"Can I get you anything else?" He smiled at me from across the bar as I popped the last french fry into my mouth. Without waiting for my response, he continued in a more somber tone. "I don't know if I ever got the chance to tell you how sorry I am about Emma. She was a fine woman."

Since I had food in my mouth, I nodded my thanks.

John polished a spot on the bar. "A dear friend. Did a lot for this town. Spunky, too." He smiled but didn't quite manage to erase the sadness in his eyes. "You and your sister are a lot like her."

I smiled at the compliment. "How's Alma doing?"

He shook his head. "Eh law, she's caught herself a bug."

"I hope she feels better soon."

"Fact is, she hasn't felt like herself since Emma Rae passed. Alma's the one found her, you know."

"Blake told me."

"Hated to leave her home by herself tonight, but my regular bartender had to go see about his sister up in West Virginia. I had to get Moon Unit to hold down the fort long enough for me to go to the council meeting. How about some key lime pie?"

"Sounds great." I watched his calloused hands slice and plate the pie and set it in front of me.

I took a bite of my pie, letting the cool, tart sweetness melt on my tongue. "Mmmm. Delicious." I smiled. "I hear Gram had a Roaring Twenties party last month. You and Alma make it?"

John laughed. "We wouldn't have missed that. Alma made a right smart flapper."

"I think Gram was already planning her next soiree. I found the guest list she was working on at the house. Who knows what her next theme would have been?"

He chuckled. "Hard to say."

"I declare, so many new people have moved to Stella Maris over the last few years, it's going to take me a while to get to know everyone. Gram had names on that list I didn't recognize."

John looked at me quizzically. "Most of the folks that came to Emma's parties are old friends. There've been a few new faces, I guess."

I shrugged, put a finger to my temple, and offered him my Ditzy-

Blonde Look. I practice this look in front of the mirror. It doesn't come naturally, but it serves me well. "Some of the names were in, like, shorthand or something—just initials. Who are 'HC' and 'SD?'"

The smile vanished from John's eyes and the corners of his mouth lowered by degrees. He busied himself wiping up the bar. "The only person I've ever heard called HC was Hayden Causby, and you wouldn't a been likely to've run across him at a party of Emma Rae's."

"The shrimper from over in Mount Pleasant?"

Mount Pleasant is a fishing and shrimping hub situated across the Intracoastal Waterway. The Causby family had been prominent in the shrimping industry for generations. Last I'd heard, Merry had been dating Hayden Causby's grandson, Troy.

John took a moment to answer. "Yep. But she musta meant someone else."

"Did Gram know Hayden Causby well?"

John kept wiping. "I reckon she did. He ran with me an' Stuart an' them for a while when we were kids. 'Bout the time Emma and Stuart were dating." John's tone and expression suggested he'd taken a bite of something spoiled.

"Stuart?" I knew exactly who John must have meant, but I needed to hear him say it.

"Stuart Devlin."

Stuart Devlin was Michael's father, the town's mayor for years, and architect of the zoning laws that protected the island to this day. I vaguely recalled he and Gram had dated in high school. But Stuart had been killed in a sailing accident when Michael was in second grade. He had to be the SD Gram referred to, but what could a man twenty-five years dead have to do with Gram's death two weeks ago?

I flashed my ditzy-blonde look. "All y'all were friends?"

"I never said that." He reached for the portable phone. "Think I'll call and check on Alma."

"But if she's sleeping, the phone will disturb her," I said. I was feeling plenty guilty for dredging up memories John wanted left buried. If my hunch was right, Hayden Causby figured into John's ancient marijuana arrest. John Glendawn was a dear soul, and I had played him. "Why don't you let me watch the bar for you for a few minutes?"

"I don't know..." He considered my offer. "It's easy enough to take a beer out of the cooler or pour a glass of wine, but what if somebody wants a drink?"

I grinned. "Fix you a 'rita?"

"Huh? Well, okay, that's what we sell the most of, I guess." He opened the gate at the end of the bar and stepped back to let me in. He moved to the other side of the bar and took my place on the stool, watching as I mixed the tequila, lime juice, and Grand Marnier. I wet the outside of the glass rim, salted it, and garnished the result with a slice of lime. With a flourish, I placed the drink on the cocktail napkin in front of him.

John looked at me through squinted eyes as he tasted the concoction.

"Perfect," he declared. "I don't say that about anybody's 'ritas but my own. Where'd you learn to do that?"

"I tended bar for two years during college to help with expenses. Don't mention it in front of my mamma—she prefers to let it slip her mind."

He took another sip with a big smile on his face, the past filed neatly back in the past. "Why didn't you say so? I'll be back quick as I can."

"Take your time."

"Thanks." John waved and was out the french doors.

Business was slow that night at The Pirates' Den. A few couples lingered over dinner. Zeke Lyerly and three of his cronies occupied the front corner table closest to the bar. They were working on a pitcher of margaritas. Maybe not their first.

When I heard the words "sexy French missionary," "anaconda," and "nuclear missile," I chuckled.

Zeke's exploits were legendary, although the more colorful tales were the ones he told himself—the ones no one could confirm. Zeke could entertain you with vivid accounts of his years as an Army Ranger, his adventures as a prize-winning bull rider, and his heyday as an almost-famous NASCAR driver. According to Blake's calculations, if everything Zeke said were true, he'd have been two hundred thirty-five years old.

John was gone less than five minutes when I heard the front door open and close. I turned to see Michael coming around the end of the bar. I felt myself flush. We hadn't spent five minutes alone since the day he married Marci.

"Hi," he said, with a confused look. "Where's John?"

"He'll be right back. Can I get you something?" I offered him my brightest smile.

He grinned as he slid onto the barstool in front of me. "Are you taking over here, too?"

"Just helping out a friend," I said. "John was short a bartender and needed to check on Alma."

"Bud Light, please."

I reached for the beer and a frosted mug, grateful for something to do with my hands.

"I didn't realize you were in town until you showed up at the council meeting." Those dark-chocolate eyes found mine.

Time shifted, and I was back on campus and in love for the first and only time in my life. I'd known Michael growing up. He was Blake's best friend. But my sophomore year at Clemson, he became much more.

"I didn't think it would be appropriate to come to call." This was the feeling—this ache for him coated with anger—that made being back home so hard.

"Liz—" He was going to apologize again. I could still read him as well as I could ten years ago.

"Don't." I hated that my eyes watered. "I don't ever want to talk about it. It's done."

Irritation crept into his voice. "*You* decided we should see other people. *You* started seeing Scott." Now his eyes had that dangerous look—the one that made my insides go all liquid.

"I had been out with him *once*." I hated myself for the quiver in my voice. "And only because of that stupid fight."

"That's not the way he told it."

"He's a liar."

"That much we agree on." He studied his untouched beer for a moment. "Scott Andrews gets what he wants, one way or another. I never even went on a date with Marci. She came up to visit you just before Christmas break."

"That was the last thing I ever invited her to do, besides take a running leap off the Cooper River Bridge."

Marci and I had never been friends, but when I was young, idealistic, and ignorant of the ways of sociopaths, I tried to be nice to her—she was family, and Mamma encouraged it. Hence, Marci's visit to Clemson that had brought me so much grief.

"I saw you with him..." Michael ran his hand through his hair. "I'd had too much to drink, and she was all comfort and joy."

"I'll just bet she was."

"The next day she was gone, and six weeks later I got the phone call. What was I supposed to do? She was carrying my child."

"You did exactly what she knew you would do—the honorable thing." I tasted the bitterness on my tongue.

"And then, she was so broken up when she lost the baby..."

"Did it ever occur to you that there might not have *been* a baby?" You can bet the family silver on that one.

"Not at the time." He picked up the beer and downed a third of it.

"So when you figured it out, why did you stay married to her?"

"By that time, you were engaged to Scott." He took another long swallow of the beer. "What difference did it make?"

We looked at each other far longer than could be considered appropriate. Everything that might have been ran through my head. I wanted to shout at him that I was divorced now, and he knew this full well, so why, exactly, was he still married to that devious little witch? But pride held my tongue. If he didn't want me enough to fight for me, I didn't want him either. The steel slid back into my spine.

"Look," I said, in a tone that masked what I felt, "this is ancient history. We're going to have to get used to living in the same town. It's good we cleared the air."

I saw the wall go up in his eyes. He finished his beer and slid the mug towards me. "I'd like another."

I reached for the beer. "So, Marci's pretty pissed off about Gram's will."

"That's a fair assessment. What Emma Rae had was hers to do with as she damn well pleased. Besides, it's not like anyone expected her to die. To hear Marci talk, you'd think she was expecting fast cash and had already written checks against it."

I wasn't a bit surprised. Marci had always been a greedy, grasping little bitch. I studied Michael. He didn't talk like a happily married man. I should've been ashamed of the joyous backflip my heart took. Why the hell had he stayed married to her? A neon light in my brain flashed "tell him the bitch tried to swap him for some land." If he'd said one thing I could have latched on to, and somehow interpreted to mean he still loved me, I would have told him.

A tall waitress with very red hair stepped up to the end of the bar. "I need a pitcher of margaritas and a couple of Mich Lights." If she was surprised to see me behind the bar instead of John, she didn't comment on it.

I filled her drink order while Michael sipped his beer. He watched her walk away and then turned to me. "So. What became of Scott?" The wall was still there, but there was a challenge in his eyes.

"The liar worked seventy hours a week, played golf with his business associates, and dragged me to an endless parade of social occasions where all the *right* people were networking. And he slept with his secretaries, the wives of the men he screwed over in business deals, and a few of my so-called friends."

"He stayed busy."

"I should never have married him." I was on the rebound. Thank God I didn't say that out loud. I rediscovered the key lime pie in front of me. I put some pie on my fork and then rested the fork on my plate. "So you're in construction, right?"

"Residential, mostly, but sometimes I do small commercial projects. That's what I wanted to talk to John about. He wants me to enclose his deck."

"Why didn't you finish school? Being an architect was your dream."

He looked away. "Never had the time. I like being a contractor just fine," he said. "Does that amuse you?"

"Why would it?"

He shrugged and drank deeply from his beer mug.

We both looked up as John came back through the french doors. "She was sleeping like a baby," he announced. "Everything okay in here?"

"Just fine," Michael answered. "Got yourself a new bartender, I see."

"You didn't have one of her margaritas, did you?" he asked, eying the beer mug on the bar. "You must notta, or you wouldn't be drinking that. You want to take a look at this deck with me?"

"Sure thing." Michael hesitated. "I guess I'll see you around."

I nodded. "See you around."

I picked up my fork to commence stress eating as I watched them disappear onto the deck. A large bite of key lime pie missed my mouth and slid down the front of my suit. "Shit."

It served me right. Mamma raised me better than to ogle someone else's husband. But in my heart, he would never belong to anyone but me.

By the time I left The Pirates' Den, it was after nine. There were maybe eight cars in the oyster-shell parking lot. Two of them, a Lexus and a Camry, sat side by side in the corner of the lot, near the road, with the Camry on the far side of the Lexus. One of the motors was running, but it was hard to tell which. As I walked towards the Escape, David Morehead, Merry's embellished cohort, slid out of the passenger side of the Lexus. I only saw his silhouette, and might not have recognized him except for the man purse. He moved in a stealthy posture, not standing to his full height, around the back of the Lexus to the Camry. Before he even opened the door, the Lexus pulled out of the lot.

I hopped into the Escape and pulled onto Ocean Boulevard behind the Lexus. Within a half mile I'd caught up with it. I didn't follow it long. Better not to make the driver suspicious.

All I needed was the license plate.

ELEVEN

Back at Gram's house, I poured myself a glass of pinot noir. Rhett was snoozing in his bed in the sunroom. He seemed lost in doggy dreams, so I didn't disturb him. I took my wine into my new office and logged on to one of my subscription databases. Seconds later, I knew that David Morehead had been meeting with Adam Devlin outside The Pirates' Den. Adam was Michael's older brother, but they were nothing alike. I didn't know Adam well, but I'd never liked him. He'd married Colleen's older sister, Deanna. She was the closest thing to an angel you'd find this side of heaven. I'd always held the opinion that she deserved better.

At first blush, it seemed reasonable that David and Adam might have legitimate business. After all, Merry and David's project was to be housed on a sizable piece of Devlin land. But why would Adam and David be skulking about parking lots? People with nothing to hide meet inside the restaurant, not in the dark shadows outside.

I typed interview notes from my conversation with John Glendawn. Then I set up profiles for Hayden Causby and Stuart Devlin. A records check confirmed both were arrested at the same time as John Glendawn back in 1961. But, while Stuart and John were both charged with simple marijuana possession, Hayden was sentenced to fifteen years for possession with intent to distribute. Interesting, but what did it mean? Maybe Merry could fill me in on some of the Causby history—if she ever spoke to me again.

Next, I checked up on David Morehead. Something about that guy was nagging at me. I knew I'd seen him somewhere before, but I couldn't place where. His proximity to Merry's schizophrenic project—and his clandestine meeting with Adam Devlin—made me leery of David and the New Life Foundation. I Googled both. I came up with nothing on him, but plenty on the foundation.

The New Life folks had several camps across the country dedicated to helping at-risk teenagers. The website didn't mention gangs or felons, but maybe they didn't advertise that clientele. No high-rise facilities appeared in any of the photos. In fact, their operations looked more like campgrounds. There was no mention of David Morehead, or any of the executives, for that matter. It was all about the kids—success stories and testimonials.

The nonprofit was registered in New York, with a Quincy Owen as contact at a Lake George, New York mailing address. Three clicks later, I had a phone number for Mr. Owen, but it was too late to call.

The pinot noir was silky on my tongue. I savored a long sip and stared out the front windows. Gram was my client. She was the victim. As often happens, the victim would have to be a subject of the investigation. I sighed and set up a profile for Gram. Hers was the lone missing council member's name on the list. And she was the one who'd been murdered. Whose name would she have written by her own on the legal pad?

I was pondering that when the stairs creaked.

I listened hard. Old houses make settling noises, right?

Squeak.

Now it occurred to me how odd it was that Rhett was asleep when I came in. He always greeted me at the door. I eased open the bottom drawer of my desk and retrieved Sig. Then I crept over to the french doors opening to the foyer. I hadn't been upstairs since I'd come home, so the landing lights weren't on. I couldn't see past the first three steps.

The light switch for the foyer was by the front door. To turn it on, I'd have to pass in full view of anyone on the steps.

Creak.

"Marci? That you? I have a gun, it's loaded, and I'm a pretty fair shot," I said, in a chatty tone.

Creaks, squeaks, rapid footsteps. Someone scrambled back up the stairs and across the landing. I crossed to the door and flipped on the lights. A glimpse of denim disappeared down the hall to the right, towards Gram's room. Marci wouldn't run from me—she'd confront me.

I bolted up the steps.

Gram's bedroom door slammed closed.

I sprinted to the door and tried the knob. Locked. Where were the interior keys? No time to pick a lock.

I rammed my shoulder into the door. Yeouch! That was stupid. The doors were solid mahogany. Why the devil would an intruder lock himself in Gram's room? There was no way—yes, there was a way out.

Back down the hall I dashed, taking the stairs two at a time. At the landing, I swung around and flew down the hall towards the back of the house. I threw the deadbolt in the sunroom and burst out onto the deck. I looked up at the balcony outside Gram's room. The french doors stood open, and no sign of the intruder. I knew—because I had done it myself as a child—that one could climb from the balcony onto the handrail of the deck using the wisteria trellis. But this was a dicey maneuver, not something you did in a hurry. No one except a monkey could have already climbed down and disappeared into the night.

I waited, panting.

Nothing.

Damnation.

Back into the house I ran. Through the sunroom, down the hall, up the stairs. I pulled up short. Gram's bedroom door stood open.

Sonofabitch. I'd been had. The intruder waited until I was outside, then walked down the steps and out the front door.

I eased down the hall, Sig drawn, and into Gram's room. I cleared the closets and her bathroom, then closed and locked the balcony doors. Room by room, I checked the rest of the house. All the windows and doors were locked. And no sign of forced entry. How the hell had anyone gotten in?

I went back to Rhett. I ruffled the fur on his back and called his name. He rolled over and yawned, but didn't waken. I reached out to put my gun on the coffee table, but stopped short. A box of Benadryl sat on the edge of the coffee table. A box I hadn't left there. The intruder wanted me to know he gave Rhett Benadryl—something that would wear off shortly and wouldn't hurt him.

Anyone that thoughtful was probably not a killer. My prowler was not likely Gram's murderer. And it damn sure wasn't Marci. She'd have poisoned Rhett for spite. Nothing seemed missing, and the burglar made no attempt to harm me—just the opposite. He'd avoided a confrontation. Then what did he want?

With the house secure and Rhett sleeping off the Benadryl, I snugged Sig in the back waistband of my slacks, grabbed a flashlight, and went to look for signs of entry outside.

I stood in the circle drive and stared at the house. If I were going to break in, how would I do it?

I'd pick a lock. But that was a specialized skill set—not nearly as easy as it looked on television. If someone had picked a lock, it was either a professional thief or possibly another results-oriented PI with relaxed standards about occasional breaking and entering.

If I couldn't pick locks, how would I break in?

I circled the exterior of the house looking for ideas. Blake was right about one thing, motion detectors illuminated the entire yard as I walked. When I reached the north lawn, I walked up the stone path to the garage. The side door was unlocked. I hadn't checked it earlier—it hadn't occurred to me. I turned on the lights and walked up the steps to the door leading to the mudroom. Something was on the top step. I bent down for a closer view.

It looked like a chicken nugget. I stood and quickly surveyed the garage below me. A box of car rags sat on a shelf at the foot of the steps. Perfect. I retrieved a rag and used it to pick up the lump. It was, in fact, a chicken nugget. My intruder likely slipped Rhett a bite through the pet door, called to him, watched him eat it, and then given him another treat with the Benadryl inside.

I sat on the top step, leaned back, and stuck my arm through the pet door. Barely a stretch to unlock both the knob and the deadbolt. With that mystery solved, I retraced my steps, locking the door to the yard behind me. It didn't have a deadbolt. The knob-lock was accessible through the pet door just like the one at the top of the stairs. Maybe a security system wasn't such a bad idea.

I walked back around to the ocean side of the house. What brought Gram outside the night she was killed? I stared under the deck and switched on the flashlight. Something sinister, with tiny cold feet ran up my spine. A wave of nausea hit me. This was where it had happened, on a night much like this one. The wind would have been howling.

I shined the flashlight on every square foot of the storage area. Frame by frame, I looked for anything out of place. Just like in the daylight, there was nothing here but firewood and sand. My gaze slid past the stacked logs, then back. I eyed the wood.

I'd seen things hidden in far stranger places.

I ran inside and came back with latex gloves and a pair of heavy gardening gloves I found in the storage room. I blew into the gardening gloves and shook them out. Who knows what might have nested in there, or who wore the gloves last, or how fastidious his sanitary habits were? I slipped on the latex gloves and the gardening gloves over top.

Log by log, I unstacked the wood, tossing each piece into a pile behind me. Thirty minutes later, I was sure there was nothing but wood. It took far longer to restack it than to take the pile apart. When I finished, I stepped back and swept the flashlight once more around the area for good measure. I'm nothing if not thorough.

As I backed out from underneath the deck, something glinted in the flashlight beam. Something in the sand, a few feet in front of the woodpile. I stepped closer, brushed the sand away. It was a silver, heart-shaped locket on a dainty chain—must have been buried. In moving all that wood around, I'd uncovered it.

I pulled off the gardening gloves and lifted the necklace out of the sand. The clasp appeared broken. Inside was a picture of a man I'd never seen before. The image was small, but the smiling subject appeared to be somewhere in the neighborhood of sixty. A tanned, vibrant sixty.

Back in my office, I labeled a plastic bag, slipped the locket inside, and sealed the bag. A rift of blues from my iPhone signaled Nate on the line. The photo of him on the screen had been taken at Artisphere, an arts festival in Greenville, the year before. He was sprawled on a quilt in the grass at The Peace Center Amphitheatre. We'd been listening to a local jazz band and munching on street food. I smiled at the memory and slid the arrow across the touch screen to answer his call.

"Hey, you," I said.

"What's going on down there?"

I hesitated. Nate and I didn't keep secrets from each other. But if I told him I'd just chased off a prowler he'd worry. This long distance partnership was still very new. "Ahh, not much. Family drama, a prowler, small-town politics, you know."

"A prowler?"

"It was nothing. You should have been at that town council meeting—*man*."

"A prowler in the yard or someone in your house?"

"He left in a hurry, no worries there. Hey, I found a locket near where Blake thinks Gram was killed." I stared at the piece of jewelry in question. "I think it must have been hers, but I've never seen it before. Or the man whose picture is inside it."

"Give it to Blake. Now tell me about the prowler."

I sighed and told him about the prowler.

Nate was so quiet I thought the call had dropped.

"Nate?"

"Yeah. I'm here."

"You know I can take care of myself. This was nothing, really."

"Got it." Nate's tone rarely betrayed what he was thinking. He sounded calm, relaxed.

"What's new with you?" I knew I sounded a shade too bright.

"Not much. Closed the file on the Walker divorce."

"That was a messy one."

"Yeah, but adultery pays the rent."

"True."

"I'm supposed to fly to Vegas tomorrow to chase down a lead on Atticus Vardry's granddaughter."

"Wow, that trail's been cold for months. Wait, what do you mean you're 'supposed' to fly to Vegas?"

"I mean I have an airline ticket, and the client would very much like for me to ascertain if the heir to his considerable fortune is currently performing as a showgirl at the Jubilee show. But I'm considering heading south instead."

"What? No—I'm fine. Perfectly fine. And this is the first lead we've had on her in—"

"I know, months." He sighed. "Are you sure you're okay? I know you can handle prowlers. It's your family that worries me."

I had no doubt he was referring to Michael. He considered him yet another example of my bad romantic decisions. Although Michael was not technically family, Nate liked to remind me he was my cousin's husband by calling him family. "I can handle things here. Go to Vegas. Let me know if it's her. I'd love to close that case."

"Fine. Stay safe."

"You, too."

"Talk to you soon."

"Goodnight." I pressed end to disconnect and held the phone in both hands. For the first time since I'd arrived home, I felt lonely.

TWELVE

I got up at five the next morning to run on the beach. Rhett woke fine as frog hair—well rested and itching to frolic—so I took him along. I dropped a robe across a beach chair for later, and we warmed up with a jog around the north point of the island. We passed Sullivan's Bed and Breakfast, then Simmons' Inlet as we rounded the point and headed south along the Intracoastal Waterway to the marina where my brother still slept on his houseboat. I detoured through the marina parking lot and then hit sand again on the other side of the boat slips.

At Heron Creek, I turned and headed back the way I came.

We rounded North Point and ran south, towards town. I passed The Pirate's Den and half a dozen houses before the shore veered inland. From there, it was two miles to the spot where Main Street dead-ended into the dunes and I turned towards home. Round trip it was a five mile run, and I needed it. I was pent up.

Gradually the sky lightened enough that I could make out the clay-colored sand beneath my running shoes. I ran, like I run most mornings, until the endorphins flooded my brain. When I felt the rush, I jogged up the beach to the spot right in front of my house, took off every stitch of my clothes, and splashed into the surf. Rhett had better sense than I did. He got his paws wet, then scampered back up onto the beach.

I hadn't swum naked at sunrise since I was eighteen. Fully sane people would tell you this is a dangerous indulgence, but I was one with the ocean creatures. I was God's own mermaid.

The waves were rough that morning, so I didn't go in far. I swam parallel to the shore a few hundred feet, fighting the current, and then turned back. I rode a wave in and pulled myself out of the brine, water sluicing off me in a sensual caress as the surf splashed at my back. The fluffy robe I'd left on the canvass-and-wood beach chair felt like a warm cloud. I wrapped up and sat down.

The *woosh...splash* rhythm of the surf was therapeutic. Rhett chased foam, and I wiggled my toes in the sand and let my mind drift while the sun came up. This was where I'd always found peace. The ocean was my drug of choice. How had I possibly lived so far from it for so long?

It was fully light when I heard footsteps on the walkway behind me.

My first thought was that it was stupid of me to be on a deserted beach at sunup without a weapon. Someone killed Gram not far from where I sat. Fear coiled in my stomach. Perhaps I hadn't been taking Blake's concerns for my safety seriously enough. I slid down and turned in the chair to peer over the top.

I recognized the masculine form coming down the steps as my brother. Rhett, who hadn't opened his mouth, scampered with tail wagging towards Blake. Relieved, I turned back towards the ocean as he trudged through the wide belt of soft sand. A few waves later, I heard the gentle smack of bare feet on wet sand. Blake settled his beach chair beside mine and sat down.

"You know you're making me crazy," he said.

"I'm not trying to."

"I saw you run past the marina. Can you not wait until daylight?"

"If I did, it would be light outside when I take my morning swim."

"And that would be bad because...?"

I gestured toward my pile of clothes in the sand. "After daylight you get a lot more walkers."

He stared at me for a long moment. "I think I'll just go ahead and shoot you myself."

I laughed out loud.

"This is not funny, Liz."

"So, what did Merry say last night after I went back into the meeting? I bet she's mad as fire at me. You guys cut out of there so fast I didn't get to talk to either one of you."

Blake rubbed the back of his neck. "She's upset. I'm sure she'll get over it."

"I know enough to know she's not being straight with me about her little project. But you know. Why won't you tell me?"

Blake watched Rhett romp by, chasing a shorebird. "Because I know she will, eventually, and I know it's harmless."

"What she described to me wasn't harmless."

"You'll see her tonight at dinner, right? At Mom and Dad's? If she doesn't tell you everything by then, I will. Fair enough?"

"Fine." I kicked sand at his feet. I wasn't really focused on Merry at that moment. Inside my head, a debate raged about whether to tell Blake about my intruder, and if I should show him the locket and the list. I was afraid he'd take the locket away from me, and I needed it for the time being. On the other hand, I had promised my brother I'd bring him anything I found—in exactly those words. But I hadn't said immediately.... But the locket needed to be dusted for prints, something I couldn't do. I sighed, resigned to handing over the evidence. Well, some of it, anyway.

"Someone broke in last night," I said casually, "but it was a benevolent burglar. Also, I found a locket under the deck near where you believe Gram was killed."

Blake slowly turned his head and stared at me. "What was that first thing you said?"

I'd hoped to slip that past him by distracting him with what might be critical evidence. I brought him up to speed on the intruder and the locket, but didn't mention the list. It would be counterproductive for both of us to investigate the same folks. Besides, I didn't know yet what it meant.

Blake's face was three shades of red. "This is exactly what I tried to tell you. It's not safe for you here. Dammit, at least go stay with Mom and Dad—just for a little while. "

"Blake." I kept my voice calm. "Whoever broke in here wasn't trying to hurt me. He was looking for something. I am armed and quite dangerous, really. We need to know what the intruder was looking for. If I leave, we may never find out. I'm just hoping he comes back."

He stared at me. "You're serious, aren't you?"

I nodded.

He muttered something that sounded like *freaking hot-damn mule*, and looked like he wanted to spit fire. Then he just sat there shaking his head staring at the ocean. Finally, he said, "Where's the locket?"

"Inside."

He stood and picked up his chair. I gathered my things and called Rhett.

Blake hovered over me while I pulled the plastic bag out of the desk. I handed him a pair of latex gloves.

He slipped them on and pulled the locket out of the bag. "It could have come off when she was hit," he said. He fiddled with the clasp. "Looks like this thing sticks. Might work sometimes and not others."

"Look at the photo."

He opened the locket.

"That's for sure not Granddaddy," I said.

"Nope, it sure isn't."

"But we can't say for sure the necklace belonged to Gram. Did you ever see her wear it? 'Cause I've never seen it before."

"I don't notice stuff like that. But who else would it belong to? It's not like she entertained down there."

"Murder is an equal opportunity crime, Blake. It could belong to whoever killed her."

THIRTEEN

By the time Blake left, I was starving. I scrubbed up and sanitized my hands, and then fixed myself a bowl of fresh blueberries and yogurt topped with chopped walnuts. And a strong pot of coffee.

Then I showered, put on sunscreen, and dressed for the day in white Capris, a lacey tank, and a sheer floral blouse. A little bit of sheer mineral powder, some mascara, and lipstick, and I was ready for my day. I slipped my Sig Sauer 9 inside my Kate Spade bag. I typically took Sig along as a precaution when hunting folks with violent tendencies. A murderer and a burglar were presumably still on the island. You just never knew what the day might bring.

I was standing at the top of the stairs, one foot halfway to the first step, when Colleen appeared, perched on the banister. She was dressed for spring in a calf-length, yellow polka-dot dress that buttoned down the front. Startled by both her sudden appearance and the dress itself, I nearly fell down the steps. I grabbed the rail to steady myself.

"It looks like the one I had junior year, doesn't it?" she asked.

"Remarkably."

"That's the great thing about being dead. You can wear whatever you want by just thinking about it."

"Think about something different."

Her face clouded. "I like this dress."

The dress had looked much different on Colleen when she was alive. The buttons had pulled across her ample chest and stomach. "Stuffed sausage," Mackie Sullivan and his friends had called her. Teenagers were no less cruel in Stella Maris than anywhere else. Colleen had gone through an awkward stage starting at twelve and lasting until her death in the violent currents of Breach Inlet. She was my best friend, and the memory of the taunts, teasing, and pranks she'd suffered came back at the sight of that yellow dress.

As a ghost, Colleen was svelte, her skin unblemished and radiant. "Deanna's in trouble," she said.

"Deanna? First Merry, now Deanna?"

"Stop by the hardware store."

"I've got to go to Charleston this morning—"

"Please."

I glanced at my watch. I had plenty of time. I'd planned on dropping by to see Deanna before the day was over anyway, just to say hi. Besides, Adam Devlin would be at the hardware store, too. He was on my list. "All right," I said. "But change your dress."

The hardware store had been in Deanna's family since her great-grandfather first opened the doors back in 1903. It had been modernized over the years, but still had the look of an old-fashioned, small-town hardware store: wood floors, neat rows of tall shelves, and an eclectic mix of merchandise. Deanna had kept the books for Island Hardware ever since she and Adam were married, when her daddy started training Adam to take over for him.

An electronic door chime announced my entrance. Deanna was busy behind the counter, preparing for the day's business. Petite, with shoulder-length, honey-colored hair, Deanna didn't favor Colleen at all, but she was her sister, and connected to all my Colleen memories. Well, the ones from before she died, anyway.

Deanna's face lit up when she saw me. "Liz, I heard you were home." She rushed around the counter for a hug. "It's just been too long. I barely got to speak to you at the funeral—so many people." She held me at arms-length, but didn't let go.

"Hey, Deanna." My eyes misted over. "It has been too long. But...I'm home to stay."

"Ohmygosh. I'm so glad."

I looked around, wondering where Adam was. "So...you're still keeping the books and all?"

"Yeah, but I prefer the 'and all' to the bookkeeping. Today we had a sales clerk call in sick, so I'm out front." She patted my arm and released me. "I like the decorating department—you know, paint, wallpaper, floor-covering, stuff like that. I thought about going to school for interior design, but, well, there just hasn't been time."

"How's Adam?"

Deanna's smile didn't reach her eyes. "He's fine." She glanced down and stepped back to the other side of the counter.

"And the girls? Isabella must be, what? Six by now?"

"Seven. She's almost finished first grade. And Holly's six."

"I can't believe it. I guess I expected nothing would change while I was gone."

Deanna pushed up the sleeves of her lightweight cardigan and pressed a sequence of buttons on the cash register. "Most things are the same. We're all just a little older." When I didn't respond, she looked up and caught me staring at her left arm. It was covered in bruises.

"What on earth happened to your arm?"

She pushed the sleeves on her sweater back down and focused on the cash register. "Oh, that's nothing. I'm so clumsy sometimes. I accidentally slammed it in the car door when I was carrying the groceries in." Her face bloomed crimson.

I tried to visualize how that scenario might be possible and came up empty. "Deanna?"

She wouldn't look at me. "I'm fine, really."

I've spoken to too many abused women not to recognize the marks made when a man grips your forearm way too tight and jerks you around. But I also knew if she didn't want to talk about it, I would only alienate her by pursuing it. "Well," I said, in a tone as light as I could manage, "if that car ever attacks you again, just remember, I'm trained in martial arts. Also, I carry a gun."

Deanna laughed, so I did, too.

I pulled out a business card and laid it on the counter. "Just in case you ever need my cell phone number. It's a Greenville area code."

"I'll need this to call you up so we can have lunch, won't I?"

I glanced at the floor. A palmetto bug—a roach on steroids—crawled along the edge of the counter. "Eeew." I made a face. "I haven't missed those things."

Deanna leaned over the counter and looked. "Oh my stars. We have got to call an exterminator. I'd better do it now, while I'm thinking about it. I saw a rat day before yesterday. Adam will have a fit. I'll just be a minute." She walked towards the office in the back of the store.

I followed, pretty sure that was not her intention.

Deanna glanced over her shoulder and smiled uncertainly. She stepped into the office and slipped behind the desk. For a moment we stood on opposite sides of the desk looking at each other. Her shoulders rose and fell.

She motioned me into a chair. "Adam didn't like the folks that did it last time. He said they charged too much, but I can't remember which company that was." She flipped through the Rolodex. "That's odd. There are two exterminators in here." She held one of the cards, frowned at it, and then flipped it forward, then back. "Bugs-R-Us is the company from Charleston that Adam said was too expensive. This card just says 'Exterminator,' and lists a phone number. I guess he found someone he wanted to try."

She pressed the speakerphone button and dialed. While we listened to the *brrrrs,* Deanna busied herself straightening the desk.

"Yeah." The voice on the other end of the line sounded neither courteous nor professional.

"Hello," she said, in a businesslike tone. "Is this the exterminator?"

"Who's this?" The male voice was low and hoarse.

We looked at each other. What were exterminators supposed to sound like?

"This is Mrs. Adam Devlin, from Island Hardware, here in Stella Maris?"

"Ah...yeah, Miz Devlin, what can I do for you?" He sounded confused.

"My husband may have spoken with you before, I'm not sure. But I have a problem here in the hardware store that requires your assistance."

"You want to hire me?"

"Well, yes." She stiffened. "Do you have a problem with that?"

He laughed. "No ma'am. None whatsoever."

Deanna gave me a can-you-believe-this-guy look. "Did my husband agree with you on a price?"

"Yeah. We agreed on a price."

"Well, I'd like this taken care of as soon as possible. I don't want to see that rat in this hardware store again. Do you understand?"

"Yes, ma'am. I understand perfectly."

"Whatever normal treatment you use for bugs will be fine."

"Huh?"

Deanna propped her arms on the desk and leaned in towards the phone, enunciating clearly. "Whatever process you normally use to get rid of pests will be fine. Just please take care of it as soon as possible."

"Yes, ma'am. I'll be in touch."

She shook her head as she pressed the button to end the call. "It seems like courteous servicemen are a thing of the past. I have a good mind to call up the owner of that company and have a word or two with him about the rudeness of his employee."

"That guy answered the phone. He probably works out of his house." I would have told him never mind about three words into the conversation, but I didn't tell her that.

"Well, maybe we'll wait and see. If he takes care of the bugs and the rat, who cares if he's nice? Maybe working with vermin makes you cranky."

"*Deanna.*" Adam's voice startled us. He must have come in the back door, because the chime didn't ring. He stood in the stockroom doorway, his face creased with anger. Adam was a watered-down version of Michael: not as tall, not as dark, not as handsome. "It's ten after nine, why aren't you out front? Anybody could walk right in and steal us blind."

Deanna jumped up. "I'm sorry, sweetheart. I guess the time got away from me. I'm on my way. Look who's home."

He spared me a glance. "Hey, Liz."

"Adam." I didn't feel like making nice with the jerk. I followed Deanna, but glanced at him over my shoulder.

He watched Deanna walk out front, step behind the counter, and complete the process of setting up the register as if he didn't trust her to do it unsupervised. Then he retreated into the back.

She grimaced. "Sorry about all that."

I made a dismissive wave. "All what? He probably just needs more coffee. I know I do." It galled me to make excuses for the bastard, but I could tell Deanna was embarrassed, and I wanted to put her at ease.

Her smile was brave, resigned. "It sure is good to have you home.

Let's have lunch soon. We'll catch up."

"I'd like that. You take care of yourself, okay?" I didn't want to leave her alone with Adam, but I realized how ridiculous that was. She'd been alone with him for years.

"Mmm-kay."

The prudent thing to do would've been to go talk to Blake. Maybe he could have kept an eye on things, maybe even talked to Adam about how it was bad form to bruise and bully your wife. Prudence, regrettably, is not one of the virtues I am acquainted with. I decided to gather more information before going to Blake.

I exited stage left, circled the building, and eased open the back door. I heard a drawer in the office slide open and slam closed. I slipped into the stockroom across the hall.

The stockroom, back office, and current restrooms were added to the original hardware store back before I was born. The result was a row of windows along the back wall that separated the sales floor from the stockroom. Deanna had hung curtains on the store side to block the view of the stockroom, but from my perch on a paint can, I could see her through the gap. Business was light that morning. Deanna busied herself on the computer terminal at the end of the counter.

Thirty minutes later when Adam emerged from the back, his disposition had improved. "We got a new wallpaper sample book." He smiled as he laid it on the counter. "I thought you might like to see it."

"Thanks." She studied him for a moment and then returned the smile.

"I've got some deliveries to make. Probably won't be back, so I'll see you at dinner."

Deanna stiffened, but her face remained passive.

"Call one of the part-time clerks to fill in for you if you can't get your mamma to pick up the girls, okay?" He swatted her behind.

Deanna winced. "Mmm-kay."

Adam walked towards the hall.

As soon as his back was turned, Deanna's face transformed, the doormat look gone, replaced by resolve and something else. She watched him leave. I heard the back door open and close. She was still standing there staring after him. I was shocked, but encouraged, by what I saw.

Deanna was one pissed-off lady.

FOURTEEN

By the time I snuck out of the hardware store, I was running late for my doctor's appointment in Charleston. A friend finagled me a spot on Dr. Lombard's calendar, which was a miracle on such short notice. I spent the entire trip composing an explanation that would garner sympathy from the police officer who would surely stop me for any one of the twenty-seven traffic violations I committed en route. It must have been a high-crime morning on the peninsula. I didn't get the ticket I deserved.

A trip to the gynecologist is right up there with root canals on the fun scale—if you had to undress and put your feet in stirrups for root canals. The ovarian cysts weren't new, but Dr. Lombard wanted new lab work, and of course the results wouldn't be in until next week. Same drill, different doctor. I underwent several tests that ratcheted up the humiliation factor to a point where I had a pressing need for a margarita by the time I got out of there.

Then I passed Marci the Schemer on my way out and it became a straight tequila afternoon. As I came out the door, she turned down the front walk. We both paused, like gunfighters on opposite ends of the street in an old western. I fixed her with a double-barreled stare, and she matched it. We both stepped deliberately forward. Just before we passed, her lip curled up in that sardonic grin my hand always itches to slap right off her face.

I stared her down and walked on by, my posture perfect. Neither of us spoke. What a hellish coincidence, her turning up there.

I was headed towards Hyman's Seafood on Meeting Street, thinking an oyster po-boy was the perfect complement to Cuervo Gold, when I remembered I was supposed to meet Grace for lunch. Tequila would have to wait.

While I waited for the tourists to clear the intersection at the corner of Meeting and Market, I grabbed my iPhone and selected the playlist dubbed "Play Before Loading Gun." Music blared through the car's speakers via the Sync system.

Kenny Chesney. Guitars and Tiki Bars. Deep breaths… in…out.

When I drove off the ferry onto Stella Maris, Colleen materialized in the passenger seat beside me.

The doorbells jangled a welcome as I stepped inside The Cracked Pot with Colleen right beside me. Acoustical guitar music played just loud enough to be heard over the clank and bustle of the busy restaurant. Two efficient-looking waitresses hustled among the lunchtime crowd. Moon Unit must have stepped into the back, because no one was at the hostess stand.

I took the opportunity to get a closer look at her pictures. The back wall was one colossal town-family collage. My gaze slid over the photos, taking in memories.

Colleen stopped to stare at a picture of eight ten-year-olds in front of a giant sand sculpture of a turtle. She and I were two of the proud artists.

"Liz!" Moon Unit appeared and gathered me into an enthusiastic hug. "I have a booth free, or you can sit at the counter. That would give us a better chance to chat."

"I'd love to, Moon, but I'm meeting Grace. The booth in the back would be great." I had the ridiculous urge to hide Colleen, even though I knew no one else could see her.

Moon Unit looked disappointed, but rallied. "Sure thing."

We followed her to the booth in the back of the dining room, and I waited for Colleen to slide into the bench facing the door.

Moon Unit looked at me oddly, like she was unsure what I was waiting for.

I settled in beside Colleen, and Moon Unit handed me a menu. "I love this place," I said. "It is so *home*."

Moon Unit's smile lit the room. "Well, aren't you the sweet one? It's the pictures, mainly, that do it, don't you think? Those are my treasures. Anytime it looks like we're going to get hit by a hurricane, I take every last one of them off the wall and pack them up when I leave town. They're irreplaceable, you know."

"There are pictures of everybody who's ever lived on this island, I bet. Why Moon, you're the town historian."

She smiled lovingly at the collection on the back wall. "That's the idea. The whole town pitched a fit when I remodeled this place—folks here don't care for change, you know. I figured everybody would feel more at home if they saw little pieces of their lives here. So I asked the lot of 'em for pictures. I've been adding to it ever since."

I glanced at the menu. "Hmm."

"Well, bless my soul, here I am, rattling on, and you must be famished from all that excitement last night. Iced tea?"

"Please." Much to my great sorrow, they didn't serve alcohol at The Cracked Pot.

She whirled off to get my tea and seat another party.

Sitting in a booth at The Cracked Pot with a ghost was unnerving. I had to glance out the window or down at my lap or discreetly cover my mouth so no one would see me talking to Colleen and conclude I had finally qualified for membership in the Southern Fruitcake Hall of Fame. She, of course, found this highly amusing.

"Where'd you go this morning?" Colleen asked.

I admired the flowers in the window box. "Charleston."

"What were you doing there?"

"I had a doctor's appointment."

"Why?"

"Here you go." Moon Unit slid a glass of iced tea in front of me. "I heard all about last night at the council meeting. I woulda liked to a been a fly on *that* wall. You Talbot girls stirred things up pretty good."

Colleen smirked. "Brilliant."

Ghosts shouldn't smirk. I mean, really, what do they have to be smug about? I cut my eyes at her, wondering what she meant by that remark, and then turned to Moon Unit. "Too many people have worked too hard for too long to protect this island. Stella Maris is perfect just like it is. I'm not about to sit still while *anybody* starts putting up high rises." As soon as the words were out of my mouth I regretted encouraging Moon Unit. It was Colleen's fault—she distracted me.

Moon Unit crossed her arms. "That part about how perfect this island is? For goodness sake, don't tell it. We need to keep that to ourselves better. We've had our share of newcomers the last few years. All nice people, mind you, but the transplants are starting to outnumber those of us *from* here."

"I have noticed a lot of new faces."

"You would not believe the ruckus we had, oh, I guess it was about a year ago. Some reporter from *Southern Living* 'discovered' us. Had a big article on Stella Maris called *Hidden Paradise*. This place was a circus for six months. Tourists crawling out of the woodwork, not to mention real estate people looking for investment property. The real estate folks left when they figured out no one was going to sell them any oceanfront property, and if they did, good luck getting it zoned commercial. Hopefully the tourists are reading about someplace else. You know how it is. Tourists are fine as long as they're *our* tourists. The ones who've been coming here for so long they're like family. They have respect for the island, you know what I mean?"

The doorbell announced another customer, and Moon Unit darted off before I could form a response.

"How's Deanna?" Colleen moved a wooden peg on one of the brainteaser puzzles Moon Unit kept on the tables.

"Would you leave that thing alone?" Anyone looking would have seen the bright blue pegs jump. "She's married to a grade A jackass, as I'm sure you're fully aware—you sent me over there. But I get the feeling she's had about all she's going to take from him." I took a sip of my iced tea.

Colleen looked up at me sharply. "What do you mean? What did she say?"

"It's not what she said, just the look on her face. I've investigated a lot of domestic abuse situations. I can tell when a woman is invested in the whole 'He really loves me and he swears it will never happen again' fantasy. Deanna puts on that act in front of Adam, but I don't think she buys it."

"Can't you get her to throw him out?"

"She's not talking to me. She wouldn't even admit he put the bruises on her arm. I can't just barge in there and start giving her advice."

"Shoulda told Blake." Colleen jumped another peg and flashed me a mutinous look.

"You're still seventeen, aren't you?" I was beginning to figure out ghosts don't mature much after death. "Once I tell Blake, it's an official investigation. Deanna will not thank me for that."

"Shoulda told him about that list, too."

"What do you know about the list?"

Colleen shrugged. "I know where you found it and I know whose names are on it. I think it means something just like you do."

I eyed her closely. I had the sense she knew more than she was saying, but it's hard to pin down a ghost. "Until I know what it's a list of, better to leave Blake out of it. He'll thank me later." I seriously doubted that was the case, but was trying to sell myself the idea.

"Moron."

The bells on the door jangled, and Grace Sullivan, my godmother the psychic, strolled in. Her shoulder-length platinum bob was expertly styled, her make-up understated. In her navy St. John pantsuit, she oozed elegance. Grace was the same age as Mamma, and they were both practiced at making that age hard to guess.

I stood as she approached our booth. This should be interesting. Lunch with a ghost and a psychic.

Grace dropped her purse on the empty seat, opened her arms wide and gathered me into a perfumed embrace. "*Liz, sugar.* Let me hug your neck. I can't believe you're home. It's so good to see you."

"It's good to see you, Grace."

She arranged herself on the other side of the booth. "So sorry I'm late. Phoebe was running behind this morning. Tammy Sue had a hair emergency. Tried to do her own color again, bless her heart, and it turned this hideous shade of pumpkin-orange."

Moon Unit appeared at the table with Grace's iced tea, apparently knowing her standard order. "Y'all know what you want for lunch or should I come back?"

"I know what I want." Grace looked at me. "Are you ready?"

"I'd like a Cobb Salad, please."

"I'll have the same. I *love* the Cobb Salads here, they are simply *divine.*" Everything Grace said came out sounding dramatic, in a thick Southern drawl.

"Well, thank you," Moon Unit said. "We try. I'll be back in a jiffy."

I pretended to admire something out the window and checked on Colleen. She had abandoned the peg game. I wondered briefly if she was nervous Grace could sense her presence.

Grace leaned forward. "Sugar, what's going on? You sounded terribly urgent on the phone. Are you really staying here with us?"

"I'm staying," I said. "And I need your help with something."

She reached forward and grabbed my arm. "*Tell* me."

I pulled a copy of Gram's list from my purse and handed it to Grace. "Gram was working on something. I'm hoping you can help me figure out what it is."

Her face creased as she studied it. "My name is on here? Beside Mackenzie's?"

Colleen disappeared, then reappeared on Grace's side of the booth. I flashed her an imitation of one of my mamma's looks—the one that usually accompanied the words "You'd better straighten up and fly right."

Grace laid the page on the table and rubbed her arms, as if chilled. She looked up from the list. "This is quite an odd list. Sugar, are you cold? It feels like Moon Unit turned the air conditioning on refrigerate."

"I'm fine," I said, trying not to look at Colleen.

"Who are HC and SD?"

"I think Hayden Causby and Stuart Devlin."

"Anything Hayden Causby's associated with can't be good. You're thinking this has something to do with Emma Rae's death?"

"Yes. I think she was trying to solve something, and these names are pieces to the puzzle. I just need to figure out the relationship between the names on the left and the names on the right."

"Well," Grace said, "in confidence, I can tell you that aside from the accident of birth that made him my brother's boy, I *have* no relationship with Mackenzie," Grace said. Her brother, Henry Sullivan, was the rector of St. Francis Episcopal Church.

"Y'all don't get along?"

"It's not so much that. It's more that I simply have no interest in him. I see him on holidays and so forth. He's done all right for himself, the town's attorney and all. But he really is a pompous ass, isn't he?"

I laughed out loud. "Yes, he is that."

Grace looked at the list again. "The only other thing I can think of...the names on the left are council members. Of course, the seats are traditionally kept in the same families. If I were to decide not to run again, Mackenzie would likely run for the Sullivan seat. But you couldn't draw that parallel between the others, could you?"

"No. The only names on the right side without question marks are Mackie's and Marci's. It's like Gram was sure of those connections."

Grace was quiet for a minute. "Well, this has no bearing on my relationship with him, you understand. But I have sensed for a long time that Mackenzie was in some sort of trouble."

"Sensed? Like a psychic thing, or you've noticed changes in his behavior?"

She averted her gaze, looking out the window, or at Colleen, for a long moment. "I guess you'd call it a psychic thing."

"Do you think he's having financial problems?" There had to be a reason he was mortgaged to the hilt.

"As I said, I'm not close to Mackenzie, but he is Henry's boy."

I waited.

Clear gray eyes met mine across the table. "A few years back he had some gambling problems. Henry and Nancy bailed him out with the bookies. I've bailed him out... He's been in a program. I thought it was behind him, but my sense is he's gambling again. I hope I'm wrong."

Grace leaned forward and said, "I'm having a very odd feeling, sugar. I know you'll think I'm crazy, but I'm quite sure there's someone else here with us at the table."

"I've never thought your intuitions were crazy, Grace." I looked at Colleen.

Colleen shook her head. "No matter what she says, don't say a word about me."

A tune sang out from Grace's purse. She reached in and pulled out her cell phone. "Excuse me, sugar. I'm expecting painters later this afternoon at the bed and breakfast. Hello?"

I let my gaze wander while she spoke. I jumped slightly. Colleen had switched sides of the booth again. I sighed and bit back a curse.

"Why no, it's not at all convenient for you to come now. I'm having lunch," Grace said, presumably to the painter. She closed her eyes and flung an exasperated gesture with her free hand. "Fine. I'll meet you there in ten minutes." She ended the call and slipped her phone back into her purse.

"I'm so sorry, sugar, but if I don't go and meet with these painters, they won't get the front bedroom done this week, and I've got a full house next week. Let's do lunch another day, shall we?"

"Of course."

"Take my salad home and have it tomorrow." She pulled cash out of her wallet and laid it on the table. Then, Grace looked at me intently. "You must promise me you'll be careful. You'll be fine, I'm quite sure of it. But watch your back." She rubbed my forearms, and then patted them with a wink. "I have a feeling someone else is watching it, too." She stood and gathered her purse. "And Liz?"

"Yes?"

"Merry needs to stay away from that Causby boy—Hayden's grandson—whatshisname."

I started to tell her I held little sway with Merry, but Moon Unit arrived with two salads as Grace spun towards the door.

"Grace," I said. "One quick thing."

She turned and looked at me expectantly.

"Do you know Mildred Sullivan's maiden name?" Grace and Lincoln Sullivan were second cousins. Surely she would know.

Grace cocked her head and squinted in thought.

Moon Unit beat her to it. "She was a Knox when she married the mayor. Of course, he wasn't the mayor back then. She studied art history at Converse College is what I heard. But Knox wasn't her maiden name. She was married before. I declare, I don't think I know what her maiden name was, do you Grace?"

"I never knew she'd been married before. I would have said she was a Knox when I eventually thought of it. Got to run." She turned and glided toward the door, at a faster clip than her typical gait.

"Is she coming back?" Moon Unit asked.

"Looks *so* good." Colleen eyed the salads wistfully.

"Ghosts don't eat," I said. Then I wondered for a second. I'd seen a lot of new things the last few weeks. "Right?"

"Say *what*?" Moon Unit tilted her head.

"Grace had an emergency. Could you box up her salad? I'll take it with me."

"Whatever you say, sweetie."

FIFTEEN

Colleen made herself scarce right after lunch. She had a lot of explaining to do. I was frustrated, outraged, and baffled at the ghost. But I knew it would net me nothing to call for her. She'd pop back in when she jolly well felt like it, and not before.

Fine. I had things to do at home. I wasn't kidding when I'd told Blake I was hoping the intruder came back. But I needed to be ready for him. I spent the next hour installing my router, Wi-Fi, and the network server. Thankfully, no one had cancelled Gram's internet connection.

I love technology.

Next I installed my surveillance controller. I'd purchased this unit, along with eight wireless IP cameras, motion sensors, and an RF DVR receiver a year back when the disgruntled subject of a domestic investigation turned stalker on me. He'd planned to surprise me in my loft one night, but an alert sent to my iPhone notified me when he'd crossed the threshold. I met the police there and let them in to arrest him. The surveillance system had been quite expensive, but likely saved my life that night. The party favors the psycho brought with him included chloroform, handcuffs, an ugly knife, and some plastic sheeting.

I hid motion-activated cameras in the air vents inside the house, and covered the outside with three night-vision cameras aimed at all the entries. The only alarm would be sent to my phone. If my intruder came back, I didn't want him to know he'd been caught. This likely wasn't what Blake had in mind when he suggested I install a security system, but it served my purposes.

System work completed, I washed up, filled my water bottle, and settled in at my desk. I generated invoices for my last few clients in Greenville, paid a few bills, and called the local utility companies to transfer service into my name. I tried reaching Quincy Owen at The New Life Foundation, but got his voicemail. I left a message, then tried to contact someone at one of the five camps. Apparently, office help was not in the budget. I left messages at all five locations. The nagging voice in my head about David Morehead was getting more persistent.

Mildred was another loose end. After combing South Carolina records for a marriage license issued to Lincoln Sullivan and Mildred Knox with no results, I broadened my search. Queries of North Carolina, Georgia, and Florida produced nothing.

But in Las Vegas, I hit the jackpot.

Lincoln Elisha Sullivan married Mildred Kingsley Knox on December 24, 1978. A Christmas Eve wedding in Vegas. The Nevada Marriage Index listed South Carolina under residence for both. Now why no big wedding with friends and family in her hometown or here in Stella Maris? Though it was her second marriage; maybe she had the big deal the first time. Still, the Sullivans were a prominent family. Lincoln had been groomed to be mayor from the crib—well, that was my impression anyway. He was ten years older than my parents, so what did I know about him, really?

Mildred's divorce record came up on the first try. Oh, hello. William Alexander James Knox was granted a divorce in Charleston County on December 23, 1978. One day before Mildred married the mayor. Moon Unit's earlier statement echoed in my head. "Of course, he wasn't mayor back then."

In a town the size of Stella Maris, there had to be a juicy reason no one knew anything about Mildred's background. Like a hound on the hunt, I'd caught a whiff of something. I didn't know yet what it was, but I wouldn't rest until I'd treed it. For the details, I'd have to go to the Clerk of Court's office and pull the divorce file. I glanced at my watch. That would have to wait for another day.

I ran my fingers through my hair. Deanna kept popping into my head. Rationally, I knew Adam had likely been abusing her for years. Just because I was now aware of it didn't make her danger any more imminent. But Colleen's sense of urgency was contagious. Finally I gave into it, grabbed my keys and headed to the police department to find Blake.

*　*　*

When I arrived, Blake was on his way out to see Kate Devlin, Gram's lifelong friend. Blake reasoned Kate might know something about Gram's death she didn't realize she knew. And hopefully she'd know if the locket belonged to Gram. Because he couldn't get me out of his Tahoe without removing me bodily, he agreed to let me tag along.

"Did you find any usable prints on the locket?" I asked.

"None. The locket itself had been recently polished. The chain and clasp are too small."

"Damnation."

"Yep."

I gazed out the window. "Adam Devlin is abusing Deanna."

For a few moments, all I heard was the Tahoe's engine and air blowing through the air conditioning vents.

Finally, Blake said, "That doesn't surprise me. How do you know?"

I recapped what I'd seen in the hardware store.

"I'll take care of it."

"If she won't file a complaint, what can you do?"

"I'll talk to Michael."

A flock of butterflies tried to escape my stomach through my throat. "Michael? What can he do?"

"Well, he's not a town employee. If he talks to Adam, lets him know folks are noticing he's a wife beater, it won't be official. I won't have to listen to him carry on about suing the town for slander and whatnot. Michael can tell Adam that Deanna didn't say anything, but it doesn't look good, et cetera."

"I still think Adam will take it out on Deanna."

"Maybe," Blake said. "But Michael can keep a closer eye on things. Maybe he can convince Deanna to file a complaint—or kick the bastard out."

"Or both."

Kate Devlin led us through the house, out to the oceanfront screened porch. "You all have a seat, won't you?" She gestured to the wicker sofa.

"I'll be right back."

We sat as directed. Moments later she returned with a tray holding tall crystal glasses of ice, a matching pitcher of tea, and dishes of lemon and mint. After we'd been served, she settled into a large rocker. "It's awfully hot for April, don't you think?"

Kate appeared as if the unusually warm day hadn't touched her. Her crisp linen skirt and blouse were unwrinkled. Every hair lay in place, her makeup was fresh. The years had not been good to Kate, but the scars were internal. She was widowed when Adam was eleven, Michael seven. Stuart Devlin went sailing one Sunday afternoon and never returned, his sailboat lost at sea during a summer squall. Kate never remarried. She devoted herself to her boys and the coastal preservation efforts she and Stuart had held dear.

Blake shifted on the sofa and the wicker creaked. He smiled one of those closed-lip smiles that told me he was uncomfortable.

Kate was practiced at the art of small talk. "Nice having Liz home again, isn't it, Blake?"

"Yes, ma'am." His eyes danced past hers. He glanced around the porch, at his shoe, and across the Atlantic at Africa. "Ah, Kate, I need to ask you some questions, if you don't mind."

Kate stopped rocking. "Oh my, this isn't a social call then, is it? You are here in your *professional* capacity. How exciting."

"I'm looking into Gram's death." Blake rubbed the back of his neck. "I'm not convinced it was an accident."

"Blake, darlin', that's nonsense." Kate looked horrified. "Who in this world would want to hurt Emma Rae?"

"That's what I can't figure. You knew her, her entire life. I hoped you could help me sort things out."

Kate shook her head slowly and emphatically. "I am sorry. It was a freak accident, to be sure. But I can't believe it was anything but an accident."

Blake paused a moment as he reached inside his pocket. "Kate, have you ever seen this locket?" He handed her the plastic evidence bag and pulled on a pair of Latex gloves.

For a long moment she stared at the piece of jewelry. "No," she said. "I don't believe I have. Was it Emma Rae's?"

"I'm not sure." Blake retrieved the bag, pulled out the locket and opened it so she could see the picture.

Kate covered her mouth with her hand.

Lines appeared in Blake's forehead. "Kate?"

"I'm afraid I don't understand." Kate lowered her hand to her chest and brought the other to her throat.

"Do you recognize this man?" asked Blake.

"You all don't know who he is?"

"Do you?" Blake asked again.

"Well, no. I don't think so. This is all so very strange. Emma Rae was like a sister to me, and I know after Ben died, well, there just wasn't anybody else for her. There must be some explanation."

"I'm sure there is," he said. "I just wish I knew where to look for it."

Kate rose abruptly. "Blake, Elizabeth, I do apologize, but I really must lie down now. It was good of you to stop by and I'm sorry I couldn't be more help. Do come again soon, won't you?"

"Of course, Kate. Are you all right?" He closed the locket, replaced it in the bag and dropped it into his pocket.

"Yes, yes. I'm fine. Don't make a fuss now. I'm just going to take a nap." She glided into the house, her exit quick for someone who needed to lie down.

"We'll see ourselves out," I called to her back.

In the Tahoe, Blake sat a moment without starting the engine.

"That was odd," I said. "Very un-Kate of her to bolt and leave company sitting on the porch."

"What do you think upset her so much about that locket?"

"Well, it was one of two things. Either the shock of finding out Gram had a beau, or Kate recognized the person in that picture."

SIXTEEN

Blake brought the Tahoe to a stop in the station parking lot.

His handheld chirped. "Chief?" Nell said. Blake's administrative assistant and dispatcher, Nell Cooper, belonged to one of a handful of families who had lived on Stella Maris as long as ours. She allowed Blake the illusion he was in charge of their tiny office. Nell was a formidable woman—two hundred fifty pounds of groomed-to-the-nines African-American church lady with a thick veneer of Southern sass. She was also Clay Cooper's mother.

Blake fumbled with the phone. "Yeah, Nell."

"Mackie's waiting in your office. You have a five-o'clock with him about Zeke Lyerly shooting squirrels inside the town limits again."

He closed his eyes and banged his head on the steering wheel, then lifted the phone back to his ear. "On my way in the door."

He climbed out of the Tahoe, and I scrambled behind him. "Blake, while you meet with Mackie, can I just look through Gram's file? Two sets of eyes—"

"Forget it." He kept walking, the way folks do when they're shouting "no comment" to the reporters on the way into the courthouse.

Since he felt that way about it, I stopped and watched him disappear inside. I bit back a handful of words that weren't filled with sisterly love and got in my own car. As I shut the door to the Escape, I noticed a maroon Mazda across the street in the bank parking lot. The top of someone's head was barely visible in front of the steering wheel, as if they'd slid down to hide. I do this myself sometimes. I pulled across the street into a spot one row back from the Mazda. I opened my laptop and logged on to the database I subscribe to for motor vehicle information. The Mazda was registered to Deanna's dad. It was a cinch that wasn't him slouched behind the wheel. Deanna. What in blazes was she doing?

From our respective surveillance positions, Deanna and I watched as Adam walked out of the town offices, crossed Palmetto Boulevard, and headed down the sidewalk.

"This is ridiculous." I got out of the Escape, opened the passenger door to the Mazda, and slid low into the passenger seat.

Deanna squealed and reached for the door handle, then froze. "*Liz?*"

"What are you doing?"

"Minding my own business, unlike some folks."

Colleen poked her head between the front seats. Great. I bit my lip and focused on Deanna.

"I'm worried about you," I said. "I want to help. What are you doing in your daddy's car?"

"You've been home three days. How do you know this is my daddy's car and not mine?"

"We're wasting time. You're tailing Adam, right?"

She peered over the steering wheel. "He's headed back to the hardware store. He said he'd be gone the rest of the day. Half the time, when he's *supposed* to come back, he doesn't. I asked one of the stock boys to watch the store, but he left a half hour ago." She covered her face with her hands. "And Adam won't find me there."

"So what? Tell him you had errands to run."

She lowered her hands. "I'll run back in and say I just stepped out to the bank." She turned away from me. "Another lie. I've been lying to people I love all day. I lied to Mamma—I couldn't tell her the real reason I needed her to pick up the girls, now could I? You'd be amazed how easy the lie about my car giving me trouble rolled off my tongue." Her eyes met mine. They were wide and wet. "I'm not normally a liar, you know."

"Why are you following him?"

Emotions wrestled on her face. Pissed-off won. "He's having an affair."

"Who is she?" Colleen snarled.

I tried making Colleen vaporize with a look. It didn't work. "So, who is she?" I asked Deanna.

She swiped at a tear. "I don't know. Unless he rendezvoused with his mistress while I was picking up Daddy's car, he hasn't seen the hussy today. He made the deliveries, and then he stopped at the bank—which is odd, because I normally do the banking—then the professional building next to the courthouse. His last stop was the town administrative offices. I didn't dare get out of the car to see whose office he'd gone into. He might've caught me on his way out. He was in there for nearly an hour and a half. Just as I was about to leave, he came out and headed up Palmetto on foot."

Deanna grabbed the steering wheel and peered over it again. Adam tried the front door of the hardware store. It didn't open. He stepped back, scowled at the door, then tried again. He appeared to be spitting curses as he pulled out his keys, unlocked the door, and went inside.

Deanna started the engine. She turned down the alley and into the small parking lot behind the hardware store. Adam had left his car in front of the professional building, and there was only one car in the lot: a dark blue BMW with a vanity plate on the front.

Thornblade—a high-dollar country club in Greenville.

I sucked in a lungful of air. I knew exactly who owned that car.

What in the name of sweet reason was Scott doing in Stella Maris? I could count on one hand the times he'd come home with me when we were married.

Deanna parked close to the building, turned off the engine, and removed her keys from the switch. "Shoot," she said. "I forgot to roll up the windows." She put the key back in the ignition.

That's when we heard loud angry voices from the back room of the hardware store.

Colleen transported herself to the outside of the car and crouched beside it. She motioned for me to follow.

"Deanna, stay here." I opened the door, slid out, and closed the door silently. "Let me see what's going on." I knelt behind Colleen.

Deanna opened her door. "I'm not staying here by myself. What if they come out?" She mimicked me getting out of the car quietly and huddled behind me.

I sighed. I didn't like this a little bit, but there was no time to argue. Like ducklings, the three of us waddled in a row up the back steps. I turned the knob carefully and opened the door just wide enough to slip into the hallway.

The door to the office was closed halfway. Colleen propped herself in the open doorway and watched the action while Deanna and I peeked through the crack between the door and the jamb, her head over mine. She couldn't have recognized the blonde man in the expensive-looking business suit who was shouting at her husband, but I surely did.

"Look," said Scott. "I told you to wrap this up before the end of the month. Time is money."

"And like *I* told *you*, everything is under control, with the possible exception of your wife. An unpleasant surprise, her turning up here, wouldn't you say?"

"You just handle your end. I'll take care of Elizabeth."

My eyes nearly popped out of my head. *Of all the nerve.* I glanced at Colleen. She made a zip-it gesture.

"Well, you'd better," Adam said. "Because it's not just her vote on town council we have to worry about. She's mouthy. Every person we've convinced to go along with our 'good cause,' she'll unconvince. You can either persuade Liz this is for the greater good or persuade her to go back where she came from.

"Or," Adam continued, "we can do what I wanted to begin with, and take care of Frank Talbot. Get him on board, and Liz won't fight us. Or put somebody more cooperative in his seat."

Scott raised his hand. "We've been over this. I know Frank Talbot. The man is the most stubborn mule on the planet. You won't blackmail him—I don't care what you come up with. And if you try to kill him, even if you succeed without getting yourself shot—which I seriously doubt—it would never come off as an accident. Let me worry about Liz. You just deliver the other votes by the next meeting, or I will make other arrangements. Understood?" There was an unmistakable threat in Scott's voice.

"Yeah," Adam sneered. "I understand. And I'm real scared. You think I couldn't find a hundred other guys who'd want a piece of this?"

"Perhaps," Scott said. "Perhaps not. Let us not forget whose brainchild Stella Maris Resort *is*. And as you pointed out, my wife has thrown an interesting new light on things, has she not? I believe you need me as much as I need you."

Adam seemed to consider this. "Hey, we've got enough to worry about without fighting between ourselves." He grinned and reached out to place a hand on Scott's shoulder. "Let's just get this thing done, and we'll both be rich."

Scott didn't return the smile. He stared at the hand on his shoulder until Adam removed it. "I'll be in touch."

Like a scared rabbit, Deanna bolted into the ladies room, and I followed. I closed the door silently behind us. After a moment, the back door opened and closed. Thinking they had both left, I breathed a sigh of relief. Then I heard Adam's voice from the next room. The walls were thin, and even with the door shut, we could hear him clearly.

"It's me. When are you going to do it? ...Say *what*? ...No. My wife doesn't know a damn thing. ...Why would she call you? ...*Dammit to hell.* ....No, she'd never put that together. ...I'm not paying you another cent. You got twenty-five up front and you'll get the other half when it's done and I need it done yesterday. ...I don't want to know the details. Just get it done." He slammed down the phone.

We heard what sounded like Adam rummaging through papers on the desk. A minute later, we heard the sounds of the safe combination being keyed in. After what seemed like an eternity, the front door chimed opened, then shut. Adam went out the way he came in, thank heaven. If he'd seen the Mazda in the back lot, he'd have known Deanna was there.

Deanna and I sank to the floor in the dark and sat there, too numb to move. After a moment, I reached up and flipped on the light.

"What in this world is he up to?" she whispered.

"Don't tell." Colleen was sitting cross-legged in the utility sink.

For a moment, I forgot myself. "Tell what?" I wasn't sure yet what I knew.

Deanna's face scrunched. "Huh?"

"No telling what he's up to," I said.

"Whatever it is, he's in way over his head. Shady characters. Underhanded deals." Deanna stood and opened the door. She was trembling, in a trance-like state.

Fragments of the conversation we'd overheard were spinning through my head. I slipped past Deanna, crossed the hall, and went into the office. I stepped behind the desk and found a pen and piece of paper. Deanna walked into the office and sat down in the visitors' chair. I pressed the speaker button on the phone, then the redial key. I jotted down the phone number on the telephone display.

After one ring, the same snarly voice we'd heard that morning came over the line. "Now what?"

I disconnected the phone.

Deanna recoiled from it. "Oh dear heavens. Who did I speak with this morning, and what has Adam hired him to do?"

She rubbed her arms.

"What's the combination to the safe?"

"Eleven, twenty-three, two." Her voice shook. "Our first date was November twenty-third, nineteen ninety-two."

I stepped over to the wall safe, entered the combination, and opened the door. Inside, on top of the cash drawers and the ledger books, sat five stacks of hundred-dollar bills. I picked one up and fanned through it. "Here's the other twenty-five Adam just promised the exterminator. Not twenty-five dollars, not twenty-five hundred dollars, but twenty-five *thousand* dollars."

"*For what?*" Deanna choked out a whisper.

"Adam is paying our friend the exterminator fifty thousand dollars to exterminate something—some*one*."

Deanna shuddered. She shook her head. "No, this is ridiculous. There's some other explanation. There has to be. There's no way I'm married to a murderer."

Colleen stood beside her sister, arm protectively around her shoulders. "Don't push her," she said.

Deanna's eyes were wild. She looked at me for answers. I looked at Colleen and raised my palms. What did she want me to do here?

Abruptly, Deanna threw herself into homemaker gear. "It's getting late. I've got to get home before Adam wonders where I am. We've got church tonight."

She stood, pushed in front of me, and scooped up the money and crammed it in her oversized purse. "I'll hang on to this until we figure out what to do with it."

I clutched my head in an effort to grip reality. The Deanna Devlin I knew would never stuff her purse full of hit-man-payoff money. "Deanna?"

Colleen looked worried, but she didn't offer suggestions.

"Come on," Deanna said. "I'll be late for church."

We left through the back door. Deanna locked the deadbolt behind us.

SEVENTEEN

I strode toward the police station at a fast clip. As I pulled out my phone, my head oscillated like a fan, checking every direction for Scott or Adam.

Nate answered on the second ring. "Hey there."

"Nate..." I slammed into the reality of what I was about to say and stumbled.

"What's wrong?"

"I... Oh, God."

"Liz. What's wrong?"

"Scott."

"What about Scott?" Nate's tone reflected how irrelevant he considered Scott to anything current in our lives. Scott was his brother, but they'd never been close. Scott was my ex-husband, but I'd erased him from my life.

"He's here."

"In Stella Maris?"

"Yep." I had my wits about me now. No time to sugarcoat what I was about to tell my best friend. "And it looks like he and Adam Devlin are in bed together on some scheme to build a resort here."

"Interesting."

"Nate, I think they had Gram killed."

Silence.

"Nate?"

"Yeah." More silence. "What makes you think that?" Nate knew what Scott was. But murder was surely beyond what he'd ever thought his brother capable of.

"I just overheard them talking. They're about to have someone else killed, and they are none too happy I'm here."

"I'm on the next flight to Charleston. I'll call you when I know what time I land."

"Aren't you in Vegas?"

"Yeah. So is Camilla Vardry. I've got to stop by the hotel and pick up my bag. Then I'll head to the airport. I'm going to hang up and call the airline. Have you told Blake?"

"On my way to do that right now."

"Stick close to him. And stay away from Scott."

"Hell's bells. You and I have worked together for years. I expected better from you. I'm going to do my job, Nate."

Silence. Then, "I'm on my way."

I'd no sooner sat down in front of Blake's desk to tell him what just happened at the hardware store, when Nell appeared in his office doorway looking like she knew something he didn't. She usually did.

"Chief, Elvis is out front," she said. "He's been trying to get ahold of you all day."

He closed his eyes and rubbed his forehead. "Send him in."

"Blake—" I grabbed the chair arms to keep from lunging at him.

He sighed. "I'm tired and ready to go home. But if I don't talk to Elvis, he'll just ride that bike of his over to Mom and Dad's during dinner or out to the houseboat later on. Let me get this over with. Then we'll talk."

I was ready to throttle him, and might have, but in came Elvis. I hadn't seen him in at least eight years, but he looked exactly the same as I remembered. I'd swear he was wearing the same baseball cap. And he had the same unmistakable childlike quality about him.

"Hey, Chief Blake. Hey, Miss Elizabeth." John and Alma had instilled manners in Elvis from an early age, but he struggled with discerning different etiquette for different social situations. Although he was only two years younger than I was, he used the same formal manners with me as he did with Mamma.

"Busy day, huh?" Elvis didn't sit in one of the office chairs. He roamed the room, looking at pictures, the calendar, Blake's framed degree from the University of South Carolina, case notes on the dry erase board, and the view from the window as he spoke.

"It's been a real hummer," Blake said. "What's up, Elvis?"

"Miss Grace says I should tell you about The Phantom. I was going to anyway, but she made me promise."

Blake muttered something that sounded like *not Grace, for the love of Pete*, and then spoke more clearly. "She wanted you to tell me about the what?"

"The Phantom."

"Elvis, I don't believe in phantoms. Or a lot of things Grace believes in, for that matter."

Elvis stopped wandering around the room and looked at him ominously. "Well, I saw him, Chief, three times this week already. Twice yesterday and once today. And a bunch of times before then." He lowered his voice and leaned towards Blake's desk. "And there was that one time? He was at the *graveyard*."

"What does this phantom took like?"

"I think he's old. He looks kinda shriveled up and dried out. He wears regular pants and a shirt. He's got a cool baseball cap with a red flag on it. I looked it up—it's a scuba diving flag."

"Okay," Blake said.

"But I know he's a phantom 'cause he disappears before I get close enough to get a good look. He walks in the shadows, so's people he's studying can't see him. So far he's been studying Adam Devlin. And you, Miss Elizabeth. I seen him watching Miss Emma's house. He maybe studies other folks, too, but I ain't seen him."

The back of my neck tingled. "When did you see him at Gram's house, Elvis?"

"He's been following Liz?" Elvis had Blake's attention now, too.

"Yeah, he was in front of Miss Emma's house watching Miss Elizabeth, but her dog scared him away. That's a real pretty dog."

"When?" I asked.

"When was this?" Blake spoke at the same time.

"Monday afternoon, right after she got there. I tried to stay with him, but he gave me the slip."

That had been Elvis whizzing by on his bike while Rhett barked his head off at the end of the driveway. Was the man I'd seen Elvis's phantom?

Elvis said, "He went into the hardware store just a little bit ago.

But when I followed him in, he wasn't there."

"The hardware store?" I sat up straight.

"Yep." Elvis nodded enthusiastically.

"Moves pretty fast for a guy so shriveled up," Blake said. "Elvis, are you sure this isn't Coy Watson, maybe, or Dan Gregory out exercising? Doc Harper has everybody on this island walking. And they both go in and out of the hardware store a couple times a week?"

"Chief Blake, I been patrolling this island my whole life. There ain't many people live here that I don't know. And it for sure wasn't Coy Watson, nor Dan Gregory, neither. It's a phantom, I tell you, a *phantom*." Nothing upset Elvis more than people not taking him seriously.

Blake leaned forward. "Okay, okay. I tell you what. I'll keep an eye out for anybody who looks suspicious, and you call me next time you see this guy, so I can get a look at him, all right?"

"Okay." Elvis started towards the door, then stopped. "But you be careful, Chief. 'Cause he *is* a phantom."

"I'll be careful. Hey, what was he doing when you saw him at the graveyard? Are you sure this was the same guy?"

"Oh, it was him all right." Elvis nodded. "He was praying."

"Praying? Where was he exactly?"

"Up on that little hill by the big old oak tree. The one that got its picture in the magazine? You know, right by where Miss Emma is restin'. Bye now." Having told us everything he knew about The Phantom, Elvis had fulfilled his duty and was out the door.

Blake stared after him. "I don't know who Elvis's phantom is, but anyone who was praying at Gram's grave is more likely friend than foe, and almost certainly someone we know."

"Someone *she* knew. I wonder if Elvis's phantom looks anything like the picture in the locket."

"Maybe I'll have him take a look." He shook his head. "Elvis is sounding more like Grace all the time. Not everything that happens on this island is some sort of supernatural mystery."

If he only knew.

I filled him in on what had happened in the hardware store—well, most of it. I left out the Colleen parts, which maybe made things sound slightly off. About halfway into the story, he reached into his bottom desk drawer and got out his old baseball glove and a battered baseball—

one he knocked over a fence when he was eighteen. Whenever Blake was deep in thought, he tossed the baseball into the air and caught it, over and over, in some sort of rhythmic mind massage.

"What possessed you to get in the car with Deanna to begin with?" he asked.

"Will you focus on the big picture here? Scott and Adam are conspiring to kill somebody and get me off this island. They want control of the town council so they can build some kind of resort. One of them killed Gram for her land."

Blake consulted the ceiling for a moment. The ball went up...down. Up...down. "Do you think Scott somehow knew you'd inherit? Maybe planned a reconciliation so he could get his hands on Gram's land?"

"No, they were not happy I showed up."

"You own the land whether you live here or not."

"True."

"And how else would they get the land with Gram dead? You remarry Scott, and if you don't agree to his plans for the land, he could arrange an accident." Blake's eyes were hard with suspicion. "Then he'd inherit."

This hadn't occurred to me. Scott's involvement was still new, and I hadn't had time to noodle it over. Six months into our marriage, I knew Scott had character issues. But I hadn't figured him for a murderer. Now that the idea was settling in, I shuddered. "So you agree? One of them killed Gram?"

"Liz, I have no doubt Scott would kill anyone who stood between him and a pile of money. Or hire someone to do it, anyway. And Adam? Sure, I can see that. But unfortunately, there is zero evidence linking them to Gram's murder. None."

"Do you honestly think it's a coincidence they are conspiring to kill town council members to get this resort approved and Gram gets killed?" I came up out of my chair.

"Of course not. But the only evidence we have that Adam—not Scott—is *planning* to kill someone—and we don't know who—is one end of a telephone conversation you overheard while trespassing. Given the animosity you—and I—have for Scott, I'm gonna need a little more than that to arrest them."

"I wasn't trespassing. I was in a business accompanied by one of its owners."

"And you think Deanna will admit that?"

I huffed out an exasperated sigh. Scott told Adam to get the votes. The only mention of murder Scott made was Adam shouldn't try to kill Daddy. The context made it crystal clear they previously discussed killing folks. But context wasn't the kind of evidence you could take to a judge. "Well...you can haul Adam and Scott in for questioning. I'd like to question those two scum-sucking—"

"And let them know we're on to them? Then we'll never get the evidence to convict them. Sis, maybe one day you'll tell me the stuff you left out of that story. When we get to court, trust me, it will come up." He eyed me suspiciously. "We've got to get evidence. But..." He caught the baseball one last time. "We have a lot more than we had this morning. We have suspects."

"If we don't do something quick, we're going to have another dead body. We don't know who to protect, and we don't know who the hit man is. We both know the trace on that phone number will come back to a disposable cell phone. There are ways to track where it was bought, and if we're lucky, who bought it. But that will take days at a minimum."

"We have to protect the whole island until we figure it out," Blake said. "If I arrest Adam and Scott, it's not like they're going to just say, 'Oh, right, we have a contract out on Joe Blow.' And even if we make sure it's in tomorrow's paper they've been arrested, how likely is it that a hired gun will read the Stella Maris newspaper? We can't be sure the hit wouldn't still go down."

"So what do we do?"

"We make sure everyone knows Gram was murdered. Tell them the culprit is still on the island and dangerous."

"Bedlam by the Sea," I said.

"Yep. Our best defense. I'll call Vern Waters at *The Citizen* and give him tomorrow's headline."

"And when you go into The Cracked Pot for breakfast, make sure Moon Unit has read the paper. I'll drop by Phoebe's Day Spa in the morning, the other hotbed of information."

Blake called a meeting of his entire staff of three patrol officers. I sat quietly in the corner with Nell while Blake briefed Clay "Coop"

Cooper, Sam Manigault, and Rodney Murphy. Days off were canceled, and everyone would work double shifts, with patrols concentrated on council members.

It was getting close to dinnertime, and Mamma and Daddy were expecting us. I doubt Blake would have gone if our family wasn't in the high-risk group. Even though Scott told Adam to leave Daddy and me alone, there was no reason to think he would do as he was told.

"Head on over to the house," Blake said. "I'm going to take a quick spin around town. Maybe I'll spot Elvis's phantom. Once in a while, Elvis sees things before I do. His phantom could be our hit man."

It was a deceptively peaceful spring evening. The air was warm with a slight breeze blowing off the ocean. "I'll just take that spin around town with you," I said. "It's a nice evening for a walk."

He grimaced. "Fine."

We strolled down Main Street, past the courthouse and the professional building, and then crossed the street and came back up the other side. We rounded the corner and headed down Palmetto Boulevard. Blake checked doors as he went. Everything seemed to be in order. "No sign of any phantoms."

Nate called to let me know the best flight he could get had an overnight layover in Chicago. Calm Nate had been replaced by tense Nate, whom I'd never met before. He wouldn't be in Charleston until nine the next morning.

As we passed Island Hardware, Blake stopped short. "Normally, Adam and Deanna pull the big shade down on the front door."

"Yeah, well, today wasn't a normal day at the hardware store."

Blake tried the door and found it securely locked. He peered through one of the large storefront windows. All the lights were off inside, no signs of life. "No phantoms here either."

We continued to the next stop, Ferguson's Flowers and Gifts.

The sound of shattering glass and splintering wood tore through the evening.

We both spun around. The noise had come from behind the hardware store.

Blake bolted back down the street and cut through the alley between the hardware store and the dress shop.

I grabbed Sig from my purse, dropped the handbag, and took off after him.

Someone was running along the back of the building.

"Stay put." Blake shouted at me.

I ignored him and tried my best to keep up, but my Kate Spade sandals weren't designed for sprinting. As I rounded the back corner, I caught a glimpse of a darkly clad figure disappearing around the front of the Stella Maris Baptist Church.

Blake dashed after him, pushing himself to a speed I'd bet he hadn't run since high school. I stopped long enough to pull off my shoes, then made up some ground. Rounding the front of the church, I pulled up short. Blake was poised on the church's front lawn, scanning the grounds in a slow circle. "Where the hell did he go?"

He searched the area surrounding the church, but there was no sign of anyone. We tried all the doors to the church, but they were all locked except the front doors. No one was inside the sanctuary. Whoever we were chasing had disappeared into thin air.

Blake grabbed his cell phone/radio. "*Coop?*" He let go of the button and spoke to me. "He's at The Pirates' Den. Alma's Wednesday night special is Shrimp and Sausage. He was on his way there when he left the office."

After a long pause, his reply came back. "Yeah, Blake."

"Get over to the Baptist Church quick as you can. And have John call Adam Devlin and tell him to meet me at the hardware store."

I grabbed his arm and pointed to the cars in the parking lot of the fellowship hall.

Blake pressed the talk button again. "Never mind that. Adam's not home."

"On my way," Clay said. "What's up?"

Across the churchyard, a motion-activated light on the back of the hardware store illuminated the area. The window at the top of the steps was completely torn out of the wall. Shattered glass and splintered pieces of wood covered the ground below. "I'm still working on that," Blake said. "If you see anybody along the way dressed all in black, pick 'em up and bring 'em with you." He holstered his cell phone.

"One thing's for sure," Blake said to me. "That wasn't a phantom. Phantoms don't generally have to burst through windows—frame and all—to get out of places."

EIGHTEEN

I retrieved my shoes and purse. Then I let Blake convince me to go on over to Mamma and Daddy's. I was exhausted, and Blake and three patrol officers were looking for the phantom, who might also be a hit man. As luck would have it, I pulled into the driveway right behind Merry. We hadn't spoken since the council meeting, and the evening ahead loomed full of the promise of a tension headache.

Ignoring me, Merry slammed her car door and strode towards the front door. My sister radar clicked on. There was something a shade too dramatic, almost scripted, in Merry's clearly demonstrated rage.

"Merry, will you wait up?" I wanted to negotiate a truce before we went inside. I crossed the front yard at a run and caught up with her just as Mamma opened the front door and took us in with her quelling gaze.

Mamma was five-feet-four of no-nonsense. Not a hair in her auburn bob was out of place, and her makeup was skillfully applied. "Leave your situations at the door," she said. Her tone, along with the fire in her eyes, told me she'd heard all the details of last night's skirmish. She didn't favor us with a backward glance as she returned to the kitchen.

It was a long-standing rule in our mother's house that nothing controversial be discussed at the dinner table. But the Mary J. Blige lyrics Mamma used to remind us of the moratorium on brawling in the house—and her bizarre attire—took us both aback.

The animal print exercise tank top and black Lycra capri pants were so far removed from anything Mamma ever wore that we were both struck dumb. We glanced at each other, and then looked to Daddy for an explanation.

"Your mamma's been taking Jazzercise classes," he explained. "Says it's a good outlet. Helps her cope. It's got Chumley all upset. His dinner's been late every night this week, and she's started talking like one of those rappers."

I looked from Daddy to the latest in a long line of sad-sack basset hounds that had occupied the spot by his recliner since I was a child. This one was not even two years old, but the folds of loose skin and big droopy eyes made him look as ancient as his predecessors. Chumley gave a loud *woof* to emphasize his distress.

"More likely you're upset because *your* dinner's been late," Merry said. "And Mary J. Blige is rhythm and blues, not rap."

"It wouldn't hurt you to cook every now and then, you know," I informed him. "You could broaden your horizons."

"Girls, come set the table," Mamma called.

I stepped over to the sink to wash my hands. I let the water run until it steamed, then I reached for the soap. "I don't know who's more spoiled, Daddy or that dog," I declared.

"You're all ruined," Mamma retorted. "Blake called. He's going to be late. We'll start without him, but set him a place."

"What's going on?" Merry asked.

I kept scrubbing and played innocent.

"He said he'd tell us about it later," Mamma said.

"Do you have any sanitizer handy?" I asked.

Merry and Mamma exchanged a look.

"I am not crazy. I'm getting ready to handle *your* food. I'd think you'd want my hands to be clean."

Merry smothered a grin. "You just scalded them."

I fantasized about smothering her. "Fine. Don't blame me if we all come down with a stomach virus tomorrow."

Mamma took the last of the squash out of the cast iron frying pan and turned off the burner.

She glanced up as she handed me the platter. With a pained look, she offered the advice she had shared with us countless times since our sixteenth birthdays. "You girls would be amazed at how much your dispositions would improve if you'd just put on a little lipstick."

It was Mamma's philosophy that eighty percent of a girl's problems could be mitigated—if not completely solved—by putting on a little lipstick, preferably Estée Lauder.

"I'll have a Jack and Coke," Daddy called from the den. "And

Chumley here needs to go outside for a walk."

"You've already had a Jack and Coke," Mamma told him. "Walk the dog yourself, and then come open a bottle of merlot. Merry, use the green napkins. Liz, here, these serving dishes can be put in the dining room."

I delivered them, and popped into the family room to grab my sanitizer.

In short order, we were seated around the dark mahogany dining room table. Fresh yellow tulips graced the centerpiece and soft candlelight flickered off the prisms of the dimmed crystal chandelier. Mamma offered her hands to Merry, on her left, and me, on her right. Following deep-seated tradition, we joined hands and bowed our heads.

As was her custom, Mamma returned thanks. "Father, bless this food to our use and us to thy service. And please smile down on us tomorrow and make The Most Fabulous Spring Bazaar Ever a huge success. To the glory of thy name, amen."

Daddy looked at Mamma. "What do you have for Chumley to eat? The gravy on that steak might upset his stomach."

"I broiled his piece," she said. "He really shouldn't have fried foods at all."

"Mamma, please tell me you did not broil that ridiculous hound a piece of steak." I stared open-mouthed at her.

"Liz, close your mouth, darlin', that really is unattractive. Of course I did, I just told you he shouldn't have fried foods. I broiled a piece for Rhett, too."

"*We* shouldn't have fried foods," Merry said.

"Speak for yourself." I closed my eyes and savored the first bite of steak and gravy.

We all looked up as Blake came through the front door.

"Hey, everybody. Sorry to be late." Blake kissed Mamma on the proffered cheek and slid into his place at the table.

"What kept you?" Mamma picked up his plate and shoveled on steak and gravy.

"Somebody broke out of the hardware store."

"Broke *out*?" Finally, Daddy's interest had been captured by something other than his dog.

"Believe it or not. From what Adam could tell, nothing was taken.

The back window sure was destroyed, though. Somebody was locked in and smashed a chair through the window to get out. Probably just some teenage prank, but..." The look on his face said he didn't buy what he was saying.

I thought it prudent not to tell Mamma I had been involved in a police chase. Apparently Blake agreed.

"Why would you automatically assume that teenagers are responsible?" Merry demanded.

"Why not just open the window and crawl out?" Daddy always favored simplicity.

"According to Adam, the back windows haven't worked in years. They're painted shut. The front windows are display only. And all the doors have keyed deadbolts."

"Sounds like a fire hazard to me," I said.

"I've raised Adam's fire-safety awareness," Blake said.

"Whoever it was probably went home with at least a few scrapes and scratches. I'll ask around tomorrow morning," Mamma said.

A guilty teenager could not hide from the Stella Maris grapevine. But Elvis's "phantom" was looking good for it to me. Adam and Scott both left through doors.

"Whoever it was hightailed it out of there pretty fast," Blake said. "They weren't hurt too bad."

"Enough now. Eat your dinner, it's getting cold." Mamma had piled a small mountain of food on Blake's plate while he wasn't looking.

Daddy glanced up at Merry as he slathered butter on a biscuit. "How's that roommate of yours?"

Neither Blake nor Daddy particularly cared for Merry's roommate, Kristen, though the reasons always seemed vague to me.

Mamma shot Daddy a warning glance.

"I'm just asking after the girl, Carolyn. Just being polite." He reached for the blackberry jam. "She still selling drugs?"

"Daddy," Merry said. "Kristen is a pharmaceutical sales rep. You make it sound like she's pushing crack on a street corner. I *assure* you that is not the case."

"So you tell me," Daddy said.

After a moment, he tried another approach. "Could be your sister will be needing a roommate. Your grandmamma's house is awful big for one person to ramble around in."

A forkful of squash froze halfway to my mouth.

"In case you've forgotten," Merry said. "I have a house of my own. I'm not moving in with Liz."

"Save you some money," Daddy said.

"Frank, enough." Mamma patted her lips carefully with her napkin. "Did you girls get a look at my azaleas?"

"They are breathtaking, Mamma, as always," I said. "Something else that sucks the breath right out of your lungs is that billboard of Merry's on I-26."

I'd noticed the sign on my trip in on Monday. It featured a man in a coffin, surrounded by elaborate floral arrangements and six women in funeral attire, one of them my sister. The caption in three-foot letters read, "Are you positive you're negative? Call Teen Council of Charleston at 1-800-GET-TESTED."

"It's a good picture of her." Daddy cut a bite of steak. "The TV commercials are better, though. Merry's got real screen presence, don't you think?"

"What I *think*," Mamma said, "is if we can't find something more pleasant to discuss, perhaps we should enjoy our dinner while we each silently reflect upon the topic of our choice."

Merry's work at Teen Council involved several programs that upset Mamma. She preferred not to know about teenage pregnancy, sexually transmitted diseases, and drug addiction. My mamma has a big heart, and she works tirelessly for the less fortunate, but the less she knows the happier she is. In her world, the less fortunate are all innocent victims of circumstance.

"I shouldn't have brought it up," I said. "It's just so outrageous, it's funny."

"It would be more amusing if everyone in the picture was a member of someone else's family," Blake said.

"Would you like to hear the STD statistics among teenagers in Charleston County?" Merry bristled.

Mamma stood abruptly, picked up her plate and left the room.

Silence hung heavy in the dining room as we finished dinner.

I searched for a safe topic of conversation. "Anybody want cake?"

"Where's that cake at?" Daddy grasped at the cake like a life preserver. "Coffee would be good with that, wouldn't it? That poor little hound has got to be fed, too."

I rose, stacked the dinner plates, and joined Mamma in the kitchen. Several minutes later, Mamma waltzed calmly back into the dining room brandishing a three-layer chocolate cake with cream cheese frosting and fresh raspberries. Mamma served and I passed around the generous slices of cake. Like a gentle breeze of nitrous oxide, the decadent confection dispelled the fog of ill temper, and serenity returned to the dining room.

I grinned. If Mamma ran the world, everyone would be happy. Fat, but happy.

"This is wonderful." Merry relished her first bite.

"Ummph." Blake offered his ultimate compliment.

"Ohmygosh. It's been so long since I had this cake, I'd forgotten how good it is." I closed my eyes.

For the next thirty minutes, the conversation never strayed from the scrumptious dinner, the exquisite azaleas, and The Most Fabulous Spring Bazaar Ever. Only after everyone finished dessert and coffee, the table was cleared, and the kitchen cleaned, and after we meandered one by one into the homey family room and settled into the overstuffed sofa and chairs, did Blake tell Mamma, Daddy, and Merry about the next day's headlines. Everyone got quiet. It still felt surreal to be discussing Gram's murder.

"Of course," Blake said, "there won't be any mention of Adam or Scott. We have no evidence against either of them. But I need to keep everyone safe while we sort this out."

Mamma was appalled. "I never did care for Scott. He has far too high an opinion of himself. But Adam Devlin? Why, his family helped build this town. I just can't believe it."

"Doesn't make any sense," Daddy said. "If they thought they'd ever get their hands on your grandmamma's land...that's just foolish. Scott's a jackass, but he's a smart jackass. He had to've had a better plan."

For a change of pace, Mamma brought up another not-during-dinner subject.

She crossed her wrists in her lap and raised her chin. "Esmerelda, suppose you fill us in on this youth camp that has the entire island in an uproar. Somehow I had the impression you were building a fellowship hall for local teenagers. But I've heard three different stories from three different people today, none of which sounded remotely like what you told me."

"Fine," Merry said. "I'll be happy to tell you about it. You all act as if I've been trying to do something behind your backs. I've tried to talk to you about this, but none of you had time to listen. Now, suddenly, I have your attention. I don't know why—"

"Merry, you know your father has a limited attention span, please get to the point," Mamma said.

Merry flushed, swallowed hard, and started again. "It's simple. The Devlin family has agreed to donate land at Devlin's Point for a camp for at-risk youth. The facility's purpose will be to get inner-city kids away from the gang and drug culture to show them a glimpse of a better life."

Warming to her topic now, she continued. "We have an opportunity to share our world with kids that would otherwise never get to visit a place not covered in concrete and asphalt, a place without danger of being hit by a stray bullet every time you go outside."

I crossed my arms. We'd be the ones hit by stray bullets.

Merry raised her palms, her face lit with passion. "If we can show them a life outside of the violent drug culture, we can make a real difference in their lives."

My heart softened. I'm not against helping kids. I just don't want our home to become a battleground.

Merry's eyes held mine. "The New Life Foundation is a nonprofit organization that only accepts kids who have never been convicted of a violent crime."

I processed her last few words. Blood surged to my head and my eyes felt as if they might pop out of their sockets.

Merry rolled right on past my shock. "They approached me to run one of their other facilities. I was so excited about the concept, I asked them to consider a new camp here instead. If the facility is built on Stella Maris, they've promised me the director's position."

I could not have been more stunned if Merry had sprouted snakes in her hair. She quickly averted her eyes.

"You said there would be convicted felons—"

"Well, it's possible that—" Merry searched the corners of the room.

Daddy stood. "You don't need to build *facilities* to go camping. You can go camping anytime you like—take anybody you want to." He looked at Merry long and hard. "Although I'd like to see that."

Merry was not known for her love of the great outdoors.

"The hound needs to go for a walk." Daddy brushed past us, leash in hand and dog in tow.

I stood and planted myself in front of my sister. "You said rival gangs. I had visions of shoot-outs on the beach dancing in my head. You deliberately mislead me. *Why*?"

"Umm...let's go for a walk on the beach. You must have misunderstood." Merry jumped up and grabbed a quilt from the back of the chair. Shoving it into my arms, she pushed me towards the front door.

I shoved the quilt back at her. I grabbed my purse, fished out Sig, and stuck it in the back of my Capris. We made for the door.

"Elizabeth!" Mamma must have seen the gun.

"Hold it." Blake sprang to his feet. "Walk on the beach? Did you miss the part about the hit man?"

"It's okay," I called over my shoulder. "I'm armed."

NINETEEN

Colleen joined us on the front porch. "Let her explain."

I shot her a warning look. "Scram."

Merry stopped walking and turned toward me. "Liz, please—"

"Not you." I waved my hands wildly in front of my face and kept walking. "Damn mosquitoes."

"Oh."

Colleen did a backflip and floated upward. She flew in a circle around us, then darted around, mimicking a mosquito. "I'll leave, if you promise to hear her out."

I shooed her away with both hands. She disappeared in a dramatic spray of fireworks.

"They're not bothering me at all," Merry said.

I inhaled a lungful of salt air and savored it a moment before exhaling. "There was one really big one. She's gone now."

It was a clear evening. A million diamonds glittered in the velvet sky over Stella Maris. We ambled the two blocks from Mamma and Daddy's house to the beach. Per my agreement with a ghost, I waited for Merry to explain herself. She wasn't in any hurry. Suddenly I wasn't either. It had been a long day.

I tossed the quilt onto the sand at the foot of a nearby dune. "I'm going to leave this here while we walk."

This after dinner ritual, stargazing on the beach, was one of our favorites from grade school until I left for college. It felt warm and familiar, and strange at the same time, as if we were watching two other sisters link arms and stroll up the beach. The music of the waves crashing on the sand soothed my nerves.

"So, what do you think?" Merry didn't look at me.

Laughter bubbled up from my chest. "You mean about the youth camp? Or the halfway house for felons from rival gangs?"

"The youth camp."

I sighed heavily, loath to disturb the peace of the evening with a heated debate. I chose my words carefully. "I think you are an incredibly giving person, who sincerely wants to make a difference in the lives of kids who otherwise might not have a chance. And, I cannot imagine why you would give me such a distorted version of your plan."

When Merry didn't answer immediately, I continued, searching for the words that would convey what I felt yet not alienate my sister. "But, I have to tell you, I have a huge problem with the idea of developing Devlin's Point for *any* purpose. Opening that door is like opening Pandora's Box. Before you know it, Stella Maris will look like Myrtle Beach. You know what they say about unintended consequences." The resort that Adam and Scott were plotting was fresh in my brain.

"No." She gave me her trademark sarcastic look. "What?"

"They're unintended."

"We can't freeze this island in time, Liz."

"Sure we can. Haven't you heard? There's this new tree-hugger bitch on the town council."

Merry laughed and shook her head. "My sister, the crusader. I can't believe I set myself up for this."

"What do you mean by that?"

"I've missed you," Merry said, in her best baby-sister voice. "You're home now, but there's no way you'd have stayed. And Mamma and Daddy aren't getting any younger, you know."

"Exactly what have you done?"

She took three more steps and stopped. "Well..."

"*Merry...* "

"Remember last night at the council meeting, when I volunteered for Gram's seat?"

"Vividly." I could feel my left eyebrow creeping towards my hairline.

"Well, I never intended to actually take it."

"What?"

"Can you imagine how breathtakingly boring those meetings are? You couldn't pay me enough. You have so much more patience than I do."

I closed the distance between us by half. "You set me up."

"Well... yeah."

"All that concern about an outsider on the town council—I knew that didn't sound like you."

"Actually I'd love to see somebody from anywhere *but* here on the town council. But that wasn't the most important issue last night."

"You manipulated me into volunteering for that seat. You gave me some ridiculous version of your plan, knowing I'd do anything to stop you. Why did you think you had to trick me into staying here?"

"Call it insurance. It worked, too."

I burst out laughing. She'd snookered me. It had been a while since I'd let that happen. I should have been mad. But to be mad at Merry for manipulating me was to be forever mad at Merry.

Merry laughed too. We laughed until tears rolled down our cheeks and we couldn't catch our breath. We held our sides, and held each other up.

Finally, I wiped my eyes. "Just to be clear, I'm glad I'm home, but I was planning to stay."

"You say that now, but—"

"My loft is on the market."

"Really?"

"Really," I said. "And I owe you for all the Tuesday nights I'll be discussing wild hogs and water towers."

"What?"

"Never mind." I kept forgetting which things Colleen had told me. I started walking back the way we'd come. "Couldn't you have just called me and said, 'Hey Liz, since you're home and all, why don't you take Gram's seat on town council?'"

"Oh yeah, that would have worked."

We walked in silence for a few minutes before I stated the obvious. "But you had to know I'd have serious reservations about development...even for a good cause."

"I was betting I could talk you into it."

"That was a bad bet."

"We'll see."

I was relieved she seemed content not to pursue the topic. Normally, Merry was like a dog with a bone when she wanted something, especially something related to her work. I changed the subject before Merry could change her mind. "Are you still seeing Troy Causby?"

"Oh hell no," Merry said. "I broke that off a month ago. I'm through my bad-boy stage."

Troy Causby had lived on the periphery of our childhood. He had cousins on Stella Maris, and he'd occasionally shown up at the beach or at a church potluck. Troy had always seemed to envision himself as James Dean. I'd bet he practiced his surly look in the mirror. He'd been in trouble a few times—underage drinking, pot—nothing serious. Lots of kids go through rough patches and grow up to be pillars of the community. Something about Troy, though, had always screamed bad seed to me. I thought Merry deserved better.

"What made you see the light about Troy?"

"I never thought he was Mr. Right, but you've got to admit, he sure is *fine* to look at. He was Mr. Right Now. Now he's Mr. Can't Shake Him Loose."

"Send Blake to convince him."

"I don't need my big brother to solve my problems for me. I can handle it." Merry stared down the beach into the darkness.

"Why do I sense you're not so sure that you can?"

"Because you always think I can't handle things myself. It's your nature, you're my big sister."

"It's more than that. You sound worried."

Merry wrapped her arms around herself. "He's just... a little scary sometimes."

"What do you mean?"

"He went a little nuts when I broke it off."

"Like how?"

"He got really mad, shouting and throwing things. The next day, he brought flowers, ready to play kiss and make-up. When I wouldn't let him in, he threw the flowers at me and told me I'd be sorry." Merry shuddered. "That was a month ago, and he's still following me."

Merry stopped, turned, and looked out across the water. "The thing that really scared me, though, is he came to the door a couple of weeks ago. Two in the morning. I think he knew I was just inside, watching him through the peephole and listening. He said, 'Nobody treats me like shit and gets away with it. You'd better watch yourself, Merry. I know how to hide bodies so they're never found.'"

"And you didn't call Blake right then because *why*?"

"I told you, I can handle it."

"I don't think we'll find that very comforting when we're looking for your body."

"He was just trying to intimidate me."

"How do you know? It sounds to me like he's unbalanced."

"I think he is, a little, but not enough to kill me and hide my body."

"I'm telling Blake."

She spun on me. "No, you're not. This is my problem and I'll handle it. I shouldn't have told you."

"You should have told me and everyone else you know, and then told Troy you told everybody."

Merry sighed. "Maybe. But the good news is, the thing Troy wants most in this world is to leave South Carolina and never look back. He might already be gone."

"Isn't all of his family here?"

Merry snorted. "Troy's not big on family. He hates the shrimping business. His dad made him work on the boats summers growing up. Troy isn't cut out for manual labor. He wants to go to Hollywood and be in commercials."

"That's his big dream? Commercials? Not a TV show, or movies, but commercials?"

"Yep. He thinks he can make a pile of money doing beer commercials. Beer and trucks. He says for commercials all you have to do is look good."

We both laughed. "What about your roommate, Kristen? Why do Dad and Blake dislike her so much? Have I ever met her?"

"No, she went to school with me at College of Charleston, but we weren't close. After I bought my house, money was tight and I needed a roommate. I mentioned it on Facebook a couple times. Eventually, Kristen called me. She's a little odd. Hard to read, but she's okay. She pays her rent on time and does her share of the housework. And she's been very encouraging about my youth camp. I think she's going to work there with me."

I playfully bumped into her. "So you don't want to move in with me?"

"Oh please. One of us would end up dead and Blake would have to put the other in jail."

We had made our way back to the quilt. Merry grabbed one side, I grabbed the other, and together we spread it on the soft sand. "Seen any shooting stars lately?"

"I haven't been star gazing in forever. I'm really glad you're home." I took Sig out of my capris and laid it on the quilt. We sprawled out and soaked in the night sky and the sounds of the surf.

Finally, Merry sighed and asked, "Do you think you'll miss Greenville?"

"Some things I'll miss." Nate came to mind.

"How is that partner of yours?"

I almost laughed out loud at how she read my mind. "Nate's good. He's actually on his way here right now."

"Do tell!" Merry's tone bathed that information in intrigue. "Clearly, you married the wrong brother."

"Marrying Scott was a mistake. But Nate and I are friends—he's my best friend. We're strictly platonic."

"Damn waste. You're still pining after Michael, aren't you?"

"Afraid so."

Merry made a disgusted noise, and we both fell silent and listened to the waves. I considered telling Merry about Colleen. I'd told my sister things I would never tell anyone else. But I wasn't ready to talk about Colleen, even to Merry.

"So why don't Dad and Blake like Kristen? You never said."

"*Your* father doesn't like her because she has two piercings in each ear. As for Blake, I don't know. He's never really said. Just that there's something about her he doesn't trust. I think it's big-brother paranoia. We grew up in this safe little world where everybody knows everybody."

"Maybe, but Blake has been off the island before. He has good instincts." I shrugged. "But, he can be protective. He pitched a fit at me this morning for running before it was light out. Well, that and skinny dipping."

"Oh man. I haven't been skinny dipping since you and I went in September."

"It was a new moon, pitch-black out," I said, remembering. "Not like tonight."

I stood up. "It's bright as broad daylight out here."

Merry took off her sweatshirt as she scrambled to her feet. "Anybody would go skinny dipping when it's pitch-dark out."

"It would take a real exhibitionist to swim naked when it's this bright." Off came my shoes, followed by my jeans.

Merry threw her bra on top of her pile of clothes. "Yeah, or somebody completely crazy."

"And her sister." I darted towards the surf. "First one in gets the quilt on the way back."

Together we splashed into the waves, laughing and whooping in wild abandon.

TWENTY

I slogged through the whole bedtime beauty routine, and then collapsed into the cloud of pillows and goose down that was my bed. And then I remembered I hadn't put my phone on the charger or changed the setting from silent. All those fancy surveillance alerts wouldn't do any good if I couldn't hear them.

I switched on the bedside lamp and leaned out of the bed to grab my purse from the floor. This maneuver nearly landed me headfirst beside the purse. In a gravity-defying move, I drug myself and the tote/purse back up onto the bed. I scrambled for my phone, which I typically keep in a side pocket. But not tonight. Tonight, I'd tossed my phone in my purse at Mamma's house, while Merry and I sorted through the clothes we hadn't put on standing on the beach.

I jammed my hand down in the tote, felt around, and came back with a familiar leather-cased iPhone. I slid it out of the case, pressed the home button, and let fly a string of curses.

The picture on the wallpaper was one of Merry, Blake, Mamma, Daddy, and me, from Thanksgiving. It was a great picture—I had a copy of it in a frame in a box somewhere. But it wasn't the one I used for wallpaper on my phone.

The phone in my hand was Merry's. As often happened, we had independently chosen the same phone and the same case. We must have mixed them up in the clothes jumble. Damnation. I threw back the covers and pulled on my clothes, cursing the whole way. I had to have my phone, and I had to have it back that night.

I tried dialing my phone from Merry's, but, of course, it was on silent mode. Merry wouldn't notice she had the wrong phone until she went to use it. I crawled into the Escape and headed, eyes half closed, to my sister's house.

Two blocks from Merry's house on Magnolia Lane, I squinted and leaned over the steering wheel. Was this another crazy-assed dream?

Colleen was perched on top of the bougainvillea-covered arbor in Merry's front yard. She must have sensed me approaching. She jerked her head around, saw me, and popped into the passenger seat. "What are you doing here?" she asked.

"Back at you."

"You're not supposed to be here."

I was still a block away. I pulled to the curb, under a big live oak and cut the engine. "Why not? What's going on?"

Troy Causby leaned against the doorframe of Merry's neat white cottage. It had been a while, but I recognized him.

"What's he doing here?" It registered then that Merry's car wasn't in the driveway. A white Ford Expedition was parked there beside a gray Honda. Where the hell was Merry?

"Merry's in trouble. I'm here to help. You'll get in the way."

"Merry's not here, Colleen. If she's in trouble, where is she?" But I knew then, where she must be. Merry discovered the phone mix-up, and was likely ringing my doorbell at that very moment, wondering where the hell *I* was.

"Whatever happens, it happens here." Colleen faded out.

I slipped Sig into the back of my jeans and Merry's iPhone into my pocket. I eased out of the car and pressed the door closed. As fast as I could go while remaining quiet, I navigated the edge of neighboring yards in the direction of Merry's house. Using trees, cars, and trellises as cover, I approached with caution. Two houses away, someone's dog went to barking.

I slipped behind the big magnolia at the corner of Merry's house. Behind me, someone shouted at the dog. He gave three more barks, then all was silent except for the voices on Merry's front porch. Colleen appeared beside me.

Troy's voice had a wheedling quality. "Come on, Kristen, let me in. She's over at her folks' house. They'll be yappin' all night."

Where had I heard that voice?

Kristen—I only knew who she was because Troy called her that, and she was in my sister's house—stood in the doorway, which was opened just far enough to see her. "And she might be home in any minute. We're not going to blow this deal. We're too close. Adam would be furious—"

Colleen and I looked at each other. Adam.

"You're really hot when you're mad," Troy said. "Actually, I think the boss would expect me to be here. That's the idea, right? Keep an eye on the prima donna."

"Wrong," Kristen said. "I'm supposed to monitor the situation here, since you were dumb enough to get dumped. You're supposed to be responding to problems, not creating them."

"Not my fault she broke up with me. But if she shows up, I'll just say I came by to beg her again to take me back. She wasn't here, so I cried on your beautiful shoulder."

"It was stupid—and unnecessary—for you to get involved with her to begin with."

"Are you jealous, baby?" Troy traced one finger down the side of her neck and across her shoulder. "You and me been a team a long time. She's just business. Quick as we get our money, you and me will be on a plane, and South Carolina will be nothing but a little redneck state on the other side of the country. Let me in, now."

"I know what you have in mind, Troy, and there is no way we could talk our way out of getting caught. You'd better go. Come back and play the lovesick puppy when she gets home." She tried to close the door, but he had slipped his foot over the threshold.

"It's been a long time, darlin'. I know you want me. I can see it in your eyes."

Kristen tilted her head. "Look, why don't we just go somewhere else?"

"That wouldn't be half as much fun. It's kinda excitin', thinking about gettin' caught, doncha think?" This time, his finger moved across her chest, lightly stroking her.

Kristen moaned and closed her eyes. Troy continued to caress her while he pushed the door firmly with his free hand. He slipped inside and closed the door behind him.

I looked at Colleen. "Are you sure we need to see this?" Merry's phone chimed. *Shit.* I pulled it out of my pocket. Battery life was at less than ten percent.

"You need to leave," Colleen said.

"Like hell I will. You said Merry was in trouble. I don't get it, seeing how she's not here, but—"

"If you're staying, let's find a window."

I was afraid to leave and afraid not to leave. Colleen was a ghost, and I was operating on the assumption she knew things I didn't.

I crept past the high kitchen window, over to the den window, and raised my head just enough to see through the sheers. Luckily, the window was open, so I could hear.

I hadn't missed much.

The lovers were locked in an embrace just inside the front door. Troy's mouth clamped down on Kristen's neck like he was a vampire. She arched her back, molded her pelvis to his, and clutched his shoulders, which was, I'm sure, the only way she kept her balance. In one motion, he lifted her and she wrapped her legs around his waist. His mouth never left her neck as he crossed the living room and pinned her to the wall. Thrusting, grinding, grunting, and groaning ensued.

Kristen left a trail of hungry kisses down his neck and chest as she released her legs. He stepped back, allowing her room to maneuver. She unbuckled his belt and slid down his jeans, and he returned the favor. Stepping out of her lacy panties, she kicked them out of the way.

Beside me, Colleen covered her eyes and peeked between her fingers. Maybe it was easier for me to watch because I'd tailed and photo'd so many cheating spouses.

Kristen hooked her arms around Troy's neck. She hopped back up, wrapped herself around him like a squid, and reattached her mouth to his.

A car door slammed. Merry.

I turned towards the front of the house.

"Stay put," Colleen said.

I hesitated. She sounded like she knew what she was doing. Would I make things worse by being there?

At the sound of a key in the lock, the lust-crazed pair froze mid-gyration.

I sucked in my breath as Merry blew through the door.

She had no doubt recognized Troy's Expedition in the driveway, because she was already steamed. "Kristen, why did you—"

They both stared at her, still frozen in the incriminating, half-clothed position against the living room wall. For a moment, nobody spoke.

Merry regained her wits first. She slammed the door and shot death rays from her eyes at Kristen. "You have ten minutes to get everything that belongs to you and get out of my house."

Then the Wrath of Merry rained down on Troy. "You, get out. Now. And if I ever see you again, you'd better not come within punching distance."

"You tell 'em, baby sister." I murmured. "Colleen, I need to get in there."

"Not a chance," said Colleen.

Troy shoved Kristen off of him and fumbled with his jeans. "Now Merry, this isn't what it looks like..."

Getting caught was evidently more exciting in theory than reality.

Kristen stumbled, then scrambled for her clothes.

Merry fisted her hands on her hips and cocked her head to the side. "Oh really? If you weren't having sex with my roommate, exactly what were you doing, Troy?"

I could almost hear the poor little hamster panting as he ran for dear life in the wheel that no doubt powered Troy's brain. "I came to see you, baby, but you weren't here. I needed someone to talk to, and Kristen felt sorry for me and let me in out of the kindness of her heart. I..."

Merry's eyes threatened to roll all the way back into her head. "Oh I can see how kind she was being."

Troy whined, "That's not how it was. I guess I got carried away...in my loneliness. Merry, you have no idea how hard these last few weeks have been on me."

I thought I might gag—I purely hate a whiney man. So does my sister.

"Oh please," Merry said.

"No, I mean it. I went a little crazy. Truth is, I was forcing myself on Kristen here just now. I guess if she wants to call the police, I'd understand." He gave Kristen a look that said *Play along. Play alonnng.*

Merry crossed the room and stood behind them, placing them between her and the door, as if to shoo them out. "I don't know what kind of idiot you take me for, but that is the biggest crock of shit I've ever heard. Get out. Now."

She turned that same look on Kristen. "You've already wasted two minutes. You now have eight. I recommend you start packing."

Kristen gulped, and took a tentative step down the hall. She stopped and looked at Troy.

The Genius was evidently frantic to convince Merry that Kristen was the innocent victim of his grief-induced lust. "Now Merry, you don't want to do that." He turned and stepped towards her, grasped her arm, and looked at her with an odd combination of pleading and menace.

"Don't you dare touch me." Merry pulled away from him with such force that she stumbled backward.

The backs of her knees caught the edge of the coffee table. All four of us watched in horror. Merry seemed suspended in mid-air, then crashed to the floor, cracking the back of her head on the fireplace hearth. For the second time in five minutes, Troy and Kristen froze.

I pulled out Merry's phone. Dead. Dammit. Dammit. *Dammit.* I unholstered my gun and took a step around the tree, towards the porch.

Colleen appeared in my path.

"What the hell? I've got to help her."

"You can't go in."

"What? Why?"

"If you go in, you'll all three die. You, Merry, and Kristen."

"How do you know that?"

"I don't know how I know. I just know. Stay here."

"Dammit Colleen."

"I can't let you go in."

"You can't stop me." I tried to push past her, but I couldn't. An invisible wall came up. It was like pushing against a big mattress. I beat on it and kicked it. Colleen disappeared, but I couldn't move past the wall.

"Come back to the window."

I looked over my shoulder and Colleen was peering inside.

"Why can't I just shoot the bastard and call 911?"

"Because he will shoot you first. Then he'll kill Merry and Kristen. You're not supposed to be here. You cannot intervene. *Trust me.* Come back to the window."

Because she was a ghost, I did as she said.

"If you promise to stay here, I'll go in," she said. "But if you come in there, I'll protect you first and anyone else second. Got it?"

"What can you do?" I whispered.

"We're about to find out."

Colleen walked through the side of the house and went to Merry's side. Merry was motionless. In shock, Troy and Kristen stood over her, staring. Colleen slid one arm under Merry's head and brushed her forehead with the fingertips of her other hand.

Screaming, Kristen ran towards the phone, resting on its cradle on the kitchen counter. Troy met her there. He grabbed the phone with one hand and Kristen's arm with the other. "What do you think you're doing?"

Now I knew that voice. Troy Causby was The Exterminator.

"I'm calling nine-one-one. She's hurt," Kristen said.

"Wait a minute. I need to think."

Kristen jerked at the phone. "She'll die while you're trying to concoct some story where you're not responsible."

Troy jerked back. "I'm *not* responsible. You saw what happened. She tripped. It was an accident."

"I'm not going to stand here arguing with you. Give me the phone." She grimaced, and looked at her arm. "You're hurting me."

His panic took on a layer of threat. "She's probably already dead. They'll never believe it wasn't our fault. Her brother's the fucking chief of police. I'm not going to jail."

Kristen hesitated.

Troy let go of Kristen, reached across the counter, and ripped the old-fashioned phone jack off the wall. He glanced back at Merry. He crossed the room, knelt down, and felt for a pulse.

"She's dead."

I drew back as if I'd been slapped.

Colleen's head snapped up. "No, she's not. Don't listen to him. He wants Kristen to think that. She's just stunned. *Do not come in here.*"

Kristen screamed, "No, no, no." She doubled over and rocked back and forth crying.

Troy went back and stood in front of Kristen, placed both his hands on her arms—gently this time—and met her eyes. "Look, we can't help Merry now, but we can help ourselves."

Kristen sobbed quietly and shivered.

The Exterminator rubbed her arms. "You're upset. I understand." He kept his voice calm and soothing. "Go to your room and get your purse. You've got to pull yourself together enough to drive. Go over to my place and wait for me there. I'll take care of Merry and get there as soon as I can."

"What are you going to do?" Kristen choked out.

So intent was Troy on dealing with Kristen that he didn't see Merry stir, but I did. Tears of gratitude welled up in my eyes. Colleen pressed her fingers against Merry's eyelids, presumably to keep them closed so Troy would think Merry was still unconscious.

His next words turned my blood to ice water.

"I'm going to hide her body," the bastard said. "You don't want to know where."

Kristen shook her head violently. "No."

"Look at me, Kristen. We've got to clean this mess up or the boss's associates are going to be ditching *our* bodies. You get that?" His snake eyes burned into hers. "Remember...you're the one that told me she wanted to open a camp on the beach. You started this whole thing. We're in this together...right?"

She raised and lowered her chin twice.

"No one will ever know we were even here tonight. No one is *ever* going to know, right, Kristen?"

Again, as if his puppet, she nodded.

Colleen looked at me again. "Ignore him. Merry's going to be fine."

Troy pushed Kristen towards her room. "Go on, now, get your purse."

Moving like a robot, she did as she was told.

Colleen kept her fingers pressed to Merry's eyelids, and whispered into her ear.

The Exterminator ran his fingers through his hair and stared at Merry.

Kristen shuffled back into the room carrying her purse.

"Be careful," he admonished her. "Don't speed, and don't run any stop signs. If you get stopped looking like that, the cop will remember it when Merry turns up missing. Go straight to my place and stay there."

"Okay." As if in a trance, she floated out the door, closing it behind her. A moment later, I heard the Honda start.

Troy turned his attention to Merry. Ignoring the magazines, pictures, and candles that had been scattered by Merry's fall, he lifted the coffee table and dropped it in the corner, off the pastel braided rug. He pulled the edges of the rug from underneath the furniture legs.

A fierce look on her face, Colleen appeared to be whispering the same thing, over and over into Merry's ear. She turned her head slightly and met my eyes. She raised her voice so I could hear. Soothingly she said, "One chance to escape. Wait for it. Focus on staying limp."

Troy stood over Merry and Colleen and took a deep breath. He lifted Merry and laid her down at the edge of the braided chenille rug. Colleen and I stood helpless as he folded the end of the rug over Merry, tucked it underneath her, and rolled her across the floor, wrapping her in the rug as he went. He looked relieved once she was fully concealed in the rug.

Colleen bent over the rug and chanted, "Stay still. Stay still. Stay still…"

Troy strode to the front door and left the house, closing the door behind him.

Merry must have heard the door close, or maybe on some level she heard Colleen shout, *"Now!"*

Merry flopped like a fish out of water, trying to loosen the rug. She rolled herself backwards, opposite the way Troy had wrapped her up.

"Help her," I hissed.

But Merry tumbled, still dazed and unsteady, out of the rug and scrambled to her feet. She bolted for the back door.

"No!" Colleen shouted. A silver aura appeared around her body.

I stepped back in wonder.

The light shimmered and tiny sparks of gold flew from Colleen's fingertips as she reached towards Merry with both hands. "He's driving around back. He'll catch you there."

Merry stopped and turned.

"She can't hear me," said Colleen. "She thinks the thought occurred to her. Stay quiet."

My instincts were screaming at me to shout at her, but I didn't know what the consequences might be.

Wildly, Merry's eyes searched the room. She took in the ripped out phone jack. She lunged for the fireplace poker, grabbed it, and dashed to the french doors that led onto the back deck. She peered out.

"Lock the door," Colleen said.

Merry threw the deadbolt, and darted away from the door.

"Where's my cell phone?" I whispered. "Tell her to call Blake."

"She left it on the porch at your house with a note." Colleen looked at me hard. "Stay put."

Grasping the poker in both hands, Merry flattened herself against the wall beside the front door. When he came back in, she'd be ready for him.

TWENTY-ONE

Colleen stared out the french doors. "He's pulled the Expedition around back. He's unloading a bunch of crap onto the deck. Looks like he didn't plan on having to dispose of a body this evening. We got golf clubs, a gym bag, a toolbox, dirty clothes, and a bunch of wadded-up fast food bags."

For what seemed like hours, we waited. Colleen watching, and Merry and I straining to hear, each rooted to our spot. Then, footsteps on the deck. Troy crossed the deck and tried the back door. He cursed quietly, but emphatically.

Cursing non-stop, he backed off the deck.

Seconds later, I heard a car door out front. Footsteps clicked on the walk.

Colleen spun towards the front door, a question in her eyes.

The door opened.

Kristen stepped in.

Merry brought the fireplace poker down on her head.

Kristen crumpled to the floor.

Merry stared down in horror. Then, thinking astonishingly fast on her feet for someone with a gash in the back of her head, she grabbed Kristen's feet and pulled her over to the rug. Adrenaline—or possibly Colleen—now in the driver's seat, Merry rolled Kristen up in the rug exactly as Merry herself had been only moments before.

Without a backward glance, Merry picked up Kristen's purse and slipped out the front door. Seconds later, the Honda purred to life.

TWENTY-TWO

"Why did Kristen come back?" I hissed at Colleen.

"I don't know." Colleen stood in the middle of the room, ears perked. She turned slowly around in a circle. "A better question is what happened to Troy. Stay there. He's armed. If you try to leave now, he'll see you when he comes back around the house. I don't understand what's taking him so long."

"He probably heard the car and waited."

Colleen nodded. "He probably thought it was a neighbor and didn't want to be seen."

Praise God, Merry had made good her escape.

Footsteps on the front porch.

Colleen's eyes glowed red. "Remember—*no matter what*—do not come in here. If you come in here, you die tonight."

The front door opened. Troy came inside and closed it behind him. The silencer made the gun in his hand look huge. I held my breath and ducked a little lower.

Later, I wished in my bones I'd gone inside, regardless of Coleen's dire predictions and freaky eyes.

A muffled moan came from the rug.

Troy's eyes riveted to the bundle.

The middle of the rug heaved then both ends jerked wildly. Muffled screams fought their way through chenille.

Troy crossed the room in two long strides and stood over the mound.

The rug rocked and rolled forward.

Troy pointed the pistol at the end of the rug, squinted, and recoiled as far from the gun as he could.

I ducked, turned, and braced my back against the house.

I covered my face and slid down the side of the house to the ground.

Pfft-pfft. I barely heard the shots.

TWENTY-THREE

Maybe he'd hit her in the arm. Through the rug, it would be hard for him to tell. Shaking, I peeked over the windowsill. The rug wasn't moving. Troy unlocked the deadbolt on the french doors and opened both sides. He heaved the rug over his shoulder and staggered out. As soon as he cleared the doors, Colleen shouted, "Run, *now*. Go home. Merry's there. Let Blake handle Troy."

Then Colleen went wherever Colleen goes.

I sprinted back to the Escape, made a u-turn, and sped home.

Kristen's Honda was in the driveway. I pulled in behind it and ran up the steps. Merry was curled in a ball on the porch by the door. I knelt and crushed my sister to my chest. Then I got us both inside and bolted the door.

Since that was not the time—if ever there would be a time—to explain to Merry I'd been consorting with spirits, I listened as she sobbed out what happened. "I thought I saw your car down the block," she said at one point.

I shook my head. "Someone else must have one like it."

"I don't know what made me think to lock that door," she said. "I started to run out back. But something just told me not to, you know?"

While she talked, I hugged her for dear life. Then I dialed Blake.

He made it from his houseboat in record time. The three of us sat huddled together in the sunroom. Merry and I on the loveseat, Blake on the adjacent sofa, as Merry repeated the story. Rhett paced the room like a sentry, sniffing corners.

"What does Troy drive?" Blake asked.

"A white Expedition," Merry said.

Blake reached for his cell phone and radioed Rodney Murphy.

When he finished giving the description of Troy and his vehicle to Rodney, he turned back to us. Blake leaned in and spoke gently to Merry. "Troy's dad is a shrimper. I know he has access to several boats. Do you know if any of them was docked here tonight?"

"Sometimes he'd use his dad's speedboat to come from Shem Creek," Merry said. "But then I'd pick him up at the marina. He was driving the Expedition. He came over on the ferry."

Blake said, "We've got to find him before he dumps Kristen somewhere. You probably just stunned her with the poker, but she needs medical attention. If she wakes up before he gets where he's going... Do you have any idea where that might be?"

I couldn't tell them she'd been shot. It wouldn't have changed anything anyway. Troy still had to be found.

Merry shook her head. "No, all I heard him say is that he was going to get rid of the body. *My body.*" She dissolved into violent sobs.

I tightened my arms around my sister and rocked her back and forth. "It's okay, you're safe."

Blake stood, eager to join the hunt. "Look, I don't know where this asshole is, or what his plans are, but if he finds out that's not Merry rolled up in the rug, he's going to come looking for her."

Visions of the Exterminator still danced in my head. "I know."

His eyes bored into mine. "If Kristen regained consciousness, he may already be looking for Merry. The first place he'll come is here, then Mom and Dad's. I've got to go find him. I can't leave the two of you here alone. Please don't ask me to do that." Blake knew me well enough to know I would not take kindly the idea of being run out of my own home.

I muled up. "I installed a security system. We'll lock up behind you, and you can have somebody drive by every now and then."

Blake got loud. "Liz, be reasonable. This is a small island. I don't have a fleet of patrol cars at my disposal. Right now, I need everyone I have to hunt this asshole down."

"Be sure to call when you find him. I can't wait to get my hands on that—"

"I can't leave here until I know that the two of you are safe. Please, for once in your life, listen to me."

Merry asked, "Where do you want us to go? You said yourself he'll go to Mom and Dad's if he doesn't find me here."

"But there's safety in numbers, and Dad has a nice collection of shotguns. You'll be safer there than you are here."

I wasn't happy about the idea, but the beseeching look on Blake's face won me over. "I'll pack an overnight bag. It'll just take a minute. Go on...I'll call when we get there."

Blake said, "I'll call Dad and tell him you're on your way."

I gently extricated myself from Merry and tucked the afghan around her. "What about Kristen's car? That's the first thing he'll look for. Even if we put it in the garage, the doors have windows."

Blake thought for a moment. "I'll park it at the ferry dock. If he finds it there, he'll think she caught the last ferry over."

"The keys are on the coffee table," Merry said. "But it's nearly out of gas. I didn't think I'd make it here."

Was that why Kristen had come back? Did she need money for gas? She'd taken her purse, but maybe for whatever reason she didn't have money.

Blake picked up the keys and turned towards the kitchen. "There's some in a gas can in the garage."

"Blake?" I said.

"Yeah?" He stopped and turned, impatience on his face.

"Be. Careful." I gestured with both hands for emphasis. "He has a gun."

"What? How do you—?"

I shook my head. "Later. Just trust me. He has a gun. Troy's the Exterminator."

He swallowed a curse and glared at me. "Later, you'll tell me how you know that."

TWENTY-FOUR

The morning after Merry's close encounter with a nine-millimeter, I slipped out of Mamma and Daddy's house just before five and drove home to check on Rhett. I couldn't take him to Mamma and Daddy's. Chumley did not play well with other dogs.

I unfastened Rhett's electronic collar and took him with me on my run. Mamma's voice in my head kept admonishing me about how reckless it was, running alone that particular morning. But I needed to run. It helped me think, and I had a lot to sort out. Besides, my instincts told me that Troy was holed up somewhere sleeping off a very bad night.

When Rhett and I ran past the marina, Rodney Murphy and Sam Manigault were waiting by Troy's Expedition in the parking lot. No sign of Troy. I didn't stop. There was nothing in that Ford I needed to see. I let Rhett romp in the surf while I swam, but no watching the sunrise for me. I hurried back to Mamma and Daddy's, hoping to get there before I was missed.

At six fifteen, I got a text from Nate: Flight delayed. ETA 11:45. Sit rep?

My situation report would not fit in a text message. Besides, there was nothing he could do from Chicago. I replied: Complicated. Tell u when I c u. I'm fine.

I poured myself a cup of coffee and went outside to the screened porch. I settled into the swing and pondered what in the name of sweet reason I was going to tell Blake.

Before I could work that one out, Colleen dropped by.

"Would you like some coffee?" My words were coated in sarcasm with sprinkles.

"No thanks." She leaned back into the cushions on the swing.

"I need some straight answers from you or I'll be checking myself into the nervous hospital before noon."

"What?" She looked all innocent.

"First of all, why are you back here, on earth, on the island? After all these years?"

"Colleen Stevens, guardian spirit." She held out her hand for a shake.

"*You*...are my guardian angel?"

"No. Angels are unique creatures. Dead people don't turn into angels any more than they turn into zebras."

"So what exactly is a guardian spirit?"

"Anyone who has passed from the mortal world to the immortal world and has been sent back on assignment to help or protect someone. Or someplace."

I considered getting a swig of something out of Daddy's well-stocked cabinet for my coffee. "On the outside chance I am *not* stark-raving mad, and you *are* actually sitting there, *what* you are is my guardian spirit?"

"No. I guard Stella Maris. If you were my assignment, you would never have gone out with Scott—much less married him."

I closed my eyes and drew in a deep breath. What if she disappeared again? My eyes flew open. "Why are you popping up in my dreams?"

"Your dreams are your own. That's between you and your subconscious."

"So what was all that about last night?"

Colleen sighed. "Like I said, I protect the island. Sometimes, I protect people who live here as a part of that overall assignment."

"Sometimes?"

"Sometimes."

"Where were you when Gram was murdered?"

Colleen's eyes misted. "Look, I just do what I'm told. I go where I'm told, when I'm told. I'm not privy to the big picture."

"Why wouldn't you let me shoot Troy? I could have taken him out and Kristen would be alive, and this would be over."

"That's what you *think* would have happened. See, you weren't supposed to be there. Every time one thing gets changed, something else doesn't unfold the way it's supposed to."

"Why was I there if I wasn't supposed to be?"

Colleen shrugged. "To quote the bard, 'There are more things in Heaven and Earth than dreamt of in your philosophy.'"

"I'm pretty open-minded."

"This gets into the whole good versus evil thing. We'd best leave that for another day."

"Are you saying evil forces switched my phone with Merry's so I'd come to her house and get involved in a shoot-out with an ex-shrimper?"

"I didn't say that. But it's one explanation."

I was feeling a little light-headed. "Okay then."

"Most people—even those who believe in ghosts—have never had a conversation with one," she said. "Just imagine the possibilities of all that could exist that you don't know about."

I had no answer to that. "Did Adam, Scott, or Troy kill Gram?"

"I don't know. Maybe."

"You're not here to help me find who killed Gram, are you?"

"That's not part of my assignment, but I'll help if I can. You know I will."

"But your agenda is preventing Adam and Scott from building a resort."

"Yes."

"And protecting Deanna."

"That's not really part of my assignment, either. But there's some crossover here. Deanna's involved. Normally, I'm not allowed to intercede on behalf of family. Or anyone, really, unless it's specifically part of my assignment. I'm new at this." She shrugged and looked apologetic.

"So tell me everything you know about what Adam and Scott are up to. I get that Kristen and Troy go way back. She must've told him Merry wanted to open a youth camp, and he told Adam." The dream popped into my head, the one where Michael had his arms wrapped around Merry. She'd been enjoying it—then she started struggling. It was Adam she'd gotten in bed with—metaphorically speaking—not Michael. The dream had been a foreshadowing of Merry's unwitting involvement with Adam's evil plans.

I pulled myself back to the present. "Sometime after that, Troy started dating Merry, and the Devlins agreed to donate land for this camp. But what's in it for the Devlins?"

"That's what we have to find out. You're the detective. Right now I don't know any more than you do. I'm not omniscient. I'm a guardian spirit, not God."

I stared at her for a long moment. "Have you seen Him?"

Colleen glowed. "Of course."

"What does He look like?"

"I can't tell you anything about Eternity. That's one of the rules."

"Oh."

"No time for pouting."

I pushed the floor with my feet to rock the swing. "Wait, what do you mean, 'You're the detective?' Are you here to help me, or do *you* need *my* help. In a professional capacity?"

"A little of both, I guess. We each have our role."

I pondered that. "Last night, you knew things. Like Merry had left my phone on the porch. Are you clairvoyant?"

"Not exactly. I'm given tasks that are limited in scope, like last night to help Merry. I'm given information relevant as I need it. I needed to know about the phone, so it popped into my head. Sometimes I pick up on things not directly related to a task—like a radio channel I accidently tune in to or something. Sometimes I can read minds. But my most reliable skill is snooping without getting caught." She grinned. "Kinda like you do, only it's easier for me."

"Can you read my mind? Right now?"

"Yeah. You're thinking you're still asleep and this is a dream."

"Wow."

We swung for a minute in silence.

"That thing you did," I said, "where you put an idea in Merry's head..."

"Throwing thoughts. That doesn't always work either. I'm still learning how to use my tools."

"What have you been doing for fourteen years?"

"That's not nearly as long as you think it is. I've been in training. This is my debut assignment."

"Why can't you just read everyone's mind and figure out what's going on?" It seemed pretty simple to me.

"I told you. I can't always read minds. And, I have to know whose mind to read."

"We have some candidates."

"And they have to be thinking about what I want to know."

"I see your point."

"And I have to be with them. I can't do it remotely."

"And you don't know where Troy and Kristen are." I was getting it. Colleen looked grim. "I know where Kristen is."

My stomach clenched remembering the pfft-pfft of the silenced pistol. The chains creaked as the swing moved back and forth.

"Wasn't there anything you could do for her?"

"I don't have the kind of powers that angels do. All I can do is try to point you people in the right direction and pray."

"How do you know what the right direction is?"

Colleen gave me this Mona Lisa smile. "Let's just say I get stronger hints."

"What was that wall thing you did, where you wouldn't let me go inside Merry's?"

"A force field. That's the first time I've ever done one, and I can't keep it up long—it takes practice to build endurance."

"Has anyone else ever seen you?"

"No. I only get one POC."

"One what?"

"Point of Contact."

I stared for a minute at the line of crepe myrtles in the backyard. "Colleen?"

"Yeah?"

"Why were you swimming in Breach Inlet?" This question had been bothering me for fourteen years.

"All the tequila in my system didn't tip you off?"

"You drank tequila?" At seventeen, Colleen was a teetotaler.

She met my gaze, and then dropped her eyes to her lap, where she became interested in her fingers. "I shoulda figured they'd keep that quiet."

"Are you telling me you killed yourself? On purpose?"

"Not one of my finer moments."

"Why?"

"I guess I lost sight of the big picture just long enough to get it done. I didn't grow out of the awkward stage as fast as you did. I was weary of trying to morph into something my parents could be content with. I was lonely, miserable. Seventeen. After Deanna got married, Mom and Dad focused on me full time, trying to fix me. Dermatologists, diet consultants, a personal trainer. The psychologist was the last straw."

Tears slipped down my cheeks. "How could I not have known you were that desperate? I've always agonized about not going to the movies with you that night instead of going out on a date. I thought, if only you'd been with me it never would have happened. I used to think you'd been murdered by some serial killer."

Colleen shook her head sadly.

"Once or twice it occurred to me you might have done it on purpose, but I just wouldn't let myself think that. Now I know it was my fault."

"No." She shook her head vehemently. "It was my fault. No one else's."

The back door opened and Mamma stepped onto the porch.

Colleen faded away.

"Good morning, sweetheart. I thought I heard you talking to somebody out here." Mamma took in my tear-streaked face and frowned in concern. "Liz, honey, everything's going to be all right."

She sat down beside me in the spot Colleen just vacated and wrapped her arms around me.

I rested my head on Mamma's shoulder while she stroked my hair and made soothing noises just like she'd done every time I was hurt my whole life—provided I was in petting range.

"Come on inside, honey," she said. "Let's get you some breakfast. I've got grits and eggs and bacon and biscuits and gravy and baked apples."

That's my mamma—no problem is so bad a little gravy won't cure it.

She led me into the kitchen. "After a good hot breakfast, and a little lipstick, you'll feel much better."

Gravy and lipstick. All a girl needs to make it through.

Blake was already at the table. His lined face and red eyes betrayed his lack of sleep. His hair was damp from the shower, and the change of clothes Mamma still kept in his old room were neatly pressed.

He looked up from the platter of breakfast in front of him.

"Any sign of him?" I asked.

"We scoured this island most of the night. Found his Expedition parked at the marina. Forensics is processing it now. His golf clubs, laundry, and a load of trash were piled up on Merry's deck. Seems pretty clear he made room in the Ford for something large."

"He must have left by boat."

"John's Chris-Craft is missing."

I sat down across the table from him. "He'll turn up. I bet they find that boat at Shem Creek."

"Nah, Mount Pleasant Police already checked. Charleston PD checked the City Marina. The sheriff's department is searching docks and marinas along every inlet, river, and creek within range, but that's a lot of waterfront to cover."

Mamma set a plate piled high in front of me. "You children eat your breakfast."

Blake eyed me over his coffee cup and then set it down. "We need to talk."

"I know."

"I've got a briefing with the patrol team at seven-thirty. I'll be gone about an hour. You'll be here when I get back?" The look in his eyes said *you'd better be here.*

Colleen joined us at the breakfast table.

I looked away from Blake, to what he no doubt believed an empty chair. "Sure."

He stood and carried his plate to the sink. "Liz..." his voice held a warning.

"What?"

Colleen said, "Hurry up and eat, would you? We've got places to be."

Blake drained his coffee cup and put his dishes in the dishwasher. "I'll see you in an hour." He was out the back door before I could think of anything to say that wouldn't get me committed.

I didn't intend to lie to him. It just worked out that way.

TWENTY-FIVE

I closed the door to the Escape, put the key into the ignition, and waited. Seconds later, Colleen joined me. "Hardware store," she said.

"Look, my priority is finding out who killed Gram, and why. I'm reasonably certain that Troy, Adam, and Scott are the culprits, but to prove that, I've got work to do. You've got your assignments, I've got mine. I can't just go chasing around with you all day."

"All right, but you'll be sorry you missed this."

I rolled my eyes. "You're the guardian spirit."

She gave me that smug grin.

I backed out of my parents' driveway. My iPhone automatically connects to the Sync system whenever I get into the car. Through the car's stereo system, I heard Nate's special ring. I pressed the button on the steering wheel to answer the call. "Hey. I thought you'd be in the air by now."

"After they delayed the flight three times, they canceled it. I'm re-booked on another flight, but it doesn't leave until four-forty-five." Tension coiled in Nate's voice.

I took a deep breath and tried to sound normal. "What time do you get in?"

"Not until around ten tonight. I've got a stop in Atlanta."

"Do you want me to pick you up?"

"I'll rent a car at the airport. What's going on there?"

"Too much to get into over the phone, but nothing for you to worry about. I'll catch you up tonight."

"I'll call you from Atlanta. Stay safe."

"See you soon." I pressed the button to end the call.

Five minutes later, I pulled into a parking space in front of Island

Hardware. They weren't open for business. It was only seven-thirty. "Now what?"

"We go inside." Colleen did her pop-out-and-in-again trick and was standing in front of the door.

"Maybe you can walk through doors, but I can't."

The smart aleck grabbed the large brass door handle, pressed down on the thingamajig and pushed open the door. The door chimed. I took a step backward, but she just breezed right on in. She didn't say a word. Just smirked.

I looked up and down the street, and then followed Colleen inside and shut the door behind us. The store appeared deserted. Colleen gave me the shhh sign and ducked behind the first row of power tools.

"I wonder where they are," I whispered.

"Deanna's taking the morning off. The jerk is out back talking to the insurance agent. Now be quiet."

Sure enough, a few minutes later, the back door opened and Adam called out, "Thanks...bye."

We crouched down and peered around the end of the aisle. Ten minutes later, my legs were cramping, and Adam was still in the back.

"Stay here." Colleen mouthed in exaggerated lip movements. She stood and walked across the store and down the back hallway. Why didn't she just talk out loud? No one could hear her but me.

I heard muffled noises, like someone moving things around. I sat cross-legged on the floor about the time Colleen strolled back in.

"What's he doing?" I mouthed.

She leaned down and whispered, right in my ear. "He's tearing that office apart looking for the money."

"Why are you whispering?"

"So you will, too. If I speak to you in a normal voice you'll forget to whisper."

Suddenly the front door opened, heralded by the electronic ding-dong, and then slammed shut.

Colleen crouched beside me, and we peeked around the corner.

Michael stood inside the door oozing fury. "Adam!"

Adam came down the hall and onto the sales floor with a curious look on his face. "Hey Michael, what's up?"

The raging-bull look on Michael's face must have registered with

Adam. He stepped behind the counter, putting it between him and his brother.

"Why don't you tell me what's up, brother?" Michael's voice was deceptively low and calm as he crossed the room to stand directly across the counter from Adam.

Adam glanced around the store. He looked torn between relief there were no customers around and alarmed. "What do you mean?" He laughed nervously.

"I found something of yours." Michael flung a wallet down on the counter.

Adam picked it up and inspected it. "My wallet. Thanks. I thought I'd lost it. Been looking everywhere for it."

Michael placed both hands on the counter and leaned in towards Adam. "Not. Quite. Everywhere."

My blood temperature dropped to below freezing, and I wasn't the one Michael was mad at.

"Where'd you find it?" Adam looked like a possum just before an eighteen-wheeler rolls over it: bewildered and transfixed.

"Under my bed." Michael ground out the words.

"How—"

"Oh, I think it's pretty obvious how. Tell me something, brother. What were you thinking about when you were screwing *my* wife in *my* bed? Did it make you feel big? Isn't one woman enough for such a big man? Or did you just like taking something that was mine?"

"Now, Michael..." Adam held up his palms and took a step back.

"Don't bother to deny it."

Adam just stood there, staring at Michael. The corner of his mouth inched up in an odd little grin.

"I don't know why I didn't see it before." Michael pounded his fist on the counter. "How long?"

Adam started to speak, hesitated.

"How long, Adam?"

"About a year."

Michael pulled his fist back and drove it squarely into his brother's left jaw.

Adam flew backward. He slammed into the shelves on the wall and slid to the floor with a loud thud. Small plastic buckets of screws, nails, nuts and bolts rained down on his head and shoulders.

"Well, guess what? You can have her." Michael laughed harshly. "Hell, you could've had her a long time ago if I'd known you wanted her. I hope you enjoy her now that you won't be screwing her in my bed. Because I don't sleep there anymore."

I could not control the big grin spreading across my face. The Halleluiah Chorus played in my head.

Adam hadn't bothered getting up.

Michael looked at him like something he'd stepped in and gotten on his shoe. "You and Marci deserve each other."

Michael walked out and slammed the door behind him.

Colleen and I looked at each other.

After a minute, we heard Adam pick himself up off the floor. He stumbled back down the hall, cursing under his breath.

I jerked my head towards the door and Colleen nodded.

We hightailed it out of there.

TWENTY-SIX

Colleen faded out a block from the hardware store, leaving me to noodle over how my adulterous cousin figured into the epidemic of chaos infecting the island. There must be a connection, or why would Colleen have shared that particular piece of information? Why did she always disappear before I could think of the questions I wanted to ask her?

I hadn't had much sleep the night before, and I needed caffeine. Not just coffee, but something with an extra shot or two of espresso. With all the pinballs banging off the corners of my brain just then, a chat with Moon Unit would have sent me into tilt.

The Book & Grind, a bookstore and coffee shop, had opened two years ago in the old drapery and upholstery shop between Phoebe's Day Spa and the dry cleaners. I decided to give it a try. The rich aroma of espresso permeated the air and beckoned me to the counter. I ordered a triple mocha latte to go. Lighthouse Park—the city park just south of Devlin's Point—provided a quiet place to think. I parked the Escape and opened the moonroof.

Here's what I knew: Gram suspected something was going on with the town council. Adam and Scott were working on a scheme to build a resort on the island. It would take four votes to change the zoning and allow oceanfront commercial development. It appeared Adam had hired a hit man—Troy—to kill another council member, but who? Who did Adam want on the council instead and where would the other votes come from?

The weirdest piece to the puzzle was Merry's camp. It had to be connected. Adam somehow convinced the rest of his family to donate land for the youth camp on Devlin's Point. I had no idea what he stood to gain from such a thing, but it was important enough to him that he had

Troy and Kristen spying on Merry. Plus, Adam had been surreptitiously meeting with David Morehead outside The Pirates' Den.

Maybe Adam figured Merry would get the ban on beachfront development lifted for her camp, then he could build his resort on Gram's land, North Point. No way would Kate Devlin—or Michael—sit still for a resort on Devlin's Point. But maybe the youth camp was the proverbial camel's nose under the tent.

Gram must have figured out the resort scheme. Maybe they tried to buy the land first, and that had tipped her off. My gut said Adam hired Troy to kill Gram to get control of her land, her town council seat, or both. A plan I had complicated. If Merry hadn't shanghaied me, and the seat had gone up for special election, who would have run?

The caffeine kicked in.

Adam was having an affair with Michael's wife, Marci the Schemer. Marci thought she was going to inherit Gram's house and land. Hell, she even tried to trade me Michael for the land. Adam evidently felt confident he controlled Marci, which meant she was involved in this mess right up to her perfectly arched eyebrows. But was she a co-conspirator, or was Marci the Schemer being manipulated?

Marci's house was only four blocks away. She would be at work. If I snooped around, what evidence might I find that she was guilty?

My stomach felt like I'd eaten a bad fish as I stared at the Craftsman-style house Michael shared with Marci. Well, until that morning anyway. I wondered if she knew he wouldn't be sleeping there that night. Marci had done all right for herself—although evidently she didn't see it that way. What would possess any woman married to Michael to sleep with Adam? It had to be about money. Marci always thought the world owed her mink and caviar. We'd never been close, but I used to feel sorry for her. The landscape of her childhood was sown with bad seeds.

Marci's mother, Daddy's sister, Sharon, fell in love with a surfer who showed up in Stella Maris the summer she turned seventeen. Paul Miller was tall, tanned, toned and untroubled by any ambition higher than the waves of the Atlantic. He got a job mowing and mulching for Granddad to pay for surfboard wax and weed. Aunt Sharon knew if Granddad found out they were seeing each other he'd fire Paul—and possibly shoot him—so they kept it a secret.

When she turned up pregnant, they took off on an extended beach tour. Marci told me once some of her earliest memories were of a nudist colony near Daytona. They lived like coastal gypsies until Marci was school-aged, and then came home. Gram and Granddad did the best they could to help Paul and Sharon. But normal was more than Paul's free spirit could bear. One day he just took off, and nobody had heard from him since. Aunt Sharon cuddled up to vodka, and Marci started sneaking swigs when she was twelve. I know, because she used to offer me a taste and tease me when I wouldn't try it. Aunt Sharon drank more and more until her liver gave out. She died three months after Michael and Marci were married.

Marci might be family, but I'd stopped trying to be her friend when she sank her claws into Michael, something I'd never forgiven her for. She took Michael from me because she saw an opportunity to take something that was mine, and for no other reason. Finding out she was cheating on him—with his own brother—brought ambivalent feelings. On the one hand, I was giddy that she could be so stupid. Her infidelity would certainly be the end of her already unstable marriage, which meant Michael would soon be free. On the other hand, I was pissed she could hurt him that way.

With a resigned sigh, I opened the car door and got out. I glanced up and down the oak-lined street, crossed it, and approached the front door. I was reasonably sure Marci was at work. It was after nine on a Thursday. On the outside chance I was wrong, I rang the bell.

The door opened to reveal the petite form of my cousin, dressed in jade-green silk lounge pajamas with a matching robe hanging casually open. Hell's bells. What was she doing at home?

For a moment she just stood there, glaring at me with one eyebrow cocked, her full lips in their permanent pout. I looked evenly into the hardest eyes I'd ever seen. It was like we were playing some weird game of chicken right there on the front porch.

Finally, Marci the Schemer spoke. "Well, well. Look who's come to call. Have you decided to take me up on my offer?"

Lord, my hand itched. I quelled the urge to smack her. Deep breath. "I was hoping we could talk for a few minutes." That was the last thing I was hoping for.

Marci shrugged. "Why not?" She stepped back to let me in.

"I should have called, but—"

"But you were in the neighborhood?" Marci cut me off with a sardonic half-grin as she led me into the living room and waved me towards the sofa. She curled herself into an over-stuffed chair.

"Yes, actually. I was." I felt queasy. I was inside the lair of the beast. But I was also in Michael's home, surrounded by things he touched every day.

Marci gave me an *oh-please* look.

"I wanted to talk to you about Gram."

"What is there to talk about? She's dead. You have everything you want."

I glared at her. Not quite everything. "Look, Marci, no one was more shocked by her will than me."

"But you're sure not sorry about it, are you?"

"It's unfortunate you feel you didn't get what was rightfully yours, but that really wasn't what I wanted to talk about."

"I shouldn't imagine that it was. Exactly what *do* you want?"

"Have you seen this morning's paper? Gram was murdered. I was hoping you might have a clue why."

"That article is absurd." Marci scowled. "Who would want to kill her? She was a little old lady, for heaven's sake. She walked on the beach and puttered with her flowers. There was nothing remotely interesting in her life, much less anything sinister enough to cause someone to kill her." If Marci knew anything about Gram's death, she had polished her acting skills.

"So it seems." I was offended at her characterization of Gram, but I smothered the impulse to react. "Did you ever see her wearing a silver, heart-shaped locket?"

"Not that I recall, why?"

"I found one near where she was killed. There was a picture in it of a man. I wondered if you might know who it is."

Marci looked surprised. "Where is the locket?"

"Blake has it."

"Why?"

"I guess he thinks it's evidence. It must have come off after she was hit over the head."

"Hit over the head? I thought she fell down the steps."

"I saw her heart necklace." The voice came from the foyer.

We both turned to stare at Elvis Glendawn, who had appeared in the doorway.

"Elvis? How did you get in?" Marci gaped at him.

"Well, Miss Marci, I was supposed to mow the yard this morning, like I do every Thursday. Michael, he's usually in the kitchen, sometimes we have breakfast together. But this morning, I knocked and knocked, but Michael never came and I guess you didn't hear me."

Marci looked at him like he was a palmetto bug.

Elvis shifted nervously from one foot to the other. "One time before Michael didn't hear me cause he was in the den and he told me I shoulda come on in. So this morning, I came on in like he told me to, only I can't find him."

"That's because he's not here." Icicles formed on Marci's breath.

Elvis took a few steps backwards. "I didn't mean to do anything wrong, Miss Marci."

"Elvis," I said. "Did you say you'd seen Miss Emma's locket?"

"Oh for Pete's sake, Liz. You can't pay any attention to what he says."

I cut her my top-of-scale withering glare. "On the contrary, I'm sure Elvis would never tell us anything that wasn't true. Elvis, did you see Miss Emma's necklace?"

Elvis glanced from me, to Marci, to the door, apparently trying to decide if he should make a run for it. His eyes met mine and he gulped. "She showed it to me one time. She said not to tell anyone. It was our secret, but since she's gone now, I guess I can tell. I mean, if it might be important, I guess you should know about it."

"Did she say who was in the picture?

"No, she just said it was a very nice man," Elvis said.

"You didn't recognize him?"

He shook his head slowly.

"Could he be the phantom you told Blake and me about yesterday?"

"Phantom?" Marci said. "Of all the—"

"Hush up," I said to her. I turned back to Elvis. "What do you think?"

He shrugged. "I never got close enough to the phantom to see his face. And I only saw the picture in the locket that one time. I can't say."

"Enough of this nonsense. Elvis, go mow the lawn. If my cousin wants to play Nancy Drew with you, she can do it on her own time."

He turned and beat a hasty retreat.

"I should be going. If you think of anything that might be important, let me know."

"Didn't you say Blake was investigating this? Have you been deputized?"

"I'll let myself out." I strode out of the room and out the front door, leaving nearly as quickly as Elvis had only moments earlier.

With one hand on the car door handle, something made me pause. Call it my suspicious nature. I looked around, half expecting Colleen to pop back in, but I was alone on the street. Why *was* Marci home today? Not likely because the newspaper headlines scared her. I hadn't gotten the chance to rifle through Marci's things, but since I was here anyway, why not see what she was up to? With an eye out for Elvis, I jogged across the front yard and slipped around the side of the house. The tall windows were open, inviting the breeze. I knelt and peered into the first room I came to. The living room, now empty.

I crept along the side of the house. The next room back was a bedroom. I could hear movement, but no one was in sight. I jerked lower as Marci stood up. She'd been looking under the bed.

Marci stretched languorously and smiled a self-satisfied smile. She sashayed over to the closet and rumbled through it for a moment, as if looking for something. The shrill ring of the telephone startled her.

She hesitated, and then picked up the phone. "Hello?"

Marci licked her lips slowly. "I'm heading out of town for a few days. Going to see an old friend in Savannah. Why?"

"Why no, did you want to talk to him?" she asked innocently.

She smothered a giggle. "He was gone when I got up. I haven't spoken to him today."

Her eyes widened. "He *hit* you?"

She sat down on the edge of the bed, a look of pure delight on her face. "That *is* odd. I wouldn't have thought he'd have *hit* you."

She lay back on the bed and ran her fingers through her hair. "No, he won't be coming back."

Marci regarded her manicure. "No. He won't. Because I'm calling a locksmith to come over and change all the locks. Right after I call my attorney. I've been abandoned."

She cradled the phone on her neck so she could check the polish on both hands. "You heard me. I don't want him back. On the contrary, I arranged for him to find your wallet under the bed to get him to leave. Since my bitch-cousin got the house and the council seat, and you're hedging now about leaving that puritan cow you married, I've had to improvise. I need to keep this house."

Marci arched an eyebrow. "Of course, I'll need your help to make ends meet, but that won't be a problem will it?"

She rolled her eyes at something he said. "We'll have to be careful for a while. Right now, he can't prove a thing in court. He gave you your wallet back, didn't he?"

Marci reached for the bottle of lotion on the nightstand. "Good. You didn't admit to anything, did you?"

She stopped in mid-motion, with a large dollop of lotion in her hand. "Was anyone else in the store while he was there? Did anyone overhear you?"

She visibly relaxed, but looked disappointed. "I see."

She gestured impatiently with her left hand. "Without a witness, he can't prove a thing in court. If he could, I might not get the house." Something in her voice smacked of Marci making it up as she went along. Something was off. She listened for a moment.

Marci sat up. One hand went to her chest. "That never seemed to bother you before. As a matter of fact, I got the distinct impression that the fact I was your brother's wife made me much more attractive."

Her shoulders and chest rose and fell slowly, like she was taking deep slow breaths. "You got what you wanted. And now, I'm getting what I want. Out. Michael has way too much pride to stay married to me now. *Ciao Baby.*"

She hung up.

A second later she sprang up and dashed through what must have been the bathroom door. The next sound I heard was retching. I didn't know what had upset her stomach, but I knew what upset mine.

TWENTY-SEVEN

As I pulled away from Marci's house, I wondered where Michael was working that day. Like a teenager, I had an overwhelming desire to drive by and just look at him. Or maybe I could think of an excuse to be there...maybe he'd pour out his heart to me about his cheating good-for-nothing wife. This insanity is why I'd stayed in Greenville for so long. Michael made me irrational.

With more self-control than I thought I possessed, I resisted the urge to do a grid search of the island for new construction. Instead, I swung by Phoebe's Day Spa to make sure everyone knew the island was on high alert. The smell of sandalwood greeted me when I walked into the old five-and-dime Phoebe had transformed into a five-star retreat. An appointment desk in the foyer sat empty, so I went on back.

The large room in the center of the spa housed hair, makeup, and nail stations. An indoor waterfall gurgled in the corner. Tropical plants, Polynesian art, and lots of sheer draped fabric gave the place an exotic feel.

Grace sat with her hair half-foiled in Phoebe's chair. Otherwise, the place was empty. Phoebe painted color on a section of Grace's hair while Grace read aloud from *The Citizen*. "Stella Maris residents should take necessary precautions to ensure their personal safety."

"You know things are serious when folks cancel appointments with you," I said.

They both looked up.

"Liz, sugar," Grace said. "Come hug my neck." She put the newspaper down and opened her arms. With tasteful makeup and manicured hands, Grace was elegant, even with foils sticking out of her head at odd angles. "I'm so sorry about lunch yesterday."

"What is it with you Southerners and necks?" Phoebe asked. "If you're not hugging one, you're threatening to wring one. Hey, stranger."

"Hey, yourself," I said. I hugged Grace, careful not to get hair color on me, and then hugged Phoebe, too. She was roughly my age, and with her three-inch platform shoes, my size. The two-inch accent stripe in her long, black hair was purple that day.

"Grace, weren't you just in here yesterday?"

"Well, yes I was," she said. "But that was just for a wash and style."

I looked at Phoebe. "Did the rest of your clients call in scared?"

Phoebe said, "Nah. Nobody booked appointments today. Everyone who isn't working at your mother's bazaar is shopping there. I let my staff have the day off."

"With the news about Gram being murdered in the paper, I figured everyone would buy bread, milk, and flashlight batteries and hole up at home. That's what Blake was hoping," I said. "I'm worried about the turnout for Mamma's bazaar. She's worked so hard..."

"Oh, don't worry about that." Grace waved dismissively. "Everyone will come out for The Most Fabulous Spring Bazaar Ever—you mark my words. It's in the church, you know. Folks will feel safe there. Besides, there's safety in numbers. That's what I've told everyone, anyway."

"And of course, they think you have the inside scoop."

Grace tried to look offended. "Well, you know I do." Then she turned serious. "I knew Emma Rae didn't fall down those steps. I told Blake that to begin with."

"Do you have guests this week?" I asked her. If she had a crowd at the bed and breakfast, she'd be safer.

"Two couples," she said. "Some retired folks from Ohio, and two young ladies from Virginia."

"Good. Stick close to home—except for the bazaar, of course. There's safety in numbers." I tried for a grin, but didn't quite execute it. I needed to call Blake and check in so he wouldn't worry. He'd still be mad, but at least he wouldn't worry about me.

"I'm not in any danger."

"Grace, whoever killed Gram was trying to shove some zoning changes through the town council. Anyone who would've opposed that is in danger. *You* are in danger. You've got to take this seriously."

"Why, of course, I take it seriously," Grace said. "But I'm not the one in danger. I could sense it if I was."

"Grace, I know you have a gift. But I also know you have blind spots."

Phoebe had been quiet far longer than usual. "I'm wondering why neither you nor Willa saw this coming." Willa Butler was the closest thing our island had to a voodoo priestess, heavy into signs and portents.

Grace pondered that for a moment. "You girls are quite right. This entire affair blindsided me. It often works that way. The people closest to me are the ones I don't read well at all." She looked at me. "I'll be careful, sugar. I promise."

I hugged her again. "Thanks. I just couldn't stand it if anything happened to you, too." When I pulled back, I caught the edge of Grace's black and white polka-dot drape and it came loose.

"Watch it, will you?" Phoebe said. "I get hair color on that St. John pantsuit and you're buying her a new one." Phoebe laid down her paintbrush and picked up the drape.

"Wait now," Grace said. She fiddled with her necklace and smoothed the top of her suit. "All right."

Phoebe adjusted the towel that had been rolled into a collar protecting Grace's neck, put the drape back on her, and fastened it.

I straightened. "Phoebe?"

"Yeah?"

"Did you ever see Gram wearing a silver locket?"

"I never saw her wearing it," Phoebe said. "But I know she had one."

Grace and I both squinted at her.

"What?" Phoebe grimaced.

"How do you know she had one?"

"She lost it in here, couple weeks before she died. I didn't know who it belonged to. I laid it aside and asked clients when they came in if they knew whose it was. The next time she was in—the last time she was in—I asked her and she said it was hers. She was sure happy to have it back."

"Is that important?" Grace asked.

"I think it is," I said.

TWENTY-EIGHT

I left Phoebe's Day Spa and hustled back to Gram's for a wardrobe change. Stella Maris is a small town. No matter how many new people had moved in over the last few years, I was still far from a stranger. Snooping incognito seemed like a reasonable precaution. Typically, when working undercover, I dress as a generic utility meter-reader. It's a common PI disguise. Put on khakis, a brown work shirt and a cap, and as long as you carry a clipboard and look busy, few people will question you.

As I pulled into Gram's driveway, I wrestled with calling Blake, and decided against it. It was easier to get forgiveness than permission. If I spoke to him, we'd have a big fight about how I needed to stay where he could keep an eye on me, et cetera—and also about last night. I had work to do, and no idea whatsoever what I was going to tell him about last night. How could I explain I saw the whole thing go down at Merry's, but didn't intervene, without mentioning Colleen?

Once I was trés incognito, I grabbed stakeout essentials (small cooler with water and Diet Cheerwine, Dove Dark Chocolate Promises, can of Lysol, extra hand sanitizer, and my camera) plus a few of my favorite toys (Taser, binoculars, and eavesdropping equipment, and, of course, Sig).

Troy had left the island, and law enforcement officers all over the state were looking for him. Scott had likely gone back to Greenville after he delivered his message in person to Adam. Adam was the only one of my axis of evil available for surveillance. My instincts said he was also the genesis of this whole endeavor, even if Scott was the financier.

Time to find out exactly how much evil Adam Devlin was the root of.

I didn't think I'd been home long enough for Adam to know what I was driving, so I took the Escape. I'd swap off and take Granddad's van for my next stakeout. I drove through the parking lot behind the hardware store. Deanna's Volvo was there, but not Adam's Lexus. I pulled into a parking spot and called just to be sure.

Deanna answered. "Island Hardware."

"Hey, Deanna. It's Liz."

Silence. I imagined she was reliving our close call the evening before in the back room and not finding it pleasant.

I plunged ahead. "Say, listen. We should talk. Can you get away for lunch?" Now, of course I knew this wasn't gonna happen, or I wouldn't have asked. Deanna would avoid me for a while if she could. That would make denial easier to hang onto.

"No. I have to stay here. Adam's home sick, so I'm here by myself until three. Then I have to pick up the girls. Let's do it another time, okay?" Her tone brightened, as if we were discussing any ordinary lunch date. I wondered if she still had that twenty-five grand in her purse.

"Sure thing," I said. "But Deanna..."

"Yes?"

"Just be careful, okay?"

"You too," she said breezily. "Bye now."

Adam was home sick my Great Aunt Fanny. He probably was ashamed for customers to see him. Which was a problem, since he likely wanted an alibi for today. He was expecting someone to be murdered soon. Jerk was probably home with an ice pack on his eye. I wondered how he'd explained that to Deanna. Probably hadn't. He probably left and called her to say he was going home. Which meant she would think he'd gone to see his mistress. Would Deanna try to track him down again?

I pondered whether to stick around or go hunt him myself. What I needed was a second set of eyes. I needed Nate. Since he was still in Chicago, I'd have to settle for who I could get. "Colleen?"

Miracle of miracles, she popped into the passenger seat. "Nice outfit." Bray-snorting ensued.

"Thanks. Can you hang out here with Deanna for a while and let me know if she leaves?"

"I can try."

"I'm sorry?"

"I can stay unless I'm given an assignment. Then I'll have to go."

"All right. But try to let me know if you have to leave."

"Okay." She faded out, presumably to pop into the hardware store.

I zipped over to Sea Farm to see if Adam was really at home, which, of course, he wasn't. Thinking that might work to my benefit, I circled the block and parked one street over. Then, I took a stroll around the neighborhood, which was deserted as far as I could tell. Everyone was at work or school. Sea Farm was predominantly a neighborhood of young families. Either they hadn't read the paper, they didn't feel personally threatened, or they wanted to be out and about to gossip with their friends. The stay-at-home moms were likely at the bazaar. I slipped through an adjoining back yard into Adam and Deanna's.

I hopped up onto the back porch of their two-story Victorian and examined the lock on the door. Given a little time, I could have let myself in. But through the paned top half of the door, a light on the alarm panel blinked red. The system was armed. Hell's bells. I guess Blake was right. Some folks on Stella Maris did have alarm systems. Bypassing one was complicated, and something I did not have the equipment for.

I thought for a moment, and then went back to the car. What I did have in my toy box was a butt set—a device that would identify Adam's phone line for me in the phone company's junction box—jumper wires to tap his line, and a digital recorder that would store all of his phone calls for me. The ones that went through the landline anyway. I realized if he were smart, he'd use a disposable cell for his criminal activity. On the other hand, I'd heard him talk to Troy on the hardware store phone. He even had his number in the rolodex. Adam wasn't the smartest criminal I'd seen.

The junction box was three houses down. Thank goodness the subdivision had underground utilities. Access would be easier. It took me less than thirty minutes to install the jumper wires. I sealed the recorder in a plastic bag, with only one small hole for the wires, and hid it in the pampas grass Adam's neighbor had no doubt planted to hide the telephone junction box. Lots of people do this—they camouflage the utility boxes with landscaping. It makes my job easier.

Most of the time I try my best to stay within the law. But when absolutely necessary, I do indulge in the occasional breaking and entering, wire-tapping, et cetera. But since my motivation is pure, I can sleep at night. I suspected Adam of hiring Troy to kill Gram. I *knew* Adam was plotting to kill someone else. I needed to stop him. For me, the moral lines were clear.

I climbed out of the pampas grass, brushed off my clothes and looked around. Still not a soul. If anyone had asked what I was doing, I would have spun a story about investigating noise on the phone line, or a gas leak. In the days of outsourced technicians, no one looks for a recognizable logo on your shirt.

My gaze settled on the recycling bins and trashcans at the end of each drive. The collection crew hadn't made it down Adam and Deanna's street yet. I dashed back to the car and pulled out a large trash bag from my handy stash of Heftys. I moseyed over to the Devlin trash containers. Nothing in the recycling, but that was always the way. The dirt was invariably in the nasty trash.

I held my breath and opened the trashcan. First, I sprayed the contents with half a can of Lysol. Then, I pulled out the three kitchen-size white bags and stuffed them in my extra-large lawn-and-leaf bag. I closed the can and lugged my treasure back to the Escape, where I stowed it in back for later inspection. At least with the trash double-bagged it wouldn't stink. I hoped.

I climbed into the driver's seat and slathered myself with sanitizer. Where might Adam be? After this morning's drama, not likely with Marci. The only other place I could think of was onboard his sailboat, *The Conquest,* which was moored at the marina. That destination in mind, I started the car and pulled out into the street.

Colleen materialized in the passenger seat. "Deanna's on the move. She got one of the part-time clerks to fill in for her. She's on her way home."

"And she won't find Adam there. The question is, does she know where to find him?"

"If she goes looking, she must have an idea."

"True." I drove slowly around the block. Then, I wended my way through the neighborhood and circled back. I passed Adam and Deanna's house just as she pulled into the garage.

There was only one way in and out of Sea Farm by car. I pulled into the Shell station on Inlet Drive just past the entrance and parked at a right angle to the road so that I could turn either way. I'd give Deanna an hour. If she didn't come back out, I'd head to the marina.

Thirty minutes later, Deanna's blue Volvo rolled to a stop at the intersection of Sea Farm and Inlet Drive. She crossed Inlet and headed down Palmetto Boulevard. I let one car between us and followed. When we circled the park, the car between us turned right and continued down Palmetto Boulevard. Deanna continued around the park to Main Street and bore right, towards the ferry dock. We were right behind her. I wondered if she'd seen my car the day before when I'd parked behind her in the bank lot.

Moments later, she pulled into the ferry parking lot. She pulled close to the front, near the ferry, and I hung back.

"Looks like we're going off island," I said. "But she's not looking for Adam, or she wouldn't be in her own car."

"Unless she couldn't borrow one."

I conceded the point with a tilt of my head.

I stayed a couple of cars back once we exited the ferry. Traffic was heavy enough to keep a couple of cars between us, but light enough that I could keep her in sight. This got more difficult when she headed into Charleston.

I got caught by a light and lost sight of her on King Street. Where was Deanna headed?

I looked at Colleen. She had a look of intense concentration on her face. "White Point Gardens," she said. "Step on it."

I tooled down King Street as fast as traffic would allow, which was not nearly fast enough to suit me or Colleen. She was tense, her eyes worried. She gripped the armrest on her right side and the console on her left.

I turned left on South Battery and started looking for Deanna, her car, or a parking place. It was a sunny spring afternoon, and White Point Gardens—the park at The Battery—had an assortment of college kids, housewives with preschoolers, tourists, and locals playing hooky from work.

"What was she wearing?" I asked.

"A navy sailor dress. Matching shoes and hat."

"In the hardware store? The last two days she had on slacks. Wherever she's going, she dressed for it before she left the house. Doesn't sound like tailing-your-cheating-husband attire."

Colleen said, "Keep going. Park on Murray."

I turned right on East Battery, then rounded the tip of the Charleston peninsula onto Murray Boulevard.

Colleen pointed. "There."

Deanna was making her way through the park in purposeful strides, her shoulder bag clutched tightly to her body. Every few steps she glanced over her shoulder.

I pulled over and parked in front of a cannon.

Deanna sat down on a bench under a huge live oak. Her posture was perfect, her purse on her lap.

Colleen turned in her seat to look behind us. "Troy." She pointed towards the battery.

"Where?" I twisted to see.

A man leaned casually against the black metal railing that ran across the High Battery. From that distance, I couldn't make out who it was. I pulled out my binoculars to have a look for myself.

It was Troy all right. "He's got balls of brass, wandering around Charleston in broad daylight. I'm calling Blake." I reached for my iPhone.

"No." Colleen's eyes were frantic. "I don't want Deanna caught with him. She has that money."

"*With her?*"

"Maybe. I hope not. Just wait."

I vacillated. I understood Colleen's instinct to protect her sister, but Troy was a killer. "Let's see what he wants with her." I pulled out my eavesdropping equipment, put on the headphones, and positioned the receiver. Then I raised the binoculars again.

Troy chewed a toothpick in the corner of his mouth and watched Deanna. He was hiding in plain sight—who would look for him in the park with tourists and college kids? I couldn't make up my mind if he was the dumbest hit man in the history of the world or crazy like a fox. We'd been there ten minutes when he crossed East Battery and sauntered over to the park bench where Deanna waited. He flashed her a smile. "Mind if I sit down?"

She stared up at him for a ten count, but said nothing.

"Mrs. Devlin?" he said.

"Yes, please sit down. Mr. ah..."

"It's better you don't know my name. Why don't you just call me Mr. Exterminator?"

Deanna didn't look at Troy, didn't turn her head. "I'm sure I'd feel quite silly doing that."

Colleen asked, "Are you recording this?"

"Yes," I said.

"She doesn't recognize Troy Causby?" Colleen asked.

"Deanna's four years older than us. Troy's, what? Two years younger? Their paths probably never crossed."

He leaned forward, propping his elbows on his knees. "Lady, you're wasting my time. You called me, remember? And while we're on that, please tell me you didn't call me from the hardware store again."

"Of course not. As soon as I realized who...*what* you were, I...I've watched enough *Law and Order* to know better than to use my home, business, or cell phone. I used a pay phone, and remembered to wipe both the phone and the coins I used free of fingerprints."

He laughed out loud.

She blushed bright red. "My husband is not going to be giving you any more money."

He leaned in closer to her and lowered his voice. "Is that a fact?"

She raised her chin. "Yes, it is. He doesn't have it to give. His funds have been...confiscated."

"By who?" he asked.

"If you want the rest of your money, you'll have to deal with me."

He leaned back on the bench, stretching his arms across the back. "Your old man said you were too dumb to figure out what was what. Guess he was wrong. But it might notta been too smart for you to call me. What's to stop me from telling him about this little meeting?"

"Money. I told you. I have it. He doesn't."

Colleen whistled. "Jeez-Louise. Do you believe her?"

"Shhh," I said.

Troy said, "And what do you want?"

"I want my life back and my children safe."

"What's that got to do with me?"

"First of all, I want to know what he was paying you to do," Deanna said.

"No way, lady. You could be wired eight different ways."

She hugged her purse tighter. "I believe I know *what* he wanted you to do. It's the *to whom* and *why* I'm interested in."

Troy said, "I don't have any idea about the why. The boss don't confide in me."

"Liar," Colleen said.

"Shhh," I hissed.

Deanna sat silently.

Troy said, "You'll have to figure why yourself. Are you saying you'll give me the rest of the money just for the *who*?"

"Not exactly," Deanna said. "I want the *who* right now. And I want your word that you will not do *anything* to this person. As a matter of fact, I want you to guarantee his or her safety."

"Now how am I supposed to do that? I'm not a freakin' guardian angel."

She locked eyes with him. "Let's just say that this person had better not suffer any unusual misfortune while you're still around, mmm-kay?"

"Who the hell do you think you are? Angelina Freakin' Jolie?" He looked away, then back. "Assuming I agree to this, what else do you want? And when do I get my money?"

"I want you to follow my husband, find out what he's up to. I know he's having an affair. I want to know with whom and I want pictures. I also want to know what else he's mixed up in that involves the need of your...services."

"The why?"

She stared him down. "Exactly, the why. Beyond that... I'm sure my husband will get his just desserts. As soon as I get the results I need, you will get your money."

"I'm not a private detective."

Deanna said, "I imagine you'll make do. There has to be a certain amount of skulking about in your line of work."

I shook my head. I could not believe how cool Deanna was. Adam must have hit her one too many times. Something had pushed her over the edge.

Troy said, "Okay, I understand what *you* want. All *I* want is enough money to get out of this place and never come back."

"I think that's a very good idea." She turned and looked across the harbor. "Now, why don't you tell me who you think should be in the dunk tank this year at the Fourth of July celebration?"

"What?" He scowled at her.

"I *said...*" she turned her head and looked at him, one eyebrow raised. "*Who* do you think we should have in the dunk tank this year?" She winked at him.

Colleen rolled her eyes. "Dear heavens."

Troy said, "Oh, ah...I think you should get that lady from the bed and breakfast, Grace Sullivan." Without another word, he tipped his imaginary hat, stood, and left.

"*Grace.* Grace was the target." I laid down the binoculars and started the car. "We need to tail him while I get ahold of Blake."

"No need," Colleen said. "He's going back to Stella Maris. Besides, we'll lose him in the crowd. And Grace is safe now. Deanna told Troy she has the money. He's not going to kill Grace if there's nothing in it for him."

I looked over my shoulder. He was walking fast in the opposite direction, and I was headed down a one-way street. I sighed, picked up my iPhone and dialed 911.

"What's your emergency?"

"You have an APB on Troy Causby of Mount Pleasant. He's walking away from White Point Gardens on East Bay. Please send help."

"What's your name, please?"

"That's East Bay, just north of The Battery. Troy Causby. Please hurry."

I hung up. I was sure the operator had my name and number on the screen. I couldn't tell her anything else, and I needed to call Blake. If the Charleston PD called me on it, which I doubted, I'd explain later.

I dialed Blake and got his voicemail. "Blake, Grace was the next target. Make sure she's got protection."

I stowed my eavesdropping equipment. "Colleen, I know Adam abuses Deanna. I've seen the bruises," I said. "Deanna told Troy she wanted her children safe. He abuses the girls, too, doesn't he?"

Colleen's lip trembled. "They're family. If I interfere, I'll be reassigned. Please don't ask me about that."

"But you sent me to the hardware store because Deanna was in trouble."

"That's what I told you. But Adam was there, too. And stopping his plans is part of my assignment. And if he's in jail for fraud or something, everything will be okay. There are gray areas. I just can't cross the line."

"Okay, let's don't talk about it anymore." But I had my answer. And I knew why Deanna had been pushed to the point where she would deal with a hit man. She was protecting her children the only way she knew how.

And she was less afraid of Troy than she was of Adam.

Colleen seemed calmer, but still sad.

"Hey," I said. "It's going to be okay. We're going to get Adam's ass locked *up*."

She smiled.

I slipped my phone into its mount on the console.

Colleen stared at the iPhone. "Got any Michael Jackson on that thing?"

"Sure." I glanced at her sideways. "Have you seen *him* since he passed?"

"Wouldn't you like to know?" There was that smirk again.

TWENTY-NINE

I had another stop to make while on the peninsula. Colleen listened to the end of *Man in the Mirror* then faded out. I parked in the Cumberland Street garage and strode down Meeting Street. The Charleston County Courthouse is a Georgian white-brick-and-stucco edifice built before the Revolutionary War as the South Carolina Statehouse. The Declaration of Independence was read from a balcony overlooking Meeting Street. In the late 1700s when the state's capitol was moved to Columbia, the building was converted to a courthouse. Through Herculean preservation efforts, it has survived fires, hurricanes, and earthquakes to preside over the heart of downtown Charleston.

I popped in the Meeting Street entrance and made my way to room 143, the Family Court Clerk's office. With the case number in hand, I didn't have to scroll through rolls of microfilm to locate the file I needed. I gave the case number to the twenty-something clerk with an educated manner that raised my suspicion she was overqualified for her job. Who knows what she suspected about me? My drab, meter-reader ensemble is not my best look. Five minutes later, she handed me a tape with instructions on how to print the pages I needed. I thanked her and hurried over to the film reader. I resisted the urge to read while I pulled up each page and pressed print. I paid my fifty cents per page and took the copied file back to the car.

I lowered the windows, then scanned through the wherefores and whereases until I found what I was looking for. The dirt. The divorce itself was a no-fault divorce, based on a year's separation. More interesting were the reasons enumerated by William Alexander James Knox as to why Mildred should receive none of his considerable assets.

Mr. Knox alleged that Mildred had entered into the marriage in a fraudulent manner, not informing him of her past employment as an exotic dancer at The Pussycat Gentlemen's Club in Myrtle Beach. Her stage name was Miller Dawn. Additionally, Mr. Knox made note of Mildred's extramarital affair with one Lincoln Sullivan.

Holy shit. Mildred the Moral, the Stella Maris authority on social decorum, had been a *stripper*? If the file had said Mildred was from the constellation Draco, I could not have been more shocked. I laid the file on the passenger seat, exited the parking garage and drove back to the ferry, pondering Mildred and her colorful background.

Everyone has secrets. Most people have reinvented themselves a time or three. And I'm a firm believer in leaving skeletons in their closets. Unless those skeletons bear directly on my case. I didn't know yet if Mildred's dancing days were relevant or not.

But here's what I did know: Mildred's past had the potential to embarrass the mayor. Mackie's gambling had the potential to embarrass—and financially harm—the Sullivan family, including Grace. Any number of things in Marci's past or present might embarrass Michael. John Glendawn's past with Hayden Causby and Stuart Devlin was common knowledge, but there was still plenty I didn't know about what happened back then. The common denominator for the names in column B on Gram's list seemed to be that they made a council member vulnerable. Had Gram suspected someone of attempting to blackmail council members?

Had someone tried to blackmail her?

THIRTY

I went back to Gram's to change. Mamma would've given me the always-dress-like-a-lady lecture for sure if she'd gotten a look at my frumpy work clothes. Besides, I needed to unload Adam and Deanna's garbage from the back of the Escape. Typically, for a garbage grab to net me anything, I had to lift it for several weeks. Taking Adam and Deanna's that morning had been an impulse, and I wasn't expecting much. But you never know.

Several tarps lay folded neatly on wire shelves in the corner of the garage. I spread one of them over the workbench. Then I pulled on a pair of latex gloves and a dust mask and went to work. One by one, I sifted through the Devlin household trash bags. I detest this part of my job. That afternoon, I missed Nate something fierce. More often than not in Greenville, he'd taken pity on me and done the garbage sorting.

Of course, Adam was a shredder—or maybe it was Deanna. Either way, coffee grounds, shredded documents, and tissues were the biggest volume items in the bags. There were two empty prescription bottles, an antibiotic for Holly and Xanax for Deanna. That explained how she coped, anyway. The only other pharmaceuticals were an empty blister pack of antacid and an almost-full bottle of something called "Ephed-Dream," which promised to make you very thin very quickly. According to the label, the primary ingredient was Ephedra extract. Wasn't that stuff illegal? Deanna had always been obsessed with her weight. I hoped she wasn't taking this stuff along with Xanax.

I tossed everything except the empty Xanax bottle and the Ephedra. Those, I placed in a plastic bag. Then, I cleaned up my mess and went upstairs.

I needed a bubble bath.

I started the water running and lit a few stress-relief candles. I poured in lavender bubble bath and some Lancôme Aroma Calm bath oil. Then I threw in a fizz ball. The more products you put in the tub, the better. After digging through all that trash, I considered pouring in some Clorox.

I sank into the water and closed my eyes. I rested my head on a bath pillow and let my arms and legs float.

The doorbell was ringing when I stepped out of the tub. I pulled on my robe and peered out of the second-story window. In the driveway was an unfamiliar Jeep Cherokee. I tensed. It couldn't be Nate. He hadn't even left Chicago yet. Surely when Scott told Adam he'd handle me, he hadn't meant he'd send someone on over to kill me.

The doorbell rang again, three times in rapid succession. I reached for the phone.

Then, Michael stepped off the front porch and looked up at my bedroom window. I waited about a nanosecond. I fumbled with the plantation shutter, the curtain, and the window. He waited patiently, hands on hips, while I raised the sash.

"Let me in," he said.

I was safe up in my perch, and unsure what waited downstairs. I hesitated.

"Liz." Even from that distance, I could read that look. It matched the yearning in the pit of my stomach. Oh, God, how I wanted him. How long I had wanted him. But...surely he didn't think he could crook his little finger and I'd come running just because he'd suddenly discovered what I'd figured out when I was six years old—that Marci was not to be trusted.

I wrestled with the urge to run down the stairs and fling myself into his arms. "What do you want?"

"I saw Robert Pearson this afternoon."

I waited.

"Can I please come in?"

"I don't think so."

"Fine. We can do this your way. As soon as Robert can get me out of this mess, you and I are getting married."

"Is that a fact?" I felt lightheaded, but somehow it wasn't with a pure joy.

"Yes. The last time I let you decide something, everything went straight to hell."

He had me there. But there were things I needed to know. "Why did you stay married to her?"

"For stupid reasons. The problem, for both of us, is that Marci doesn't make enough money as a bank teller to support herself. She has no immediate family and no close friends. I couldn't bring myself to set her out by the curb, but I didn't want to give her the house I built myself and half of my business, either. Those reasons have recently become less compelling."

I persisted. "But why are you here *now*?" As much as I wanted him, I didn't want him only because she'd cheated.

His shoulders rose and fell. He looked down, then up at me, a pleading look in his eyes. "Ever since I saw you at your grandmother's funeral, I've been fighting the urge to kidnap you and run away. When you stayed in Greenville, I figured you'd made your choice. Even if you didn't want Scott, you still didn't want me."

"But—"

"Let me get this out."

I gestured for him to continue.

"I know you didn't come back home because of me. But I looked in your eyes Tuesday night and knew that you still felt something for me. I came here to find out what."

"But why this afternoon? Why not yesterday or tomorrow?"

He hesitated. "This is not why. This is not about *her*. It's about us, okay?"

I raised an eyebrow and tilted my head.

"She's been having an affair with Adam for the last year."

I pressed my hand to my throat and tried hard to look shocked. "Are you sure?"

"Yeah, I'm sure. I found his wallet under my bed this morning."

"I see. And you ran straight over here, did you? Tell me something, Michael. Where would you be right now if you hadn't discovered your brother's wallet under your bed this morning?"

He had no answer ready for that.

The longer we talked, the happier I was I hadn't let him in. Just who did he think he was dealing with, anyway? Did I look like a backup plan? Had he even confronted her yet? "Does she know you know?"

"No. I just left. I found the wallet, packed a bag, and left before she woke up."

"What did you do with the wallet?"

"I gave it back to Adam."

"I'll bet you did. Did Adam admit the affair?" Of course, I already knew the answer, but I was trying to get him to tell me as much of what I already knew as possible. That would simplify things.

"Yeah. But, like I told Robert, I don't want to drag this out in court. I don't want my mother embarrassed by a scandal. I just want to use it to bargain with Marci."

"I see." I knew, and he should have, that there would be no bargaining with Marci the Schemer. "She'll get an attorney. If you can't prove adultery, I'm not sure how much bargaining power you've got."

"That's what Robert said. He wants me to get proof."

"How do I know you're not here just because she pissed you off?"

"Liz, I've never loved anyone but you. I've lived a lie so long I'd begun to believe that's all I could hope for. But then you came home. If she hadn't cheated, I still would have left. Maybe not today. But make no mistake, this—us—is inevitable. Marry me, Liz. I'm lost without you."

I smiled a teary smile. "Come back and see me when you have that divorce. We'll talk then." I slammed the window shut.

"Liz, wait," he shouted.

I closed the plantation shutters.

"Liz!"

I crawled onto my bed and propped against the headboard. I pulled a pillow to my chest and cried.

THIRTY-ONE

The combination of not nearly enough sleep, repeated adrenaline rushes, and emotional drama caught up with me. Somehow, I dozed off. I woke with a start and glanced at the clock. Hell's bells—it was after two in the afternoon. I hadn't had lunch. I had work to do. My family would be worried about me. And I was missing The Most Fabulous Spring Bazaar Ever, which had commenced that morning, homicidal maniacs on the loose notwithstanding.

I'd no sooner gotten dressed than someone started hammering out *Chopsticks* on the doorbell. Of course, I just knew it was Blake, or possibly Michael again. I wasn't expecting anyone else, least of all my ex-husband, holding a dozen yellow roses—my favorite. I stared at him through the peephole, hoping I was hallucinating.

"*Scott?*" I reacted and called through the door before thinking it through. Damn. I should have let him think I wasn't home. I did not have time for this. I took a deep breath and opened it halfway.

"The one and only." He shoved the roses in my direction and flashed me his best imitation of an appealing smile.

I crossed my arms and didn't take the flowers. "What are you doing here?" I was relieved he had roses and not a gun.

"I miss you, kitten. I guess I didn't realize how much. Lately, it just all seems so final."

I drew my head back and studied him for a moment. Even if I hadn't known what he was up to, I would never have fallen for that lie.

He took a step towards me. "I talked to Nate this morning. I had to pry it out of him where you'd gone. The next thing you know, I was headed down here." His voice deepened to a husky drawl. "You sure are a sight for sore eyes. Come on, baby, let me come in. Can't we just talk?"

Scott was a smooth liar. He had to come up with something to explain how he knew I was home. But he hadn't thought that lie all the way through. No way Nate would have ever told Scott where to find me. Rhett materialized by my side. The low, warning growl indicated he remembered Scott well.

"Talk? About what?" I said.

He pressed the roses into my arms.

"This is insane." Reluctantly, I took the flowers.

He grinned that cocksure grin of his.

I gave him my spare-me look. "Let me get something to put these in." I opened the door far enough to admit him into the foyer. I didn't want to arouse his suspicions by showing him I was afraid of him.

Rhett backed up but braced to pounce.

"Wait right here," I admonished Scott.

Moments later when I returned from the kitchen, he was gone. "Scott?"

Rhett barked from the sunroom.

"In here," Scott called. "I hope you don't mind, I made myself comfortable."

I hustled down the hall, thrashing myself for letting him in the door. What the hell was I thinking?

There he sat, on the sofa, looking up at me with his innocent look.

"I do mind. You're not staying that long. Look, I'm sorry you drove all this way, but we said everything we had to say months—no, years—ago. This doesn't make any sense."

"It makes perfect sense," he said. "When Nate told me you were staying down here indefinitely, it snapped me to my senses. As long as we were both in Greenville, the split didn't feel permanent. But with you taking up residence here, I guess it's sinking in. If we don't patch things up now, we never will."

"Scott—"

"Come back with me, Liz. Let's start over. We'll leave right now and go someplace in the Caribbean. Then we'll go home together. I'm not asking you to make a commitment now. We don't have to get remarried until you're sure. But just give me another chance." As he was speaking, he'd stood and crossed the room, and now stood way too close.

My, my. Two marriage proposals in one afternoon. So this was his plan. Another female might have been swayed by the pleading look in his blue eyes. But I'd been inoculated.

Rhett's barking became more urgent.

I backed away. "Scott, I am not going anywhere with you. You are going to leave now, do you understand?"

"Okay, okay. I'll go. For now. I can see this has been a shock for you. I'll call you later. Maybe we can have dinner."

"No, we can't."

Something shifted in his eyes.

Alarmed I may have pushed him too far, I softened my tone. "Please go, Scott."

"I'm not going back to Greenville without you." He backed slowly down the hall, not taking his eyes off me. "I'll be at the Stella Maris Hotel, waiting."

"It's not going to change anything." I followed him, resisting the urge to shove him out the door.

"Don't say that, now." He tried for charming, but I felt chilled. He stepped across the threshold to the porch. "You come see me when you change your mind. Anytime now, you hear?"

I closed the door, locked it behind him, and leaned against it.

Arrrhhh! I dug my fingers into my hair. I took a few slow, calming breaths, and then went into my office. I called Blake and, thankfully, got his voicemail again. I left him a message letting him know I was fine, and I was working, and I was so, so sorry, and I would see him later that evening at Mamma and Daddy's. Blake would be steamed I'd been gone all day when he'd asked me to wait for him that morning—which now felt like three years ago. But he would get over it.

I grabbed a banana and a glass of tea to hold me over and went into my office. I pulled out Gram's list and studied the names and, in particular, the question marks. If my hunch was right, Gram had been sure that Mackie made Grace vulnerable, and Marci was Michael's vulnerability. Mildred and Olivia each had one question mark, indicating perhaps Gram suspected there was something that could be used against Lincoln and Robert, but wasn't quite sure. Evidently, she hadn't uncovered Mildred's prior occupation.

Gram was even less sure that John Glendawn's history with Hayden Causby and Stuart Devlin could be used against him—they had two question marks. And apparently Gram had considered Merry a possibility—though a long shot with three question marks—as leverage against Daddy. Or maybe she thought Merry could convince Daddy to go along with a zoning change that allowed her to build her camp. That made sense. But I would have put four or five question marks there. Convincing Daddy to go along with oceanfront development was not a likely scenario.

I pulled out my phone and tapped Quincy Owen's saved phone number, with no real expectation he would answer.

He picked up on the second ring. "Quincy Owen."

"Mr. Owen. Glad I caught you. This is Liz Talbot calling from South Carolina."

"Oh, right. The private investigator."

"Yes. Am I catching you at a bad time?"

"No, no. I'm sorry I haven't returned the call. I'm in the middle of a new project that's pretty much consumed me, I'm afraid. Down your way, actually."

I had a sinking feeling. If this camp turned out to be legit, I'd be left with a lot of loose ends.

"That's what I wanted to speak with you about."

"You from the Upstate, are you? Could have sworn you said you were calling from the Charleston area."

"Wait." I scrunched my face so hard I could feel the wrinkles setting in. "I'm calling from Stella Maris, near Charleston. That's where you're planning your new camp, right? On Stella Maris?"

He chuckled. "I wish that were possible. We're building a camp in the foothills near Lake Jocassee. A benefactor left the property to the foundation in her will."

"Mr. Owen, does David Morehead work for your organization?"

"Who?"

"David Morehead."

"Never heard of him."

"How about Merry—Esmerelda—Talbot? Are you by chance trying to recruit her for a project?"

"She related to you?"

"Yes. She's my sister."

"Sorry, I haven't had the pleasure."

"That's what I needed. Thank you for your time."

I leaned back in my chair and pondered the New Life Foundation. Merry was one of the smartest people I knew. She would have researched these folks on the web. And she would have found exactly what I'd found. Pictures of pristine campgrounds and happy teenagers. And she would have called David Morehead back on the number he gave her. Many people used cell phones for business these days. That wouldn't have raised her suspicions.

I pulled up the South Carolina Secretary of State's webpage and did a query on New Life Foundation.

Oh my, my. The New Life Foundation *of South Carolina* popped up.

With Adam Devlin as the registered agent.

It was not a nonprofit organization.

THIRTY-TWO

St. Francis Episcopal is the oldest church on Stella Maris. It's built of stone with a steeple and stained glass windows. The gym doubles as a fellowship hall. The Most Fabulous Spring Bazaar Ever was still in full swing at three o'clock when I pulled into the parking lot. Tables of pickles, jams, casseroles, and every homemade or hand-stitched thing under the sun spilled out of the gym and onto the shady lawn. Throngs of people examined the merchandise and chatted with their neighbors.

I smiled and waved my way into the gym and tried to find Mamma. I needed her to see me, preferably after I'd purchased something. The noise level in the gym was deafening. I picked up snatches of conversation as I worked my way through the crowd.

"...just can't believe poor Emma was murdered..."

"...serial killer...running loose..."

"...strange lights over the ocean..."

"...all be murdered in our sleep..."

"...my Tom has all our guns loaded..."

I spotted Kate Devlin behind a table selling her chicken potpies. I could see stocking up on those. I pushed through the crowd in her direction. I slid behind two women engaged in earnest gossip, and smiled brightly as I popped out of the crowd and landed right next to Michael.

Kate smiled at me, but continued talking to her son. "Where have you been keeping yourself, son?"

Michael glanced at me. Tacitly, we agreed to keep things simple just then. "Hi, Liz," he said. "Good to have you home."

I tingled from head to toe. My mouth was so dry I struggled to make it work. "Hey," I said. "I didn't mean to interrupt. I'm just here to get some of your mamma's pies. I'll just browse. You all go on and visit."

I focused on the pies and casseroles.

Michael turned back to his mother. "Mostly I've been working, Mamma. How are you feeling? Are you taking care of yourself like you're supposed to? You look a little weak."

"Yes, I've been following the doctor's orders precisely, and aside from feeling a bit drunk from the medication Warren gave me for my heart, I feel fine."

"You've cut back on the caffeine like he said, right?"

"Warren Harper is an alarmist," she said. "Always has been."

"Have you been walking, like he told you?"

"I walked this morning. Early. Before your brother came by."

Michael stiffened. "How is Adam?"

I was wondering myself if she'd seen him before, or after, Michael blackened his eye.

"He seemed in a stew," Kate said. "But you know your brother. Always in a stew about something. He was by before breakfast."

Michael visibly relaxed. "What was bothering him?"

Kate's smile diminished somewhat, and she glanced down at her folded hands. "He didn't want to talk about it, whatever it was. After I told him Blake had been by asking about Emma Rae, that's all he wanted to talk about."

"Emma Rae Talbot?"

"Yes." Kate glanced at me. "Blake has some farfetched notion that Emma Rae was murdered."

Michael asked, "What does that have to do with Adam?"

Kate shrugged. "Nothing more than it has to do with any of us, I suppose. I guess he was concerned for my safety. And poor Emma Rae..." Kate turned towards me. "She was one of my dearest friends, you know."

"Listen, Mamma," Michael said. "Adam didn't say anything to upset you, did he?"

"Why, no. He hasn't mentioned anything in months about that other nonsense. It's a moot point now, anyway. I told you, I'm donating two hundred acres of that land for a camp." She turned to me and smiled. It was an odd little smile. I couldn't quite read it. "Merry's camp."

Michael nodded. "That's for the best."

What nonsense was she talking about? I gathered my wits. I needed to buy my pies and get Michael out of there so we could compare notes. "Kate, I can't tell you how much I enjoyed that potpie you brought by the other day. It was delicious. These freeze, right?"

"Well, of course."

"I'll take half a dozen. And two of the chicken rice casseroles. Do you have a bag?" You should never shop for food when you're hungry. That banana hadn't gone far. I was starved.

Kate did the math, took my money and bagged my food. I thanked her, motioned Michael with a nod, and headed towards the back of the gym, leaving him to say goodbye. Foot traffic was chaotic. People were not sticking to the whole "walk on the right-hand side" rule. I hadn't gone three steps before I was feeling claustrophobic. I hate crowds. They make me feel like I'm suffocating, perhaps because I'm afraid to breathe. You just know a third of the people in any given herd have something contagious. I had an impulse to bolt for the nearest door.

Michael came up behind me. "Here. Let me carry that bag. You've got a month's worth of food in there. Maybe you'll need some company for dinner to help you eat it."

"I doubt it. I'm a healthy eater. And I can carry my own bag, thanks." I stopped walking. "Look, we need to talk. *Not* about us, not now. But there's something I have to tell you. I just have to say hey to Mamma, and then we can get out of here."

A concerned look crossed his face. "Okay. Your mamma's in the back, at the information booth, near the quilts."

We pressed though the crowd in that direction. It seemed like hours before I caught sight of Mamma. I waved through the crowd. We negotiated our way over to the information table.

"Well, there you are," Mamma said. "Your brother's been looking for you."

"I know, Mamma. I tried to call him. Several times. I'll see him tonight at your house. What a great turnout." I offered her my brightest smile. "I've been shopping up a storm." I lifted my bag.

"Well, I'm glad you made it," she said. She turned to Michael and her smile widened. "How are you, Michael?"

"I'm fine, Carolyn," he said. "Looks like the bazaar's a big success. Congratulations."

"Thank you so much. A lot of folks had a hand in it, of course. Liz, did you see the quilts?"

"Not yet, Mamma, but I'm going to right now. And I just have to have some of Alma's bread and butter pickles. I've only made it half way around the gym." I could tell I had only partially redeemed myself by showing up late in the afternoon. "I'll see you later at the house, okay?"

"All right then." She eyed me like she might inventory my purchases later.

Michael and I found a quiet spot outside on a bench under a live oak. "What's wrong?" he asked.

"Tell me what 'other nonsense' Adam has been bothering your mother with."

He gave me an odd look, but answered. "Adam has tried, several times now, to bully her into going along with developing Devlin's Point. Last winter when she was still on town council, he had some harebrained scheme to turn Devlin's Point into a high-dollar resort, and he was trying to badger Mamma into voting for a zoning variance when it came before the council."

I nodded.

Michael said, "Of course she wouldn't have any of it, but he hounded her for weeks. I didn't know anything about it until Mamma broke down and told me. He didn't want me to know."

"I'll bet he didn't."

"The whole thing was crazy. It would've taken more than Mamma's vote to pass something like that. But he insisted he could get the other votes. Said we'd all be billionaires. Mamma was so upset she resigned from the council. That's when I took over her seat."

"How do you suppose he was going to get you to go along with this scheme?"

"No idea," Michael said. "I really believe he had a lot to do with her heart problems back last winter. That's when it all started, right about the time he was carrying on with all this."

"You'd expect him to be mad as fire about your mamma donating the land for that youth camp, wouldn't you? Seems like he'd never be able to build his resort."

"I think that's her intention."

"But he's not mad about it, is he?"

Michael shrugged. "We haven't discussed it. That alone tells me he's not. Seems like he'd be hounding me to help him talk her out of it."

"But in fact, he's in favor of the camp. He's been lobbying on Merry's behalf."

Michael grew very still. He stared at me for a long moment. "Why would he do that?"

"Because Adam *is* the New Life Foundation of South Carolina. If your mamma deeds that land to the foundation, she's deeding it to him. And it isn't a non-profit. The whole thing is a bait-and-switch."

"Son of a *bitch*." Michael stood. "I'll put a stop to that right now." He stormed back into the fellowship hall.

My phone sang out Nate's ringtone. I glanced at the time as I answered the call. It was almost four. "Hey. Are you boarding?"

"No." Nate bit out the word. "No, I'm not. There's weather in Atlanta. The airport is backed up. They pushed my departure twice, then cancelled the flight."

"Oh, Nate." I felt sick that he was living this airline nightmare on my account.

"I'm going to see if there's a flight on any airline that will get me to Charleston tonight. I'll call when I know something."

"All right. I'm so, so sorry."

"Not your fault. Tell me what's going on there."

My head spun. "Adam and Scott are using Merry as a front to get the land for their resort. Merry's not involved, although she was almost killed last night."

"She okay?"

"She's fine. Her roommate is not. I'm fine. Oh, and Scott dropped by earlier. He wants me to run away with him to the Caribbean. This is all such a mess. I'll explain everything when you get here."

Silence.

"Nate?"

"Scott dropped by where?"

"Gram's house."

"You were there alone, weren't you?"

"Nate, what is wrong with you? You of all people know I can take of myself."

He sighed. "Our typical case load doesn't involve murderers on the loose. We're usually working to get the guy *out* of jail. Because we think he's innocent. Correct me if I'm wrong, but that's not the shape of this situation, is it?"

"Nate? When the guy in jail is innocent, the murderer is on the loose."

"Usually you have backup. Me."

"I'm fine. Trust me. Let me know when you get another flight, okay?"

"Where are you now?"

"I'm at the church."

"Why?"

"My mother's bazaar."

"What—never mind. Where is Blake?"

"He's working. He's trying to find the guy Adam and Scott hired to do their dirty work."

"I thought you were going to stick close to Blake."

"Nate, there is no way Blake is going to take me to work with him. Trust me."

"I'll call you." He hung up.

I sat there, focusing on breathing in and out, enjoying the shade of the live oak and a few moments of peace. Then, my phone vibrated.

An alert. Someone had breached my security system.

THIRTY-THREE

I pulled up the live feed while I ran for the car. A man in khakis, a blue golf shirt, and a ball cap peered in the window of the pass-through door to the garage.

I slipped the phone into its mount on the console and started the car. I glanced from the rearview mirror to the screen while I backed out of the parking spot. I turned right on Palmetto. Before I could hit the accelerator, the Dodge Caravan in front of me braked to a stop. I peered around the minivan. SUVs and minivans were backed up as far as I could see. Between traffic coming and going to the bazaar, and the soccer practice car pool, the island was in gridlock. Why weren't these people holed up at home? Stella Maris residents might have been panicking, but they weren't letting it interfere with their daily routines. Every parking space in sight was taken. I couldn't even get out and make a run for it.

I growled in frustration and picked up my phone for a better view of what was going on at home.

My uninvited guest had disappeared from the screen. I pulled up a multi-pane view of the three outdoor cameras. A horn blared. I glanced up. Traffic had moved a foot. I rolled forward, and then turned back to the screen. He was on the deck now, approaching the sunroom door. The camera faced the door, so I could only see him from behind. Turn around, turn around, *turn around.*

He tried the sunroom door, then cupped his hands around his face and looked inside. He jumped back. Rhett was no doubt on the other side raising hell. The prowler looked around the backyard, and up and down the beach, presumably to see if anyone was around to catch him in the act.

The cap was pulled low. Between that and his wrap-around sunglasses, I couldn't tell anything about his face except he wore neither mustache nor beard. The cap had a scuba diving flag on the front. Elvis's phantom. He'd been at the house Monday and Rhett scared him off. Odds were, he was also my intruder from Tuesday night. He'd known Rhett would be inside and come prepared.

I looked up just as the Caravan in front of me rolled forward. The light at Palmetto and Anchor must've changed. Traffic started moving, but my speedometer still didn't break ten miles an hour.

I glanced back at the phone. The Phantom reached inside both pockets and pulled out a set of keys and something white, about the size of a baseball. He laid the white object down on the deck. The corners of a napkin fell open. I banged the steering wheel with my left hand. He had more treats for Rhett. Hopefully, he realized now he didn't have to drug that particular golden retriever. Snacks and a belly rub would buy anyone unmolested access to the house.

The Phantom fished through the set of keys, tried one, then another. On the third try, he opened the sunroom door. Hell's bells. He must have taken a set of keys when he was in the house Tuesday night. There'd been an extra set in a drawer in the kitchen.

Rhett sprang through the door. I couldn't hear him barking—there was no sound on the feed—but I could see he was giving the intruder what for.

The man knelt, reached for one of the treats, and held out his hand to Rhett.

Rhett sniffed his hand, then scarfed down the treat.

The Phantom patted Rhett on the head, pointed to the napkin with more treats, and went inside and closed the door.

Rhett wagged his tail and wolfed down the contents of the napkin.

Traffic stopped again. I switched the feed to the indoor cameras.

The Phantom passed quickly through the sunroom and foyer, moving from one pane on my phone to the next. Then he disappeared. The upstairs cameras were in my room and Gram's. I waited. A moment later, he appeared in Gram's room and opened the top drawer in her dresser. He slid his hands through the contents, then closed the drawer and went to the next one. What was he looking for?

Another horn honked. I'd reached the outskirts of downtown, and traffic was moving again, though still not fast enough to suit me. I was too close to the Caravan, and I knew it. I gritted my teeth and backed off.

The Phantom was working on Gram's chest of drawers, methodically checking each drawer. When he finished, he moved to the nightstand.

Finally, the Caravan turned left at the end of Palmetto and I turned right on Ocean Boulevard. I pulled to the edge of the road in front of the hedge. The engine was quiet, but I didn't want to risk my prowler hearing me coming. I slipped my phone into one pocket, my keys into the other. I opened the door, and was halfway out of the car when I reached back into my purse and grabbed Sig. I was almost positive this phantom prowler wasn't dangerous. But I wouldn't bet my life on it.

I tucked Sig in the back waistband of my pants and darted around the end of the hedge. I dashed across the grass to dampen the noise of my approach. Rhett came sprinting from around the house to greet me. Midway up the drive, he remembered we had guests and commenced barking.

"Shhh!" I hissed loudly, to no avail. Dammit, dammit, *dammit!* My prowler would no doubt be headed for the door. I was in no mood to chase anyone.

The Phantom had come in from the back of the house, but Tuesday night he'd come in through the mudroom and left via the front. How would he leave today? I darted around back.

Rhett passed me, circled back, and chased ahead. He sprang up the deck steps, and I took them two at a time. Rhett barked emphatically at the back door. I wasn't sure how long it took Benadryl to take effect, but he showed no signs of being drugged.

"Hush now," I said. "Sit. Stay."

Rhett sat, but wiggled, squirmed, and yipped.

The intruder had left the door unlocked. I pushed it open and listened. The house was quiet. I slipped in and tiptoed towards the foyer. He'd have to come downstairs to access any of the three doors.

I slipped Sig out of the waistband of my pants. Holding the gun with both hands, I pointed it towards the floor and started up the steps.

The stairs creaked.

Nate's blues rift rang out from my phone. *Shit.* I let the phone ring; it would go to voicemail. I abandoned stealth for speed and raced down the hall towards Gram's room.

Sonofabitch.

One side of the french doors stood open, curtains pulled back. I crossed the room and looked out. I scanned the balcony, trellis, and deck. No sign of anyone. He couldn't have climbed down the trellis and slipped away that fast, could he?

I listened again. All was quiet, the house felt empty. I checked Gram's closet and bathroom. Empty. Room by room, I cleared the house. No one there but me.

How in the hell had he gotten away that fast? He must have climbed down the trellis, but he sure made quick work of it.

I went back out to the deck, where Rhett still sat, struggling to contain himself.

"Good boy." I knelt, laid down the gun, and hugged him.

Released from the command to stay, he charged down the steps and over to the south yard. He stopped just short of the boundary his collar allowed and barked into the forest. No doubt, that's where my prowler went. The big question was what had he been looking for?

I pulled out my phone and listened to the voicemail from Nate. Unable to book another flight that night, he'd taken a shuttle to a Hampton Inn. He'd rebooked for tomorrow and would land in Charleston at 8:20 Friday evening.

I went back inside and locked up. Then, I went into my office and logged onto my laptop. I pulled up the recordings for each camera to make sure I hadn't missed anything while I was driving, and to confirm how the intruder escaped. Sure enough, he'd been looking under the bed when his head jerked towards the window—presumably when he'd heard Rhett barking as I ran towards the house. He walked straight to the french doors, opened the one on the left, and stepped out onto the balcony. He'd likely started down the trellis as soon as I went in the back door. I didn't think Elvis's phantom was quite as old as Elvis thought. I watched the recordings several times, zooming in for a better look, but still had no idea who my prowler could be.

I debated calling a locksmith, but decided against it. If my prowler wanted in badly enough, he'd get in, and I'd rather not have to deal with a broken window. Besides, what I really wanted was to catch him in the act and find out who he was and what he was looking for.

Could this phantom have been looking for Gram's list? I doubted it. Who would've known she'd made such a list? I headed upstairs to conduct my own search.

I hesitated at the door to Gram's room. I hadn't been in this room since Gram's death, except in pursuit of the intruder. The peaceful retreat awaited its occupant's return, as at the end of any normal day. The bottles and jars on the antique dressing table had only a light coating of dust, and the four-poster bed, with its celadon toile duvet and dust ruffle, piled high with pillows, looked freshly made. I steeled myself.

Systematically, I went through every drawer. I checked the drawer bottoms for envelopes taped there, knowing full well that Gram had nothing to hide in such a fashion. I searched her room as if she were a complete stranger. I went through her bathroom, looked in the toilet tank, and checked the medicine cabinet.

An hour later, I'd found nothing of note. I glanced at my watch and sighed. I'd have to search the closet and the rest of the house later. If I didn't hie me back to Mamma and Daddy's house soon, Blake would have an APB out on me. If he didn't already.

THIRTY-FOUR

A symphony of tree frogs and crickets greeted me when I stepped out of the Escape in Mamma and Daddy's driveway. I blinked at the scene in front of me.

Daddy rocked slowly back and forth in one of the six chairs that lined the porch. A shotgun lay across his lap, a glass of what looked like Jack and diet in his hand, and Chumley the faithful basset hound lay at his feet.

A posse of friends and neighbors gathered on the front porch and dotted the lawn. Each of Daddy's buddies carried a shotgun, rifle, or sidearm, and sipped liquid fortification. Several drank from Mamma's good crystal. A couple had wads of tobacco in their cheeks, and periodically spit into the mulched azalea beds. Others patrolled the perimeter of the lawn and tromped through Mamma's hostas. Too many dogs to count sniffed each other and marked territory.

Daddy glowered at me. "High time you showed up. Something wrong with that fancy telephone of yours?"

"I'm sorry, Daddy. I meant to call." I was feeling really guilty just then for worrying my family. I wasn't accustomed to having people waiting at home for me while I worked.

Blake opened the front door and glared at me as if he'd like to eviscerate me but was just too tired. "I ought to wring your neck."

"Could you maybe do that later? We need to talk."

He looked from me to Daddy. "Everything all right out here?"

Daddy took a sip from his glass. "Just fine."

Blake massaged his neck. "Dad, maybe everyone would be safer inside their own houses. This looks like an accident waiting to happen."

"Son, I've been handling guns since before you came into this world. So has everybody out here. If somebody's coming for Merry they'll have to go through us." He looked at me hard. "If they want Liz, they'll have to find her first. If they're coming for me, I'm waiting for 'em."

Blake shook his head and stepped back to let me inside the house. He shut the door behind us.

"Grace?" My eyes searched his.

"We're watching her. She's fine."

"Where's Mamma?" I asked. No way had she seen what was going on out front.

"Upstairs," Blake said. "She was exhausted from the bazaar. She brought home plates of chicken and dumplings for dinner. Yours is in the kitchen."

I peeked out the front window for another look. "Holy crap."

"You don't know the half of it," Blake said. "Zeke Lyerly's in that bunch."

"Oh hell."

Zeke Lyerly had lived across the street from Mamma and Daddy for two decades. Zeke used his gun to expedite things. When he found a nest of yellow jackets in his front yard, rather than bother with the usual chemicals, he and Daddy shot into the rotted tree stump where the yellow jackets made their home. This proved less harmful to the yellow jackets than to Zeke and Daddy, who each suffered a dozen stings.

I closed the blinds. "Can't you run those crazies off?" I asked.

"Even Troy isn't stupid enough to mess with that bunch. Unless I'm willing to arrest the lot of them—Dad included—all we can do is hope for the best and stay out of the line of fire."

"Did you say there were dumplings?" I was starved. I headed towards the kitchen.

"Where the hell have you been all day?"

I opened the refrigerator and pulled out a carryout box. Where to start? I grabbed a fork and dug in. Even cold, chicken and dumplings were my weakness. "Where's Merry?"

"On the screened porch." His tone of voice telegraphed exactly how much patience he had left.

"If we go out there, I'll only have to tell this once."

He sighed and waved his arms in a shooing motion.

I scurried out to the screened porch.

Curled up in the wicker chair, Merry pulled the quilt she was wrapped in tighter. I suspected the quilt was more for emotional comfort than against the non-existent chill. "Hey," she said. "Where've you been?"

I settled onto the swing with my dumplings.

Blake sprawled across the loveseat. "So." He looked at me. "Elvis tells me he ran into you at Marci's. Not only did you not stay here today like I specifically asked, but you've apparently appointed yourself my special investigator."

I gave him my why-didn't-I-smother-you-when-we-were-little look.

He ranted on. "I have successfully done my job without your help for years. Please refrain from conducting your own investigations—wait." He got this terrified look in his eyes. "You're not planning on opening up shop *here* are you? Taking cases..."

"What else would I do?" I looked at him straight down my nose. He hates it when I do that. "A girl's gotta eat."

He glared at me.

I sighed. Between bites of dumpling, I edited on the fly. "Okay, this morning, I was worried about Deanna, so I dashed out to the hardware store to check on her. I didn't plan to be gone long..." And so it went. I filled them in on everything I'd learned that day, leaving out anything to do with Colleen or phone taps. I let Michael's proposal slip my mind. I also left out how Deanna had been consorting with known criminals. My story was that I'd accidentally run across Troy at White Point Gardens, and overheard him talking to someone I didn't recognize.

I looked up from my dumplings. From the expression on Blake's face, I knew that he knew I left plenty out. In my line of work, it's frequently necessary to lie to people. I've discovered, despite my raising, I have an affinity for it. BS flows quite naturally from my lips. But Blake's BS meter was calibrated to a higher sensitivity than most.

I pushed against the brick floor of the screened porch with my foot. The swing obliged and resumed rocking me.

I swear, steam rolled off my brother. "You were close enough to Troy to hit him with a rock. When your call went to voicemail, you could have called Nell, had her get ahold of me."

"And what would you have done? You were thirty minutes away, for Pete's sake. I called 911. I *tried* calling you."

Blake took deep breaths and struggled for control.

I took the opening. "Adam needed two separate and distinct things, both nearly impossible to come by: Land that doesn't belong to him and the zoning to develop it. This whole camp charade was for Kate's benefit, no one else's."

"The head of The New Life Foundation has never heard of David Morehead," Merry repeated slowly.

I shook my head. "I'm so sorry, Merry."

Calmer now, Blake looked at the ceiling. "So, net-net, the youth camp was a scheme to get Kate Devlin to deed Devlin's Point over to Adam so he could develop it. And, Marci is sleeping with Adam, and we care because he probably planned to finagle her onto town council where he'd control her vote. That plan blew up, so now Marci is using Adam to ditch Michael. Well I'll be scattered, smothered, and covered."

I nodded. "Oh, and Elvis didn't recognize the picture in the locket."

"He told me," Blake said.

"I don't believe any of this," Merry said, like she really did, but wanted her shock noted.

Colleen decided to join me on the swing. "David Morehead," she said. "Think."

A wisp of something fluttered through my brain. I turned to Merry. "I have seen David Morehead somewhere before, but I can't place where."

Merry seemed to be melting in despair. She held her head up with the heel of her hand, her elbow propped on her knee. "He said he was from their corporate office in Los Angeles."

"Hmmm." I consciously smoothed the crease from my brow. "I know our paths have crossed. How did you say he first contacted you?"

"He called me. Said he was the VP of Recruitment."

My hand went to my mouth. "I just remembered where I've seen him."

"Where?" Blake asked.

"Scott's office in Greenville. It's been a year or so, but I'm sure it was him. I went by to speak to Scott. I needed his signature on some papers. We finally had an offer on the house, and I was eager to get it finalized. He was in a meeting, and I had to wait.

"His office door opened, and out came this guy. He stopped in the doorway to finish his conversation with Scott. What stuck in my mind was how ridiculously well groomed he was. A whole tube of gel in that blond spiked hairdo, clothes off the cover of GQ so smooth it looked like he'd never sat down in them. And those rings..."

"He's a metrosexual," Merry said.

"A *what*?" Blake snorted.

"A heterosexual male who grooms himself like a woman," I said.

"Whatever," Blake said. "I don't want to hear about the guy's grooming habits *or* sexual preferences. What was he doing with Scott?"

"I remember Scott telling him to have a safe flight back to Los Angeles. That's what triggered the memory. I don't have any idea what he was up to then. But we know what Scott's up to now," I said. "And this guy is knee-deep in it."

Merry crossed her arms over the top of the quilt. "Maybe that's just a coincidence. They could have grown up together or known each other in school."

Blake said, "Seriously, Merry? You're smarter than that."

"Merry," I said. "Think back to the first conversation you had with David Morehead. Did he somehow plant the idea of a camp here, lead you into it?"

"I am not some ignorant, easily-led child."

I met and held my sister's eyes. "Of course you're not. But you've been scammed, nevertheless. It happens, even to smart people, Merry. You expect people to have honorable intentions because you do."

After a long moment, Merry looked away. Two tears slipped down her cheeks and she angrily brushed them away. "They offered me a position in Wyoming. I told David I was flattered, but I didn't want to be that far away from home. He asked if he could keep me on their prospects list, for future camps closer to home. I asked where he thought they might be expanding. He said they were looking for property along the east coast." Merry shook her head in disbelief. "It just seemed perfect."

Merry cursed under her breath. "At first, he was resistant. He said it would be impossible to get all the approvals they'd need, even to buy the land. I told him I was sure I could get it approved, that the people of this island would support it if it was presented right, and if it came from an insider. Me." She sat quietly for a minute. "I went to Kate Devlin and asked her to donate the land. It was to be environmentally friendly, not some high-rise."

"That's it," I said. Kate would never go along with developing Devlin's Point for a resort. But an environmentally friendly camp for at-risk kids, that was a whole nother story.

Merry said, "They played me for a fool. Scott told them exactly which buttons to press. That *bastard*," she ground out through clenched teeth.

Scott was responsible for this whole mess, no doubt. He was the one in charge, the one who controlled the money. The Stella Maris Resort was his brainchild—I'd heard him remind Adam.

But the one who got Merry involved was Kristen. *You're the one that told me she wanted to open a camp on the beach,* Troy had said to Kristen. *You started this whole thing.* I hadn't worked out a way to tell Merry and Blake that part just yet.

Blake stood to pace. He did that when his ball and glove weren't handy. "They must have planned to use you to get the land zoned for development, too."

"It's not Gram's land they were after," I said. "It was her vote. Adam's been trying to develop Devlin's Point for years. But it doesn't belong to him. It belongs to Kate. He must have given up trying to talk her into it and decided to trick her out of the land instead." Something tickled the back of my brain. Something still didn't quite fit.

Blake looked at me for a long moment. He was trying to pick apart what I'd just said. "You think Marci was in on it?"

"Of course she was. Why the snotty little bitch tried to—" I caught myself. I didn't want to say out loud that Marci had tried to barter Michael to get her hands on a chunk of land. Land she would presumably have offered up for development as soon as the ink was dry on the deed.

"Tried to what?" Blake asked.

"She..." I made a rolling motion with my hand. "She tried to cut herself in. Tried to get herself installed on the town council so she could earn a cut by greasing the skids for all the approvals they'd need."

"Uh-huh." Blake cut his eyes at me.

"Any word on Kristen?" I asked.

"None," said Blake.

Merry wailed, "It's all my fault. Whatever's happened to Kristen is all my fault. I never should have rolled her up in that rug."

"And if you hadn't," I said, "Troy would have known immediately you were missing. You probably wouldn't have made it as far as Gram's."

"Merry, none of this is your fault," Blake said.

"It's mine," I said. "I brought that jackass Scott home in the first place."

Blake said, "If it wasn't him, Adam would have found some other dealmaker. Or he would've found Adam."

"Any sign of Troy?" I asked.

Blake shook his head. "Nope."

"He has to be on the island. That's the only way he can finish his contract and get paid." I knew, but hadn't told, that his contract had now evolved from killing Grace to following Adam. If he were to be trusted, which he was not. But still, if I could get Blake to tail Adam, he might stumble over Troy.

"If he's here, we'll find him," Blake said.

I said, "If Scott, Adam, and Troy see things are falling apart, they could turn on each other. Do you have someone watching Adam?"

"We're checking on him regularly."

"I wonder what Troy's driving," I said. "With his car impounded and all."

Blake said, "Could be anything borrowed or stolen—boat or car. Mount Pleasant PD attempted to contact his dad, but he's out of town. There're a few family member cars on our watch list. I've got someone posted at the ferry dock."

I nodded slowly. "It's a blessing Stuart Devlin isn't alive to see Adam try to undo his life's work. This may kill Kate."

Blake sighed hard. "That poor woman's been through a lot."

"Which other votes do you think Adam was counting on?" I asked.

Blake said, "I think he could've gotten the votes for the camp. Then there would've been a bait-and-switch after the property was deeded and the zoning changed. Merry's camp was a Trojan Horse."

"Yeah," I said, "that's what I thought, too. But what was to stop the council from rescinding the new zoning? That's where he needed leverage. Who would've sat still for that?"

"Definitely not Dad," Blake said. "And not Grace, which is why they needed her out of the way. I wonder who they planned to replace her with."

"Mackie," I said. "Gambling debts. Check it out."

Blake looked at me like I'd sprouted a second head.

"Just check into it, okay?"

Blake held up both hands in a stop gesture. "Fine. I'll look into it."

"That leaves Michael—not a chance. John—I can't believe it. Robert...."

Merry said, "And Lincoln Sullivan. The mayor votes if there's a tie."

Blake and I both looked at her.

"Yes, he does," I said. "And he's vulnerable to blackmail."

"How?" Blake asked.

"Why?" Merry spoke at the same time.

I looked from Blake, to Merry and back. I didn't typically gossip about things I learned during investigations. Loose lips and all that. But Mildred's past, and Lincoln's resulting exposure, were a part of this investigation. Part of what had gotten Gram killed. Besides, I felt guilty about all the stuff I hadn't told Blake and Merry.

I filled them in on Mildred's stage career as Miller Dawn at the Pussycat Gentleman's Club.

"You're making that up to get me to laugh." Merry giggled.

"Oh, but I'm not, baby sister."

"Oh, man." Blake squeezed the back of his neck and rolled his shoulders. "That's an image I didn't need in my head."

"Well, she *was* quite a bit younger," I said.

Then we all burst out laughing. When we'd stopped holding our stomachs and crying, Blake said, "I'll talk to all the council members—and the mayor—tomorrow."

From beside me on the swing, Colleen smiled.

I stood and stretched. "I can't keep my eyes open another minute."

Blake proceeded to read me the riot act on how I should stay at Mamma and Daddy's until further notice. I was too tired to argue.

I dragged myself upstairs and called to check in with Nate.

"Hey." He picked up on the first ring. "Where are you?"

"I'm at Mamma and Daddy's house. Blake is here. Daddy and his shot-gun-toting cronies were on the front porch last time I looked."

"I feel much better now," he said dryly. "Get some rest and call me in the morning."

"Will do. You get some rest, too. Goodnight."

After an abbreviated bedtime-beauty routine, I crawled between the sheets and fully expected to pass out. But my brain was in overdrive. I couldn't shut it down. After hours of trying to visualize a staticky TV screen, I slept in starts and fits.

THIRTY-FIVE

At five the next morning I was on the front porch stretching. No sign of Daddy or his posse. I sucked in a deep breath of salt air and let it out slowly. Cleansing breaths. The last few days had left me a lot to cleanse. Deliberately and emphatically, I ignored Blake's directive and left the house unaccompanied, while it was still dark outside no less. I was nursing an irritation at my brother for his overbearing nature. Troy Causby couldn't pick me out of a lineup after all these years. Besides, he had no reason to hurt me. And Scott was trying to woo me, not kill me.

I ran the two blocks to the beach, then north towards home. I fed Rhett, gave him some attention, and continued my run around North Point. The eastern sky turned pink, and the rising sun backlit the scattering of slate-colored clouds on the horizon. The cool morning wind blew through me, the irritation, stress, and fatigue slipping away on the breeze.

When I approached the marina, the sky was lighter than it had been the last few mornings. Ahead of me, an eclectic assortment of boats was docked. Everything from fifty-foot sailboats to jet skis. The docks were quiet at that hour, which was why the movement caught my attention.

A tall, gray-headed figure emerged onto the deck of what appeared to be a forty-two-foot Pearson sailboat.

I watched him as I drew closer.

He stood on the bow of the sloop and stretched towards the morning sky. There was a certain elegance in both the classic vessel and the way the man moved. I figured him to be somewhere over sixty, but remarkably agile. He executed a set of stretches as easily as I could have.

I headed out across the dock towards the old sailor and his boat.

I'd always admired Pearson sailboats, and his dark-blue-hulled sloop was a beauty. I wanted a closer look, at the sailboat and its captain. I'm an inquisitive sort by nature, a trait that comes in handy in my line of work.

I slowed my step as I approached him and tried not to be too obvious in my curiosity.

His skin was tanned and wrinkled, but something—perhaps his apparent exceptional health—gave him a glow.

As I walked alongside the boat, he stopped stretching, turned, and smiled, as if he'd been expecting me. The smile didn't reach his eyes. Grief lived there.

"Good morning." His warm, soft, brown eyes locked onto mine like a laser guided missile, stopping me in my tracks. He swiped his cheeks and tried again with the smile.

"Good morning." I stood there waiting. For what, I had no idea.

He walked over to the edge of the boat and extended his hand across the rail. "Name's Tom. Tom Davidson. Care for a cup of coffee? Freshly brewed..."

I took his hand and returned his smile. A warmth radiated from him that was irresistible. And those *eyes*... "That would be wonderful. I haven't had mine yet, and I still have a few cobwebs floating around in my head."

"Welcome aboard." He stepped to the side and helped me over the railing. "Have a seat," he indicated a spot in the cockpit. "I'll be right back."

I settled into the soft tropical cushions that lined the roomy cockpit. I could hear Mamma's voice inside my head, warning me that he could be an ax-murderer. *After all, Ted Bundy was quite the charmer, now wasn't he?* I dismissed Mamma's worries. If this guy was a serial killer, I was slap out of luck.

He climbed out of the cabin a few moments later with two large steaming mugs. "Cream and sugar?"

"Yes, please." I took the brightly painted pottery mug gratefully. "This smells divine."

He disappeared below deck once more, returning momentarily with a small pitcher of cream and a sugar bowl that matched the mugs.

I chuckled to myself.

"Everything all right?" he asked.

"I'm just surprised you have two mugs that match, let alone a cream and sugar set. Most men I know aren't that coordinated."

He settled in across from me. "Ahh. Well, the customers like it."

"Customers?"

"I run a charter boat service, day sails mostly, in the Virgin Islands."

"Wow, what a life."

"It's pretty special, I must say." He studied me.

"Where are my manners?" I held out my hand. "Liz Talbot."

He clasped my hand in both of his. "Of course." His expression changed for a split second, but I couldn't read what was there.

"Have we met?"

"No, I've never had the pleasure. You remind me of an old friend."

"Anyone I know?"

He smiled enigmatically. "What brings you out so early this morning?"

"I run most mornings. I love the beach at sunrise."

"My favorite time of the day." He smiled and sipped his coffee. "I like to get my morning routine done while everyone else is still asleep. At my age I need the edge. I have to stay active or the age creep will get me."

"Age creep?"

"If you sit still too much, old age creeps up on you when you're not looking."

I returned his smile with a wry one. "I'm aging fast lately myself."

"Yeah, me, too." A look of profound sadness crept into his eyes. "Only I can't afford much of that."

I sipped my coffee. "I've been to the Virgin Islands once. St. John. One of the most beautiful places I've ever seen. We took a day sail to Jost Van Dyke."

"With one of my good friends, no doubt. I do the Jost trip myself, but I'm sure I'd remember you. How long ago were you there?"

"About eighteen months ago. My grandmother had been there a few times. She always talked about how beautiful it was. I went down with a group of friends and rented a house on the north shore. Are you from St. John originally?"

He looked away. "No, I grew up not too far from here. But I've been in St. John for so long..."

"What brings you here?"

"Business," he said. "Stella Maris is beautiful as well."

"Yes it is. I'm afraid I've taken it for granted for too long. We stop appreciating the things we love the most."

"Regrettable, but true."

We sat companionably, neither talking, just savoring the coffee and the morning, each lost in our own thoughts. Realizing I'd dallied longer than I should have, I set down my coffee cup and stood. "I really have to be getting back. My family will worry about me if I'm not there when they wake up. It was so nice meeting you."

He took my hand in both of his and enfolded me in that wonderful, warm smile. "God's peace, Liz Talbot. It has been my pleasure to have you aboard the *Gypsy Wind*."

"How long will you be here?"

"That remains to be seen." The sadness crept back into his eyes.

"Well, thanks for the coffee." I withdrew my hand and climbed back over the railing to the dock. With a wave, I turned back towards the beach.

THIRTY-SIX

From his customary place at Mamma's kitchen table, Blake scowled as I walked through the back door. "Where have you been? I should've known you'd be up wandering the island before dawn. Since I *specifically* asked you not to go out by yourself, you just had to do it before I got up to stop you, didn't you?" He'd slept in his old room the night before, but apparently not well.

"I went for a run on the beach." I slipped into my chair. "I'm fine."

Mamma flipped a pancake. "You'd better do as Blake asks, Elizabeth. That Causby boy is still running loose. Have some consideration for those of us who care about you." Mamma's eyes were round with hurt.

"I'm sorry, Mamma. I didn't mean to worry you."

I inhaled the aroma of Mamma's hot-off-the-griddle blueberry pancakes. My mouth watered as she set a plate in front of Blake, piled high and slathered in butter. A wide stream of warmed maple syrup flowed down the sides of the stack.

He closed his eyes as he took the first bite. He grunted his appreciation. "Ummph...umph."

I rolled my eyes. "I swear, you put food in front of him and he loses the capacity to form words."

"*I* understand what he's saying." Mamma patted him on the shoulder. "You eat your breakfast now. You need some more coffee?"

Mouth full, Blake shook his head.

Mamma set a plate down in front of me and I winced. "Mamma, sit down and eat your breakfast. You don't need to wait on us. We're all capable of feeding ourselves."

"What she means is we can *serve* ourselves. None of us can make pancakes like this." Blake roused himself from his pancakes to fire a round back at me. "Liz and Merry can wash the dishes."

Daddy looked at me. "Where is Merry? It's almost seven o'clock. Go see if she's awake."

I snorted.

Mamma cast me a disapproving look.

"Merry doesn't know that seven o'clock comes in the morning," I said.

On cue, Merry shuffled into the kitchen clad in cow-print pajamas and pig slippers, her hair jutting from her head at odd angles. "Unnnh." She grunted indignantly. "If you people have to get up before dawn, can't you at least be quiet about it?"

Blake stopped in mid-motion and stared. "Did you sleep standing on your head?"

Merry telegraphed a curse from half-opened eyelids.

The telephone rang, saving Blake from verbal assault. Daddy answered on the third ring, an indication of how wrong things were that morning which, on the surface, seemed so normal. A sedentary creature, Daddy never roused himself to answer the phone if someone else was in the house. Apparently sensing some new peril on the other end of the line, the man of the house took the call.

"Blake." Daddy handed him the phone. "It's Sonny Ravenel over to Charleston."

Blake and Sonny went way back. They'd been friends growing up. Sonny was now a detective with the Charleston Police Department. Blake laid his napkin by his plate and stood. He took the phone and stepped into the den.

"Speaker phone," Colleen shouted from the top of the refrigerator.

I jumped up and pressed the speaker button on the phone's base.

Blake was oblivious. He'd evidently wandered far enough through the house that he couldn't hear the speaker. "Sonny."

Mamma and Daddy stared at me as if clearly I'd been possessed by demons. Such a lapse in manners—to eavesdrop on a family member's conversation—it was unthinkable. Nonetheless, no one moved to turn the speaker off.

"Morning Blake." Sonny's voice boomed into the kitchen. "Nell told me where to find you. Thought I'd keep this off the scanner for now. Couldn't get you on your cell, got one of those damn fast busy signals."

"What's up?" Blake asked.

"You'd better head on over this way quick as you can."

My stomach knotted. I was hoping they'd apprehended Troy Causby, but something in Sonny's tone said he didn't have good news.

"That Kristen Bradley you've been looking for?"

"Yeah?"

"Some fancy S.O.B type, light in his loafers you ask me, out walking his foo-foo rat dog this morning. Had a ruffled dress on, damnedest thing I've ever seen. The dog, not the guy...or whatever."

I clenched my teeth, willing Sonny to get to what someone from South of Broad had to do with Kristen.

"Anyway, he lets the little yappy dog off his leash to go take care of business. Fifi won't go unless he has privacy or some such bullshit. He makes a beeline for this construction site over near Waterfront Park— somebody apparently thinks we need more condos on this peninsula."

We all stared, transfixed, at the phone.

"They're just getting ready to pour the foundation. Fifi starts digging around, yapping...works himself into a frenzy. Won't let the guy put him back on the leash. He digs and yaps and digs and yaps and guess what he digs up?"

"What?" Blake asked. But we all knew the answer.

"White female, mid-twenties. A real looker. No ID. Two gunshot wounds to the head."

Merry let out a low moan and sank into a chair. Mamma grabbed the counter for support. I covered my face in horror.

"You sure it's Kristen?" Blake asked.

"No ID on her, but it sure looks like the driver's license photo you've been circulating. We're at Prioleau and Middle Atlantic Wharf."

"I'll be right there." Blake stepped back into the kitchen and laid the phone down on the table. We looked at him expectantly. His eyes bored into mine for a moment. He swiveled to Daddy. "I've got to go over to Charleston for a while. Keep Mom and the girls here with you until I get back. I'm going to send Coop over to keep an eye on things. He'll be out front in a patrol car. *No one* is to leave this house until I get back or call."

Daddy looked sheepish. "We...ahh...overheard."

Blake gaped at him.

Daddy nodded towards me. I still stood by the phone base.

Blake smothered a curse. He looked from me to Merry. "Do I need to spell this out for you two?"

Merry's eyes grew and watered.

"The person who put her there intended for it to be *you*, Merry Leigh. The person I am going to identify at that construction site could easily, but for the grace of God, have been you."

He spun on me. "Do you get how serious this is? This is not some schmuck getting some on the side."

"Enough Blake." Mamma moved to Merry's side and placed her arms protectively around her shoulders. "Go do what you have to do. Merry and Liz will stay here with us. Call as soon as you know something definite."

I turned away from him. Outside the window, squirrels were helping themselves to Mamma's birdseed.

Blake came up behind me and spoke softly, but in lethal tones. "Two gunshots to the head." He let that sink in. "How did you know Troy had a gun? You said I should be careful, because he had a gun, and he would use it. You told me that the night it happened. How did you know?"

I turned to face him. "I can't tell you," I whispered.

His anger was palpable. He faced the room and spoke loud enough for everyone to hear. "I've got to get moving," he said. "Troy may know who he buried at that construction site in Charleston, and he may not. He may have buried Kristen in the rug without ever unrolling it. If not, he's figured out by now that you, Merry, know enough to send him to prison. He's capable of just about anything to avoid prison."

"She gets it, okay? We all get it," I said.

"I'll call when I can." He looked around the room at each of us and headed out the back door.

THIRTY-SEVEN

My mamma should have been a drug pusher. She approached Clay Cooper's patrol car, goods in hand. "You poor little thing. You couldn't have had time for a proper breakfast, running over here on such short notice. You take this now. There's no reason why you can't keep an eye on things here and have your breakfast at the same time."

I'd walked outside with her to deliver the blueberry sin. "Hey, Clay."

He didn't take his eyes off those pancakes. "Hey, Liz."

Clay knew as well as any of us that resistance was futile, but he made a perfunctory attempt. "Now, Mrs. Talbot, I'm pretty sure Blake would prefer me to stay focused on securing the premises and not be distracted by this fine stack of pancakes."

"Nonsense. You eat your breakfast."

I could see Clay's mouth watering as he reached through the patrol car window and eagerly accepted the piled-high plate of hot blueberry pancakes and bacon. Clay needn't have worried. Blake knew better than anyone the only way Clay could get Mamma to go back in the house and lock the door was to take the plate and commence eating. Grinning from ear to ear, he did just that.

"Thanks, Mrs. Talbot. This looks mighty fine. To tell the truth, I did miss my breakfast this morning."

She reached into the car and patted his shoulder. "Bless your heart. I am so sorry you had to come running out on our account. But I do feel so much safer with you out here." She cast a quick look over her shoulder at Daddy, only a few dozen feet away in his front-porch rocking chair. It wouldn't do for him to think she doubted his ability to protect us. A little louder, she added, "My Frank has everything under control,

I'm sure. Nobody will get past him. You just enjoy your breakfast, now."

He lifted another forkful. "Yes ma'am. But, uh, Mrs. Talbot, ma'am, if you and Liz would please go back inside, I surely would be much obliged. I have strict orders. You and the girls are not to cross the threshold, and, uh..."

"Yes, of course. We're going right now. You just let Frank know when you're finished. He can bring the plate in. You've got coffee, now, right?"

"Yes ma'am, I got a thermos full right here. Now please, if anything happened to you all on my watch, Blake wouldn't have to kill me. I'd personally throw myself right off the Cooper River Bridge."

I took an appraising look around our peaceful, oak-lined street where nothing bad ever happened. I shuddered and put my arm around Mamma's waist. "Come on, Mamma. Let's get back inside."

The squawk on Clay's radio was so loud and shrill that it not only startled Mamma and me, but brought Daddy out of his rocking chair on the front porch.

Mayhem ensued.

Chumley lunged one basset-hound length forward and barked in the direction of the car. His leap positioned him squarely between Daddy and the front porch steps. Chumley yelped as Daddy tripped over him and went sprawling down the steps, shotgun flying. As it hit the ground, the gun discharged. A flock of birds rocketed out of the live oak.

Focused on the radio, Clay evidently didn't see the source of the shotgun blast. He threw open the door. Pancakes hit the pavement. Clay scrambled out of the car, pulling his pistol from the holster. He visually swept the area, crouching, gun clasped in both hands, arms locked forward.

Merry came flying out the front door. "Daddy," she gasped. She ran down the steps as Mamma and I rushed to his side. He was sprawled half on the sidewalk and half in the azalea bushes that lined it.

Mamma reached his side and knelt beside him. "Frank, are you all right?"

"Cracked my damn knee," Daddy muttered. He groaned, but managed to navigate from a full spread-eagle sprawl to a semi-sitting position. He looked up. "What'd I hit?"

Reassured by the fact that he was not only conscious, but sitting up, we breathed a sigh of relief. Chumley, however, went from bark to full howl.

"Maybe a tree limb," I said. "Likely nothing but air."

"Clay, are you there? This is your mother. Answer me right now." Nell Cooper, having initiated the fracas when she tried to raise Clay on the radio, dropped all pretense of radio protocol.

Clay swept the area once more in a complete circle. Slowly, eyes darting around the perimeter, he holstered his gun and reached for the radio. "Yeah. I'm here. What's up?"

"You'd better get over to Marsh Point. Willa Butler called in. She was out jogging this morning and says she saw something in the marsh."

Clay's voice took on an impatient edge. "Well, Mamma, what did she see? I'm on duty here. I can't go running over to the marsh on a wild goose chase. This is serious business."

It was as likely as anything that Willa the Voodoo Priestess wanted someone to come take a gander at suspicious patterns in the marsh grass.

"Well, son, she *says* it's a dead body. I don't reckon it gets any more serious than that."

What in the name of sweet reason is going on? I couldn't imagine anything more unbelievable than a second body being discovered that morning. Willa had to be mistaken. I sent up a silent prayer for circles in the marsh grass, or some other such harmless nonsense that made up the fabric of our world.

Clay looked at us, then at the ground. He rolled his lips in, heaved a sigh, and then shook his head. "Hang on, Mamma," he said into the handheld. He lowered the unit and dialed, then raised it to his ear.

We waited.

After a minute, Clay gave his cell phone/radio the evil eye. "Damn fast busy signal," he said. "I can't reach Blake. Rodney's guarding Grace Sullivan. Sam's supposed to be catching a few hours' sleep." He turned in a circle, either stalling, or praying for an idea. He shook his head, slow and wide. "Mmm, mmm, mmm."

Finally, Clay spoke into his radio. "Mamma, call Doc Harper and ask him to meet me at the scene. And wake up Sam and send him on over, too. I need backup."

Clay squared his shoulders and strode across the lawn to our circle of Talbot women hovering around the slightly scuffed man-of-the-house. Clay cleared his throat. "Uh, Mr. Talbot, we seem to have a problem over at Marsh Point I'm going to have to go investigate. Now I know Blake didn't want the ladies to leave the house, but I've got to believe that, given a choice, he'd rather me take y'all along than leave you here. This is a little out of the ordinary, sir, but if y'all wouldn't mind..." He turned to Mamma. "Ma'am?" He moved quickly to the car and opened the door for her.

"Just a second, I have to get my purse." Mamma dashed back towards the house.

His knee miraculously healed, Daddy hopped to his feet and retrieved his shotgun.

Chumley promptly stopped howling and scampered towards the car. He leaped into the patrol car and positioned himself squarely in the middle of the front seat. He barked once to indicate his impatience with the rest of us.

Clay's eyes widened and he spun around. "Oh, ah, Mr. Talbot, that would be against regulations, sir. I'm afraid we'll need to leave the, ah, dog here. There just wouldn't be room."

Daddy grimaced and addressed the hound in question. "Get out of there now. Come on." He turned to Clay. "I'm afraid this might not be easy."

Mamma returned with her purse. She looked at Clay apologetically as she slid into the backseat. "We can try to get him out, but it's likely to take a while. I'll have to go get a hot dog and lure him out."

"I'll just pick him up and sit him back on the front porch." Clay reached for Chumley, who turned and locked eyes with his would-be captor and growled.

Daddy raised his eyebrows. "I wouldn't recommend that. Chumley doesn't normally bite, but all this excitement's got him a little high-strung."

Clay hesitated. "Oh, all right, everybody in, and let's go."

Merry and I climbed in the backseat with Mamma, and Daddy joined Clay and Chumley in the front.

Doors slammed and seat belts clicked. Mamma reached into her oversized purse and pulled out her cosmetics bag. She rummaged for a minute and then pulled out a tube of Estée Lauder Forward Fig and passed it to me. "Honey, put on a little lipstick, you look pale."

I knew it was pointless to argue that no one at the crime scene would notice I hadn't put on lipstick. I accepted the slender gold tube without a word of protest.

"Pass that on over to your sister when you're finished." Mamma patted me on the leg and faced front, ready to proceed now that a cosmetic emergency had been averted. Then her head swiveled back to Merry. Mamma's hand came to her throat and a look of horror slid over her face. Merry was still clad in cows and pigs, her hair defying gravity.

As the car started moving, Chumley commenced woofing again. With Daddy in the front seat toting a shotgun in one hand, his other arm around his hound dog, and the three of us in the back primping, Clay headed towards the marsh.

THIRTY-EIGHT

When dead people are not turning up all over the place, my brother is as easy-going a guy as you'll ever meet. The morning Willa found the body in the salt marsh, his stress level peaked. Mamma, Daddy, Merry and I were standing on the bank when Blake pulled the Tahoe to a stop behind Clay's patrol car.

The look of relief on Clay Cooper's face when he saw Blake was so dramatic it would have been comical in any other situation. He stood knee-deep in muck, about twenty feet out into the marsh on the western side of Stella Maris. I could tell by the way Blake worked his jaw he was biting back a curse. He pulled on his gloves to go to work as he walked across the grassy edge of the marsh, making efficient use of the time by chewing Clay out along the way.

"What were you thinking bringing my *mother* to a crime scene?" His eyes bored a hole through Clay. "I am a reasonable man, Coop, and I know there is no way you could've left my sisters at the house. I *understand*, having lived with them for thirty years, that *they...*" he motioned towards me and Merry with a sweeping gesture, "are as reasonable as a pair of mules. But what possessed you to put my mother in a patrol car and bring her out here to look at a corpse?"

Normally, I would've had plenty to say to Blake about his attitude, especially that mule remark. But I kept my mouth shut.

A mournful howl rose from the direction of Clay's car. Blake stopped and stared in disbelief at Daddy. Chumley hopped up and hung his head out the window, paws on the doorframe. "Aw, for the love of Pete, the dog, too? *Dad.*"

"Well, he hopped up in the car and wouldn't get out. Coop needed to get over here lickety-split, and well..." Daddy shrugged.

Mamma chimed in. "For heaven's sake, son. We don't have much experience dealing with dead people showing up like uninvited relatives. I'm fine, Liz and Merry are fine, and your daddy and his hound dog are just peachy-keen. Don't bother about us." She gave him a look that clearly indicated the subject was closed.

Blake flashed Mamma an exasperated look as he passed the crowd of onlookers gathered at the edge of the marsh. I felt sorry for my brother. He didn't have time to deal with us. For the second time in one morning, a dead body required his attention.

Blake waded out to where Clay and Sam watched Doc Harper examine the body. Thankfully, Doc had made a makeshift screen from a sheet and nearby bushes, shielding the gruesome sight.

Clay found his voice. "Look Chief, it was a judgment call. It appeared to me, with all hell breaking loose, it'd be best for your mamma to be here with me and Sam and your Daddy, than back at the house with just your Daddy. I'm real sorry you don't see it that way."

Blake held up his hand. "You're right. I'm sorry. Doc, what've we got here?"

Doc Harper looked up. "Couple of gunshot wounds to the head. Point-blank. Probably been dead eight to ten hours. Face is pretty messed up, but I've been treating him ever since I got my medical license. It's Adam Devlin."

Adam Devlin? Lightning seared me in the chest and radiated through my body.

"Oh my sweet Lord," Mamma said.

"He got his wallet on him?" Blake asked.

"Yeah. A couple hundred bucks and three credit cards in it," Sam said.

Troy. It had to've been Troy. He'd been following Adam for Deanna. Maybe Adam caught him and things went bad. Troy shot Adam and I did nothing to stop it. I stood quietly and watched as Blake and Sam taped off the scene and pored over the area. Coop took pictures of the drag marks from the road to the marsh, and made shoe impressions. Doc Harper ministered to the body.

After what seemed like hours, Blake stepped back from the yellow ribbon. "Coop, you and Sam finish up here with the Doc. Then head back to your posts. I'm going to take my family home and then go talk to the

Devlins."

"I don't think that's gonna be necessary." Clay looked over Blake's shoulder.

I followed Clay's gaze to see Michael slogging through the marsh towards them. I quashed the urge to run to him. We had all the drama we could handle.

"New plan," Blake said. "I'll stay here with Doc and Sam. You take Mom, Dad, and the girls home and stay with them. When we finish up here, I'll go with Michael to see Deanna and the rest of the family."

"Okay, Chief." Clay turned to round us up.

"And Coop?"

"Yeah, Chief?"

"Get your car cleaned up. That hound dog of my daddy's is an awful drooler."

THIRTY-NINE

Clay took us back to Mamma and Daddy's around ten that morning. As we piled out of the car, Mamma said, "I think I'll make some chicken salad and devil up some eggs. Anybody want a glass of iced tea?"

"Mamma," I said, "what I need is a nap. I haven't slept much all week."

"I'm wound up," Merry said. "How can you possibly sleep, after...that?"

Mamma patted my cheek and looked at me, eyes filled with concern. "You go straight upstairs. I'll fix us some lunch, and you eat when you're ready. Merry, you can help me in the kitchen."

"Thanks, Mamma," I hugged her.

Behind Mamma's back, Merry cut me a look that said she suspected I was up to something.

Mamma said, "Frank, now you be quiet and let her sleep."

I headed for the stairs, feeling guilty as a whore at a tent revival. I locked my bedroom door and crammed the essentials—iPhone, Sig, water bottle, sanitizer, and a USB drive—into a small backpack. Just in case Mamma made Daddy break down the door if I didn't answer her knock, I scribbled a note. Then I climbed out my window onto the screened porch roof. I crept down to the edge and grabbed a limb of the nearest oak. Merry waved at me from the kitchen window as I swung down. I dropped to the ground and offered her a pleading look. She made a shooing motion with her hands. I brushed my hands off and scampered away.

I couldn't take my car—Mamma and Daddy would've known I'd left. They were traumatized enough already without having to worry about me again today. If Troy had killed Adam, he'd want money from Deanna sooner rather than later. I headed towards the Atlantic. I'd run on the beach, then cut through the park at Devlin's Point. Fortunately, I hadn't changed out of my running clothes.

I picked up a bike trail at the edge of the park. Colleen appeared beside me, jogging along in a snappy green running suit.

"I've never known you to run before," I said.

"It's easier when you don't have to actually breathe. Cut through here." She darted down a dirt path to the left.

I rolled my eyes and followed. She was the guardian spirit.

After a minute she slowed and held a finger to her lips. She tip-toed off the path. Wood smoke lingered in the air. Colleen crept up to a sprawling live oak with branches that nearly touched the ground. Ivy clumped around the base, its tendrils climbing partway up the trunk. Colleen faded out and reappeared on a limb about thirty feet up. She motioned for me to join her. I fisted my hands on my hips and cocked my head at her. She flashed me a look of exaggerated patience.

I approached the tree, avoiding the ivy as much as possible. "This better not be anything that makes me itch," I hissed. I grabbed the lowest limb. It wasn't all that difficult. Moments later, I was perched on an adjacent branch on the other side of the trunk.

"Where are we?" I murmured.

"Ground Zero for a youth camp," Colleen said. "Or a fancy resort."

In a small clearing below us, someone had put up a tent. A canvas chair sat near the front flap.

"Who's camping out?" I asked.

"Troy. I've been looking for him everywhere. Finally found him while you were at the marsh."

"Did he kill Adam?"

"I don't know. Shhh."

We waited. A few minutes later, we heard him stirring inside the tent, then he emerged. He wobbled, almost fell. He'd taken to drinking Crown Royal directly from the bottle, and the bottle shook as he raised it to his mouth. He took a generous gulp and wiped his mouth with the back of his hand.

He leaned forward and squinted through the trees. Patches of burgundy were visible between the oaks and pines. A car was wedged into the woods on a path that led from a dirt road in the park. Troy nodded, apparently satisfied. Evidently, he'd parked the car in the woods.

He pulled out a cell phone and tapped in a number. While he waited for someone to answer, he took another swig of Crown. After a few moments, he cursed the phone and pressed a button. "That's fine, old man. You get home, go ahead and report your truck stolen. Cops'll find the fucker next time they dredge the fuckin' Cooper River. Commandeered me a new ride. Ida left your piece-of-shit truck on the street, that woulda tipped 'em off to what I'm driving. So I *rolllled* it into the river. I'm a thinker." He tapped his temple with a finger from the hand holding the cell phone. "That's my *edge* over all you losers. Slavin' your lives away catching little bitty shrimp in a great big net. I'ma make a shitload of money in Hollywood."

Colleen and I looked at each other and rolled our eyes. It was getting easier and easier to visualize Troy on an episode of *World's Dumbest Criminals*. How had Adam come to hire this genius to kill someone? It was obvious he wasn't a professional hit man. More like an inept thug willing to kill for money.

He set down the bottle of Crown, held the phone close to his face and selected a stored number. He put the phone to his ear and waited. After a minute, he screwed up his face like he was about to cry. "Kristen, I don't know where you are, but when you get this call me, okay?"

Troy hiccupped into the phone. "Sugar, I'da never hurt Merry. That was an assident. I coulda smoothed everything over. Hatten I always smoothed things over? If she hatten fell and hit her head. Call me. Hollywood won't be the same without you." He pressed a button to end the call.

So Troy didn't know Kristen was dead. He thought he buried Merry at that construction site. That was a blessing. As long as he kept on thinking that, Merry was safe.

Troy sat there staring at the phone for a minute. Then, he squinted at it and selected another number.

He pulled the phone back up to his ear. "It's me."

He scowled. "What the hell you crying for? It's done."

"Deanna," said Colleen.

Troy said, "Quit your blubbering and lissen. I need to collect *pretty* damn quick. I got no idea who he was screwin'. But it don't make a damn any more. The rat is dead. Get me my money and I'm outta here."

Rage seized his face.

Colleen said, "She hung up on him."

He threw back his head and roared. "Aaahhh!" He threw the phone on the ground. "Will some damn thing just go like is s'posed to?"

He paced the campsite, kicking pinecones. He picked up the bottle of Crown and took a swig, then he stumbled towards the car. He stopped, backtracked, and picked up the phone, muttering curses. Then he weaved in the general direction of the car.

He was leaving. I needed to stop him. I turned on the tree limb and reached with my leg for the next lower branch.

"What are you doing?" asked Colleen.

"I'm going to detain him and call Blake," I hissed.

"Ummm..." Colleen apparently weighed the wisdom of this plan.

The car door squeaked when he opened it.

I navigated the tree limbs as quickly as I dared, not looking down. I'm not a big fan of heights, mostly because I have this pressing urge to fling myself to the ground. I've always wondered what that was all about.

The engine started.

I moved faster, slipped, grabbed a limb and hung on.

"Be careful," Colleen said, her voice tense.

"I am." I growled. "Find out what kind of car that is." I dangled, not daring to look down. I stretched my right leg and reached for a branch I thought would bear my weight. My foot caught hold. I focused hard on the limb above the one my foot rested on, let go with my right hand, and swung for it.

I felt the tree bark under my palm and held on tight. I looked down. I was spread-eagled twenty-feet above the ground.

I clamped my eyes shut. I turned, let go with my left hand, and threw all of my weight towards the near-parallel limbs that supported the right side of my body. I teetered, steadied myself. Three deep breaths later, I continued my descent. A mere six feet off the ground, I slipped and hit the sand flat on my stomach.

The wind knocked out of me, I laid there a moment. Then I braced my palms under me, preparing to push myself up.

That's when I saw the snake.

It was a pinkish-tan with darker brown bands. A copperhead. It had frozen in its path through the ivy at the base of the oak.

My face was six inches away from its tail, which started to shake.

I launched myself backwards, away from the tree, landing on my ass not nearly far enough away to suit me. I scrambled to my feet and backed off into the clearing where the tent stood. Had Troy been looking in his rearview as he drove away, he would've seen me. I did not care.

Colleen appeared beside me. "It's a Honda Accord."

I stared at her, breathing hard and shaking.

"What's wrong with you?" she asked. "You're eyes look sorta scary, like maybe you've snapped."

"Snake." I pointed to the tree.

"Eeeww." She took a step backwards.

I shuddered. After a long breath, I pulled out my phone. It was eleven o'clock. I tried calling Blake three times, and paged him. He didn't answer, likely because he was in the middle of doing notifications. I left him a voice mail telling him where Troy was camped, what he was driving, and that he wanted Deanna's twenty-five grand. I'd explain that later. Somehow.

Damnation. Someone needed to nab Troy. Since I had no car in which to give chase, I called Nell Cooper. Maybe Clay or Sam could intercept Troy. When Nell asked how I'd come by this new information, the call got staticky, then dropped. Damn cell phones.

I checked the tent. Nothing but a sleeping bag and some McDonald's trash. "I'm going over to Deanna's," I said. "Odds are that's where Troy's headed."

"I'll meet you there," Colleen said. She disappeared.

I took off at a run, giving the ivy-floored live oak a wide berth. On the way to Deanna's, I mulled how I'd been headed there to begin with, before Colleen made me take a detour through the woods, fall out of a tree, and nearly get bitten by a snake. Seemed Colleen's involvement was sometimes more helpful than others. She'd told me herself that she wasn't omniscient. Sure, she knew some things I didn't, but I was learning that simply following her directions wasn't always the best course. But how to know which to follow?

A block into Sea Farm, I slowed to a walk. Surveillance would be difficult without a car. Protecting Deanna from inside the house seemed the best option. Hopefully, there wasn't a crowd. As I approached the house, I noted there were no cars in the driveway or in the street out front. If Troy was at Deanna's, he'd likely parked a street or two over. I didn't see his car, but I didn't have time to search the entire neighborhood either.

On the front porch of Deanna's two-story Victorian, I took a moment to smooth my hair and wipe my hands on my black Lycra capris. My reflection in the window confirmed what I already knew—I looked a sight. I rang the doorbell.

After a full two minutes, I rang again, and then knocked.

No response.

I cupped my hands and put my face to the window. No sign of anyone. Also no signs of violence, which was good. But Deanna had been home when she took Troy's call earlier. Or had she? He could have called her on a cell, though I hadn't seen her with one.

I ran around back and looked through the window in the back door. The alarm system was armed. Okay, maybe Deanna hadn't been at home, or, if she had, maybe Troy had scared her and she'd taken the girls and left. Either way, the alarm system wouldn't be armed if Troy had broken in.

I trotted down the block to the phone junction box, where I'd hidden the recorder the day before. A quick glance up and down the street confirmed that I was still alone. I knelt, pushed back the pampas grass, and disconnected the equipment. Cramming it my backpack, I hit the sidewalk.

It was almost noon. Mamma would be knocking on my bedroom door with a chicken salad sandwich and iced tea any minute. I broke into a run.

FORTY

A block from Mamma and Daddy's, I pulled out my iPhone and called Merry on hers. "Get Mamma and Daddy into the kitchen and distract them while I slip in the front."

"You owe me. I've been in the kitchen for the past two hours. Shredding chicken."

"Anything you want." I was not climbing another tree that day.

"I'll text you when it's clear."

"I love you."

I waited behind a weeping willow in the front yard. Seconds later I received a one-word text. "Go."

I slipped in the front door and tiptoed up the stairs. Straight to the shower I went. Never had water and soap felt so good. I scrubbed like I was washing snake off of me along with the sand and sweat. I pulled on a pair of navy capris, a lacy green tank, and a sheer white blouse. Then, I suspended my primping to see if I had snagged anything useful with my phone tap.

There were four calls on the recorder. The first was date-time stamped 8:08 p.m. from the night before.

"Hello?" Deanna said.

"I won't be home for dinner. I'm going into Charleston." Adam's voice made me queasy after seeing his body in the marsh only hours before.

"Where are you having dinner?"

"None of your damn business, that's where."

"When should I expect you?"

"When you see me. And if you have any more questions, you'd better keep them to yourself unless you want a taste of my belt when I get home."

I recoiled from the digital recorder. For the first time I wondered if Deanna could possibly have killed him herself.

Deanna didn't respond.

"Kiss the girls goodnight for me. You hear?" His voice still had a threat in it.

"I will," she said, in the vocal equivalent of a poker face.

A click ended the call.

The second call was date-time stamped at 10:13 the night before.

"Hello?" Deanna answered.

"Sweetheart, are you feeling any better?" A female voice.

"Yes, Mamma, I'm fine," Deanna said. "Really. Please don't worry about me."

"You're just so keyed up. I wish you'd reconsider and take the medication the doctor gave you."

"Mamma, I flushed those things down the toilet. I can't believe I even had that prescription filled. You know I don't like to take pills."

Her mother sighed. "Never could get you to even take an aspirin."

"No telling what that stuff does to your kidneys."

"Well, you just call me if you need me. Hear?"

"Mmm-kay. Love you."

"Love you too, sweetheart. Bye now."

"Bye bye."

Click.

Huh. So she hadn't taken the Xanax. She'd flushed it. Did she buy the Ephedra and toss it as well? But why flush one and throw the other in the trash?

The next call was the one I overheard Troy make that morning. Deanna's side of the call consisted of her sobbing and hanging up on Troy in mid-sentence. So she had been at home when she spoke to him.

The fourth call was also from Troy. He must have called her back after he left the campsite. I must have missed her at her house by seconds.

"Hello?" Deanna said, her voice now slightly slurred. Odds were, someone medicated her against her will and the drugs were kicking in.

"Lady, if you know whass good for you, you won't hang up on me this time," Troy said.

"Just a moment, please." She must have covered the phone, because her voice was muffled. She was speaking to someone else. "I'll be right there."

She spoke into the phone again. "Does your mamma know how you speak to ladies?"

"I was you, I'd shut the fuck up. Me, I've had a couple a really bad days, and I've got no patience whatsoever with any a your la-tee-da bullshit. I did the job. I want my money *right now*."

"Why that's absurd, I never asked you to do a single thing except follow my husband and find out who he was sleeping with. As a matter of fact, I vividly remember telling you not to hurt anyone." The word "vividly" came out mangled. Deanna was definitely on something.

"I don't know what kind of game you're playing, but we both know what you meant. Trust me, it's in your best interest to bring me my money so I can get the hell out of Dodge."

"I don't know what kind of drugs *you're* taking, Mr. Exterminator, but everybody knows I would never consort with criminals, let alone hire someone to kill my husband. The idea is ridiculous."

"Shut up. Bring the money over to White Point Gardens, to the place we met before. It shouldn't take you more than an hour to get there. I'll be waiting. If you don't show up, I'll be coming after my money. If you make me do that, somebody else is going to get hurt. *Got it?*"

What was it with Troy and White Point Gardens? Why wouldn't he just come get the money? He was already on Stella Maris. But he'd know Deanna would be surrounded by family and friends. She'd be hard to get to without him being seen, and arrested.

Deanna said, "Why don't I bring a picnic along? I've got a lovely shrimp salad in the refrigerator that Mrs. Smithers brought over. That's one thing you have to say about Mrs. Smithers, she is always prompt with food for the bereaved. I bet she keeps things made up just in case someone keels over. Why, if you hadn't knocked off my Adam, someone else might have ended up with this shrimp salad, so, I guess, in a way, I really owe you some of it. Do you prefer yours on the little croissants or toast points?"

"Lady, you are seriously disturbed. Just get my money over here. And if you know what's good for you, you won't bring along *shrimp* of any kind."

Click.

Great. By now Troy was back on the other side of the Cooper River. At least Deanna was safe, for now. Whoever she'd been speaking to when she put her hand over the phone must have taken her and the girls somewhere else. But I needed to make sure she didn't go to meet Troy. That way, he'd come back to Stella Maris to get his money, and we'd have him.

I finished my hair and makeup, and was just about to head downstairs when Nate called.

"Hey. You get some rest?" I asked.

"Some. What have I missed?" Calm Nate was back this morning.

"Willa Butler found Adam Devlin dead in the salt marsh this morning. And someone found Merry's roommate's body in Charleston."

"What the hell? Is there a serial killer in Charleston County?"

"It's beginning to look that way."

"Have you seen any more of Scott?"

"No."

"Well, there's one good thing," Nate said. "Unless there are more delays, I should be in Stella Maris around nine-thirty. Should I go to your parent's house?"

If Nate were here, no one could object to my staying at Gram's. "No. Come to Gram's house. You remember how to get there?" We'd driven by when he came home with me for the funeral.

"I can find it. See you soon."

Merry was in the kitchen, nibbling on a chicken salad croissant. "You won't believe this, but I saw a rat in here earlier."

"Thanks again. If I'd had to climb in my bedroom window, I'd probably have broken my neck. It's been a rough morning. I'll fill you in later." I reached in the refrigerator and pulled out the chicken salad and a plate of deviled eggs topped with olives. "Do these have cream cheese in them?"

"Of course."

"Yum. I'm starved." I made myself a sandwich and added three deviled eggs to my plate. "Where are Mamma and Daddy?"

"After the rat incident, Mamma needed to lie down. Daddy's on the front porch standing guard."

"Heard from Blake?"

"No."

I poured myself some tea and perched on a bar-height chair at the opposite end of the butcher-block work island from Merry. I propped my pink-tipped toes on the chair between us, beside her red ones. Then, I pulled out my iPhone and called Blake.

For once, he answered when I called. "What fresh hell is this?"

"If that's the way you feel about it, I won't bother checking in anymore."

"Tell me you're still at Mom and Dad's."

"I am. I'm sitting in the kitchen, eating a chicken salad sandwich. Oh, man this is good chicken salad. Mamma just made it." Okay, that was mean. He probably hadn't had a chance to eat lunch.

"Then how, exactly, do you happen to know that Troy Causby is driving a burgundy Honda Accord and may be heading towards Deanna's? Or that he was camping in this tent over on Devlin's Point that I'm standing next to? Nell was a little fuzzy on the details. She said the call broke up." Blake's tone indicated his familiarity with my vagary/dropped call technique.

"Well, I did pop out for a bit. But Mamma thinks I was napping, so don't tell."

"If you were close enough to hear where he was headed, why didn't you shoot him in the kneecap or something until I could get here?"

"Well, I tried. It's a long story. Anyway, where's Deanna?"

"At Kate's," he said. "With Sam in a squad car out front. Grace is over there, too, to answer the phone and handle food drop-offs. Works out. We can watch her and Deanna with one unit."

"Let Sam know Deanna might try to slip out."

"Why would she do that?"

"To meet Troy and pay him. He wants her to come over to White Point Gardens and bring the money."

"Why would she even consider doing that?"

Hell's bells. I kept forgetting what I had and hadn't told Blake. Lying to subjects and witnesses had become second nature over the years. Lying to my family was altogether different. "He threatened her. He knows Adam had the money to pay him. He told Deanna if she didn't bring it to him, someone else would get hurt." That was the truth, just not the whole truth.

"I'll alert Sam, but she's asleep. Doc Harper gave her something. She was loopy for a while. Then she crashed. Look, I gotta go. Stay put." He hung up before I had to answer that.

Merry finished her croissant and started into the cookies. I ate my sandwich, relishing every savory flaky bite. Nobody makes better chicken salad than Mamma. Then I downed the three cream-cheese-and-olive deviled eggs. Finally, I reached for the cookie jar and extracted two of Mamma's double-chocolate-chunk delights.

Merry and I sat silently munching. After the fourth time I sought comfort in the cookie jar, Merry raised her eyebrows. "You're stress-eating," she informed me.

"And?"

"You're going to scarf them all down. Pass that cookie jar over here."

I complied. "This is infuriating." I had reached the limit of my patience with being babysat, which, admittedly, I had only suffered long enough to eat my lunch.

"It seems to me we'd be safer if we weren't just sitting here in the most likely place Troy would come looking," Merry mused.

"Exactly." I pointed my cookie at her. "Adam's dead, Scott, so far, is trying to seduce me, not kill me, and Troy is in Charleston."

"Really?" Merry tilted her head. "How do you know that?"

I shrugged. "I ran across that information while I was out. The less you know, the less you'll have to remember to forget."

"*Liz.*"

"I'll tell you everything later. Right now, why are we sitting here packing on the pounds?"

"We're humoring your brother and your father." Merry took another bite of cookie.

"I'm all done humoring them. Let's get out of here." I stood, ready to make a break.

"And go where? What scheme lurks in that devious mind of yours?"

"Me devious?" My eyes went wide with innocence.

"Spare me."

"Fine." I chewed my last bite of cookie as I concocted a plan. "I'd like to know how Adam and Scott got mixed up with each other."

"Why don't you call Scott up and ask him?"

"Like he'd just tell me. That snake is at the bottom of this whole mess. Come on." I stood up, slid into my sandals, and grabbed my purse. "We're going to hunt him down."

Colleen appeared, sprawled across the work island, one hand propping up her head.

I closed my eyes and huffed my exasperation.

"What?" Merry asked.

"Nothing." I made for the door.

Her timing always impeccable, Mamma entered the kitchen just in time to catch me with one hand on the doorknob. "*E-liz-a-beth.* Where do you girls think you're going?"

I said, "Mamma, I can't possibly sit still another second. We're going shopping. We'll be fine, for heaven's sake. It's broad daylight. There are too many people out on Main Street this time of day for Troy to abduct us. Besides, I've got a pistol in my purse."

"Oh, I feel much better now." Mamma took a step towards us, hands on her hips, fire in her eyes. Then, she seemed to deflate. "I am just too undone to argue with you. Please be careful."

"We will, Mamma. Please don't worry. Back soon." I called over my shoulder as we hurried out the door.

"Love you," Merry added.

"Put on some lipstick," Mamma called after us.

FORTY-ONE

I slid into the driver's seat and reached to stow my purse in the back. There sat Colleen. I jumped so high I hit my head on the top of the car. I growled at her.

Merry knocked on the window.

"You'd better let Merry in," Colleen said. "Don't talk to me—just listen."

Merry opened the door and stepped in. "Where are we headed first?" She buckled up.

"To the police station," Colleen said.

"*What?*" I looked in the rearview.

Merry looked at me. "I said, where to first?"

"Merry should have a look at that locket. See if she recognizes the man in the picture," Colleen said. "It's in the evidence room."

"To the police station," I said.

"Right." Merry laughed. "No, really."

I squared my shoulders and started the car. "To the police station."

"Are you nuts? Wait—don't even answer that. I thought we were going to look for Scott?"

"We are. Right after we stop by the police station."

Merry and I continued our debate even as we walked into the police station. Colleen was elsewhere, again.

"Blake is going to lock us up in one of those jail cells just to keep us where he can see us," Merry said in exasperation.

"Maybe," I replied. "But he won't keep us long. Trust me, he's never had high maintenance prisoners before."

"This is a mistake," Merry insisted.

I stopped abruptly three yards in front of Nell's desk and looked at Merry. "Do you want to see the picture or not?"

"Well, yes, but I *thought* we were going to find Scott."

"This was on the way and it won't take a minute."

"Unless we're incarcerated."

Nell's head swiveled back and forth between us with each volley. Finally, she interrupted. "Is there something I can help you girls with?"

"Is Blake here?" I asked, knowing full well he wasn't.

"No, he's out hunting down that lowlife trash, Troy Causby."

"Fantastic."

Nell drew up her entire face into a pucker. "Did you want to see your brother or not?"

"Not really," Merry said.

"I see," Nell said. "Is there anybody else you don't want to see?"

"Nell," I said, "actually, what we want to see is the locket I found at Gram's house. I gave it to Blake, but Merry's never seen it."

Nell stiffened her posture and braced her hands on the desk. "You'll have to take that up with the chief. That locket is evidence in an ongoing investigation."

"When will he be back?" Merry asked.

"That's anybody's guess," Nell said.

"Where is he?" I asked, pretty sure he was still at Devlin's Point.

"That's police business," Nell said.

I bristled. "Nell Cooper, Blake is our brother, and if he's in some kind of danger, we have a perfect right to know."

"If Clay was in trouble, you'd want to know, wouldn't you?" Merry chimed in.

"Did I *say* he was in danger? If Blake wanted the two of you to know where he was headed, he'd have said, 'Nell, call up my sisters and give them my itinerary for the day.' But that's not what he said."

"What did he say?" Merry asked.

Nell tilted her head forward, and looked at us from under her eyebrows. "Why don't y'all just head on back over to your mamma's house where you're supposed to be?"

I turned to Merry. "I think we'd better call Mamma. If Nell's worried, I'm sure Mamma would want to know what's going on. Maybe she and Daddy had better head on over here, too."

Merry read my mind. "Good point. I'll call her right now." She pulled her cell phone out of her purse and began to dial.

"Hogs in lace, *no*." Nell stood up muttering under her breath none too quietly. "Upsetting your poor mamma. Your crazy daddy would have that messy ole hound in here." She reached in her top drawer and brought out a key ring. "You just stay right here. I'll get the locket. It's already been printed. I guess it's all right for you to look at it."

She walked down the hall and returned with a plastic evidence bag. Not taking any chances, Nell had put on a pair of latex gloves. "You can look, but you can't touch." She slipped the locket out of the bag and laid it on her desk.

We leaned over the desk. "Would you open it please?" I asked.

Nell muttered something I couldn't make out, but she opened the locket.

Merry stared at the picture.

I glanced at the picture. I did a double take. I leaned in closer, apparently obscuring my sister's view.

"Hey," Merry protested.

"Nell, thank you so much for all your trouble. We'll be getting out of your hair now." I backed away from the desk and bolted for the door, dragging Merry behind me.

Once outside, Merry stopped in her tracks and turned to face me. "Would you mind telling me what that was all about?"

I grinned.

"Spill it already. You look like you've got the biggest pot and the answer to Final Jeopardy."

"I know whose picture is in the locket."

"*What?*"

"Come on." I hopped behind the wheel of the Escape. "We're going to the marina."

FORTY-TWO

I zipped into the marina parking lot and pulled into a space near the docks.

Merry stared straight ahead, gripping the door handle. "You're *sure* this is the guy in the picture?"

"No doubt. He's the guy."

"All right, then. Let's go talk to him."

We got out of the car and walked down the dock.

"That's his boat right there, *The Gypsy Wind*." I pointed. "But I don't see him. He's probably below deck."

"How does one knock on the door of a sailboat?"

"I don't have a clue."

We stood there on the dock for a moment, looking at each other. Finally, I shouted, "Ahoy."

Merry giggled.

I cocked my head at my sister. "Do you have a better idea?"

"Not really. If we climb on board to knock on the cabin door are we trespassing?"

"Probably. But he doesn't seem like the type that would have us arrested."

We hesitated, and then both climbed over the rail. I took the lead, and we stepped down into the cockpit. "Mr. Davidson?"

All was quiet on the boat. I knocked on the teak panel that served as a door to the cabin. "Mr. Davidson?"

"He's not here," Merry said. "Come on, I don't feel right being on his boat uninvited."

"All right, we can come back later."

"Did you say he's from St. John?"

"Not from there, but he's lived there for a long time. He's from around here, originally." I climbed back over the rail and onto the dock.

"*Where*, here? Do you mean the U.S. mainland, South Carolina, the Charleston area, or Stella Maris?" Merry made the small step over the gap between boat and dock appear like a death-defying act.

"He didn't say, exactly, but I had the impression it was the Charleston area. We'd know him if he was from Stella Maris."

"That depends on how long he's been gone. He's a lot older than we are."

"True."

Merry slipped into the car. "*Now* can we hunt my ex-skunk-in-law?"

I started the engine and gripped the steering wheel with both hands. "Yes indeed."

FORTY-THREE

I parked in the small lot behind the Stella Maris Hotel. It was more of an inn, really. But the Rivers family, who had first opened it in the 1950s, had named it the Stella Maris Hotel, and the sign still proclaimed it that, so we all went along.

We crossed the wide ceiling fan-cooled front porch and entered the lobby. Alicia Rivers Manigault, a tall redhead, sat behind the front desk reading a paperback novel. We had been classmates all through school. Alicia had dated Blake for a while, and Merry and I had considered her a predatory female. Since Alicia was now happily married to Sam Manigault, with two-year-old redheaded twin boys, we assumed our brother was safe. Anyway, we needed her cooperation, so we unholstered our most honeyed tones and brightest smiles on the way in.

"Hey, Alicia, how are you?" I asked.

Alicia offered us a perfunctory smile. "Fine, and you?"

"We're good. How are those adorable twins of yours?" I asked.

"Why, they're just...adorable. What can I do for you?" Alicia appeared already tired of the effort to be pleasant, and eager to get back to her book.

"Well, Alicia, my estranged husband has been staying with you all for the last few days. I need to speak to him, family business and all. Could you tell me if he's still here?"

"As far as I know he is," Alicia said. "He hasn't checked out, anyway."

"Well, then, we'll just go on up. What room would that be?" I smiled so sweetly I made myself queasy.

"Twelve. Top of the stairs to the right."

"Thank you so much. You've been a real big help."

"No problem." She seemed to be silently willing us to hurry on up the stairs and out of her sight. "Here—why don't you take a key just in case? If he's out, you might have to wait a while. He told me to expect you." She laid the spare key to room twelve on the counter.

Merry and I exchanged a look. Scott. So sure of his irresistible charms he actually told Alicia I'd be coming by. Whatever. This was unexpected good fortune. I snagged the key and we glided across the lobby and up the stairs as quickly as possible without actually bolting.

We stood in front of the door to room twelve and looked at each other.

"What are we going to say to him if he's in there?" Merry asked.

"We're going to ask him what in the name of sweet reason he's up to."

"And you think he's just going to tell us?"

"No, I'm hoping I'll have to shoot him."

Merry's eyes widened.

"No place vital, I still want him to be able to talk. I'll probably start with the kneecap. I hear that's quite painful." I pounded on the door.

After a moment, Merry pressed her ear to the door. "I don't hear anyone moving around in there."

I put the key in the lock and opened the door slowly. "Scott?"

Convinced he wasn't in the room, we entered and closed the door behind us.

Merry peered into the closet. "From the looks of things, he's still in town."

I looked over her shoulder. A suit, two shirts and a pair of khaki pants, along with a pair of tennis shoes. I went to check out the chest of drawers. "Yeah, unless he left in such a hurry he abandoned his clothes."

I walked over to the desk. "But he wouldn't have left this." I sat down at the desk and opened the laptop. "Listen at the door in case he comes back."

"Won't he have everything password protected?"

"Yep." I typed in "BigKahuna9" and snickered when it worked.

When the computer finished booting, I clicked on the email icon. I skimmed through his inbox, but nothing immediately caught my attention. I had better luck in his sent items folder. The subject line on the first item was "Stella Maris Resort Project." I read for a moment. I turned to Merry. "You'd better come look at this. I'll listen at the door while you read."

Merry switched places with me and read the e-mail on the screen. It was time stamped at 11:38pm on Tuesday night, and addressed to the VP of New Projects at Scott's firm. Merry read silently for a moment, and then erupted. "That sonofabitch."

She read aloud. *"It appears from David Morehead's report that, while there may be a slight delay due to unforeseen circumstances, the strategy of going through one of the local residents to transfer the property is a success. There may be some initial backlash from the local residents when the project is fully laid out, and the youth camp proves unfeasible. However, any resistance should quickly be mitigated by the positive impact to the local economy."* She swiveled towards me. Merry was wild-eyed and seething.

"There's our proof," I said. "It looks like you were the 'local resident' being used and I was the 'unforeseen circumstances.'" I crossed the room and nudged her out of the chair. Scott could come back any minute, and we needed more information. "Let me poke around a little more."

Merry rose and paced the floor. She cursed Scott and all his ancestors while I searched the computer for anything else related to Stella Maris.

"Jackpot," I murmured. "Here's a folder of saved e-mails named 'Stella Maris Project.'" I scanned the sender and recipient fields. "Here's one from Adam Devlin."

Merry moved to read over my shoulder. *"Imagine running into you at The Pirates' Den of all places. It's a damn good thing your girlfriend saw that article in* Southern Living. *I'm glad you finally see the potential here. I'm confident I can deliver the votes we need to get Devlin's Point rezoned. The key is to make sure the project stays under the radar until the property is transferred. Using Esmerelda Talbot to get the land donated to the namesake corporation is the right approach. I've found someone local we can use to monitor the situation and let us know if she gets suspicious. In return for the property, per our agreement, New Life Resorts will pay me ten million dollars up front, plus a ten percent interest in the Stella Maris Resort."*

I was getting nervous. "We've got to get out of here. I'm going to forward this to myself, Blake, and Nate, along with the other one from Tuesday. Go back and listen at the door."

I was closing the laptop when Merry whispered loudly, "Someone's coming."

I was pretty sure Scott was not, himself, a murderer, but I wasn't willing to bet my life on it. "Hide. In the closet."

Merry slipped into the closet and shut the door just as Scott put his key in the lock. I arranged myself in my most seductive pose on the bed.

Scott could hardly have looked more self-satisfied when he opened the door and found me sprawled across the four-poster bed with a come-hither smile on my face. "Hi ya, big boy," I purred.

"Well hey, kitten. About time you showed up." He looked around the room. "I thought the girl at the desk said your sister was with you."

I bit the inside of my cheek. I despised it when he called me kitten. Then again, I despised everything that came out of his mouth. "No, just little ole me. I wanted to surprise you." Honey dripped from my lips.

"And a pleasant surprise you are. Well, now, I knew you'd come around. But you sure took your sweet time." Confident in his skills with women in general, and his ability to schmooze me in particular, he didn't stop to ponder my complete and utter change of heart. He loosened his tie and sauntered towards the bed.

I stood on my knees and put my arms around his neck. "You know what I want?" I whispered in his ear.

"Baby you know I do." He pulled me to him and his mouth covered mine.

I kissed him just long enough to be convincing and then turned my head and whispered in his other ear. "Champagne."

"What?" His breath was ragged.

"I want some champagne." I pulled back far enough to look him in the eyes. "You know how I love it. This is a celebration, right?" I looked at him pleadingly.

"Well, sure, kitten, but, you've already got me wound up, and they don't have room service here."

I pulled back and gave him my most alluring pout.

"Oh, all right," he said. "But where am I going to find chilled champagne on this island?"

"Edwards Grocery has it. It's not far at all, just go to the stoplight and turn left down Palmetto. It's just a few doors down on the right."

"Are you sure—?"

I placed my finger over his lips. "Shhh. I'm going to change into a little something I picked up at Victoria's Secret this morning just for you. I was remembering how partial you are to black lace." I lowered my chin and looked up at him through my eyelashes. I flashed him a particularly feline smile. "Go on now. I'll be waiting right here for you."

He kissed me once more. "I'll be right back," he promised. He was out the door.

I waited a ten count then opened the closet door.

Merry grinned at me wickedly. "Kitten?"

"Don't start."

"Remind me to ask you where you learned all that stuff."

"Remind me to wash my mouth out with Clorox. Come on, let's get out of here."

I cracked the door and looked out. No sign of anyone. We tiptoed down the stairs and out the front door. Thankfully, Alicia wasn't at the front desk.

We ran around back, hopped in my car, and hightailed it out of the parking lot.

FORTY-FOUR

"*I was remembering how partial you are to black lace,*" Merry mimicked, and burst into wild laughter for the umpteenth time since we'd peeled out of the hotel parking lot.

I glared at my sister and considered putting her out of the car. "This is the thanks I get for sacrificing myself to save your skinny hide. For all we know, that jackass is a murderer. He could have shot the both of us and thrown us in the marsh just like Adam."

"Will you please watch where you're going? If you drive us into the marsh, your Academy-Award-worthy performance will have been for nothing."

I turned back to the road ahead. "I barely even crossed the line."

"Whatever."

I'd been driving without a destination in mind, intent on getting away from the hotel. "Let's go by Gram's for a while. If this Tom Davidson was so important that she wore a locket with his picture in it, there should be some other trace of him in her things."

Of course. How had I been so dense? "That's it!"

"What?" Merry asked.

"Gram's beau was my prowler. He didn't mean me or Rhett any harm. He just wanted to remove all traces of himself from Gram's before I stumbled onto evidence of their affair. And that's why he said I reminded him of an old friend. He meant Gram."

"You're brilliant." Merry grinned. "But then, you are my sister."

I drove the short distance to Gram's house and parked in the circle drive. Rhett came bounding from the backyard to greet us. We cooed at him, petted him, and scratched his tummy. The sun slipped behind a bank of towering cumulonimbus clouds. I squinted at the sky. "I think I'll close the moonroof. Looks like a storm's brewing. Maybe we should just check in with Blake." I reached for my cell phone.

"All right, but my story is you made me come."

"What?"

"Everybody knows how bossy you are."

"And everybody also knows how devious you are." I dialed Blake's cell phone. After five rings, his voicemail picked up. "Hey, Blake. It's Liz. Call me and give me an update. Please. Merry and I were going stir crazy, so we've gone out for a while. We're fine. We're at Gram's. It's about two o'clock. Talk to you later. Oh. And whatever you do, make sure somebody keeps watching Deanna."

Merry gave me a quizzical look. "Why does someone need to watch Deanna?"

Without missing a beat, I said, "She could be in danger." I switched on the light in the foyer. Deanna. Something about the Xanax and the Ephedra nagged at me. I stepped towards my office. "I just want to check something before we get started. You want something to drink?"

"Yeah. Vodka maybe, after that scene at the hotel."

"Whatever you want. Bring me a Diet Cheerwine, will you? In a glass?"

"Sure."

"Hey—"

"I know. Wash off the top of the can before I pour it in the glass. Got it." I could hear Merry rolling her eyes.

I sat at my desk and pulled out the plastic bag with the Xanax bottle and the Ephedra. I updated the label on the bag, indicating I had opened it with the date and time, and pulled on a pair of latex gloves. Doc Harper had prescribed the Xanax the week before. The bottle of Ephed-Dream had likely been purchased online, but that seemed very un-Deanna. She hated taking pills, and she wasn't the type to order controversial items over the internet. I checked the FDA website and verified that Ephedra had been banned in 2004. There was a long list of side effects—including death. Hell of a side effect. Most of the problems appeared liver or heart-related. Then I Googled Ephedra and found that you could indeed still buy it online. Likely from suppliers in other countries, though the websites didn't always indicate that. Like any illegal drug, you could probably buy it locally from a guy who knew a guy. Her recent out-of-character behavior notwithstanding, I couldn't see Deanna buying this stuff. Maybe Adam bought it for her, as a not-so-subtle suggestion she lose a pound or two.

I opened the bottle. It must have been previously opened. It wasn't sealed in any way and no cotton in the top. The label advertised 120 tablets. I peered inside, then dumped the contents onto my desk calendar. The caplets were white and oval. I flipped a few of them over and studied the markings. Odd. "M 447" was engraved on some, but not all of the pills. Using a pencil eraser, I counted them. Ninety of the pills had no markings. Thirty had the engraved code.

Merry came into the office and set a glass of Diet Cheerwine on a coaster on my desk. "What are you doing?" She reached for the Ephedra bottle.

"No." I snatched it away.

She jerked her hand back. "What?"

"That's evidence."

"Of what?"

"I'm not sure yet. Thanks for the drink." I picked up the glass and downed a third of it.

"You're welcome." Merry plopped onto the sofa, right where Marci sat Monday when she came by to try and sell me Michael.

"What is up with you?" Merry asked.

"Nothing." I pulled out my phone and loaded the Pill Id application. I took a photo of the pills with the markings. Seconds later, the image of the caplet appeared on the screen with the message "identified." Below the picture of the pill was the text "Benazepril 40 mg." I tapped the information button.

Well, well. Benazepril was an ACE inhibitor used to treat high blood pressure.

I took a photo of the plain caplets and sent it to Pill ID. After analyzing for maybe twenty seconds, the screen displayed the message "unable to identify."

I sat back in my chair and took another long drink of Cheerwine. Merry stared at me with a less-than-patient look.

"I'm sorry," I said. "Just let me get this put away." With the pencil, I scraped the pills back into the bottle.

"What's with the pills?"

"That's what I'd like to know."

"You're not going to tell me, are you?"

"Not until I know if they're important." I returned both bottles to the evidence bag, and locked it in my desk.

"Fine." Merry sipped her drink. "Where should we start looking for evidence of the man in the locket?"

"Well, whatever this relationship was, it was a secret. We won't find pictures of him in her albums or on the wall in the sunroom. So I guess we start in her room."

We finished our drinks and started up the stairs. I didn't tell Merry I'd already searched most of Gram's room. There was a chance I'd missed something. Two sets of eyes and all that. "I'll take the closet."

"I'll take the dresser." Merry spoke in a near whisper.

"This the first time you've been in here?"

She nodded.

I hugged her and rubbed her arms. Then we went to work.

We searched in silence, each alone with our own memories. The closet was a large walk-in affair, roughly the size of a studio apartment. There were built-in drawers and shelves, along with several hanging bars of various heights and lengths. I started at the front left, and was halfway down that side, examining every bag, box, basket and drawer for anything that might provide a clue when I noticed several hatboxes on the top shelf, pushed to the back. I used a small stepstool and climbed up to examine them. The first two had, of all things, hats. The third proved much more interesting.

I carried the box back into the bedroom and settled into one of the comfortable chairs in front of the fireplace. "Come check this out."

"What did you find?"

"Letters."

Merry abandoned the dressing table. "From who?" She sat down in the matching chair across from me and reached into the hatbox to see for herself.

I had been scanning the first letter I pulled out. I gasped and lowered the letter to meet Merry's gaze. "Stuart Devlin."

FORTY-FIVE

I swung open the door to The Cracked Pot with more than customary urgency, sending the doorbells into a fierce clanging. Both Moon Unit and Alma Glendawn nearly jumped a foot straight up from their perches on opposite sides of the counter.

"Hey, y'all—" Moon Unit started towards us.

"Hey, Moon Unit, Alma. Listen, we'd just like to look at your pictures for a minute if that's okay." I eased past them to the photo collage. Merry smiled, waved, and followed.

"Well, sure. You looking for anybody in particular?" Moon Unit asked. She and her mamma followed us to the back wall.

"Stuart Devlin. The most recent picture you have."

"Well, honey, that would be close to twenty-five years old. You remember Stuart passed on a while back?" Moon Unit looked at me like maybe I was Not Quite Right.

"I was only six at the time, so I don't remember what he looked like. Do you have a picture of him up here?" I asked.

"Oh, my yes. Several." Moon Unit studied the floor-to-ceiling photo array of decades of island life. "I guess this is probably the last one taken of him." She pointed to a picture of three men and three women dressed in evening attire, and posing for the picture in front of what appeared to be the Devlin home. "That was taken the night of the Rose Ball in 1986. I was too young to remember it, of course, but I believe this was only a week or two before he died, right, Mamma?"

Alma looked at the photograph that Moon Unit was pointing to. She smiled wistfully. "We danced until after one in the morning. The Rose Ball is one of Charleston's most ritzy annual charity events."

She stepped closer to the picture, and touched the Plexiglas. "We rode back to the island in Stuart's speedboat, flying across the moonlit water, laughing as the salt spray hit us in our faces. That night we felt like teenagers again. Afterward we walked up the beach to The Pirates' Den. John opened the kitchen and fixed breakfast for us in his tuxedo. It was one of the happiest times of my life.

"We all looked quite spiffy, didn't we?" For a moment she was lost in the memory, and no one disturbed her reverie. Smiling through the unshed tears, she continued. "That's Stuart," she pointed to the tall dark-haired man on the far left of the picture, "and Kate, of course, and Ben and Emma Rae, and that's John and me. Two weeks later, Stuart was dead."

"Do you think that's him?" Merry asked.

I studied the picture carefully. "Yes, I'm almost positive. Can we borrow this for a little while?" I asked Moon Unit.

"Well, sure, I guess, but what in the world..." Moon Unit opened the hinged Plexiglas panel that helped preserve her pictorial island history and removed the picture.

"I'll explain it to you later. Right now we've got to find Blake."

"He's over at the station," Alma offered. "He was walking in over there with Michael Devlin when I passed by on my way here."

"Thank you so much, both of you." I smiled at them as I moved towards the door. Merry was already three steps in front of me.

Distant thunder rolled across the sky.

FORTY-SIX

Colleen waited for us in the backseat of the Escape. When I climbed into the driver's seat, she put her hand on my shoulder. I couldn't exactly feel it, but I saw her through the corner of my eye, and I was becoming more in tune to her presence. Merry slid in on the passenger side.

I'd been so excited to discover who Elvis's phantom, my prowler, and Gram's beau actually was, that at first, it hadn't hit me what that meant. I sat there behind the wheel thinking about Michael.

Merry tapped the dash with her palm. "Liz? Let's go talk to Blake. What are you waiting for?"

"You heard what Alma said. Michael's with him."

Merry started to say something, then bit back whatever it was. "Oh." She sat back in her seat. "Oh."

"Yeah."

"I need to think about how to handle this. The bottom line is, who killed Gram? I don't want to cause unnecessary pain. Stuart *seems* like a great guy. Elvis said he was praying at Gram's grave. Either he's a complete psychopath or he's completely innocent. Then, there's Kate and Michael to consider. They just lost Adam. They've thought Stuart was dead for twenty-five years. I don't know what the story is there, but unless it connects to Gram's death, we've got no business meddling in it."

"What a hot mess."

It was indeed that. And it reminded me of another touchy area I wasn't sure I should wade into. Merry's name on Gram's list. I looked down at my hands. "Merry?"

"What?"

"Don't take this wrong, okay?"

"O-*kaaaay*."

"Remember last night, when we were talking about how Adam would need leverage with at least four town council members after they found out about the resort?"

"Yeah, why?"

"Can you think of *anything* they could have used against Daddy?"

Merry turned to stare out the passenger window. After a moment, she said, "I can think of something they might have tried to blackmail him with."

"Something I don't know about?" I'd been so sure Merry and I didn't have any secrets from each other.

"Some things you don't talk about over the phone. Or bring up when you only have a few hours together."

I waited.

"Six months ago, one of my kids got into trouble. Serious trouble. His name was Jeremy. He was a sad case, been from one foster home to another most of his life. Abused, neglected. But such a sweet kid, you know? And smart. One day his latest foster mother ties up one of the younger kids, a seven-year-old girl, and puts her in a closet. The little girl cries. The bitch stuffs a rag in her mouth and shoves her back in the closet. She's afraid of the dark." Tears rolled down Merry's cheeks. "Jeremy was twelve. He'd been in that closet before. When he tried to let her out, the foster mother starts beating him with a cane. Jeremy snapped. He fought back, took the cane away from her. She ended up dead from a crushed larynx. Jeremy caught a ride over to Isle of Palms, took the ferry and came to me. The police were looking for him everywhere. It was all over the news. You probably heard about it."

"I did, but I had no idea he was one of your kids."

"I couldn't turn him in. He'd been in trouble before. They were talking about trying him as an adult. He hid out at my place for three days. I was harboring a fugitive. Probably could be charged with aiding and abetting and who knows what all."

"But he turned himself in, right? I read about it in the paper."

"I was desperate. I went to Daddy and asked him for the money to hire Jeremy a lawyer—a good one. A public defender would've talked him into pleading out."

"And?"

"Daddy made a donation to Teen Council for Jeremy's defense."

Merry turned to look at me. "Then Daddy hid Jeremy under a tarp in the back of his pickup and drove him back to Charleston and dropped him off at the lawyer's. They arranged for Jeremy to turn himself in."

"Has he gone to trial?"

"No." Merry smiled. "Those lawyers earned their fee. They raised all hell with DSS. By the time they were through, the District Attorney's Office looked like they were abusing kids, too. All charges were dropped. Jeremy's in a good home now, and so are the four other kids that were living with that monster. But Adam could have threatened to go to the authorities and tell them Jeremy was with me for three days. I could've been in real trouble."

"How would he have known?"

"Kristen." Both of us spoke at the same time.

"She acted cool about it at the time," Merry said. "I never told her Jeremy was the kid in the news, just that he was one of my kids. But his picture was everywhere."

"Did Gram know about this?" She must have—that would explain Merry's name on Gram's list.

"Daddy might have told her. I didn't."

"Interesting."

"What?"

"Adam wanted to pursue blackmailing Daddy, but Scott vetoed it."

"Huh. Scott knows Daddy well enough to know he'd never be blackmailed."

"I guess. But he must have had four other votes wrapped up if he had a card he could choose not to play."

Merry sucked in a deep breath and blew it out, making her lips vibrate in a *pflubbbbb* noise. "I need a drink and a bubble bath."

Colleen patted my arm. "You need to go soak a while, too. Take some aspirin, and that nap you never got around to this morning. That was a nasty fall you took out of that tree."

FORTY-SEVEN

I took Colleen's advice: bubble bath, nap, and aspirin. Then I accepted Michael's dinner invitation. In the wake of his brother's death and the preceding adultery-related blow-up between the two of them, Michael needed a friend. One he wouldn't have to explain things to. I suspected he had other things on his mind as well. My emotions were a jumble, and I didn't have the luxury of time to sort them out just then. But I had questions for Michael.

We were at The Pirates' Den, tucked away in a corner table with a great view of the ocean. It was a hard question to ask the man you've been in love with your whole adult life, especially given our recent history, but it had to be asked. "Do you think it's possible your father's alive?"

Michael choked on his margarita. "What would make you ask that?"

Thunder, no longer distant, rolled from south to north and back.

"I think I had coffee with him this morning."

"And where exactly did you and Dad have coffee?"

"On his sailboat."

"His sailboat." Michael dipped his chin and looked at me from under raised brows. "Are you seeing ghosts now?"

Oh boy. We weren't going there. "I went for a walk, early this morning, before breakfast. I walked past the marina and he was out on his boat, stretching. Something about him was so familiar." I squelched an impulse to reach for Michael's hand. "It's obvious to me now why. You have his eyes and his build."

"Liz, this is crazy. Why would he pretend to be dead for twenty-five years and show up the same day Adam is killed? Do you know how insane that sounds?"

"I don't have any idea why, but Gram knew he was alive."

"How do you know that?"

Before I could answer, Blake pulled up a chair. "Mind if I join you?" Blake raised his hand to our waitress. She made her way across the room. "Another glass and a pitcher of margaritas, please, Casey."

Blake leaned back in his chair and sighed. "Long day." He nodded at me. "Coop radioed me the minute he discovered you and Merry snuck out on him. What did you do, drive through the backyard?"

"I was careful of Mamma's flowers."

He shook his head.

"Hey," I said. "Did you ever talk to the mayor and the council members?"

"Some of them." He nodded. "As you mentioned, the mayor's wife never did study art history at Converse College. Mildred got her degree in exotic dancing. Mayor would've done about anything to keep that quiet. And I gave him my word that I would."

Michael took a long drink from his glass.

"And," Blake said, "Mackie in fact has some gambling-related financial problems that most likely would've been used to convince him to fill Grace's seat and vote any way Adam wanted. But we'll never know for sure."

John Glendawn delivered the margaritas himself. He placed the large pitcher in the middle of the table and set a glass down in front of Blake. A few seconds later, John was back with a large platter of chilled shrimp. "This'll hold you for a while." We smiled tired, grateful smiles and handed around plates.

"I got several interesting emails this afternoon," Blake said quietly.

"All the evidence you need should be there."

"I'm not sure how admissible it will be. You were obviously breaking and entering into his hotel room," Blake said.

Out of nowhere, Merry dropped into a chair and popped a shrimp into her mouth. "We were not. Alicia gave us the key."

"But you were uninvited."

"No we weren't," I said. "He specifically invited me." As soon as the words were out of my mouth, I regretted them.

Michael tensed beside me.

I looked directly at him, but spoke to the table. "Everyone here knows how much I detest Scott Andrews. We were there to look for evidence, which we found. As a legal point, however, he gave me an open invitation. And, he hasn't changed the password on his computer. He is well aware I know it."

"You should have seen how she got us out of there—" Merry laughed.

I kicked her under the table. I didn't know yet what the future held for Michael and me. But I didn't want him believing I'd been cavorting with my ex-husband, a man Michael despised.

Blake said, "Michael and I did some research this afternoon. Get this. The board of directors for the New Life Foundation of South Carolina consists of Scott, Adam, and Marci. The majority stock holder is New Life Resorts, which is a whole different animal."

Michael said, "It's a chain of luxury resorts, with a twist. All of their properties are in remote areas, and they are into that New Age stuff. I think Shirley McClain might've done some of their ads. They sell this back-to-nature, cure-what-ails-you, and talk-to-your-dead-relatives kind of package to the enlightened wealthy set."

Blake said, "Adam was apparently willing to do about anything to bring one of their properties to Stella Maris."

John pulled up a chair and piled some shrimp on a plate for himself. "I can vouch for that."

Four versions of surprised look stared at him.

"What do you mean?" Blake asked.

"He tried to blackmail me to vote for the damned fool idea," John said.

"How?" I asked. "With what?" I couldn't fathom what would make John Glendawn vulnerable to blackmail. It couldn't be something that happened when he was a kid.

John snorted. "He seemed to be sufferin' under the notion that because of that trouble Stuart and me got into three lifetimes ago with Hayden Causby that he could threaten to hide some drugs here, and then phone in an anonymous tip and have me busted. Seemed to think folks would believe I was running drugs out of the restaurant. I never intended go along, but I'm sure he thought I would."

"Why didn't you say something?" I asked.

John shrugged. "I figured if he tried that stunt, I'd just tell the truth and let Blake here sort it out. I'm an old man. It just seemed too farfetched anyone would take me for a drug dealer. Now maybe that was risky, but that's the way I was gonna play it."

"Looks like he thought he had a lock on several votes." Blake gave me a sideways glance. "But they didn't count on Liz moving home."

I shook my head. "I'm not sure they ever counted on the Simmons vote. For sure, that's the way Marci wanted things to go down, and it would have benefitted Adam, given him more leverage. But I'm not convinced that was ever part of the plan. Scott was too unconcerned about me being here, taking the seat."

Merry said, "He just thought he could handle you." She smothered a grin.

Blake shook his head. "They were looking to develop Devlin land. If they weren't after Gram's vote, why would they kill her?"

I set down my glass. "I'm not sure they did."

"You think somebody else had a completely different motive?"

"I'm not sure yet," I said. I didn't want to get into that just then. I was still processing the possibilities. "But if her murder wasn't part of their scheme, by process of elimination, the other council member being blackmailed would have to be Robert."

The table was quiet for a few moments while we chewed on that thought along with our shrimp. Casey arrived to take our dinner orders. Craving comfort food, I ordered my favorite, shrimp and grits. Most everyone else went with the lowcountry boil, a regional concoction of shrimp, andouille sausage, corn on the cob, potatoes and whatever else John felt like throwing in the pot, cooked in beer and spices. One of the house specialties.

"What I don't get is who killed Adam?" Michael said. "It doesn't make sense it was one of his partners."

"Sure it does," I said. I stopped myself. I was too tired to filter my mouth. Anything related to Deanna's involvement with Troy and everything Colleen was off limits.

Blake said, "It could've been one of them. Everyone he was blackmailing also had a motive, but I'd bet my last dollar none of them are killers." He raised an eyebrow at John. "I'm also betting they have alibis."

John set down his glass. "I was here until after 2:00 a.m. It takes a while to put this place to bed. A couple of the boys who work in the kitchen were here. Besides, I told you, I wasn't playing his game."

"No offense," Blake said. "I'm just checking off my list. That's what they pay me for."

John nodded.

"So." Michael stared at his margarita. "Looks like the three remaining mysteries are: Did Adam and Scott have your grandmother killed, what did they have on Robert, and who killed my brother? I swear it wasn't me, my solid motive and lack of alibi notwithstanding."

Michael picked up his drink, then paused, glass midair, and met Blake's gaze. "Another thing I don't get is how he thought he was going to get this by Mamma. I mean, after she donated the land, was he just going to turn around and say, 'Guess what, you've been had?' Mamma was dead-set against any resort. She would've had twenty lawyers on top of that, screaming fraud."

I said, "Adam must've thought of that. No doubt he had a contingency plan. Whatever it was, we may never know."

Michael shrugged. "True."

Casey delivered dinner. We were all famished, and a contented silence settled over the table while we dug into our entrées. When I came up for air, I nudged Blake. "I know the whole state is looking for Troy by now, but what about Scott?"

"I had Sam swing by the hotel an hour ago. He wasn't there, but he hadn't checked out, either. Alicia's supposed to call if he comes back. I had Nell send out an APB on him, too. At the least, he's involved in a conspiracy to commit murder, attempted murder, and blackmail."

I breathed a sigh of relief. "He was still on the island as of early this afternoon, and he had no reason to leave. He had no clue we were on to him."

Merry smirked. "Yeah, Liz did a good job of convincing him of that."

Merry was fortunate I had not yet developed the ability to fire death rays from my eyes.

"He'll turn up," Blake said. "He's too arrogant to believe us backwoods yokels would figure out what he's up to."

"What about his flunky?" I asked. "David Morehead."

"We have an APB out on him, too. But no one's seen him since

Tuesday night. He could be anywhere by now."

Michael put down his fork and napkin and looked at Blake. "Liz and I were going to head back to Mamma's. Check on her and Deanna and the girls. You want to come along, see if Deanna is up to talking?"

"Are you about ready?" Blake glanced at Michael.

"Whenever you are."

John stood and gathered a tray full of dishes. "I'm just going to check on things in the kitchen."

As soon as John was out of earshot, Merry turned to Michael. "Michael, would you ride with us over to Blake's office for a minute, please?"

"*What?*" Blake scowled.

"Merry," I said through gritted teeth. "I've already spoken to Michael about this."

Michael looked from me to Merry. "I don't understand."

"I wondered if you'd take a look at my grandmother's locket, at the picture inside," Merry said.

"Why?" Michael and Blake spoke at the same time.

I put my hand on Michael's arm. "This is what I started to tell you. We think the man in the picture is your father."

"What?"

"This is too much, even from the two of you." Blake slid back his chair.

"Just listen. Merry and I went over to Gram's this afternoon. We were looking for something that would give us an idea of who this man in the locket is. What we found was...most unexpected. There was a large box filled with letters. Love letters, going back about fifteen years."

"From who?" Michael asked.

"They were each signed 'All my love, Stuart.'"

Michael shrugged. "That's a common name."

"Yes, but...well, we read a few of the letters." I pulled one of the letters from my purse and offered it to Michael.

Michael stared at me wordlessly. He did not reach for letter.

Merry plowed ahead. "Unless there was another Stuart who lived on Stella Maris until twenty-five years ago, who knew Gram, and had children named Adam and Michael, who was married to a Kate, then your father is alive."

FORTY-EIGHT

The storm that had threatened all evening settled in just after dark. Blake, Michael, Merry and I dashed across the parking lot of The Pirates' Den through the driving rain and jumped into Michael's Jeep Cherokee. Michael grasped the steering wheel tightly with both hands for a moment, and then started the engine and turned on the headlights and windshield wipers.

From out of nowhere, a figure covered from head to toe in a hooded, yellow rain slicker appeared on a bicycle in front of the Jeep. The rider skidded to a stop just before Michael put the car in gear. "What the devil?" He rolled down his window as the figure abandoned his bike where it lay and ran up to the side of the Jeep.

"Michael," Elvis yelled. "Where's Chief Blake?"

Blake leaned across the console. "Right here, Elvis. What's wrong?"

"I almost missed you," Elvis said. "Miss Nell told me you were over here having dinner. I couldn't get you on the radio."

"I guess I didn't hear it in the restaurant, Elvis. *What's wrong?*"

"It's the Phantom. I trailed him back to where he lives. I just saw him. He's on this pretty boat down at the marina. I had him staked out. But Miss Nell wouldn't call you. Hurry, before he leaves." Elvis started moving back towards his bike.

"That's him." I reached around the seat and grabbed Michael's arm. "That's the guy I had coffee with this morning. That's Stuart Devlin. It's got to be. Go, Michael."

Merry reached over and slapped Michael several times on the shoulder for emphasis.

Blake said, "Elvis, go inside and get dry. Your mamma will skin me alive if I let you go chasing off in this rain."

"But Chief Blake—" Elvis protested.

"I'll go over there right now and check it out, okay? Good job, buddy. You did a real good job. Now go inside."

"You'll go right now?" Elvis asked.

"I'm on my way," Blake said.

Michael rolled up the window. We waited long enough to see Elvis pick up his bike and head towards the front door of the restaurant.

"Will you please step on it?" Merry slapped Michael's shoulder again.

"Esmerelda, if you don't stop beating Michael like your mule I will get out of this car and open your door and physically remove you from the backseat and place you, none too gently, on the asphalt." Even as Blake said the words, Michael backed out of the parking place and headed towards the marina.

"No." Colleen appeared between Merry and me. "Deanna's in trouble. She went home. You have to go there now. " As suddenly as she had appeared, she vanished.

"I think we should see about Deanna first," I said. "She might have decided to go home. We should go on over there now, before it gets any later. Then we can go by the marina."

Michael didn't take his eyes off the road. "No," he said. "We settle this now."

"Michael, please. I've got a bad feeling—"

Blake started dialing his phone. "I'll call and check on things." He spoke to Grace for a few moments, and then hung up. "Deanna got Sam to take her home an hour ago. Said she needed to be alone."

"That's odd she'd leave Holly and Isabella tonight."

Blake shrugged. "The girls are asleep at Kate's. Doc gave them a sedative." He pressed the talk button on his radio. "Sam?"

"Yeah, Blake?" Static distorted Sam's voice.

"You at Adam Devlin's?"

"Right out front."

"Stay there. Call me if you see anyone near that house."

"Roger that."

We drove silently for a few moments, the air inside the car electric with the anticipation. I tried calling Deanna. I knew if Colleen said she was in trouble I needed to get over there fast. But how to make Michael and Blake believe me? "Deanna's not answering, and voicemail didn't pick up. Please, can we just swing by there?"

Michael didn't answer. There was someplace else he had a compelling need to go.

FORTY-NINE

Only moments before, the rain had been coming down so hard the windshield wipers didn't improve visibility. Gradually it subsided to a drizzle. Michael pulled the Jeep into a parking space as close to the dock as possible.

Blake said, "Do you think there's any chance it's him?"

"Oh, I'm dead certain it's him," Michael said simply.

We all stared at him, stunned, for a moment. The windshield wipers squawked across the glass.

"What changed your mind?" I found my voice.

"It's his boat. That's the same boat he left on twenty-five years ago," Michael said. He opened the car door. "Stay here. All of you. For right now, at least, this is between him and me."

Blake, Merry and I were uncharacteristically quiet for a minute after Michael slammed the door and ran down the dock.

Finally, I said, "That's pretty brazen. Stuart must not have been too concerned about being found out if he sailed back home on the same boat that was supposedly lost at sea."

Blake shrugged. "Not many people would recognize it after all this time."

I thought about it. "Someone might have thought there was a boat in the marina that *looked* a lot like Stuart's old boat, but who would dream it was really him?"

"Let me see that letter." Blake cracked his door to turn on the interior light.

I handed it to him. He read for a few moments.

"I don't know which I'm more shocked about," Blake said. "That Stuart Devlin is alive, or that Gram had a love affair with him for what, fifteen years?"

"Here comes Michael," I said.

Michael climbed back into the Jeep. "We missed him."

"What now?" Blake asked.

"Let's go check on Deanna." I remembered the urgency in Colleen's voice. I had to get to Deanna's house.

"Not tonight," Michael said.

"Agreed," said Blake. "I say we wait for your Dad to show up."

I opened the door and hopped out. "Y'all wait here if you like. I'm going to Deanna's." I took off running while they were still deciding if I was serious.

FIFTY

I hesitated at the edge of the marina parking lot. The marina is on the northwest side of the island. Sea Farm, Deanna's neighborhood, is on the southeast point. I was roughly seven miles from her. Even if I ran through yards and hopped hedges, it would take me at least an hour to run it—the town was an obstacle course between us. My car was at Mamma and Daddy's house. It would be quicker to run home and get Gram's Caddy.

I darted up Marsh View drive as the rain began to grow heavier. Within five minutes I was on the front porch. I retrieved my spare key from inside the bell of a wind chime and let myself in. Rhett trotted out to meet me and I ran right past him. I pulled up short in the hall. Stuart had taken Gram's spare set of keys from the kitchen drawer. My keys were in my purse, in the back of Michael's Jeep. *Damnation.*

I'd violated my own cardinal rule: I'd left my gun, my phone and my keys behind. I had no means of protection, and no means of communication once I left Gram's house. Dammit. Think. *Think.*

The van. The keys to Granddad's van were in his desk. My desk. I bolted into the office and flipped on the light. Rhett chased after me. The keys were in the top drawer. I grabbed them and headed towards the kitchen. Through the mudroom and down the steps I flew. Rhett followed, barking admonishments.

I climbed into the van with a prayer it would start. After a little encouragement, it roared to life. I pressed the button on the remote clipped to the visor to open the garage door. When it was high enough to clear the van, I backed out, threw the van in drive, and hit the accelerator.

Rain now poured from the sky in buckets. I fumbled for the windshield wipers. When they came on, I swerved to miss a palm tree. Even with the wipers on, I could barely see ten feet in front of me. At the end of the driveway, I turned left down Ocean Boulevard. Palmetto would have been a shorter route, but would have had more traffic, and several stoplights I didn't dare run in this weather.

At the end of Ocean Boulevard, just before Devlin's Point, I turned right and navigated through a series of side streets towards Pearson's Point—the point of the island where Sea Farm had been built. I was almost halfway down Pitt Street when a Jack Russell terrier bolted in front of the van. I slammed on brakes.

A blinding white bolt split the oak on the corner. Thunder, combined with the simultaneous crack of the lightning strike nearly deafened me. The oak exploded, branches flying in every direction. The trunk split, half of it falling directly in front of the van, the other half landing in someone's front yard. In the headlights, debris fluttered to the ground. The end of a sizeable limb rested inches from my windshield.

Had I not braked for the dog, the van and I would have been under the shattered tree trunk.

To stave off hyperventilation, I took slow, measured breaths.

I couldn't drive around it. I backed up to try another route. The van sputtered and stalled, as if on cue. Hopping in the seat to encourage it, I turned the key. The engine made a grinding noise, then fell silent. I climbed out. I was close enough now to make a run for it.

The quickest route was straight down the beach to Sea Farm, then into the neighborhood. Deanna's house was only three blocks off the water. When I hit the beach, I took off my shoes and ran as hard as I could, staying close to the water where the sand was firm. Lightning split the night sky, severing it from pole to pole, and rendering me momentarily blind. I kept running. The rain soaked my clothes. By the time I turned off the beach, my knit top and jeans had absorbed so much water I felt like I was weighted down by chains.

I stopped to catch my breath, hands on my knees and breathing hard, under the porch of the first house I came to. I wrung as much water as I could out of my shirt and darted up the street.

Colleen waited for me on Deanna's back porch. "Troy." She pointed at the broken pane in the back door.

I shivered. The last time Colleen and I encountered Troy in a house at night someone ended up dead.

I darted off the porch and around to the front of the house. Sam Manigault should've been parked out front. But he wasn't. Michael, Blake and Merry should've beaten me here in the car. Clearly, Michael didn't start the Jeep and peel out right behind me, or he'd have caught up with me before I got out of the marina parking lot. But *surely* they eventually followed me. But the street in front of the house and the driveway were empty. I pulled up short. No time to think about it. I doubled back, slipped in the back door, and closed it silently behind me.

The shrill ring of the phone startled me.

Footsteps. Someone was in the foyer.

I tiptoed from the kitchen, through the dining room, and stopped at the edge of the foyer. I leaned back sharply. Troy was just ahead of me. He stood at the entrance to the living room. Beyond him, Deanna sat calmly on the sofa, sipping tea. She didn't look surprised to see Troy.

The phone rang again. She sat her teacup down and reached for the portable phone on the coffee table.

"Don't answer that." He waved his gun at her.

Damnation. I needed my gun.

She shrugged. "If I don't, the police will be here in five minutes. You tripped the alarm when you broke the window."

"D—"

"Don't swear in my home," she ordered calmly, like she was talking to a sassy kid.

He wavered. "Answer it. Tell them you set it off accidentally and everything is fine. Screw it up and I'll shoot you first, and then go upstairs and visit with your daughters."

Deanna stared him down and reached for the phone. "Hello... Oh, yes, I'm sorry. I set it off accidentally. It was stupid of me... Rubber Duck... Thanks, you, too." She pressed 'end' and laid the phone back on the coffee table.

Troy said, "Now get me my money and I'll be on my way. Nobody has to get hurt."

"Why on earth would I give you money?"

"Don't play games with me, lady. I did the job, just like you asked, now I want my money."

Before Deanna could form a response to his demand, the lights flickered. Then the house went completely black. A glance out the window told me the streetlights were out, too. The storm had taken out the power. I blinked, willing my eyes to adjust to the darkness. Lightning briefly illuminated the room. Troy hadn't moved. I prayed Deanna realized she had the advantage now. She knew this house and he didn't. She needed to move. If he couldn't see her, he couldn't shoot her. All she had to do was to stay alive until the cavalry arrived.

I was only a few steps from the front door. The stairs were behind me. I stole over to the door. I waited for the thunder, then closed my eyes and bit my lip as I disengaged the deadbolt and the knob-lock. Either we'd need a fast way out or Blake and Michael would need a fast way in. I backed up the stairs, out of the foyer. I was poised to stage a distraction if help didn't arrive soon.

Deanna said, "Not only did I *not* ask you to kill my husband, I specifically told you no one was to get hurt."

"We both know what you meant."

Deanna sounded firm, not scared. It must have been the shock. "I can only assume in your messed up criminal mind, you mistook what I asked you to do, which was to *follow* my husband. Nothing I said can be construed by any reasonable person to have been a contract for murder."

Troy said, "I'm not gonna stand here and argue with you. Get me the money. Or your little girls are going to grow up without a mommy, but with some interesting memories from this evening's entertainment."

Something in the kitchen clattered. They both froze. My ears strained to determine its source. A bolt of lightning revealed the dripping wet figure stepping into the foyer. Troy now stood between the figure and Deanna. He took a step to his right and waved the gun back and forth from one to the other in the dark.

"What I can't figure out," the newcomer said, "is why you're trying to collect payment for a job you didn't do."

Stuart Devlin. What was he doing here?

"What is this?" Troy demanded.

Stuart said, "I was there. You didn't kill anybody."

FIFTY-ONE

While Stuart had Troy distracted, I came down the steps and backed out of the foyer. I didn't think Stuart or Deanna had seen me, but the main thing was Troy hadn't. I circled back through the dining room and into the kitchen. Crouching low, I scanned the family room for Deanna. The lightning flashes were coming closer together, making it difficult for my eyes to adjust to the dark. I shivered in my soaked clothes.

Desperation rose in Troy's voice, eerily disembodied by the pitch dark. "Look, I don't know exactly what you wanted done. And I don't know who the hell this guy is. But I know you offered me twenty-five grand to do *something,* so you must have the cash handy. Get it," he growled menacingly.

Thunder crashed over our heads. Lightning lit the room long enough for me to realize that Troy was advancing on Deanna.

Colleen appeared across the room in a silvery-lit aura. "Over here," she cried.

I darted across the room, bumped into a table and knocked over a lamp. I dove behind a chair just as Troy fired a shot in my direction. My stomach roiled at the *pfft* sound.

"Who's there?" Troy yelled.

"Tell him you're Merry's ghost," Colleen said.

My voice sounded enough like hers. He'd fall for it. "It's me Troy, Merry." I peered around the edge of the chair.

"Merry?" Lightning flashed. Troy took a step in my direction. Horror fought with wonder on his face.

"Is that the same gun you shot me with, Troy?"

"*Merry*...baby, I swear I never meant to hurt you."

"You never meant to roll me in a rug, shoot me in the head, and bury me at a construction site, Troy?"

"It was Kristen. It was all her fault."

In a flicker of lightning, I saw movement behind Troy. Stuart was creeping up behind him, poised to pounce. Troy must have sensed him approaching. He spun around and raised his gun.

I screamed as the next shot rang out. Stuart fell to the floor. Troy turned and fired again in my direction.

"You can't kill me twice, Troy." I laughed wildly.

Thunder crashed and lightning exposed the fear on his face. "What do you want?"

"Leave here. Leave Deanna alone."

For a moment, all I heard was the rain.

"No," he said. "I want my money. Now." Simultaneous thunder and lightning punctuated his demand. Through the strobe of lightning, he moved towards Deanna.

I picked up the lamp I'd knocked over and threw it at him. I missed by a couple of feet, but he turned towards the crash.

The lightning came so quickly now that the room was almost continuously lit.

Standing, Deanna raised a revolver. Hell's bells, Deanna had a gun?

Troy looked back just in time to register surprise.

"No!" Stuart and I shouted at once.

The blast was so loud I felt it in my teeth.

Troy crumpled to the floor.

A pungent cocktail of nitroglycerin, sawdust, and graphite hung in the air.

Stuart jumped up.

"You're all right." I'd been certain he'd had been shot.

Stuart said, "I'm fine. I ducked just in time. He thought he got me."

Stuart knelt by Troy. I stepped towards Deanna.

"No pulse," said Stuart.

"Oh my Lord," Deanna said. "I...I didn't mean to fire the gun. I only wanted to scare him off."

I put an arm around Deanna. "Hey there."

"Hey, Liz." Deanna sounded deceptively calm, as if her limit for shock had been overdrawn.

Stuart crossed the room. He took the gun from Deanna and tucked it in the back of his pants. "It was a reflex," he said. "He threatened your children."

Deanna tilted her head sideways. "Who are you?

He sighed. "There's no time to explain everything to you now, but I'm your father-in-law. I'm Stuart Devlin."

"Oh, mmm-kay." Deanna nodded. She sat down on the sofa. "Adam's dead. His also-dead father just helped Merry's ghost distract the now-dead hit man enough for me to shoot him." She wept loudly. "I didn't know Merry was dead."

I sat beside her. "Merry's fine, Deanna. Troy just thought he hurt her. I pretended to be her ghost to distract him."

"That was smart." Deanna smiled through her tears.

"Thanks." I smiled back at her.

Colleen hovered behind the sofa, arms draped across her sister's shoulders. "That's fine, take the credit."

"Hello, Liz." Stuart looked at me, and then knelt on Deanna's other side and spoke softly, looking her in the eyes. "You don't know me. You have no reason to trust me. But I'm here to help you."

Deanna rested her head in her hands.

Someone pounded on the front door. "Deanna?" Blake called out.

"In here," I called out.

Stuart stood. The door slammed open. Blake, Michael and Merry dashed into the family room. They all stopped just short of stumbling over Troy and each other as the next flash of lightning revealed the body on the floor.

Merry gasped.

"What the hell?" Michael stared at his father in disbelief.

Stuart handed the gun to Blake by the barrel. "He's dead. He left her no choice. He threatened Deanna and the girls."

"Who are you?" Blake took the gun and stepped closer.

"I'm Stuart Devlin. My boat is docked over at the marina. I'm just in from the Virgin Islands for a few weeks. Personal business..." His voice trailed off as he looked at Michael.

Blake spoke into his handheld and called for backup, Doc Harper, and the crime scene techs. "We need more light in here," he said.

Deanna said, "There are two Coleman lanterns on the top shelf of the pantry."

Blake jerked his head in the direction of the kitchen. "Merry."

Deanna looked up at Merry. "I'm so glad you're all right."

Merry gave me a questioning look on her way to the kitchen. "I'm glad you're okay, too, Deanna."

Blake looked at Deanna. "*Are* you all right?"

"Y-yes."

"Whose gun is this?"

"It's mine," Deanna said.

Blake scrutinized her. "I see. And you had it handy, did you, when Troy came by for a surprise visit?"

Stuart said, "Her husband was killed only this—"

"I'd rather hear from Deanna, if you don't mind."

Merry stepped back into the room. She set the lanterns on opposite sides of the room. The fluorescent light added to the otherworldly ambience.

Deanna gestured towards Troy. "The alarm company called when he opened the door. I gave them the panic code. You guys got here quick." She looked at Blake.

Blake shook his head, confused. "We never got the call. I guess the alarm company couldn't get through. The phone lines must have gone out right after they called you. We've got trees down on Ocean Boulevard and Palmetto."

"But then, why are you here?" Deanna asked.

Blake stared at me. "Something just told us you needed help."

I said, "Where is Sam Manigault? Wasn't he supposed to be out front?"

Blake rubbed the back of his neck and winced. "Communication failure. He's in front of Kate Devlin's house."

"What took you guys so long?"

Blake gave me a look of exaggerated patience. "Like I said, trees down on Ocean and Palmetto. Live power lines are across the road in two places. We had to drive around the carnage, twice. Deanna, exactly what happened here?"

"I sh-sh-*shot h-h-h-im.*" Deanna's face drew together. She covered it with her hands and sobbed.

Michael was still staring at his father. "Why?" he asked.

Stuart sighed. "The answer is quite complicated. Perhaps we could discuss it later."

"Perhaps." Michael glared at him. "And then again, maybe it really doesn't matter why."

Blake raised his hand in a halt motion. "Getting back to the body on the floor, just for a moment, can I get some agreement please between the parties present at the time as to how Troy Causby came to be dead?"

Deanna had stopped sobbing, but seemed to be in some sort of post-traumatic state. She stared, glassy-eyed, at thin air in front of her.

Blake cocked his head sideways, sighed, and rubbed the back of his neck.

"He broke in," I said. "He wanted money. He was desperate, Blake. I showed up, then Stuart. Troy shot at both of us. He was coming at Deanna. He threatened to kill her—I heard him—and do worse to the girls. So she shot him. If I had my gun, I would have shot him. He fired three shots, one at Stuart and two at me. The gun is probably underneath him."

Stuart nodded. "It was as she said."

"The girls are at Kate's house," Blake said.

"Troy didn't know that," I said. "What would have stopped him from going there next? Deanna killed him in self-defense."

Blake asked, "Any idea why Troy picked your house, Deanna, to break into and demand money? Every law enforcement officer in the country is looking for him. You'd think he'd be trying to get as far away from here as possible. Why did he come *here* asking for money?"

Deanna breathed deep. "He had some crazy idea—"

"Can't you shut her up?" Colleen demanded.

I kicked Deanna. "He knew Adam had money in the house, re-member? Adam had hired him?"

Blake stared at Deanna for a long moment. "I need this crime sce-ne cleared, *now*. It's going to take a while to get the forensic team over here. Why don't you spend the night at your mother's house? You can come in tomorrow and I'll take your statement then. It seems to me you might want to sleep on what you have to say." He glanced from Deanna, to Stuart, then to me and shook his head.

Deanna nodded. "Mmm-kay."

Blake turned to me. "Liz, will you and Merry help Deanna get some things together for the night?"

Michael looked at me, but spoke to Blake. "I'll take Deanna to her mom's. Then I can drop Liz and Merry off."

I had a strong suspicion he didn't plan to drop me off at all. Something told me his plan involved spending the night. With a jolt, I remembered Nate should already be there.

Merry picked up the message Michael was sending me and decided to be helpful. "I'll drive Deanna's car and take her to her mom's house. We'll figure the rest out." She stood and gently urged Deanna up.

Blake raked a hand through his hair. "Fine. Michael, would you mind taking Stuart back to the marina? I'll catch a ride with Clay when we're finished here."

A look passed between Blake and Michael that I couldn't decipher. Blake addressed Stuart. "I'll need your statement in the morning, too. Nine o'clock work?"

Stuart nodded. "I'll be there." He turned to Michael. "I can walk back to the dock. That's how I got here."

Michael sighed. "There's a monsoon roaring out there. I'll drop you off."

We stepped out onto the porch. Michael dashed through the pounding rain to open the front passenger door for me. Stuart followed and slid into the backseat. I asked him to hand me my purse, which I'd left on the seat earlier. I slipped my phone out of its compartment and glanced at the screen. I had five missed calls and two voicemails from Nate.

Michael climbed into the driver's seat and slammed the door.

I dashed off a quick text to Nate: Where R U?

He replied: On your front porch.

Relief and something else I couldn't name washed through me. I texted back: Home soon.

Michael gave me a questioning look, but said nothing. He, Stuart and I sat in silence for a moment, listening to the rain hammer the car.

After a moment, Stuart spoke. "If it's answers you want, you'd better stop by the house. Some of them I can give you, but some of them will have to come from your mother."

FIFTY-TWO

Either power had been restored, or the outage had been limited to only part of the island. From the street, it looked like every light in Kate Devlin's house was on. We dashed through the gentled rain: the long-lost father, the angry son, and me, the past and perhaps future girlfriend. Nautical lanterns glowed on either side of the front door. It was as if we'd been expected on that rain-soaked, wind-battered night. Michael unlocked the door, pushed it open, and motioned me inside.

"Michael..." I gave him a pleading look. I didn't belong there.

"If I took you home now, I'd only have to repeat everything later. What's the point?"

"Mamma?" he called out. "Grace?"

"In here, Michael," Kate answered from the kitchen.

Michael led the way towards the back of the house. He stopped, turned, and spoke softly to Stuart. "Wait here. Let me talk to her first. She's fragile. She's had heart problems lately. Seeing you is going to be a shock."

Stuart snorted. "Fragile my eye. If there's one thing Katherine Sullivan Devlin is not, it's fragile." He pushed past Michael and me and into the big warm kitchen. We followed.

She sat on the sofa in front of a roaring fire, with her back to us as we entered the room. "Grace went home before the storm—" Kate stopped talking midsentence, either hearing, or perhaps sensing Michael was not alone. She turned and looked over her shoulder. Her eyes narrowed, the expression on her face pure hatred.

"Hello, Stuart," she said coldly. She turned back around to face the fire as casually as if she'd last seen her husband that morning.

What the hell? I felt like I'd stepped into an alternate reality show.

"Katherine," he nodded to her back. "Michael wants answers. I've agreed to give him the ones I have. You'll have to fill in the rest."

"What the devil are you doing here to begin with? If you'd stayed away, he could have lived the rest of his life in peace believing you were dead. Just like me." She curled her feet underneath her and pulled her quilt tighter. "I've told people you were dead for so long I'd forgotten it was a lie. You've ruined everything."

Michael stared at her in total shock.

The icy, controlled rage came from a stranger, not Kate Devlin. And one thing stood in stark reality: Stuart had spoken the truth. There was nothing remotely fragile about the creature that inhabited her body. She was fresh out of Southern gentility.

I took a step back. My instincts screamed, *Run*.

Michael grabbed my hand and tugged me forward. I balked. He reached back, put his arm around me, and pulled me farther into the room.

Kate sighed. "All of you are soaking wet. You'll drip water everywhere. Michael, get some towels."

Mechanically, Michael did as he was told. He returned with a stack of towels, took one for himself, and offered them to Stuart and me.

"Why don't we all sit down?" Stuart made himself comfortable, spreading a towel on the easy chair next to the fireplace. He blotted his face and hair with another towel and warmed himself by the fire.

Michael took a place on the loveseat and drew me down beside him. Kate arched an eyebrow in my direction, and then tilted her head at Michael.

"She stays," Michael said. He didn't raise his voice, but his tone was layered with steel. She didn't challenge him.

Colleen faded in, on the floor at my feet.

Michael stared at his mother. "You knew he was alive?"

"Of course I knew it," she snapped. "Your father and I came to an agreement—"

"Hold on there," Stuart said. "If we're going to tell this story, we're going to tell it honestly."

The fire crackled. Thunder, more distant now, rumbled low and long. "Why don't I start?" Stuart's eyes dared Kate to object.

She stared him down for a moment, and then averted her haughty gaze to the fire.

Stuart spoke to Michael. "The sad truth is I married your mother on the rebound, forty-six years ago last spring." A range of emotions struggled on his face. "I was desperately in love with someone else. We were young and foolish. I made some bad choices. She married someone else. Life went on."

I slid closer to Michael. Stuart could be telling our story. How had I not known Gram had made the same mistakes I did?

For a few moments, the only sound in the room was the crackling fire.

Stuart leaned forward in his chair. "After college I came home and tried to rebuild my life. I threw myself into work and efforts to protect this island. Your mother and I became friends." He stared at Kate hard. "She was very different then. Perhaps she was adept at playing a role."

Kate sniffed.

"Maybe I fooled myself into believing I loved her. Not the passionate, all-consuming kind of love I'd let slip through my hands, but a companionship. A partnership. I thought it would be enough."

Kate radiated hatred, but remained silent.

"We went about the business of building a family. We were happy enough, or so I thought. We shared our love of our beautiful children. We both loved this place, this island. It could have been enough for a lifetime of contentment."

Were these the kinds of things Michael had told himself after he married Marci the Schemer?

Restless now, Stuart stood to pace. "But it ate at you, didn't it, Kate, that I had loved someone else? I never deceived you. But you just couldn't stand it, could you?"

"I loved you, you sonofabitch," she lashed back at him, her voice dripping venom. "I loved you the way you loved her," Kate said. "I thought you would grow to love me the same way. I deserved that. I picked up the pieces of your broken heart. I gave you sons. Me, not her. But it meant nothing to you. *I* meant nothing to you." Kate glanced at me with loathing, as if I were my grandmother's proxy.

I snuggled up to Michael. Colleen wrapped her arms around my legs. I could almost feel the embrace.

Kate ranted on. "And she was right here. Always right here. Always a part of our lives. It was too much." Kate's anger had built to a crescendo. Abruptly she fell silent and sat back on the sofa, as if the wind had gone out of her. She averted her eyes and seemed to withdraw inside herself.

"In time," Stuart said, "it became obvious we were never going to be anything but miserable. The envy ate at your mother. Day by day, she hated me more. It was corrosive. As you boys grew older, it became harder to keep up the façade. Divorce was inevitable."

Stuart stopped pacing. "But I was certain she was devoted to you children. I couldn't conceive of taking you away from her, even if that had been an option in those days."

He took a deep breath, and looked at Michael, beseeching him to understand what would come next. "I decided to take some time alone to sort things through, figure out how to proceed. I was going to spend a few weeks on the sailboat. It turned into six. I called home and she told me what she'd done."

A satisfied smile crept up Kate's mouth.

Stuart's voice grew ragged. "She told everyone I'd gone out for an afternoon sail and never returned, that I was missing at sea. After the Coast Guard searched for several days in the wrong direction, I was presumed dead. She told me you boys thought I was dead. Had adjusted to it, she said. What's more, she'd already filed a life insurance claim. I was worth more to all of you dead than alive. God help me, I let her convince me to leave it alone. I just never came back. I have regretted that decision every day for the past twenty-five years. Whether or not you can ever believe me or forgive me, I love you very much, and I loved your brother."

Kate turned bright red and appeared to be literally seething. "All you ever cared about was that two-faced whore Emma Rae."

I jerked back, as if slapped.

"*Mamma*," Michael said.

"I did my best to raise these boys by myself. Perhaps you should have been here to help. Perhaps Adam would have been a better man if he'd had a father."

"You didn't give me that choice now did you?"

"You should have loved me. I earned that."

Stuart looked at her sadly, and not unkindly. "Love isn't something you earn, Kate. It's something you feel."

"I once loved you as much as I hate you right now."

Stuart shook his head. "After the children came, you became indifferent to me. Children require a lot of attention, I know. But you were obsessed with them, to the exclusion of everything else. You pushed me away."

"You were too hard on them. You expected too much."

Stuart turned red and raised his voice for the first time. "That's what was wrong with Adam, don't you see that? You never expected enough. You gave him everything. He never worked for anything his entire life. And what did he turn into?"

"Don't you dare sit here in this house after all these years and attack my son. He isn't even buried yet. *Our son is dead.*" She approached a screech.

"I knew the minute I read the account of Emma's death in the paper that Adam had a hand in it. As much as he was given, it was never enough. Always scheming, always trying to make that big pile of money he thought would make him happy."

The smug look on Kate's face struck me as odd.

"Now, hold on just a minute," Michael said. "How do you know anything about us?"

"That was the one condition I gave your mother, the cost of my absence. She wrote me weekly, for twenty-five years. I still have every letter. I know about every touchdown you ever made. And every time she bought Adam's way out of trouble."

Kate sat mute, her gaze averted.

Stuart sat back down. "And then Emma discovered my secret, quite by accident. Or perhaps providence. It was through Emma I knew Adam was trying to wrestle the family land away from you."

"That Jezebel," Kate spat. "How dare she criticize my son? It's her fault he grew up fatherless."

Colleen sensed my growing anger. "Keep quiet," she said. "Let her talk."

And then I knew.

Stuart said, "You can't lay that one at Emma's feet, Katherine. That was your choice and yours alone."

"I guess you're completely innocent, aren't you?" Kate asked.

"That's just like you. You abandon your children and make it my fault."

He met her gaze. "Well, I could have come home, I guess. But if I had, my children would have grown up without a mother instead of without a father, because you, my dear, would have gone to jail for insurance fraud."

Kate glared at him defiantly. "If you had wanted to come home badly enough, you would have found a way."

"Perhaps." Stuart looked at her for a moment. "Lord knows my hands aren't clean. If Adam had been raised differently, he might still be alive. He didn't understand actions have consequences, he never had to face any. His obsession with the almighty dollar led directly to his death, to the death of the finest woman I've ever known, and to that of two of his co-conspirators."

"Do you know who killed Adam?" Michael asked. "What makes you think he killed Emma Rae?"

"When I arrived home shortly after Emma's death, I started investigating. I wanted to verify my suspicions. I felt honor-bound to stop Adam from doing what he seemed determined to do, destroy the quality of life on this island.

"My worst fears were confirmed. I overheard enough of the conversations between him and his partner, Scott Andrews, to know they conspired to either kill or blackmail everyone who stood in their way."

I couldn't help myself. "It was you who broke out of the hardware store, wasn't it?"

"Yes. When you and Deanna left, I was locked in."

"And you broke in to Gram's, looking for the letters."

"I'm sorry I gave the dog Benadryl. At first I wasn't entirely sure he wouldn't bite. But I'd never hurt him."

Michael asked, "How is it Adam never recognized you hanging around?"

"It's been twenty-five years, son. I've changed. Would you have recognized me? If you didn't know first that I was alive? If you weren't looking for me?"

Michael shrugged, then looked away.

"As far as those two were concerned, I was just a scruffy old man in a ball cap hanging around The Pirates' Den. John's a different story."

"John knows you're alive?" Michael asked.

Stuart nodded. "He pegged me the second time I showed up at The Den."

"They talked about this scheme of theirs in public?" Michael asked.

Stuart shrugged. "Some. Sometimes I slipped into the backroom at the hardware store. Sometimes I listened when they talked on Adam's boat. Got me one of those earpieces they give to old people that helps pick up conversations. Like I said, they were going to kill or blackmail everyone who stood in their way."

He leaned back in his chair and watched Kate's face. "Even your mother."

Kate gasped. "How can you say such a thing? Adam would never hurt me. I am his mother. I raised him—"

Stuart said, "What would you have done, Katherine, when you found out Adam conned you, that you signed two hundred acres over to him to build a resort on Devlin's Point?"

Kate looked nauseous. "Michael told me all about that yesterday. I—I simply won't donate the land is all." She straightened and pulled her shoulders back.

"Ah," Stuart said. "And did you speak to Adam about that?"

"I never had the chance. I tried calling him. I would have spoken to him. What difference does it make now?"

"Probably none," Stuart said. "But what do you think his plan was? Adam had to have known you'd fight him. He would have planned ahead for that."

Like a billboard, the word "Benazepril" flashed in my brain. Could Adam kill his own mother?

"Kate," I said.

She turned her head towards me, ever so slowly. Hate radiated in my direction.

"What medication did Doc Harper prescribe for your heart?"

She drew her shoulders even further back. "What concern is that of yours?"

"Was it Benazepril?"

"My personal trials are none of your affair."

"Where's the medicine cabinet?" I started to stand, but Colleen patted my leg. I glanced at her and back at Kate. "We need to check your medications. Make sure you're taking what you think you're taking. Your vitamins, too. If I were you, I'd throw out everything in the house and buy new bottles."

"What are you saying?" Her hand fluttered up to her face.

A silver aura appeared around Colleen.

"Adam tampered with your pills."

Kate's eyes bulged, and her hand fell to her heart. "I don't believe you."

I shrugged. "You don't have to take my word for it. Have it checked out."

Stuart shook his head in disgust. "I knew he'd have killed you, just like he killed Emma Rae."

The light around Colleen shimmered.

Kate bowed back like a cobra. "You don't know everything you think you do, Stuart."

I found my voice. "Adam didn't kill Gram, did he, Kate?"

"Here it comes." Colleen held on tight.

"Why, whatever do you mean?" Kate's voice dripped glee.

My stomach roiled. "It was happening all over again, wasn't it?"

Michael turned to me. "Liz? What..."

"Phoebe showed you Gram's locket, didn't she? When Gram lost it at the day spa? Phoebe didn't know who it belonged to, so she asked all her customers."

Kate narrowed her eyes at me.

"You knew immediately once you saw the picture. And you knew that after all these years Gram and Stuart were back together. She'd won."

Kate's skin took on a blue-white cast. Her breathing became labored.

"And now," I said, "you have to decide."

"Decide what?" she hissed.

"Whether your grandchildren grow up thinking their father was a murderer, or you tell the truth." There was no way to prove what I knew she'd done, and it was not something people would want to believe. She'd have to confess.

Michael said, "Liz, I don't like what you're suggesting."

"Kate?" I said. "What's it going to be? Will Holly and Isabella—

and everyone else on this island—remember Adam, your first born, as a murderer?"

She wheezed and turned away. Her shoulders rose and fell.

Michael leaned towards Kate. "Mamma? Are you all right?"

Stuart said, "I'm almost certain it was Adam. He was abusive to his own family. He was certainly capable of murder. He had motive, means, opportunity. I'm sure after I tell Blake everything I know, he'll have no trouble finding evidence."

Kate jerked her head towards Stuart. She stared at him for a moment. "Adam is not a murderer. He did not kill your whore. I did."

I felt like I'd had the breath knocked out of me. "How did you get her outside?"

"I went there that night and knocked on the back door. Told her I'd seen a dog limp down her driveway and crawl up under the deck. Stupid bitch. Always had a soft spot for animals. She grabbed a flashlight and followed me out there, into the gale. She looked for the dog, and I grabbed a piece of firewood off the pile. I dragged her over to the bottom of the steps and smoothed out the sand. Then I remembered that cursed locket, but I couldn't find it. I wasn't sure she'd been wearing it, so I left." She looked into the fireplace. "Brought the log home with me and burned it right there."

"That's why you came by my house the day I came home." I said. "You were going to look for the locket. You weren't sure if I'd be there or not, so you brought that chicken potpie as an excuse."

The look in her eyes was pure evil. "Too bad I didn't slip some arsenic in that pie."

Stuart's face was a mixture of pain and disgust. "I knew you were capable of many things. But not murder. I'm sure Adam would have killed Emma, or tried. She stood in his way. But you did his dirty work for him, just like always."

Kate rubbed her arm. Fear leapt into her eyes. She blinked at Michael. "My arm's gone numb."

Michael reached for the phone on the table beside him, dialing as he went to his mother's side. "I'm calling Doc Harper."

"He's at Deanna's, remember?" I said. "Try his cell. Deanna's landline was down when we left."

"Why are you so helpful?" Kate spat. "Why would you care?"

"I don't want you dead," I said in a soothing voice.

Kate stared at me, hatred and a question in her eyes.

"I want to see you in prison."

Kate's eyes bulged. She clutched her chest and fell face forward onto the sofa.

FIFTY-THREE

Doc Harper declared Kate dead shortly after one that morning. He and Blake processed a body in one Devlin home and came straight to another. We told Blake how Kate killed Gram and how Adam had surprised Kate with a trip to the hereafter via pharmaceuticals. I hoped they were keeping each other company in hell.

If it had been just my word and Stuart's, I'm not sure Blake would've believed Kate killed Gram. But he believed Michael. No one would invent such a thing about his own mother.

Michael stayed at his mother's house to navigate the aftermath. He tried to get me to stick around, but I've never wanted to leave anywhere as badly as I wanted to bolt that morning.

I prevailed upon Sam Manigault to run me home. Halfway down my drive, his headlights shone on Nate's rental Fusion. A feeling of peace warmed me. I thanked Sam for the ride and stepped toward the porch.

Nate appeared at the top of the steps, Rhett beside him.

"I am so happy to see you." I started up the steps.

"Likewise. What happened where a police cruiser needed to bring you home at one-thirty in the morning looking half-drowned?"

I stopped one step below him. "I'm exhausted. Can I tell you everything in the morning?"

He moved back to let me up on the porch. "Sure."

I unlocked the door and switched on the foyer light. "There's a guestroom next to mine. I haven't checked it since I've been home, but Gram usually kept it ready for company." I started up the stairs.

Nate didn't say anything.

I stopped and turned. He stood at the bottom of the steps, duffle bag in hand, with an odd look on his face.

"You coming?"

"Sure." He glanced away, then moved towards the stairs.

My adrenalin depleted, I fell into bed around two. All systems shut down and I slept hard.

At five a.m. I slammed into wide awake with one thought in my brain: What had Stuart meant when he asked Troy why he was trying to collect payment for a murder he didn't commit? If Troy didn't kill Adam, who did?

Surely not Scott. He was capable of a great many things, but murder? I just couldn't see it. Hiring someone else to do it, yes. But Troy was the hired killer. If there was another hit man on the island, we were over quota.

Definitely not Michael. Although, he was mad enough at Adam to punch him out less than twenty-four hours before Adam was murdered. Many people might consider he had a damn fine motive. Not going there. Will not think that thought.

I looked in on Nate. He was still sleeping soundly. He rested on his stomach, with a pillow clutched under his tanned bicep. The covers had slid down to just below his waist, revealing broad shoulders and a muscled back that narrowed where it met the coverlet. I watched him breathe, mesmerized. How was it that I had never stopped to appreciate how amazingly handsome Nate was? Because he was Scott's brother? No, it wasn't that. Merry's words from a few nights before came back to me, *Damn waste. You're still pining after Michael, aren't you?*

I shook myself. I had to get moving. I splashed cold water on my face, slid into my running clothes, and put my hair in a ponytail.

The morning was clear, the wind nearly calm. I sprinted up the beach and around North Point to the marina, then slowed as I headed across the dock. Stuart was on the forward deck of the *Gypsy Wind*, doing his stretches. He was facing the open ocean, but turned towards me as I approached.

"You couldn't sleep, either," he said. "Come aboard. I'll make coffee."

I didn't move from the dock. "Who killed Adam?"

"Ah." He nodded. "Here is what I know. Adam left on the ferry at seven Thursday evening and returned on the last ferry at nearly midnight. As he pulled out of the parking lot and up to the stoplight, someone in dark clothes and a ski mask forced Adam over to the passenger side at gunpoint."

Stuart heaved a sigh. "The car turned down Marsh View Drive, followed pretty obviously by Troy Causby in a Honda. I ran after them, but by the time I caught up, the shooter was dragging Adam into the marsh. Troy drove on past, rubber-necking."

I pondered that. The eastern sky was getting lighter. Three kingfishers sailed by, low to the water, looking for breakfast. "So you couldn't tell who it was, but the only person you know it wasn't is Troy."

"It was dark." Stuart closed his eyes and rubbed his forehead. "It was a smallish man. I could've followed the killer. But I went to see if there was any help for Adam. It was obvious he was gone. I should have called for help, but Adam was in the hands of a higher power, and I wasn't ready to reveal myself."

A small man. Not Scott.

And not Michael. I knew in my core Michael wasn't a killer, but people who aren't by nature killers do it every day of the week.

Then it hit me. A small man. *Or a woman.*

Deanna? She'd been acting way out of character all week. Had she snapped? Possibly. But there was a far more likely suspect. Marci the Schemer. I shuddered. Had my sociopathic cousin graduated to murder?

I felt my phone vibrate in my sports bra. I turned and discreetly pulled it out. I had a text from Blake: MC returning car now.

Clay Cooper was bringing my car home. I'd given Blake the code to the keyless entry pad the night before. I kept a spare key in the false bottom of the console for emergencies. Bless both their hearts. I needed my car.

When I turned back around, Colleen appeared on the side of the *Gypsy Wind*, legs dangling. "Morning sickness." She yawned.

I squinted at her and thought back to Thursday morning. I'd been spying on Marci while she talked to Adam on the phone. Something made her throw up.

And Wednesday I'd passed her going into Dr. Lombard's. An OB-GYN. Was she really pregnant *now*? When was the last time I'd seen her? Thursday morning. Adam was killed around midnight. She'd told Adam she was going to Savannah. Was that the truth? If so, when did she leave?

"Changed horses," Colleen said.

"Why the hell you being cryptic again all of a sudden?" I shouted.

Stuart stared at me. "Liz, are you all right?" He stepped closer to the edge of the deck and peered down at me.

I looked up into those familiar brown eyes for a long moment. "Yes. I'm fine. Gotta run. Coffee tomorrow? You're not leaving soon are you?"

"No. No longer any reason I must leave."

Colleen faded out.

I smothered a curse.

FIFTY-FOUR

I had a strong suspicion Marci was on her way out of town, and the window of opportunity for confronting her was rapidly closing. Did Colleen plant that thought? I shook my head rapidly to clear it. It didn't matter. I ran home and grabbed my purse. No time to change clothes. I hopped in the Escape and drove to Marci's house.

What the hell had Colleen meant, *changed horses?* If Marci were pregnant, it gave her leverage with Michael. Since I'd inherited Gram's land, Marci no longer had leverage with Adam. Had she decided to stick with the Devlin she was already married to, manipulate him into finishing the deal Adam started? Marci was nothing if not adaptable.

I pounded on the front door and repeatedly jabbed the doorbell. No Marci.

There was no sign of her from any of the windows.

I debated breaking a pane on the back door and letting myself in for a closer inspection of the premises, but instinct—or perhaps Colleen—told me she wasn't there. I stood on tiptoe and peered into the garage. Her car was inside, but unless she was hiding in the trunk, she wasn't there. If she'd gone to Savannah, she would've driven. If she'd left the island, she'd either gone by boat or she'd caught a ride with someone else.

If I were a scheming witch, where would I be? If I'd killed my brother-in-law/lover, I'd only run if I thought someone was on to me. Or maybe I'd slip out of town and play like I'd been elsewhere, maybe Savannah, when the murder went down. That sounded like Marci. Either way, the smart play would've been to leave right after she killed him. Ahh. The next ferry would've been at six Friday morning, and she couldn't risk someone seeing her leave the morning after. She was depending on someone else to smuggle her out, either in an unfamiliar car or by boat.

David Morehead hadn't been seen since Tuesday night. The only other party to the Devlin's Point scheme unaccounted for was Scott.

Of course.

I climbed back into the Escape and zipped over to The Stella Maris Hotel. As I was pulling into the parking lot, Scott's BMW came flying out.

Scott gaped and Marci scowled as I passed them. Scott turned right on Main Street and hit the accelerator. They were headed for the ferry dock.

I pulled a quick u-turn and sped after them. Why would Scott run from me? He couldn't have known we were onto him. I understood why Marci was running, but why Scott? What had she told him? Abruptly, Scott turned right on Marsh View. The next ferry wouldn't leave for another thirty minutes. They were making for the marina.

I fumbled in my purse for my iPhone. I tapped Blake's name and waited. Voicemail. Damnation. I said, "Scott and Marci are headed to the marina. Marci killed Adam. I think."

Then I tried the office. Nell answered on the third ring. "Stella Maris PD. How may we serve and protect you today?"

"Where's Blake?" I yelled.

"Liz Talbot. Would your mamma approve of you yelling at folks on the telephone?"

"I need Blake *now*."

"Well, your brother's in his office talking to Mackie Sullivan. It's barely six o'clock in the morning—"

"Put him on the phone," I said urgently. "*Please*."

The BMW screeched to a stop in the marina parking lot. Both doors popped open and Scott and Marci sprang out. They ran towards the dock. Did Scott have a boat docked on Stella Maris?

Nell harrumphed. "Fine. I'll transfer your call, but—"

I parked beside Scott's car. "Never mind. Tell him to get to the marina *fast*. Scott and Marci are escaping."

There were no pockets in my running shorts. I stuffed my phone in my sports bra and grabbed Sig from my purse. Then I sprinted after Marci the Schemer and Scott the Scoundrel.

It was still early, but a few fishermen puttered around boats. Hank Johnson loosened the tie-off lines on his Boston Whaler. I was closing the distance to Scott and Marci when Scott waved a gun at Hank. He raised both hands and froze. Scott shouted something at Hank. He stepped gingerly out of the boat.

Scott spun on me. "Stop right there, Liz."

I stopped. I was also armed, but hoped Scott couldn't see that. I didn't want Hank in the middle of a shootout. I kept my arms at my side and slipped my right hand behind my leg. "What did she tell you, Scott? Why are you doing this?"

"Get in the boat, Marci," Scott said. "Liz, if you move, I shoot the old man. Got it?"

I nodded. "It's okay, Hank. They're leaving."

Hank looked from Scott to me. He kept his arms up.

Marci climbed into the boat. For once she didn't have that sardonic grin on her face. She was trying to murder me with her eyes, though.

Scott stepped onto the Boston Whaler. The engine was already idling. He loosened the remaining line and pulled the bumper into the boat. He sat down in the driver's seat. Then he turned back to face me. "I did not kill Adam Devlin. I am guilty of nothing more than pursing a legitimate business deal. But I'm not going to stay here in podunk and let your Deputy-Dog brother railroad me." He kept the gun pointed at Hank as he pulled away from the dock.

"Is that what she said? Scott, no one thinks you killed Adam." Well, I didn't think that anyway.

"Sorry, kitten. I fell for your act once this week already."

Ignoring the no-wake signs, Scott pushed the throttle all the way down and the boat darted away from the marina.

Hank put down his hands. "They won't get far," he said. "Dang gas gauge is broke. I fill 'er up before I take 'er out. Was just about to do that."

I nodded. "Good to know."

I called Blake's cell. Surely he was on the way by now.

"The hell is going on?" he said without greeting.

"Where are you?"

"Leaving the station."

"The key to the jet ski still in the console by the door?"

Blake had a jet ski tied up to his houseboat, which was at the next dock over. I was already moving in that direction.

"Why?"

"Scott stole Hank Johnson's boat."

"Do *not*—"

"Gotta go." I stuffed the iPhone back in my sports bra, and Sig in the back of my shorts. Thank God for Spandex.

I sprinted towards the houseboat. The rail was an easy vault—no time to fiddle with the gate. The key was in the console. I slipped the bracelet attached to the safety key over my wrist and grabbed a life vest from under the seat. Blake's Waverunner was tied off the bow end of the boat. I buckled the life vest as I dashed up the deck. I climbed over the rail and slid onto the jet ski.

I started the engine and eased away from the houseboat. As soon as I cleared the end of the dock, I leaned forward and went full throttle. Scott and Marci rounded North Point and raced towards Charleston. I was fast on their wake. I bounced across the waves, closing the gap. I wasn't about to let those two disappear into the Charleston area waterfront.

Scott focused on driving the boat. From her seat beside him, Marci watched me pull within a hundred feet of them. Then she leaned in to Scott. He pushed her away and shouted something. She grabbed the gun he'd stuffed in his waistband and moved to the back of the boat.

Marci planted her feet in a wide stance, struggling for balance in the bouncing boat. Then she gave that up and knelt near the motor. She braced her arms on the side of the boat and fired.

If she hit me, it would be by accident. But I still tucked myself tighter to the jet ski.

Marci fired again. The Waverunner took the bullet on the nose.

Hell fire! Blake would be pissed about that.

I pulled next to them. Marci swiveled and aimed.

I pulled a little ahead and slid my left leg over the seat. The timing had to be perfect. In one motion, I let go of the handgrips, and catapulted from the jet ski into the Whaler.

Marci got off three shots before my feet hit the deck.

I landed in a crouch, unhit.

"What the fuck!" Scott yelled.

Marci sat down in the boat and pointed the gun at me. The Whaler hit a wave and jumped. I slammed into Marci before she could regain her balance. She dropped the gun. I grabbed it and slipped it through the strap on my life vest. "That the gun you used to kill Adam?"

"Bitch," she screamed.

"Back atcha." I balled up my fist and punched her in the mouth. I shook the pain out of my hand.

"Well, well." Marci rubbed her face. "I didn't know you had that in you."

The Whaler's engine started to sputter.

Scott banged on the steering wheel. "*Motherfucker*."

The engine died.

Scott turned on me in a rage, as if it were somehow my fault he'd stolen a boat with a broken gas gauge. He came at me.

I braced, spun at the waist, and delivered a roundhouse kick to his sternum. He obliged me by falling into the Atlantic.

I pivoted to Marci. "Want to go for a swim?"

She glared at me but didn't move.

I glanced over the side of the boat. Scott treaded water a few feet away. I tossed him a lifejacket. "Wouldn't want you to drown and miss your day in court."

He seemed to be having a hard time catching his breath.

I reached under my lifejacket and pulled out Sig.

I gestured at Marci. "Why'd you kill Adam? Just between us girls?"

She deepened her sneer and rolled her eyes.

"Okay, okay." I nodded. "Hypothetically speaking, if you were screwing your brother-in-law, and expected him to divorce his wife and marry you—or at least keep you up—and you found out that wasn't in his plans, that'd piss you off, am I right?"

She narrowed her eyes. The left corner of her mouth crept up.

"That's what I thought."

Scott recovered from having the breath kicked out of him. "You bitch. You said everyone thought I killed Adam."

I bent my right arm and raised Sig, pointing it harmlessly at the sky to my left. "Marci, are you pregnant?"

She laughed. An ugly, sick laugh. "Why, yes, as a matter of fact, I am."

"You were going to try to force Michael to fill in for Adam, get the resort built, and collect on Adam's share, right?" I moved the puzzle pieces around in my brain.

"Please." She drew back her head and scowled. "Why would I tell you anything?"

I stared at her for a moment. No, Marci was done with Michael. She'd tried to barter him. That failed, and she'd arranged for him to catch her in adultery. She'd changed horses, all right, put Adam *down*. But Michael was just another discarded stud.

"You tried to frame Michael for Adam's murder. You hid that wallet under the bed so Michael would find it and confront Adam. Were you hoping for a public scene? Set Michael up as a suspect?" The thought had crossed even *my* mind. "You and Scott didn't need Adam or Michael anymore, did you? You thought all you had to do was sit back and wait for Kate to deed the land to that phony nonprofit. The two of you would've been the only remaining directors."

Marci set her jaw and looked away.

Scott was fast figuring his way out. He's bright, I'll give him that.

"That may have been *her* plan. I had nothing to do with Adam's murder, though she did want him out of the way. Tried to sweet-talk me into arranging it for her. I have proof. That's all I'm saying until I talk to a lawyer."

"What proof?" Marci snarled.

"I have several of our conversations on tape."

"Do tell." I smiled.

"Bastard." Marci spat.

"Sorry, darlin', but I've seen your work." Scott bobbed up and down as a wave rolled by. "Best to have anti-venom on hand if you pick up a snake."

Words failed me. I stared open-mouthed at him, thinking about pots and kettles. Finally, I said, "It's too bad, really."

"What?" asked Scott.

"If you hadn't let her con you into stealing a boat for her big escape, you might have walked away with no more than a few conspiracy and blackmail charges. Oh, and that murder-for-hire thing."

"I never hired anyone to kill anybody," he said.

"Tell it to the jury," I said.

Then I sat down in the driver's seat and waited for Blake.

FIFTY-FIVE

With a flick of my wrist, I sent the Frisbee flying down the beach for the hundredth time. Rhett jumped improbably high in the air and caught it between his teeth with all the skill and grace an experienced outfielder employs to rob a batter of a homerun. I was walking off Mamma's fried chicken and biscuits with gravy, immersing myself in the sound of salt water on sand and the Sunday afternoon sun. Rhett raced back up the beach to deliver the Frisbee. "Good boy." I ruffled the fur on his head.

He ran around in circles a few times, and then sprinted back down the beach in anticipation of the next throw. He apparently forgot all about the Frisbee and ran toward a male figure approaching from down the beach. I recognized him long before his features became clear. Oddly, there were no backflips in my stomach. I felt queasy. I walked towards him. Rhett jumped up to greet him, ran two circles around him, then escorted Michael back to me.

My eyes found his and something sizzled.

I welcomed him with a smile. "Looks like he fetched you."

Michael smiled back. There was sadness behind the smile, but something else, too. "I hoped I might find you out here this afternoon." He paused for a moment and glanced up the beach, then back to me.

"Listen," I said. "I understand. You've lost your brother and your mother. Your father is back from the dead. And it looks like you're going to be a father. Congratulations." I forced a smile. "That's a lot for anyone to have to absorb and—"

He closed his eyes, sighed and shook his head. Then he opened his eyes, and they claimed mine. He closed the distance between us and took my face in his hands. Gently, he rubbed my cheeks with his thumbs. "It has been quite a week." He brushed my lips with his and pulled me to him.

We held on to each other. I nestled my face into his neck and inhaled him. Seagulls flying overhead called out. A soft breeze wrapped around us, swirling from sand to sky. I'd imagined this scene so many times over the last ten years. I'd lived this moment a thousand times in my dreams.

Why did I feel so conflicted? I loved Michael, didn't I? That love—that obsession—had defined the last decade of my life. But I saw Michael with fresh eyes now. He was no longer the white knight I waited for, but the man who made me wait while he lived with another woman for vague, weak reasons. The man who, only now when he himself had been betrayed, wanted me. Anger bubbled to the surface. God help me, could it be that I'd always wanted the one man I couldn't have simply because I couldn't have him? Or did this new ambivalence have something to do with Nate, who waited for me on the deck.

I pulled away from Michael. There was a question in his eyes. I didn't have the answer. For the first time in a very long time, I wasn't sure what I wanted. I took another step back.

He dug his hands in his pockets and glanced away, towards the ocean. "I've made a mess of things."

I couldn't argue with that.

He plopped down in the sand, staring out to sea. I joined him, a foot away.

After a moment, in a practical tone, he said, "I need to get through the next week. The funerals, all the arrangements. Then Robert is going to get me the fastest divorce possible, using whatever means necessary."

"But the baby—"

"Is likely not mine. We won't know until after it's born. If it is mine, custody won't be a problem. His mother will be in prison."

"*His* mother?"

"His, hers, whatever. I don't have a preference." He leaned closer to me. "You do want kids, right?"

I was nowhere near ready to discuss children.

I felt him tense. "You don't want kids." It was a statement.

"Yes, I do. Someday."

"You just don't want one that's not yours." His voice had an edge. "Or is it that you don't want one that's hers?"

Colleen waded through the surf a few feet away. "He's yours on a silver platter. Just like you've always wanted."

"*Hush up,*" I hissed at her.

Michael slid a foot away and looked perplexed.

"Not *you.*"

He looked up the beach, then down. "Liz, what's going on? Talk to me."

I hooked my arms over my knees. "I do want kids, someday. But you're not even divorced yet." His eagerness to segue from one wife directly to another unsettled me.

"I told you, I'm working on that."

I huffed out a sigh. "Things are moving too fast. I want to get to know you again. People change, I've changed. Ten years is a long time. You might not even like me now. I'm very set in my ways."

"Pig-headed, I'd say." Colleen skipped through the foam of the Atlantic.

"What will happen to Marci's child if he isn't yours?"

"I'm not sure," Michael said. "They'll do a paternity test. He or she will still need a home. If Adam is the father, then we can probably still get custody."

"What do you mean if Adam is the father? It's you or him, right?"

"There are other possibilities." He stretched flat out in the sand and looked at the sky.

"You've got to be kidding." I flopped in the sand beside him. The sky was a cloudless, brilliant blue.

"I wish I were," he said. "I went to see her this morning. Thought she might be in the mood to bargain for a quick divorce, seeing as how any attorney who can keep her off death row won't come cheap. She was. But I had to make keeping the child part of the deal. She wanted an abortion."

"I was afraid of that."

"And, she relished telling me the child could also be Troy Causby's, or Scott's."

"I figured Scott. But Troy, too? He sure got around."

"Apparently." Michael rolled over on his side and propped his head in his hand. "If the child is Troy's, then his family will no doubt adopt. If it's Scott's—"

"His parents will get involved." I sighed. "Knowing Scott, he'll somehow avoid jail. But I doubt he'll want the responsibility of a child."

"The good news is Marci will be off the Vodka while she's pregnant. I don't think they'll be serving that in jail."

We laid there in the sand, me looking at the sky and him looking at me. Finally, I rolled my head towards him. "How are you dealing with...your mamma?"

"I grieve for her, for the loss of her." He played with the sand, picking up handfuls and letting it slip slowly out of his fist. "But I also grieve for what she did to our family. All the years I thought my father was dead. She did a number on him, on all of us. I guess I grieve most for the person I thought she was."

"What about Adam?"

He shook his head. "He was my brother in biology only. I should feel bad he's dead, but I can't. It's an awful thing to admit."

"What's awful is the kind of brother he turned out to be."

"So, what do you think constitutes a decent waiting period after your wife has a year-long affair with your brother and then shoots him? Before you marry her cousin, I mean."

"I don't think that situation is covered in Emily Post."

"I know somebody who let the real thing slip through his fingers." His eyes searched mine. "I won't let that happen to us again."

I couldn't speak. Something thick was lodged in my throat.

His eyes glowed warm and bright. "I love you, Liz Talbot. I think I always have. Ever since you were five and started tagging around after Blake and me."

"Michael, let's give this some time."

He smiled that warm smile—the one that made me hear Van Morrison singing *Someone Like You*. Then he hopped up on to one knee in the sand and pulled me up until I was standing and he was holding both my hands.

"I may be sick," Colleen said.

"Will you please *go away*?" I said.

"What?" Michael looked crushed.

"Not you." I covered my mouth with both hands and shook my head.

"Liz?"

"Michael, please stand up. I'm not ready for this."

Slowly, he stood, confusion and hurt written on his face. "I've wanted you for so long..."

Tears sprung to my eyes. "And I've wanted you, just as long. But right now, I'm not sure if it was really us I wanted, or the idea of us. I need time."

He shoved his hands back in his pockets and stared at the sand. "So, what, I should ask you out on a date?"

"Maybe," I said. "When things settle down. Right now I think I'd like to settle into being neighbors. And friends."

"Okay, then." He nodded. "I guess I need to get back to Mamma's. Dad's coming by. We have arrangements to make. Come by later?"

"Of course. I'll clean up and get a pound cake in the oven."

"Skip the cake. We've got four pound cakes already, and the day is early. Just come when you can. It's the neighborly thing."

"I will."

We both brushed the sand off. He turned and walked away.

"I always liked him." Colleen's voice was right in my ear. "If they'd let me go to college with you, you would've married him instead of Scott. But now..."

I spun around on her. "Could you at least *not* pop in during what should be private moments?"

She tilted her head and appeared to ponder that. "It would take some of the fun out of it."

"I thought you were supposed to guard the island. It isn't in any danger from Michael or me."

Colleen turned and started down the beach.

"Hey, where are you going?" I asked.

"I'm going for a walk. I want to enjoy the ocean for a while."

"You coming back?"

"Not today."

"Are you...crossing over now?"

She stopped, turned around, and gave me an exasperated look. "I've already crossed over. I told you, I'm not a ghost."

"I know, I know. You're a guardian spirit. Will I see you again?"

"Probably." Colleen smiled. "If you stay here."

"Why wouldn't I?"

Colleen glanced towards the house. "I'm only seventeen, but I think you have a lot of unresolved issues."

I followed her gaze. Nate stood at the end of the walkway, staring in my direction. How much of the scene with Michael had he witnessed? Something cold grasped at my heart and I couldn't quite catch my breath.

Colleen chattered on, "I wonder if he'd be willing to move. Long distance romances are a challenge, but not impossible. If you do stay here, you'll never be able to live on what you'd make taking clients from Stella Maris. You're going to need to drum up some business in Charleston. Go online, update your website. Don't you just love the internet?"

She grinned, spun twice, and walked away.

Reader's Discussion Guide

1) At the beginning of the book, Liz has established a life several hours away from her family and the hometown she loves. She believes the reason she can't go home is because Michael and Marci live there. Do you think she is really still in love with Michael, or after her failed marriage, does she create an idealized version of Michael and the life they might have had together?

2) Colleen and Liz were once the same age, but Colleen will be forever seventeen, while Liz is now thirty-one. How does this impact their relationship? Do Colleen's supernatural powers balance the relationship?

3) Do you think Nate is in love with Liz? If so, why do you think he has kept this to himself?

4) Michael knows he was tricked into marriage, and yet he doesn't pursue a divorce stating Marci can't take care of herself, and he didn't want to give her half of everything he'd worked for in a divorce. Is he honorable or simply living with the status quo because it's the path of least resistance, or a combination of both?

5) Liz and her sister, Merry, are quite close, yet Merry manipulates Liz without remorse, and Liz lets her get away with it. Is this a normal big sister/little sister relationship?

6) Which of Liz's immediate family members do you like best: Mamma, Daddy, Blake, and Merry? Why?

7) Adam Devlin is not a nice guy. But from his point of view, the land he wants to develop is his birthright. He would argue he should have been able to develop Devlin's Point—and make a lot of money by doing so—without having to resort to the elaborate scheme that was his downfall. At what point do the interests of a community override the interests of an individual?

8) Liz's daddy, Franklin Talbot, is somewhat of a chameleon. He's a respected member of the town council, yet at times he seems to slide into the skin of a somewhat eccentric good-ole-boy. Is this calculated on his part? Does he play the role the day demands or is he a little unbalanced?

9) Do you wish Liz had reconciled with Michael when he came to her door and she wouldn't let him in?

10) Kate Devlin is another character who is not always what she seems. Do you feel any sympathy for her?

11) Do you think Deanna Devlin knew all along what Troy Causby was? Did she secretly hope he would kill Adam, or was that her plan? Or is she exactly as innocent as she appears?

12) What do you think the future holds for Liz and Michael? Do you see Nate in her future rather than Michael?

Susan M. Boyer

Susan loves three things best: her family, books, and beaches. She's grateful to have been blessed with a vivid imagination, allowing her to write her own books centered around family, beaches, and solving puzzles wherein someone is murdered. Susan lives in Greenville, SC, and runs away to the coast as often as she can.

Her debut novel, *Lowcountry Boil* won the Agatha Award for Best First Novel, the Daphne du Maurier Award for Excellence in Mystery/Suspense, and was an RWA Golden Heart® finalist. Susan's short fiction has appeared in *moonShine Review*, *Spinetingler*, and *Relief Journal* among others. Visit Susan at www.susanmboyerbooks.com.

Don't Miss the 2nd Book in the Series

LOWCOUNTRY BOMBSHELL

Susan M. Boyer

A Liz Talbot Mystery (#2)

Liz Talbot thinks she's seen another ghost when she meets Calista McQueen. She's the spitting image of Marilyn Monroe. Born precisely fifty years after the ill-fated star, Calista's life has eerily mirrored the late starlet's—and she fears the looming anniversary of Marilyn's death will also be hers.

Before Liz can open a case file, Calista's life coach is executed. Suspicious characters swarm around Calista like mosquitoes on a sultry lowcountry evening: her certifiable mother, a fake aunt, her control-freak psychoanalyst, a private yoga instructor, her peculiar housekeeper, and an obsessed ex-husband. Liz digs in to find a motive for murder, but she's besieged with distractions. Her ex has marriage and babies on his mind. Her too-sexy partner engages in a campaign of repeat seduction. Mamma needs help with Daddy's devotion to bad habits. And a gang of wild hogs is running loose on Stella Maris.

With the heat index approaching triple digits, Liz races to uncover a diabolical murder plot in time to save not only Calista's life, but also her own.

Available at booksellers nationwide and online

Visit www.henerypress.com for details

LOWCOUNTRY BONEYARD

Susan M. Boyer

A Liz Talbot Mystery (#3)

Where is Kent Heyward? The twenty-three-year-old heiress from one of Charleston's oldest families vanished a month ago. When her father hires private investigator Liz Talbot, Liz suspects the most difficult part of her job will be convincing the patriarch his daughter tired of his overbearing nature and left town. That's what the Charleston Police Department believes.

But behind the garden walls South of Broad, family secrets pop up like weeds in the azaleas. The neighbors recollect violent arguments between Kent and her parents. Eccentric twin uncles and a gaggle of cousins covet the family fortune. And the lingering spirit of a Civil-War-era debutante may know something if Colleen, Liz's dead best friend, can get her to talk.

Liz juggles her case, the partner she's in love with, and the family she adores. But the closer she gets to what has become of Kent, the closer Liz dances to her own grave.

Henery Press Mystery Books

And finally, before you go...
Here are a few other mysteries
you might enjoy:

BOARD STIFF

Kendel Lynn

An Elliott Lisbon Mystery (#1)

As director of the Ballantyne Foundation on Sea Pine Island, SC, Elliott Lisbon scratches her detective itch by performing discreet inquiries for Foundation donors. Usually nothing more serious than retrieving a pilfered Pomeranian. Until Jane Hatting, Ballantyne board chair, is accused of murder. The Ballantyne's reputation tanks, Jane's headed to a jail cell, and Elliott's sexy ex is the new lieutenant in town.

Armed with moxie and her Mini Coop, Elliott uncovers a trail of blackmail schemes, gambling debts, illicit affairs, and investment scams. But the deeper she digs to clear Jane's name, the guiltier Jane looks. The closer she gets to the truth, the more treacherous her investigation becomes. With victims piling up faster than shells at a clambake, Elliott realizes she's next on the killer's list.

Available at booksellers nationwide and online

Visit www.henerypress.com for details

ARTIFACT
Gigi Pandian

A Jaya Jones Treasure Hunt Mystery (#1)

Historian Jaya Jones discovers the secrets of a lost Indian treasure may be hidden in a Scottish legend from the days of the British Raj. But she's not the only one on the trail...

From San Francisco to London to the Highlands of Scotland, Jaya must evade a shadowy stalker as she follows hints from the hastily scrawled note of her dead lover to a remote archaeological dig. Helping her decipher the cryptic clues are her magician best friend, a devastatingly handsome art historian with something to hide, and a charming archaeologist running for his life.

Available at booksellers nationwide and online

Visit www.henerypress.com for details

PILLOW STALK

Diane Vallere

A Madison Night Mystery (#1)

Interior Decorator Madison Night might look like a throwback to the sixties, but as business owner and landlord, she proves that independent women can have it all. But when a killer targets women dressed in her signature style—estate sale vintage to play up her resemblance to fave actress Doris Day—what makes her unique might make her dead.

The local detective connects the new crime to a twenty-year old cold case, and Madison's long-trusted contractor emerges as the leading suspect. As the body count piles up, Madison uncovers a Soviet spy, a campaign to destroy all Doris Day movies, and six minutes of film that will change her life forever.

Available at booksellers nationwide and online

Visit www.henerypress.com for details

FINDING SKY

Susan O'Brien

A Nicki Valentine Mystery

Suburban widow and P.I. in training Nicki Valentine can barely keep track of her two kids, never mind anyone else. But when her best friend's adoption plan is jeopardized by the young birth mother's disappearance, Nicki is persuaded to help. Nearly everyone else believes the teenager ran away, but Nicki trusts her BFF's judgment, and the feeling is mutual.

The case leads where few moms go (teen parties, gang shootings) and places they can't avoid (preschool parties, OB-GYNs' offices). Nicki has everything to lose and much to gain — including the attention of her unnervingly hot P.I. instructor. Thankfully, Nicki is armed with her pesky conscience, occasional babysitters, a fully stocked minivan, and nature's best defense system: women's intuition.

Available at booksellers nationwide and online

Visit www.henerypress.com for details

BET YOUR BOTTOM DOLLAR

Karin Gillespie

The Bottom Dollar Series (#1)

Welcome to the Bottom Dollar Emporium in Cayboo Creek, South Carolina, where everything from coconut mallow cookies to Clabber Girl Baking Powder costs a dollar but the coffee and gossip are free. For the Bottom Dollar gals, work time is sisterhood time.

When news gets out that a corporate dollar store is coming to town, the women are thrown into a tizzy, hoping to save their beloved store as well their friendships. Meanwhile the manager is canoodling with the town's wealthiest bachelor and their romance unearths some startling family secrets.

The first in a series, *Bet Your Bottom Dollar* serves up a heaping portion of small town Southern life and introduces readers to a cast of eccentric characters. Pull up a wicker chair, set out a tall glass of Cheer Wine, and immerse yourself in the adventures of a group of women who the *Atlanta Journal Constitution* calls, "... the kind of steel magnolias who would make Scarlett O'Hara envious."

Available at booksellers nationwide and online

Visit www.henerypress.com for details

NUN TOO SOON

Alice Loweecey

A Giulia Driscoll Mystery (#1)

Giulia Falcone-Driscoll has just taken on her first impossible client: The Silk Tie Killer. He's hired Driscoll Investigations to prove his innocence and they have only thirteen days to accomplish it. Talk about being tried in the media. Everyone in town is sure Roger Fitch strangled his girlfriend with one of his silk neckties. And then there's the local TMZ wannabes—The Scoop—stalking Giulia and her client for sleazy sound bites.

On top of all that, her assistant's first baby is due any second, her scary smart admin still doesn't relate well to humans, and her police detective husband insists her client is guilty. About this marriage thing—it's unknown territory, but it sure beats ten years of living with 150 nuns.

Giulia's ownership of Driscoll Investigations hasn't changed her passion for justice from her convent years. But the more dirt she digs up, the more she's worried her efforts will help a murderer escape. As the client accuses DI of dragging its heels on purpose, Giulia thinks The Silk Tie Killer might be choosing one of his ties for her own neck.

Available at booksellers nationwide and online

Visit www.henerypress.com for details